CHAOS

CHAOS

CONSTANCE FAY

BRAMBLE

TOR PUBLISHING GROUP

NEW YORK

CHAOS

Copyright © 2025 by Constance Fay

A Bramble Book
Published by Tom Doherty Associates / Tor Publishing Group
120 Broadway
New York, NY 10271

www.torpublishinggroup.com

Bramble™ is a trademark of Macmillan Publishing Group, LLC.

Library of Congress Cataloging-in-Publication Data

Names: Fay, Constance, author.
Title: Chaos / Constance Fay.
Description: First edition. | New York : Bramble,
Tor Publishing Group, 2025. | Series: Uncharted Hearts ; 3
Identifiers: LCCN 2024042077 | ISBN 9781250330437 (trade paperback) |
ISBN 9781250330444 (ebook)
Subjects: LCGFT: Romance fiction. | Science fiction. | Novels.
Classification: LCC PS3606.A949 C53 2025 |
DDC 813/.6—dc23/eng/20240916
LC record available at https://lccn.loc.gov/2024042077

Our books may be purchased in bulk for promotional,
educational, or business use. Please contact your local bookseller
or the Macmillan Corporate and Premium Sales Department
at 1-800-221-7945, extension 5442, or by email at
MacmillanSpecialMarkets@macmillan.com.

First Edition: 2025

Printed in the United States of America

0 9 8 7 6 5 4 3 2 1

To Bryce, David, Patrick, and Peter.
Thanks for the physics innuendo in this book
and for years of physics innuendo leading up to this book.

CHAOS

CHAPTER 1

▪ ▪ ▪ ▪ ▪ ▪ ▪ ▪ ▪ ▪ ▪ ▪ ▪ ▪ ▪

Blue-pale sunlight washes steep white stone cliffs that rise above a red grass plane. Wind ruffles the grass, flowing like the ripples of a lake. There's a certain beauty to it—if lakes of blood are your thing. They aren't mine. I like spaceships. Full of problems, all of them with solutions. Nature is messy and doesn't appreciate when you try to fix it.

Gets kind of surly when you try to fix it, actually.

I sit on a rough stone outcropping, legs dangling over the edge, and watch the undulating grass beneath me. Looks normal. Or, at least, as normal as bloodred grass gets. If you work in planet scouting like I do, you've seen grass in nearly every color the eye can sense—and a few it can't. So the red isn't disturbing. The problem is, something else below me absolutely *is* disturbing, according to the sensor in my hand. Instead of reading stone and soil and grass, the scanner reads absolutely nothing. A snowfall of static fills the entire meadow, only breaking to register the surroundings when the grass ends to pale red scrub brush and maroon-trunked trees.

The coms unit in my ear pings. My captain's voice sounds tinny and distant, like I need a new battery. "Caro, where the fuck are you?"

"One of my favorite things about our relationship is your steadfast adherence to maintaining a professional workplace, Temper." I pull the hose that runs from my backpack over my shoulder and suck down some water as I turn my datapad off and study the field below, trying to glean its secrets. I *am* on working hours, after all.

"Fine. Where the fuck are you, *please*?" Some sort of clatter comes through in the background. Probably Temper searching for a blaster so she can race out to rescue me from the literal nothing that is happening.

She worries. She has no idea what she really should be worried about, though.

"Checking out the meadow with the mystery readings. Planet scanned safe." I don't see any structure down there that could be emitting a disruption signal. Perhaps it's underground. "I wanted to see it with my own eyes instead of through a lens. Nothing stands out."

"Do you need us to come meet you?"

I stand, dusting off my coveralls with my equally dirty hands. "No, I'll come back to you."

I disconnect.

The *Calamity* is down the slope that led me to this bone-pale cliff, across a deep lake speckled with so much red algae that it's almost purple. The walk isn't that long and I want breakfast before I set out again. Not that the breakfast will be good. Micah is the only one of us worth anything in the galley and he's off-ship this mission.

A humming vibration on the interface tattoo on my forearm indicates that a new call is incoming. I stroke a fingertip down the tattoo to send the caller identity to my augmented lenses. Ven.

What the fuck?

Ven is our former captain. Noteworthy more for his exit than for any distinctive captaining. He was boffing Temper and our biology intern at the same time and, for reasons as pathetic as they are predictable, chose the intern. This led to him selling the ship to Temper and running off into charted space with his nubile little fluffball. Said fluffball grew up a little, realized Ven is a loser, and dumped him, and now Ven doesn't have a ship or a crew.

I haven't spoken to him since he left, because Temper is my friend and my captain, in that order, and I had no interest in talking to the priap. I still don't. I tap my interface tattoo to ignore the call.

Because I'm focused on stupid Ven and not the cliffside, I stumble over a patch of loose rock, dropping to hands and knees. I catch myself, one hand wrapped around a large rock. My crew would never let me live it down if I wandered out to a cliff and then accidentally toddled over the edge just because *Ven* was on the coms.

It would be a very embarrassing way to go out.

I grab that large rock that helped me steady myself and chuck it over the edge of the cliff, overwhelmed by the morbid desire to watch it fall like I almost did.

The rock crashes down and a strong buzzing noise emanates from the meadow below. Buzzing is not good. Never *ever* good.

From my position crouching on top of the cliff, I peer over the edge at the undulating red grass, now thrashing in a pattern that couldn't be created by either wind or the rock that just hit the ground.

A black cloud erupts from the grass, twisting and roiling as it hurls itself into the air. It sounds angry.

Nope. Every single kind of nope. The sound I make is probably excessively damsel-y.

I'm torn between staying frozen on the edge of the cliff, hoping I stay above their notice, and sprinting into the woods behind me on the way back to the safety of my ship. The decision is made for me as the stone I'm standing on creaks and I hurl myself bodily toward the tree line at the exact moment that the rock under me disappears, crashing straight down into the midst of the swarm of—*something*.

What are these cliffs made of? Tissue? Itzel could have warned me that this planet was the most fragile environment known to humankind. I scramble at the tree root that I caught. My legs swing over the edge of the drop, toes searching for purchase somewhere on the stone.

The buzzing is louder, a murmuration of black shapes growing larger as the cloud rises to my elevation. They're definitely bugs. Large ones. Nearly the size of my hand, with sharp charcoal wings, pyramid-shaped heads, and at least ten legs that each end with a sharp little hook. I ease myself up off the cliff and crawl closer to the tree line before getting to my feet, slow and careful as possible. One bug breaks from the rest of the twisting unreal cloud and approaches me. I look for an antenna or an eye. Any sort of detectable sense organ. Its pyramid head splits open into three triangular planes and a snakelike tongue darts out, split into three prongs at the end.

It hisses at me. Or buzzes. Or some other appropriately terrifying sound for a giant flying bug with a creepy-ass head to make. The swarm stops. Literally stops in the air like they're black stars waiting to go nova.

They don't wait long.

Two giant bugs slam into me, one at my waist, the other at my neck. The coveralls absorb some of the blow at the waist, but the bug at my neck sinks its disgusting little triangular teeth right into my flesh. I scream and bat at it, because that's what you do when a bug attacks you. When batting doesn't shake it free, I wrap my hand around its armored segmented body and rip it away.

I spin and run into the forest, ripping bugs off my body and smacking at any approaching creatures as the entire swarm shapes itself into a spiral and pierces the tree line right behind me, rolling like a wave into the sanguine shrubbery. I pull out my blaster and point it directly at the bug still clinging to my waist. Its greedy little teeth pierce the thick material of my coveralls and gnaw on the skin beneath. I'm no good with a blaster but at least I know how to pull the trigger.

The fucking thing *doesn't fire*.

I keep pulling the trigger, because the universal rule of tools is: if something doesn't work, try doing the exact same thing harder. "Temper!"

No response from my coms.

The heavy-hollow sounds of bug bodies crash into the leaves around me. The air is alive with an almost mechanical buzzing hum, and I'm peppered with collisions as I stumble over the uneven ground, battering at the swarm of bugs. If I wasn't so scared shitless, I'd be grossed out, but I don't have room in my fear for disgust. My foot strikes a scree of gravel. It slides out from under me, sending me skidding down the trail off-balance, arms flailing until eventually I crash down to my hands and knees yet again.

"Fuck!" I scream, because it feels good to scream it, but then I snap my mouth shut, because the last thing I need is one of these things trying to fly inside.

I'm not going to make it back to the ship.

"Temper?" I try the coms again, on the off chance that she stepped away.

Nothing.

"Itzel?"

Our biologist doesn't respond either.

"Arcadio?"

My breath saws in my chest. Where the hells is the crew? I start running again.

Two bugs collide on my right shoulder, both going for the same tender bleeding spot on my neck, and I duck away from them, spinning and dodging the hailstorm of charcoal bodies. One last turn and I dart out of the trees and into the wide-open air by the lake.

The swarm moves like it was choreographed—spinning in the air until it's almost a dark arrow of black bug forms. It spears down in my direction at a speed I would have thought impossible. There's only one option, and I'm just stupid enough to take it.

I dive directly into the unexplored lake, hoping it's nontoxic, hoping it houses no large predators, hoping these bugs aren't also aquatic. The dark-red algae encompasses me like a shroud. The water chills, icy cold after the adrenaline and the running and the trauma. I want to pant; I want to propel myself forward. Instead, I sink low, watching the slow ascension of bubbles as I breathe out.

Above the surface, the swarm stills. Spreads. Filaments of bugs stretch from it, searching for a sign of me. Of any likely prey. My lungs strain, tight and hungry in my chest, and still I let myself sink. Slowly, ever so slowly, the swarm diffuses, bugs looking for new territory or just coping with heartburn from all that delicious Caro-blood they sucked down.

Sparks dance in front of my eyes as I push off the squishy bottom of the lake and clear the surface, gasping for breath as silently as possible. Algae specks my skin, almost tingling. I try to ignore the sensation. Too late now to worry about poison.

It's *probably* fine.

Only, like, one in ten plants on any given planet are toxic to humans. Sometimes fewer. And that's for eating. Even fewer are toxic to touch. I drag myself up on the muddy shore, fingers sticking deep in the sludge. Out of the fresh chill of the water, a constellation of pain sparks my skin. Fucking bugs.

"Caro!" the voice roars. Not just in my coms but in my ears. My coms also. Now that the danger has moved on, of course the tech decides to work.

"Stop yelling." I hiss, hoping the coms pick it up. "You're going to bring them back."

Temper's familiar form comes tearing around the side of the lake, moving efficiently even while running in the mud. She's flanked by Arcadio, a former son of one of the Five Families, Temper's lover, and general badass.

All-around upgrade from Ven.

"She won't," Arcadio responds in a more modulated tone that only hits me via the coms. "Itzel sent out your swarm of drones to distract the bugs so we could retrieve you."

Temper and Arcadio arrive at the same time, one looking at my wounds like she's going to puke and the other like I'm a fascinating new science experiment. Arcadio strokes my captain's upper back like he's calming her at the sight of me. Who's the one who needs soothing here?

"Their heads were shaped like pyramids," I say, for want of something better. Seems noteworthy.

"I think she's in shock." Arcadio offers his completely misinformed medical opinion.

"She's absolutely in shock," Temper confirms.

"I'm not in shock. I'm cold and my heart's pounding and I might pass out."

"That's shock." Temper pokes at one of the bite marks in my neck and my eyes almost roll back in my head. "I know. I've been in it a lot."

"Coms didn't work," I mumble.

"The swarm emits some sort of jamming signal. They disable electronics over an indeterminate distance. Arcadio figured it out when we lost contact."

"That explains the blaster." I pull it out and fire into the bushes. One catches fire. "Oops."

Temper steps away to splash some water on it and then returns to poking at my wounds. "Thought you weren't heedless."

I'm *not* heedless. I'm heedfull. Heedmore. I have all the heed. Arguably too much. I save my own skin first, always. It's my least attractive trait.

. . . . .

By the time we arrive at Landsdown Way Station, the bites have faded to red spots that freckle my dark-brown skin. I run a fingertip over my forearm, tracing the surface of the inflammation. There's a hard little knot underneath the tissue that impacts the efficacy of my interface tattoo. Hopefully, once the swelling goes down, the tattoo will work properly again. As it is, it lies quiescent on my arm.

"You look better," Itzel offers as she leaves the ship, already in her civilian clothes, which are somehow more ritualistically uniform than her crew coveralls. The black hooded tunic and slim-cut pants paired with a vibrantly hot-pink belt bag certainly make a fashion statement.

"You look like a crazy person. Why do you still wear your vestments?" A long time ago, Itzel was an acolyte to a notorious cult of assassin monks who follow the Dark Mother of the Void. They kicked her out. Not because she's bad at murder. Because she managed to retain some vestigial morality that makes her upset about how *good* she is at murder.

She picks the fabric away from her chest with two darkly tattooed fingers and studies it as though it has an answer for my question. "I didn't leave the Dark Mother. I left the monastery."

"Does the Dark Mother also enjoy neon accessories?" I point at the belt bag and the equally vibrant yellow sneakers on her feet.

She squints a little glare at me. "She certainly enjoys bright red."

Guess I asked for that one. "You've been spending too much of your off time with Cyn and Micah. They've turned you mean."

Itzel gets a sort of faraway look in her eye. "I've always been mean, Caro. I simply choose to be kind instead."

I take that for the censure it is meant to be. She eyes me some more. "You need to get laid."

Demonstrably true. Also unlikely. The closest I've come in two years was a brief unrequited crush on Victor, our sometimes security expert. It didn't last long, because even though Victor is both stunning and kind, he's also a mess when it comes to women. When you see how *not* picky a man can be, it really ruins his allure.

"I'm doing fine. I'm beating the men off with sticks."

The corner of Itzel's mouth quirks. "If you're doing it with sticks, you aren't doing it right."

"I don't—!" Before I can recover and correct myself, she exits the ship. She's on well-earned leave for the next few weeks. I have no idea what—or whom—Itzel spends her leave doing. Probably don't want to.

We're all on leave now. It's in between jobs and Temper and Arcadio have Family business to conduct. So strange that I know people who have direct interaction with Family governance. I've spent so much of my life trying to keep away from the Five Families and their little games.

Arcadio might have separated from the Escajedas officially, but his sister still calls on him when extra security is needed. The upcoming Family Summit in a few months is just the sort of event where she hires him as a consultant.

Which means I'm alone in the way station and bored when Ven calls again.

CHAPTER 2

■ ■ ■ ■ ■ ■ ■ ■ ■ ■ ■ ■ ■ ■ ■

"No."

But I've already answered his call, so it's not exactly as emphatic as it could be. I'm just afraid that if I keep ignoring his calls, he'll keep calling, and then it will be even more annoying. This is a preemptive no.

"Caro, it's so good to hear your voice." Ven's smarmy grin is in *his* voice even though tension still brackets his tone. "It's been a long time."

"Maybe I didn't enunciate well. N. O. No. No to whatever scheme you're working on. No to it being a long time. No to it being good to hear my voice. It isn't and it hasn't been." I didn't expect him to irritate me so much upon first exchange. He didn't betray *me*, after all; he betrayed Temper.

He forces out a laugh. "So protective still. I made my peace with Temper, Caro. We're fine."

And yet he's calling me and not my captain. "I'm not interested in whatever you're selling, Ven."

"You will be, Caro. For the same reason you don't want to talk to me. Because it impacts those you think of as friends."

I hate him. Not the deep dark kind of hate that comes from fear but the passive kind that is bred in disgust. "Just talk, Ven. Stop playing games with your words."

The smoothness drops from his tone. Ven never did waste much charm on me. "Victor and Victory are in trouble. After

Temperance wouldn't bring me back, I had to try to make it on my own. Had to take other opportunities. Not just scouting. I brought them on for a job that needed more crew—on Shikigami."

That's Ven-language for a job that he deemed too dangerous to do himself and still wanted to get paid for. I sigh. "And yet I notice that *you* aren't in danger, just the twins. What was this job?"

Shikigami is a formerly Nakatomi-, now Pierce-run luxury prison where wealthy criminals suffer their punishment in spa-like conditions. I don't buy that Shikigami is too much for the mercenary twins to handle. Maybe they had a massage, got too relaxed, and missed a coms appointment. Then again, I put nothing past Pierce. Once, I gave them the benefit of the doubt.

Never again. None of the Five Families deserve the benefit, but Pierce least of all.

"The job was a rescue. Someone who was falsely imprisoned." Ven's careful tone breaks through my reminiscing.

I don't know how Ven would know that to be true, but I completely believe he'd trust whatever he was told. "And what went wrong?"

"I don't know." The frustration in his voice, at least, is real. "They went incommunicado as soon as they hit the prison. They got hired as guards, intended to lie low until the time came for a rescue."

"You're surprised they stopped communicating? They're in a prison, even if it is Shikigami. It's not like they're known for open coms lines." Ven was always awful at the logistics.

"I didn't expect real updates. Victory was supposed to call her cousin, played by me, for family talk."

Odds are the twins deemed that too dangerous and decided to go silent until they were done with their mission.

Ven continues undaunted, "I got a sliver of vid from a hidden camera before they went dark. It showed the inside of a lab. There were people there in cells."

Odds are high that it was just a med facility that looks like a lab, and prisoners are kept in smaller spaces while they're recovering from procedures. And yet. I know Pierce. After Cyn's experiences I know they're still up to their old games. What better place than Shikigami, a prison so dumb that it's only for Families?

Which might mean that the twins really are in some semblance of danger. Shikigami isn't exactly high security, but if Pierce is doing something shady there, they'd want to keep it quiet. That might just mean quieting the coms, but it might also be something worse.

"I need Temper and the rest of the crew to ride to the rescue. I hear you do that sort of thing now. Noble stuff like rescuing the Escajeda girl. This is basically the same thing." Ven puts on his very best persuasive voice.

This isn't the same thing. This is easier. *Much* easier. Estella Escajeda's daughter Boreal was abducted by a serial kidnapper and held in booby-trapped danger. The twins are in a fancy-people's resort. One that might be full of all kinds of juicy juicy information ripe for the picking.

"You don't need the rest of the crew; you just need me." I say it before I even fully consider the ramifications.

"Now, Caro, I know you think you're capable but—"

"No buts, Ven. You don't send a bunch of people into a prison. You send *one* person. I have the skills necessary to manipulate any tech I encounter. I'm not a physical threat. I'm not the famous scion of any Family. And—" Here I lay down my trump card, the one thing that makes me perfect for this job. "Pierce has been hunting me for years. They want me for my technical capabilities. All I need to do to get into Shikigami is introduce myself. They'll invite me right in."

"Oh. That's handy." He brightens right up.

Hasn't been handy for me the past ten standard years or so when I was in hiding, but sure, handy. Back when I was in a technical university, my senior project was sponsored by the Pierce Family. It was advertised as biohacking—a way to cure the incurable and allow humans to adapt to even more environments than they currently reside in. My sliver of the overall assignment was to figure out how to remotely access tech for emergency situations.

How could someone like me—ambitious, talented, arrogant, and so so ignorant—refuse?

It went about as well as a sane adult person might expect. Unwilling test subjects, bad results, tears. I sabotaged Pierce, changed my surname, and ran as far as a decent engine would take me toward the edges of the chart.

With the news of Pierce's experimentation on the residents of Cyn's planet, I learned that my worst mistake—my most shameful mistake—had finally come back to haunt me. It's so much nicer when shameful mistakes disappear politely.

"I want a quarter split of your collected fee; this isn't a free job."

"We already negotiated shares. I have nothing left to pay you." A wheedling tone now. "You have no idea how hard the past year has been on me."

Priap. He's negotiating with his crew's lives. Also, how pathetic one's life is has never been a valid negotiation tactic. I note that he hasn't asked how I'm doing. He never did take much interest in my life. Probably he deems it wasted effort because he knows I'm going to take this anyway. I'm not the sort of person to leave the twins in any kind of danger.

And we're between jobs, so I don't have anything better to do.

"You collect half the fee after retrieval of whomever you're rescuing. I'll take my cut then." It's like he doesn't know I'm in the business, too.

"Of course. We'll work something out." Not agreement. Wormwords that he'll use to try to wriggle his way out later. "Are you near Pierce space?"

Near enough. I can use the travel time to work on my strategy.

"I can get there soon. You said they were there on a rescue? Who was their target?"

He's silent for just a moment too long. Enough to make me suspicious. "I'll send you a vid of the target and a quick overview of the plan."

Ven's plans usually involve shooting stuff until he gets what he wants. His tool is a blaster and thus most solutions are blaster-shaped to him. We wrap up the conversation, mostly because I want to stop talking to Ven immediately. Trust him to only reach out when he's got people in trouble.

When he's gone, I open the vid. It shows a sliver of white wall with a plas-glass door in it, a flicker of sideways motion. The vid is so short that it's over just at the point I realize what I'm seeing. I scroll back and freeze the only frame of decent quality. There's a large man in a cell. The man's face is partially turned. He has light-tan skin, a jaw that looks like it could be carved from the side of a mountain, and pale eyes. A small smattering of scar tissue is visible above the neck of his white coveralls. The stubble on his head and his eyebrows indicates that his hair would be dark brown or black if it were to grow out. Without context for size, I'm not sure how big he is.

My gut says very. My gut also says that he's hot like a sun. The snippet of vid is so short I don't get much else of use. Perhaps someone smuggled it out and sent it to the man's family. I scroll back and forward again. Pause it on the man's profile. It's good that I'm alone in the station because everyone would make fun of me for staring if I was on the ship.

People assume that I like frail academic types, as though people can only be one thing. Only smart, never also handsome or brave or agile. Like I'm not the sort of person who deserves a hero type. Like I'm a side character in a holo-drama, there to crack a joke and fiddle with an engine.

Maybe I want a man with a sharp jaw, a reckless spirit, and abs you can use to scrub clothing.

He can *also* be smart.

It's healthy self-confidence like that that has kept me single for years.

I dive into research, with little more than the snippet of an image collected from the vid to try to find out more information on this rescue subject. I come up with next to nothing until I reach less than legal channels. Pierce is hard to hack. They hire the best.

Well, second best. I'm the best, but I don't have unlimited time and I can't afford attention. I can't get much information before I trigger their security. All I manage is to find a Pierce Family staffer who accidentally opened a message on their private coms instead of their Family system.

It discusses their progress on a Project Titan, best exemplified by test subject "L."

There are before and after vids of L. I project the vid to the holo-unit in my rental room. In the before vid, he's standing in a cell. They didn't bother with high image quality so I can't make out much detail, but I can tell from the way he moves that he's terrified. Right at the end the shot finally comes into focus, throwing his tense face into stark relief. It's the person from the vid Ven sent me, but not exactly. He has the same striking blue-green eyes under black brows. After that, everything's different. Smaller. He's tall but of a slighter build although it's hard to tell from the way he's hunched over. Self-protective. It's not a case of mass; even his overall dimensions seem smaller.

In the after vid, he's still in the cell and he's been changed into the version of the man I saw in Ven's vid. Roughly twice the size that he was before, with blood trickling down from a cut in his temple and vacant eyes. They paid attention to quality in the after vid. I can see every lump of scar tissue that's accumulated on the man's body, every shadow, every twitch. He's not scared anymore.

He's not anything.

I've never seen someone more in need of a rescue in my life. I still put my credits on the likelihood that the twins decided communication was too risky and went silent, but on the off chance things really did go wrong, they're both the kinds of physical specimen who would be very handy for . . . whatever this is . . . healthy and robust. It puts them at higher risk.

Victor and his twin sister, Victory, were born in a tiny colony on the dark side of a moon. They have pale skin, pale hair, and true-black eyes. Their skin is radiation resistant, but they completely lack the ability to tan. Victor's features are drawn broader than his twin's and a tiny scar slices through his left brow. She has a matching mark through her right bottom lip. It pulls her mouth down on the side, like she's always slightly doubtful.

The twins don't even have the consideration to be average sized; no, both of them are far taller than a normal person and corded with muscle, as one would expect from mercenaries. Aesthetically, it's great. Striking. They could be models if they weren't so militant.

It also means they're not the people you hire if you want to *avoid* attracting attention. Two tall beautiful violent spotlights are not clandestine.

I return my attention to the vid. Subject L is not clandestine, either. Whatever they did with him, they're not trying to make a superspy. My guess would be supersoldier. I've *got* to get into that lab.

My datapad's screen flickers out. I grimace. It's been doing that ever since I got on the station. Just my luck that the piece of shit waits to break until I don't have other options. No time for new tech. I have to rent a shuttle, make my way to Pierce space, and go be a hero.

. . . . .

The holo in the corner of my rented transport shuttle flashes a green light to indicate that my call has been accepted. Cyn and Micah pop up in all their holographic glory. I look up from the datapad I just used to message Victor and Victory—no response yet. "Hey, Cyn and Micah, Itzel and I were just talking about you the other day."

"All bad things, I hope." Cyn smiles just enough to flash the thin gap between her front teeth. The first time I ever saw her, she was embedded in a cult. The second time, she was on our ship to help us rescue Arcadio's niece and to retrieve a bounty on Micah. Needless to say, I didn't find her very trustworthy. Watching her leap into the vacuum without a suit to save Micah's life did a lot to turn that first impression around. As did the fact that she was experimented upon by the Pierce Family as a child.

"Mostly bad things," I agree with Cyn. "Sorry for the quick request, but I was hoping for an update on anything new you have about Pierce."

She's been researching the Pierce Family and Carmichael Pierce specifically for some time now.

Cyn shakes her head, short blond hair brushing against her jaw. "I don't have much of anything new. The bounty we're chasing has a friend who used to run supply to Haverhaven, the Pierce pleasure station. Anyway, this friend says there was a section of the station that was partitioned off from the rest, and that part received very different supplies."

"Let me guess: medical supplies." Shit. Of course it isn't just Shikigami. Weirdly, though, I'd rather go to the prison. Haverhaven is where the rich and famous go to play and to gamble. It's riddled with security because of the large credit transfers that it supports. No one's throwing their credits around at Shikigami. It's on an isolated planet. Nature provides security for them. I play the short vid of Subject L on my datapad, just a flash of blank pale eyes and a hard face. I can't get those eyes out of my mind.

"Got it in one." She suppresses a yawn, which Micah clearly notices. "We have to continue our search but if we want evidence of Pierce actions, Haverhaven is bound to house useful information. I'm sending everything we have to your encrypted file. Maybe you guys can figure out how to get in."

Selfishly, I was hoping she'd heard something about Shikigami that I could use. Haverhaven is a good secondary clue, but it won't do me much good at the moment. I nod.

"I'm hoping to hit something big soon. I'll send you what I get as soon as I can." It's all I can offer. If I tell them what I'm doing, they'll probably want to tag along. As though I can't handle a luxury prison on my own.

"And now, we need to sign off, because this one needs some sleep." Micah tugs Cyn closer, whispering something in her ear. The corner of her mouth twitches up.

"I thought you were sleeping better these days."

She turns back to me. "I am. You know what a worrier this one is."

Not really. Only about her. The rest of us he tells to toughen up.

"I just enjoy wearing you out, so you have peaceful dreams." Micah's voice is almost too quiet to hear. Almost.

"Gross, Micah. Keep your porny medical treatments to yourself." I close the call before any other portions of their relationship are overshared. I'm just watching the holo-feed spark down to its base when I realize that I didn't consult with Micah about the bugbites. They're all closed up, so they're probably fine. Itchy, but that means they're healing.

I spend the rest of the day scrolling through Cyn's meticulously assembled evidence file. It's nice working with someone who values documentation.

. . . . .

When I reach Pierce territory, I walk into the first embassy I find, show my real identification, and squeeze some blood into a tester, and the woman at the counter, who has green hair and slightly smudged green lipstick, just stares at me.

"I'm wanted," I provide helpfully, making sure that my hands are visible and clearly not holding weapons.

She glances at her own hands—not helpful, although she does have a lovely pale-green manicure with gold tips—and then back to me. "By whom?"

This is harder than I thought it would be. "Um. The authorities? For sabotage. Theft. Contract breaking. Probably some other stuff."

She gives me a look like this is a prank. I try to give her dangerous eyes to show that I'm a force to be reckoned with. She still isn't in the mood to reckon. "Maybe you can come back later. I'm new. I don't know what to do about this."

I sigh. Getting arrested should be easier than this. My original plan was to just get in a bar fight and see if they'd take me to Shikigami, but I'm not important enough to go there if I'm not working in a lab. So I have to reveal my true self. It feels strange after spending years as Caro Osondu to just blatantly wear my real surname, Ogunyemi, in public. "Yeah, so, I feel really bad about all the sabotage and . . . maybe terrorism? I've grown past it. My therapist says I need to take responsibility for my mistakes."

"I don't think there's a form for that." She nervously glances over my shoulder, clearly hoping a line has formed and she can get rid of me, but no such rescue is there for her.

Maybe I can flirt my way into her finally making the call that gets me arrested. I glance down at her name tag and flutter my eyelashes. "Mylanthe, that's such a beautiful name. I love your hair. So bright. Could you just call someone with Pierce at the end of their name? I promise, they'll be happy to hear about it."

"Is there something wrong with your eyes?" She squints at me.

Nice to know my flirting skills are effective as ever. "Please?"

Finally, she does. Her eyes go wide as someone speaks to her over her coms and I'm immediately escorted to a room far beneath where the way station is supposed to end.

I sit in an uncomfortable chair waiting for an amount of time. My interface tattoo still isn't working. I took off my coms before I reached the station so they couldn't trace anything back. My augmented lenses were removed for similar reasons—I don't want to bring anything into Pierce space that could be used against me. So, basically, I'm alone in a basement with absolutely nothing to entertain me besides conjuring up ever more gruesome ways for this plan to end with me dead.

I may be confident, but I'm imaginative enough to come up with a lot of ways I could be wrong.

Ven's plan was about as simple as it gets. The twins were to get hired—easy, because Shikigami is a boring job on a boring planet and they're well above the caliber of the normal applicant. They were to work long enough to get the lay of the land. Then open a cell, yoink L out, steal a ship, and leave.

It's a good thing he called me in when he did, because one does not simply steal a Pierce ship and not have a full phalanx of much better ships in hot pursuit. They're littered with trackers and nearly all able to be remote-operated in case of some sort of failure, because Pierce likes to retrieve damaged vessels even if they're full of dead crew. The twins are great, but they aren't skilled enough to strip all trackers and scrub the system's AI drive mechanisms.

Like I said, Ven understands the *pew-pew* shooting part of jobs, not the nuance. I'm not so good at the shooting parts. As I'm so often reminded, my aim has a lot of room for improvement.

I don't understand why. Aim is just pointing. It's easy! Even complete idiots can point at things.

For some reason I can't. However, I'm *good* at the nuance.

If I have access to a datapad (which Pierce will provide me, because it's how I'm useful), I'm untouchable and I can walk right out of Shikigami when I'm ready. They don't know all I've learned since the last time I was in their clutches.

I'm not saying it won't be terrifying, just that I can remote-unlock some doors and sneak where I want to go if necessary. It occurred to me to reach out to Temper and the rest of the crew, drop a line about where I'm going and what I plan to do there. But I didn't.

Temper is a protector. Always has been. She's also actually *good*. The kind of good I never thought someone from a Family was capable of being until I met her. She does the right thing, always. It inspires me to want to be better than I am. I couldn't stand it if she knew what made me run from Pierce in the first place. Or if she was in danger because of it.

Besides, this is just the sort of mission that plays to my strengths (not getting shot at or shooting) and allows me to show that I really am a fully valuable member of the crew. That I'm capable of more than sitting back with the tech while everyone else has adventures.

I set a shuttle to land on Myrrdhn, the planet that houses Shikigami, out of range of the prison's sensors. It approached the planet on a stealth trajectory. That avoids the risks of hijacking a Pierce vessel. I couldn't obtain schematics of the prison itself, beyond a message fragment that states its full capacity is over a thousand, but its actual population is in the low hundreds. Apparently, they predicted that there would be a lot more Family criminals than there have been.

The planet was scouted at some point and that report was in the planetary registry. Looks like your average cool misty climate with mountainous terrain, some small herbivore life, and one large predatory species. No images have been captured of the predator, but it's described as a positive in the scouting report—a deterrent to prisoners escaping.

That's a job for my blaster-wielding companions.

After a few hours—or what feels like a week—the holo in the center of the room activates. A Pierce-shaped and -colored face looks out at me. Carmichael Pierce. The heir to the Pierce Family. He visited us once at university, just to show off his impressiveness, and the other students and I used to call him Priap Pierce—university students love an alliterative insult. I'm sure he never knew. If he did, he's the type who would scoop our insides out with a dessert spoon and use them to season his salad. His face is pinkish and thin, his mouth is thin, and his teeth are extra large and extraordinarily white—clearly replaced after his adolescence. His hair is combed over his head in a blond swoop. There's nothing wrong with his features. Taken individually, they're all excellent. Some might consider him classically attractive. But to me, there's always been something hollow behind his light-brown eyes.

"Caro Ogunyemi. It *is* you," he greets me sourly, narrow lips twisted into a sneer. "I didn't believe them when they told me."

"It is." Better to stick with facts than get cute with Pierce. He doesn't appreciate cute things. He didn't bother to look any deeper when he encountered Caro Osondu, engineer of the *Calamity*. Back then, I was beneath his interest. I've made sure my image is hard to come across.

I have a brief flashback to Prism Way Station, the last time I saw him. Pierce had captured Micah as a way to get revenge on Cyn and settle an old score with our medic. Cyn, Itzel, and I fought our way to the edge of the ship, just as he shoved Micah through a plasma wall into the void. Cyn leapt after him. The moment when I realized I'd truly misjudged her. At the time,

Pierce's attention was focused on them. I wasn't close to him, lost in the scrum of guarda. Itzel was far more of a distraction than I was. By the time I got around to making threats, Pierce had already hightailed his ass to safety. I made sure my picture didn't linger in their security feeds.

"You left, sabotaged our system, hid for nearly twelve standard years, and then just popped up at a way station, offering yourself up like bait? I don't buy it. It's a stupid move and—whatever you are—you aren't a stupid woman."

Debatable. I *am*, however, a liar. I make my face as earnest as possible. Everything hinges on this.

"Twelve years is a long time. I grew up. Realized that what you were doing wasn't what I thought, at the time. I needed to see more of what was going on with people before I could understand that you were trying to make order in chaos."

Carmichael doesn't care about my opinion; he just wants me to tell him how smart he is—but not too quickly.

"You set us behind years with that stunt you pulled. I'd be fully justified to lock you up in Shikigami and lose the key."

I suppose that's another way to get what I'm after. A harder one that will probably put Temper on a collision course with Pierce once she hears about it. A course that will end with my captain a frozen speck in space because one does not just declare war on Pierce. I hang my head in feigned shame. "I know. I came to fix what I broke. All I can do is apologize—and work to make it better. And—well—I need credits. Your Family paid well. I don't make much scratch on the run."

Sometimes, if you tell someone exactly what they want to hear, they don't look too hard at it. Not me. I look extra hard when it's what I want to hear. That's one of those charming personality traits that has netted me threes of friends. But Pierce, he thinks peasants like me are motivated solely by credits. It's a plausible regret from his perspective.

He grins, transforming carefully sculpted features to something almost ratlike. "We won't be paying you, Caro. Not until you earn out what you cost us with your foolishness."

Perfect. He feels like he's punishing and incentivizing me at the same time. I try to appear desperate, but I'm not exactly sure what that looks like so probably I look a little sick.

I imagine Pierce gets that look a lot.

When the holo drops and the Pierce guards finally force me into the automated shuttle headed for Shikigami, an ominous cloud settles around me. I only narrowly escaped with my life the last time. This time I may not be so lucky.

The Shikigami shuttle is a plain white oval with disjointed black windows interrupting the stark snow-white of the interior surface. It's shaped kind of like a short-tailed sperm. It doesn't need massive fuel reservoirs or powerful batteries. It just needs a nudge in the right direction and an AI smart enough to get out of the way of bigger vessels.

Shiki's day-to-day activities are not publicized. I don't know how the prison is run beyond that the guards of the prison itself are all androids—powered by some form of hive-minded AI. The guards of the scientists are humans, because AI guards make scientists twitchy.

It's a sort of free-range prison where the best bunks go to the most formerly powerful prisoners and you have nothing to do except be surrounded by priaps and apply skin tonics until you die. Or until the Pierce Family decides to use you for whatever Project Titan is.

One would imagine that really relieves the boredom. I think more elaborate spa treatments are also involved. It's a weird prison but Families are weird so prisons for the highest placed within them would be weird also.

After an indeterminate amount of time, the slight adjustments of a course change register. I crane my neck and see the planet Myrrdhn. It's a greenish-white blur with rough mountains wreathed in fog and as we approach, a glistening white shape like two eggs stuck together lodged within the mountains becomes visible. Shikigami. A protrusion extends from one side of the smooth wall of the main prison. Probably the lab.

When the shuttle hits the prison's perimeter, a red light flashes on the far side of the ship, and it slips within the smooth white dock that connects to Shikigami.

The wall releases my cuffs, which part from each other, small LEDs gone dull and dead. This doesn't seem like part of the normal order of things. Why have electronic cuffs if they aren't activated? Probably I'll be blamed for breaking them. An orange android with GR52 stamped slightly crookedly on its chest enters the shuttle.

It has a vaguely humanoid head and torso, arms ending with elongated sharp black digits. It is poised with one arm extended although not pointed. It doesn't need to do anything as primitive as aiming with its arm. It aims with its robotic mind and its stun charge will use the arm as a lightning rod. One smooth black sensor encircles its entire head. Rather than legs, two thick-track triangular treads move it smoothly along the floor.

I would love to take it apart and study every single thing that makes it work.

Those cold metal fingers hover over my wrists, scanning my strangely dead cuffs. The droid emits a dismal beep. Another. The sensor on its head bores into me with a blank sort of intensity. When it speaks, its voice is flat and dull. "The cuffs have been tampered with."

Oh shit.

CHAPTER 3

I carefully regulate my breathing. Try to look innocent. Which doesn't work on a droid. "Perhaps they are defective."

Androids do not understand humor or deflection. They calculate odds. With no external signs of tampering, odds are at least even the cuffs are defective. Considering I actually *haven't* tampered with them, I hope it believes me.

A small circular saw erupts from its hand and slices through my left cuff and then my right cuff with horrifying precision. What if I'd sneezed? "Your identification was recorded in the shuttle. You will not elude us."

I remain silent, because it doesn't care about excuses. That diplomacy buys me nothing as its arm extends and something sharp shoots deep into the back of my neck. My first impulse is to clutch it and scream like I'm dying, but I'm actually *not* dying, so it's terrifying in a different way. I freeze, waiting for some basic bodily function to stop working.

Everything keeps on working. "Ow."

I glance at the android. It does not glance at me. Because it does not have eyes.

It goes back to pointing its taser fingers and gestures for me to lead it out of the shuttle. So I guess we're not going to talk about how it just injected something into my spine. Sure. That tracks.

I stumble out into the docks, hand still rubbing the back of my neck. There are two doors visible against the curved shape of the prison. The closest is small. Partway around the arc of the building, a much larger round door with a plas-glass-sculpted frame is bracketed by two tall twisted blown-glass trees. The larger door is so heavy and reinforced that it must be a direct line to the prison proper. The smaller door has a symbol etched on it and no sculpture at all. This must be where the help enters the prison.

GR52 directs me to the smaller door and, once inside, escorts me to a pile of shapeless white coveralls within. The android waits. I stare at it.

It shoots me with a taser.

Not as much power as a stun blast but enough to drive me to my knees. I crash down to the metal-grated floor.

"Ow. *Again.*" I glare at the android. The edges of the grate cut at the palms of my hands. It backs up to give me space and I push my way back to my feet.

I quickly take off my clothes and reach for the coveralls. Before I make contact, an ionic shower jet hits me like a tornado. This time, I don't fall. Good for me. Once I've been decontaminated, the android allows me to dress myself in the coveralls. They're sized for an average man, which means that they're tight at the hips and bust but also too long for me, crumpling on the floor until I roll them at the cuffs. I can't decide if this lab is funded poorly or if this is a machination of Carmichael's intended to embarrass me. It seems a level of petty attention to detail that might be beneath him. I step on a foot scanner and a zaprinter spits out a pair of soft shoes. They're fuzzy on the inside. It's like walking on clouds.

The excellent condition of the zaprinter implies the embarrassment hypothesis is accurate.

The android guides me from the room, leaving my discarded clothing in a small pile on the floor. I guess there's a housekeeping bot for that sort of thing. A moving walkway takes me farther from the entrance, threading a narrow hallway with several doors until I emerge through the farthest one.

Where I'm greeted with a view of the lab. Thank fucking be to any deity watching over me. Thank even Itzel's Dark Mother, because I am certainly floating near her void. An android, much more human-shaped than my orange escort, with glossy white chassis and a narrow pointy face, is built into a reception desk and poises its hands over a datapad—as though it needs a datapad. People build their customer-interfacing androids with a prioritization on comfortingly human anatomy before functionality.

Next to the android is Carmichael Fucking Pierce. I'm sure that's his middle name. You can't be that big a priap and not have your parents call you that at least once. His blond hair continues to be impeccable. His mouth is screwed up tight as a little fist. I'd bet that he looks like this all the time. Maybe even when he goes to sleep at night.

What the hells is he doing here? When he took my call, I assumed it was from some estate in Pierce-ville (not its real name). Oh. Maybe this is because he fucked up so bad with Aymbe, the Abyssal Abductor, that his daddy finally decided some discipline was in order. I smile, despite my better judgment.

He looks over my shoulder at the android. "Did you chip her?"

"Subject was chipped," the android's toneless voice replies. Like I'm a wayward pet.

Pierce still doesn't seem to recognize me from the Micah incident. Maybe because he still hasn't bothered to look directly at me. He continues to look at the android even though his words are clearly meant for me. "That chip contains a standard tracking beacon and a tiny explosive. Placed above your spine as it is, we don't need much explosive. You even think of going back on your newly regained fealty to Pierce, your neck will end in a large ragged stump."

That's how I know Carmichael was trained from birth to be management and not to understand anything his staff actually does. I'm familiar with this kind of chip. They don't blow your head off. That's inefficient and potentially hazardous to anyone around you. They don't *need* to blow your head off to kill you. The chip will simply neatly, catastrophically damage my brain stem, leaving me either dead or a vegetable. Pierce felt the need to dramatically embellish, which means that he wants to establish dominance both intellectually and psychologically but didn't bother to do his research beforehand.

Like I said: management.

There's something wrong with me that I consider that before I consider the fact that an android just injected a bomb into my neck, and I have to walk around hoping it doesn't malfunction. The bomb is horrifying but manageable. If I get some time alone in the lab, I can decommission it with a kludged EMP. That's the thing about bombs . . . if nothing triggers them, they can't go off.

Then, when we've escaped, I can hightail it to Micah and have him cut it out.

"Was that really necessary?" I ask, more because he expects me to than because I want an answer. "I didn't have to turn myself in. I'm here voluntarily, isolated in a prison. If you want to threaten me, you could just have a guard shoot me."

As I say it, I perform a quick assessment of the visible guards. I don't see the twins. That would be too easy, I guess.

Carmichael turns and walks away, clicking his tongue at me in what is clearly a command to heel. I do, because I have a bomb in me, and he seems officious enough to trigger it just to make a point. I reach behind my neck, rubbing first across one of the nearly healed bug bites before I find the raw edge of the injection site. My fingers come away with a thin line of blood. Super.

"I value expediency. You know you have a bomb in you, so you'll be more likely to behave. Also more motivated to earn my good graces. At such a time, I might be tempted to remove it. I'm happy to help my friends—if they help me first." He still doesn't so much as glance at me as we cross the lab.

The space is white. Maybe they like how it showcases blood spatter. At present, any blood remains unspattered on the white tile that lines the floor and walls. There is, however, a drain in the center of the room for easy cleanup. A chill traces my spine. Good rooms never have a drain in the middle of the floor. The far wall is lined with cells. Each has three white walls with a plas-glass front and very minimal facilities. Small nozzles line the ceiling, ready to dispense any number of horrifying chemicals on the men—and they're all men—within them.

I assume it's chemicals. I suppose they could be confetti cannons, ready to start the party.

From my angle, I can't see the individual prisoners well. Several men pace almost frantically, animals in too-small cages. They strike the walls when they collide with them. Several others lay in their cots, staring blankly at the ceiling. Only one stands at the front of his cell, watching everything.

It's L from Ven's vid. My throat goes tight with recognition and my fists clench against my will.

"You will be supervised as you work. Do not think you can get away with any additional sabotage. If you try—" Carmichael wiggles his thumb in the air in what I assume is a detonation gesture. I try my best to look innocent. I really should spend more time learning to fake emotions. I'm no good at it. Three guards are stationed around the room. Two near the plas-glass cells and one near a gold-lit door. They have blasters out and in hand but not pointed. I don't know whom they think they need to shoot. Probably cheap rent-a-guards trying to look like they're poised for action. It must bug the shit out of Victory to pretend to be this low-level.

Carmichael stops in front of one of the plas-glass-fronted cells and I stumble to a halt as I gaze inside. "You will not approach this subject under penalty of death. You have no need to. Meet Leviathan, our success story. Despite you wiping your old code."

It's L, up close and personal. He stares through the glass at me, gaze so intense it could lacerate, like I'm a mystery that he's trying to solve. His eyes are the expected shocking pale blue-green, like shallow ocean water, even more striking in person. They dart down to my blood-tipped fingers and then back up to my face. He doesn't look particularly sympathetic. He doesn't look like he has any feelings at all.

Leviathan is a large man. Larger than Arcadio, who was my previous reference point for big men. His shoulders look like they could barely fit through a standard doorway, and I can see the flex of muscle working beneath his spotless white coveralls as he shifts from side to side. The vid showed that he was big, but without any scale, I couldn't tell how big. This close, the very fine dark stubble on his shaved head is visible. His skin tone is the kind of light brown that could turn much darker if it ever saw sun and his hands are the size of the *Calamity*'s engine regulators. He appears like he could single-handedly tow a grounded transport ship.

If he wasn't inside a cell, looking like he wants me dead, I'd want to climb him like a ladder.

Which is a grossly inappropriate thought. He's hardly in the position to consent, and I have a bomb in my neck. Now isn't the time for climbing. It must be that false sense of familiarity from watching the video of him so many times. I couldn't stay away from the snippets of footage I managed to collect, watching them on a loop as I formed my plan. When you know what someone looks like scared, what they look like before a huge trauma, it makes you think you know them in reality. I'm glad we're here to rescue him.

His hand curls into a fist.

Carmichael chuckles a nasty little laugh. "If you try to access his cell, I won't have to detonate the explosive. He'll squash you like a bug."

"Well, that's just a waste of valuable explosives," I mutter, rubbing at the back of my neck again. I wonder if everyone here has a bomb. Seems like it would be good for productivity but bad for morale. At some point, morale always wins out.

Maybe that's where the confetti cannons come in.

"What's up with the other . . . participants? They look a little damaged."

He gives me a sour expression. "That's why you're here. In nearly every case, the subjects became violent or catatonic. On or off. This one is different. Fully within our control."

This one. As though the man in front of us is a medical dummy rather than a full human person. Considering his size, he might count as a person and a half. But they aren't going to give me access if I get all moralistic. I try to give Leviathan meaningful eye contact to convey that I'm really on his side—on the off chance that bug-squashing comment was accurate. He squints back at me like I'm blurry.

I get that reaction from men a lot.

"What exactly are you trying to achieve that impacted the subjects so severely?"

Bad question. Carmichael grabs my wrist and yanks me away from the cell, dragging me toward one of the lab benches. I yelp and stumble at the sudden contact and motion, nearly falling until I catch my balance by clutching a standing directional lamp. It tilts and goes out, eliciting an angry grunt from the scientist hunched beside it. A hammer-heavy fist crashes against plas-glass behind me, making me leap forward, jarring the table when my hip slams into it. When I glance back, Leviathan's haunting eyes are still locked on me, and some crazy stupid part of me wants to quell the vibration by setting my own hand on the plas-glass.

It's a series of examples of why Temper keeps me out of front-line situations. I'm clumsy, I'm only passable at self-defense, and I frequently have misplaced empathy.

I want to prove her wrong. Problem is—she isn't.

Carmichael releases my wrist as all three guards descend on Leviathan's cell, blasters raised, but after the one sharp knock against the plas-glass, he settles back into stable stormy observation mode. The guards retreat. I guess that's why they have weapons drawn. If he tried, maybe he really could make it out.

I brace myself against the table, hoping no one noticed my little burst of clumsy panic. *Everyone* noticed. They're staring at me. I give a little "whoopsie" grin and wave. No one waves back. Then again, these people perform experiments on prisoners. It's hardly the place one expects to find allies.

Carmichael shoves a datapad at me. "Do your best to not break anything else. And stop asking questions you don't need answers for. Work the problem. Relevant data is in your hands now. Don't ask for anything else."

"Sure. Can do." I say the words to his back. He's already storming off to make someone else's life miserable. Lucky them. My palms are sweating, my stomach feels like it's full of broken glass, and I kind of have to go to the bathroom. Now feels like a bad time to ask where it is.

I activate the datapad. It doesn't turn on. Of *course* he gave me a broken datapad. Maybe he's setting me up to fail, thinks if I can't get him a result in a certain amount of time, he's justified in popping my brain stem like a spark plug.

That's all right; I never met a piece of tech I couldn't fix.

· · · · ·

I can't fix it. *Fuck.* Everyone in the lab is giving me a wide berth, glancing from the corner of their eyes but not speaking to me just in case neck-bombs are contagious. Two people are at computerized terminals on the wall, projected screens showing something that could be sound waves. More likely they're radio waves, used to send messages. Two more technicians take packets out of a wall-mounted sterilization unit and place them beside the surgical table on a smaller magnetically fixtured table. They all seem to have functional equipment.

The lab is well stocked with new polished equipment. I don't know why I got the garbage datapad. Maybe hazing.

"Hey, my datapad seems to be out of juice." I glance around the room, hoping someone will look my way. "Do you guys have any spares?"

No response. They must have spares. My only assumption is that this really is a game of Carmichael's and no one wants to piss him off by giving me functional tools.

Okay, new plan. Someone has to go to the bathroom at some point. When they do, I'll just do a little switch-out and take their working tech. I study the test subjects. The catatonic ones are still catatonic. The other ones are still pacing and hitting walls and even harming themselves in their blind desire for . . . something. It's almost like one group of subjects possess zero aggression or energy and the others have a surplus. Leviathan is still squinting at me. You'd think they would have fixed myopia if he had it. I smile at him. Mostly to see what he does.

Look bewildered is what he does. I'm suddenly flooded with guilt. He appears so physically capable, I briefly forgot that—from his perspective—he's being tortured and I'm one of the torturers. I don't fully understand what's happening here, but I know enough to see that it's appalling. I don't know if I'll be able to stay under the radar, gather intelligence, and eventually escape with only the twins and Leviathan.

I have to stop this. I don't know how, but I'm here and I know it's happening, so I must.

"Quite the specimen, huh?" A tentative woman's voice interrupts my staring contest. She approaches from behind me. A cute button nose sits atop her little bow mouth and between large doll-like hazel eyes. Someone who knowingly does what she's doing shouldn't be so adorable. I almost prefer Carmichael. He embraces villainy with cartoonish aplomb.

"All the others came out wrong," the woman continues, pointing at the cells on either side of Leviathan for example. In the left is a man who is slightly taller than I am, built on a sturdy frame, like a spark plug. His hair is also shaved. His cheekbones are sculpted, eyes up-tilted, and freckles embellish the skin across his nose. He sits on the edge of his bed and stares directly at the wall.

I wave my arm. No reaction.

"Hey!" I yell while arm waving some more. The woman snickers. It's an ugly sound in someone so cute and it makes me feel better that at least something about her is ugly.

Still staring at the wall. He doesn't even twitch. Not that I want random test subjects to give me too much attention, but the intensity of his nothingness is off-putting. The cell on Leviathan's right contains a man pacing from wall to wall, practically vibrating with constrained energy. His wild brown hair is a shaggy uneven length and the clearly defined muscles on his shoulders and arms are in a constant state of flexure. Visibly engorged veins thread his skin. When he turns to watch us, I can see one of his eyes has been replaced with a mechanized sensor.

I don't wave my arm at this one.

"I'm Rayla Scobal, principal engineer." She sounds proud. "Principal engineer" is a title of seniority, so in a normal lab that would be a point of pride. In the human-experiment world, it makes her extra evil, because she could go anywhere else and, you know, *not* be evil. "I was surprised to hear one of the early developers was coming. I didn't expect someone so . . ." She pauses and I can tell there are a lot of things she didn't expect about me before she settles on "young. You can see the two variants we get when we try to activate the control code. Subjects are stuck in either violently aggressive or absolutely passive states. We can hack their mods, but it's clumsy, not nuanced, like the system is fighting back."

The part of my brain that likes a problem perks up but the much larger part of my brain that likes being a human with morals and ethics and stuff bops it right on the head. "How many . . . subjects . . . have you tested?"

"None of your concern." So she isn't freely offering information. How disappointing. I wonder if she was here when they first brought Leviathan into the lab. When he was a man and not a machine.

"And it's only worked with Leviathan?" That can't be his real name. Who names their adorable baby boy Leviathan? Maybe a woman who just gave birth to what must have been a large infant—although I've seen the before video. When he wasn't so large. When he was normal and frightened. "Was there anything unique about his procedure or anatomy?"

"*Lab* people!" Carmichael barks the words from across the room, clutching a datapad, glaring disparagingly between me, Rayla, and the other scientists. "I expect a report on our new arrival tomorrow morning. If she fails to perform, let's inspire her by placing her in the prison to think about motivation."

With that motivating missive, he turns and strides through a door at the back of the lab space.

"Lab people?" I raise an eyebrow at Rayla. Just making friends here. "That's a trifle dehumanizing to your team."

"Just because he's a pompous priap doesn't mean we're confidants," she snaps. There goes my hope that feminine camaraderie would make this easier on me. Not that I actually want to be friends with this adorable sociopath. One standard day isn't long to achieve results. Especially with a nonfunctioning datapad.

"Say, I don't suppose you could give me a replacement datapad? I'll help you with that problem of the toggle between modes."

She sniffs, strides across the lab with her white coat slapping in the breeze of her movement, delves into a cabinet, and returns, thrusting a device into my hands with a snide little grin. "Here."

At last.

The stupid thing doesn't turn on. Apparently she's playing the same game as Carmichael. What a fuckwaffle.

Before I try to solve the problem of the newest nonfunctioning datapad, I spare one last glance for Leviathan, still standing motionless at the front of his cell, face impassive, eyes steadily following me like *I'm* the confusing one here.

My lips part but I don't even know what I'd say if I could speak freely. Maybe try to assure him I'm not like the rest of them. That the twins and I—when I find them—will try to get him out of here and remove that awful thing in his brain that steals his agency. I don't do it. I'm here to appear like one of the other scientists. I can't ruin that illusion and squander my greater purpose just because a hunk with great eyes might want to kill me.

I've actually had a fairly large selection of hunks try to kill me. Maybe that says something bad about my general state of being.

CHAPTER 4

After a half day of questioning people and attempting to steal datapads, unsuccessfully, I have a lot more questions and not many answers. No one has offered to share *why* they're doing this but there's clearly only one reason you'd make someone change from a fluffball to a machete.

They're making supersoldiers and they're probably using prisoners as their subject pool.

I've been here long enough to hear the other guards chatting about Victor and Victory. They're still at Shikigami; they're just on night-shift duty. They don't seem to be in any trouble, which implies my suspicion that Ven overreacted is correct. No one here is on high alert. No one seems suspicious of anyone except *me*. I may be making things worse rather than better.

That's the Caro Ogunyemi guarantee.

Every hour or so, the polished white wall above the cells displays vital signs for the test subjects. Nothing too interesting except the fact that all of them, including the near-catatonic ones, are running with their vitals a little too high. Heart rate, temperature, respiration. All metrics are higher than they should be. Nothing that's unhealthy but interesting. If they were engines, they'd need a tune-up.

One scientist operates a robotic machine that lays out nearly microscopic circuitry on tiny chips. Another pulls surgical tools out of depyrogenation. I'd offer to help with that task, but it would only be suspicious. They don't have me here to haul things out of ovens. They have me here to hack people's brains.

With no functioning tech, I take a charcoal marker and write notes directly on the workbench. Nothing new, just sketching out my old code so that I can show I'm doing something. When I started my research with Pierce, I focused on viral code in androids. When a virus is embedded in a system, that network's etherwall and security protections attempt to block it. If you think of an android as a biological organism, you want to make the virus biocompatible so the immune system cannot detect it. You codematch and embed a signal that fools the machine's defenses into thinking it made the call itself.

"What do you call the test subjects?" I ask Rayla to distract her from the dead datapad on the counter in front of me. I'm starting to think they've somehow biotagged them to stop working when I touch them. What I don't understand is why. It's a lot of work just to be nasty. Then again, every time I've asked for any printed data, for calibration logs for the tech implemented on the test subjects, or for anyone to bring information up on the big display, they refuse—so I have proof that the staff of this lab is disinterested in helping me.

Rayla has been snooping over my shoulder the whole time, trying to determine if I'm implementing a diabolical plan so she can run off and tattle to Carmichael. Which, of course, I am, but I can't do much of anything until I gain enough trust to have full access, or at least privacy to hack the full access I need.

"What do we call them?" She purses her small lips. "It's Project Titan, so I suppose we call them Titans."

Ooo, exciting, finally a subject that gets her talking again. "Do they get a reduced sentence for volunteering for this research?"

She glances over her shoulder at the line of cells along the far wall and shudders delicately. "Sure. They volunteered."

The dismissive tone in her voice gives me pause. "They *had* to have volunteered, right? There are Family-based accords about how prisoners are to be treated. Especially in a place like Shikigami."

Families don't care that much about normal prisoners, but Shikigami is where *Family* criminals often find themselves. It's a plush place to spend their incarceration. Enough of the leaders are into shady things that they want to ensure that they'll be at least afforded some level of humanity in lockup.

"Don't worry about it. These guys are the worst of the worst. You don't get sent to Shiki if you're a good person." She glances back at the cells again. "I wish we could opacify the glass like we did years ago. I don't like them staring at us. It's creepy."

Sure. That's what's creepy. "Why can't you?"

"One of the angry ones killed himself. Just bashed away at the wall. We didn't know until a standard day later. They got mad at our wasted investment."

Well, that's appalling. Shikigami isn't what I expected. Far more horror, far fewer facial treatments. I guess the scientists don't get the full spa experience.

"So, the primary difference between Leviathan and the others is that his control dial works, and the others are stuck on active or just inert." I tap my chin with the marker. Accidentally draw on myself. Scrub at it with my hand. "What about their baseline personalities? Are they still present or have they been subsumed when you hack the chip?"

By which I mean, do the test subjects have any idea what's actually happening to them or are they in a semi-merciful state of oblivion? Is the man I saw in the video, the man I felt so drawn to, still there, or is it all the Titan Leviathan?

"That's not what you're here to care about. You're here to work on the control mechanism. You were the first to be able to get inside, with the impulsive suggestion you implemented in school.

We have deadlines and it doesn't look good that we've only made this work once."

I can see how that would look bad. I don't *care*, but I can see. "Sure thing." I pick up the dead datapad, carefully keeping the screen away from her. "I just need to get some scans of the subjects so I can see what's happening. Maybe their baseline chips are lower quality and lack the nuanced connections to make the changes you want."

"Their chips are fine. You don't need scans. You're starting from scratch. You can get scans if you're successful."

Fuck. There really isn't a good option here. Time to go for the hard sell. "I thought you wanted fast results. Starting from scratch won't fit your timelines. Clearly your team has been too hasty, but it will be a lot faster to find the mistake than it will be to start over and do it right from the beginning. It took me a full year in university and that was just inserting one subliminal impulse. This is much more complicated. You made it work once, so we should be comparing Leviathan to the others in order to see what the difference is."

And it would help me figure out how to undo what's been done to him.

Rayla folds her arms. "It's end of shift, and you've accomplished nothing. It's not my job to stay on overtime and hold your hand."

What exactly did she expect me to accomplish? Even if my tech was functional, one does not hack the human mind from scratch in an afternoon. Even if one *did* have a good lunch—and I had no lunch. As if remembering that cued it, my stomach lets out a loud gurgle.

Now, after ignoring me all day, the scientists look at me.

The irritation flows from Rayla's body like water and she sighs. "Come on. Eat dinner and we'll get back to this tomorrow. You're bunking in the room next to me. Don't ask me for anything, it's all in there. Mess has a nutrient printer, but its temp regulator broke a little while ago and it only prints cold stuff."

Yum. I bet the prisoners are eating better than that. "I could take a look at that for you."

Nothing to look at here. Just a helpful and nonduplicitous engineer trying to make good.

She squints at me for a moment. "It's fine as it is."

"No problem." It was probably overoptimistic to think she'd let me do that this soon.

We retreat through the door that Carmichael took earlier. It opens to a small living area with a few mismatched café tables and chairs, some overstuffed blobs that appear to be lounge chairs, a large holo in the corner currently playing a nature documentary from deep in Flores space. A creature that looks like it has more fur than flesh snuggles against a tree trunk eating a bright-blue fruit. Trust Flores to even know how to market their fluffy herbivores. A bird flies by and the puffy little creature unhinges massive jaws and bites its head off.

Not an herbivore, then.

Past the living area is a hall lined with doors. I assume they're the bunks Rayla mentioned. At the end of the hall, there's another reinforced door with a retinal scanner next to it. Probably Carmichael's personal quarters. A sudden urge to get in that space and hunt for secrets nearly overwhelms me. I know I'm here for the twins, and now the Titans, but that doesn't mean I can't take out my old nemesis on the way out the door.

Rayla pours herself a glass of a bright-orange liquor, prints out something to eat in an opaque dish, and plops herself down in front of the holo. Knowing my place in this establishment, I let all the other scientists print their cold food before I get mine. I just have it print a rice pudding and fruit.

The fruit was a mistake. It comes out textured like cobwebs. Most of the scientists cluster around the holo. Some retreat to their rooms. There appears to be some sort of holo-game happening in one of the rooms that attracts a few, wearing sensing rings on their fingers to interact with the action. I sit alone at a table by the printer, waiting for the night-shift guards to emerge.

I don't wait long. Victory is out first. Of course, she is. She's punctual like a clock. A long white braid swings down her back, a spotless black armored uniform clings to her athletic body, and the only sign she recognizes me is when her lips press together in worry. Another guard is out next. Shorter and barrel-chested. He looks at Victory with love in his eyes. Maybe lust. She's the sort of statuesquely capable person who inspires devotion. Finally, Victor emerges, hair a tangled mess, armor still open at the collar, and a grin on his face.

The twins get some stim water and join me at my table.

"You hired a new one!" Victor bellows in a voice that would be subtle to literally no one in the world. Luckily, Victor is such a womanizer, they'll probably assume it's because he wants to sleep with me, not because he knows me.

Victory's brow furrows and she takes a sip of stim, speaking in a low voice when her lips are masked behind the cup. "Why are you here, Caro?"

A cheer erupts from the holo-game room and I use it to respond. "Ven was worried when you dropped communications. He thought you were caught and couldn't do the rescue."

She makes a grumbly noise and Victor joins in. When another group outburst happens, this time from a different cute fuzzy creature eating something, Victory continues. "There is no rescue and we never dropped communications. We're here for tech, ran into a dead end. Ven played you."

That doesn't quite make sense. "No, he sent me the vid of Leviathan, the one you sent him. Why would you have evidence of the test subject if you weren't trying to rescue him?"

Victory's face stays impassive as she responds. "I sent him a long shot of the interior of the lab when we first arrived, to show the lay of the land. It's the only internal footage he has. Then I deactivated the cam because being caught with a camera is how you get dead."

I think back to when Carmichael didn't question me because I said exactly what he expected I'd say. I think of who taught me that little trick. The same priap who pulled it on me earlier. Of course, Ven cropped the vid for something that would motivate me—a hot man with haunted eyes. He knew I'd jump on a rescue when I wouldn't offer to help if he just tried to hire me. And just in case the twins weren't enough motivation, he added an innocent victim in need of aid.

I pose my guess. "You couldn't hack whatever tech you needed, and you reported that to him, so he assumed I could. That I *would* once I got here because we'd all be in so much shit that I'd have to in order to get out. I should warn you: everyone hates me, and they haven't let me use working tech. I can't do it soon."

Victor leans across the table like he's whispering sweet nothings to me. There was a time when that would have set my heart fluttering. He's a handsome man—with all the confidence of someone who's never had to work all that hard for female attention. "You don't know everything about the tech we were sent for yet."

Victory gets up, pushing away from the table, and stomps away as though she's disgusted by her brother's flirtation attempts.

"What don't I know?"

"Who hired us." His usually jovial face is uncharacteristically solemn, and he leans forward to whisper in my ear. "Frederick Reed."

Fuck. I can't come up with something better to say. To *think*. Temper's crooked brother, meddling in more Family business.

The twins go to their shift, and I go to bed without having the chance to talk more. We don't want to attract attention. I don't want to think about the Frederick Reed problem just yet. I have too many *other* problems and I need a new game plan. If they won't let me access working tech, I have to find lab notebooks. Shockingly old-fashioned but still used, because the thing about a notebook is that it isn't hackable, and it isn't auditable if you don't bring it out. It's a place to store experimental data before you're ready to write up an official report.

So, I will access data that way, I will make some sort of deduction from that, and hopefully it will get me trusted enough to access the working tech that everyone else has. At that point, I'll figure out what Reed wants and whether or not I'm willing to give it to him.

Then I'll set off all their lockdown measures, snarl their systems, steal their data, and activate the autopilot of my hidden ship to carry us off-world as quickly as it can, in the direction of the Escajedas, whom I assume will be able to do something official to help rescue the test subjects. As it is, I can't drag the catatonic ones and I can't safely get close to the other type, so I don't know what I can do for them with the limited time I have. But I'll be back for them. I'll either take the twins with me or leave them, since they have their own extraction plan.

Then, I'll do my best to kick Ven in the ass so hard that he tastes what I last stepped in.

The next morning, I hustle into the lab and manage to scoop up as much paperwork as I can get before everyone else is set up at their stations. I spread it out in front of me to study, but Rayla has other ideas.

A red light flashes in Leviathan's cell. A matching red light illuminates the reinforced door at the end of the cellblock. Rayla turns to me with an eager grin of anticipation. "You wanted to study Leviathan? Fine. We'll watch him in action."

That doesn't sound good.

Two day-shift guards position themselves in front of his cell and the plas-glass slides open. Since he's in docile mode right now, he calmly allows them to escort him down the hall and to the door. Rayla takes her datapad in hand and slips on a pair of augmented-reality glasses. The door slides open, golden illumination ringing it, and the sounds of Shikigami proper echo through the narrow portal. Mostly tinkly bell-like music and the artificial sound of waves. The prison sounds much nicer than the lab.

"What's going on?" I shuffle paper in front of me as though I'll be able to find an answer in it. I do find a schematic of Leviathan's body, riddled with tech add-ons, but I don't have time to study it before Rayla demands my attention again.

"As a way to test our Titans and to offer entertainment and distraction to the prisoners, we have enacted a gladiatorial match that occurs on a random schedule. Leviathan acts as the prison's champion. The prisoners vote on someone to send in against him."

A fancy opulent prison with gladiatorial matches. Ew. "He's never been defeated?"

"Never defeated. Their goal is to make it to that door alive. Past him. There have been survivors, but they don't go back into gen pop. We utilize them for our next Titan subjects because they've proven themselves hardy."

Gross.

"So, those two." I gesture at the catatonic man and the one who's trying to pull his own toe off. "They were survivors."

A crashing sound rattles through the open door. Rayla pulls up a holo and, through the floating image, I finally see the inside of Shikigami proper for the first time.

The prison is bright, glossy, and embellished. The large atrium in the center is stadium-sized, the walls covered in geometric white metallic panels that are decorated with iridescent paints in glowing pinks, purples, and golds. In the center of the atrium, there is a gigantic chandelier, dripping in real-glass prisms that direct light in flecks all around the open-air space, dappling all surfaces in rainbow freckles.

Rayla turns up the intensity at the base of the holo and zooms in.

The floor of the atrium is broken up with a literal maze of walls, with each panel of the maze made of a green metal that is etched and embossed with delicate leaves, as though it is a hedge. The maze provides no direct means of access to any of the lower-level chambers. Several halls stretch away from the large atrium into other portions of the prison.

Or rather, the resort. Let's call it like it is. The lab where the Pierce scientists work is far less welcoming than the "prison" itself. Just goes to show how fucked up our society is. Family criminals deserve better treatment than workers.

We're staff, they're *important*.

The rhythmic crashing is the walls of the maze beating against themselves. The maze has unfolded into a long hallway from the door Leviathan just exited to the other side of the atrium, where a squat man with slightly grown-in blond stubble stands holding a mallet. On the many levels overlooking the atrium, prisoners sit behind the railing, cheering or eating snacks. One man with Pierce-blond hair shoves a handful of some sort of chip in his mouth and then throws the bag down at the arena. The air vents between levels, sensing something unfamiliar, vacuum it up before it has a chance to fall more than one level.

I clench my hands on the table until my knuckles pop. The two sides of the long maze-formed hallway beat against each other like a heartbeat. It reverberates in my core. The golden-lit door to the lab slides shut behind Leviathan, leaving the guards on our side. Unlike the prisoner, he is unarmed.

Leviathan looks up, staring into the mass of screaming dilettantes gathered around the maze, and his face is impassive as a statue. When he looks down, straight through the undulating

metal gauntlet that leads to the elected prisoner, the man tries
to flee.

The wall behind him shoves him forward as the maze reforms
into a labyrinth. The alarms go silent.

Leviathan steps into the maze.

The prisoner takes the maze at a sprint. It's unclear whether
he believes it will give him an advantage or simply limit the time
to anticipate his demise. Behind him, walls reform themselves,
blocking retreat. He hits a dead end and is briefly trapped in a
square-walled chamber as the maze moves around him. It's like a
living thing, and as I watch the holo, I see why. It is leading them
to each other. Every turn Leviathan takes puts him inexorably
one step closer to the prisoner.

The prisoner pauses in his mad dash, looks up, eyes wide and
teeth clenched in desperation. He leaps for the top of the wall,
falls just short. Tries again. His fingers brush the top. The wall
grows another handspan, a mockery of his panicked ingenuity.
Whatever intelligence runs the maze, it's cruel. Rayla chuckles,
her fingers hovering over the datapad.

Ah. *This* intelligence.

Leviathan continues to walk, steps slow and careful, face completely impassive. He seems aware of what the maze is doing and
allows it to guide him toward the prisoner, who has now decided
to try to retreat the way he came. It's hard not to try to figure out
how much of Leviathan's action comes from a preprogrammed
behavior set or his own choices. They may have wiped personality, but he's useless to them if he's *just* an android. They need
something between the two, which means, perhaps, some of the
man remains.

They make the prisoner think he has a chance, even if he's
seen the battles that came before. Give him a weapon, create
a maze that could theoretically allow him to dodge Leviathan.
Make a spectacle of the contest. There *is* no contest. The game

is rigged and the prisoners who watch and clap and jeer know it. They want one of their own to be flattened. They want him to provide entertainment.

He picks up the pace, fists tightening around the mallet. Perhaps he can hear Leviathan breathe. The prisoner swings back with the mallet as he rounds the last corner, his face red with the effort.

Leviathan catches it in one hand. He rips it from the prisoner's grip as easily as a parent taking a toy from a child and discards it on the floor behind him. Doesn't even consider using it. That tells me a lot about Leviathan. Maybe. If, as I suspect, he's largely acting on the programming to defeat his opponent but hasn't been given more precise directives. He's not insanely violent like the man in the cell behind me. He's deliberate. Deadly.

The mallet clatters where it hits the metal, and the prisoner takes a swing at Leviathan's midsection. His fist bounces off.

Everything goes quiet. The prisoners stop whispering, catcalling, screaming. They sit and stare with anticipation. They've seen this show before. They know the ending.

I can guess it.

Rayla swipes her hand in the air, like she's flipping a switch.

Leviathan *moves*. His hand lashes out, encompassing the prisoner's neck. The muscles in his forearm tense, rippling beneath the skin. The prisoner's face goes red. He kicks out, bare toe scraping over Leviathan's knee. The big man smashes him into the maze wall. Once. Again. The prisoner's body crashes against the metal with a force almost as loud as earlier, when the maze beat itself into a frenzy.

After the fifth hit, I look away. There isn't anything more to see here. One of the guards behind me whistles, the sound low and sad.

When I finally return my gaze to the holo, Leviathan is standing in the center of the former maze, all the walls spread open.

He doesn't look at the body on the floor or the blood that stains his hands. Doesn't even wipe them off. Rayla's fingers dance over her datapad and he turns back toward the lab, plodding woodenly. As he steps through the portal into our lab and the waiting embrace of the guards, who both have blasters leveled on him, one of maze walls sweeps the body to the side, where it falls into some form of pit out of sight. Probably soon to be disposed of.

So that's Shikigami in a nutshell. Snazzy. Awful. Brutal.

I wish I'd seen Victory's eyes when she first took this place in. It so clashes with her strict good/bad mentality. She believes bad people deserve punishment. Victor's the same. Their three-handed god throws souls to the other-life with two of his three hands. One for the good and the other for the evil. As far as I know, rich people don't get to go to the good afterlife just because they're connected.

After Leviathan's complete domination in the arena, Rayla turns off the holo and I press my lips together, because anything I can think to say right now would get my chip blown. The guards lock Leviathan in his cell and finally relax, lowering their weapons.

If Pierce can make more like him, the damage isn't just the catastrophic destruction of the people like Leviathan—it's who-ever they meet in combat. This hacking eliminates fear, desire, anything that makes a soldier flinch. It can probably even be more deeply programmed, almost like an android. They can make him exactly what they want—mindless as a robot but with the ability to improvise when he must. He'll fight and keep fighting as long as he can until something stops him.

Wiping human psyches clean and then forcing them to fight to the death for you? That part is not worse than I imagined—I have a good imagination—but it's worse than I hoped. The part that's worse than my imagination is that it's not just chips that are programmed to subsume a personality. It's that my tech allowed them to hack *existing* chips. Meaning that someone could be going about their day with a translator chip or some other tech and suddenly be programmed to fight for the death for the honor of Pierce.

It's difficult not to throw up.

After the events on Herschel that led to the dissolution of the Nakatomi Family, Temper told me that she suspected they had a partner and I agreed that Pierce was the most likely. If they'd achieved their goals, Nakatomi would have snagged control of shipping lanes and possibly shared access with Pierce. I suppose Leviathan is part two of the plan.

I spend the rest of the morning diving into my pilfered notes. Some are useless to the current situation. Reaction times before and after fast-twitch muscles have been supplemented. Latency testing for command signals. It's impressive, but it doesn't tell me why they're having problems. I need to find something that seems helpful so that they'll trust me—but something that doesn't actually help them with their scheme.

Rayla snatches the Leviathan schematic away from me just as I'm finally about to study it. "This is *mine*. Carmichael told you that you don't need to study this subject."

"I have to study *something*. You gave me bad tech."

She shakes her head, fingers clutching the paper so hard that it's almost tearing. "Leviathan is my subject. Don't think I don't see what this is. You're not trying to help me. You're trying to show me up. Carmichael won't trust you. He won't ever trust you. Not like he trusts me."

Oh boy. I don't know if this is just blind professional loyalty or the biggest misplaced crush of all time. Either way, it's pathetic.

"If you won't fix anything else, fix the printer." She points back at the break area. "You said you could. I'm tired of eating cold food. If you can't do it, I'm telling Carmichael about your sabotage."

I retreat to the printer, reaching in my pocket for the ever-present multitool that isn't there because I left it with my things back on the way station. The printer is a Madahyde III, which just came out a year or so ago. I did some research into this model when I upgraded the printer on the *Calamity* with our new phy-dium credits. One of the reasons this model isn't in the *Calamity*'s galley is that its temp switch is sensitive and sometimes software updates mess up the hardware.

Once Rayla provides me with a toolbox, I gently pry the front panel open until I can activate the hard reset that sits in the mid-dle of the assembly. It'll wipe all previous programming and then we can reinstall the initial software. Not a long-term fix, but these people are monsters. They don't deserve a long-term fix.

When I hit the hard reset, the printer turns off with a depressed-sounding hum. It doesn't turn back on. I poise my finger over the button again.

"What did you do?" Rayla shoves her head nearly into the printer alongside my arm. "Did you break it?"

"I just reset it. It might need to cool down before I turn it back on."

She stabs at the button I just pressed with a stiff finger.

I rub the bridge of my nose. "That just turned it off more. The inside switch resets. It doesn't turn it on."

"You broke it. You sabotaged our printer. Do you think I'm stupid? We have food stockpiles that will last us years. You can't hurt us that easily." She's showing her pearly little teeth as she growls at me, looking not unlike the cute Flores creature from the holo last night. Probably just as rabid. Hopefully without the unhinging jaw.

"What's going on out here?" Carmichael strides out of his se-cure rooms at the end of the hall.

"Nothing," I attempt, backpedaling.

"She's sabotaging us! She didn't do any work yesterday, tried to steal my work today, and now she broke our printer!" Rayla seems far more upset at the loss of cold lunch than at my lack of work ethic.

"You gave me two broken datapads and denied me notes, no matter how often I asked," I argue. "How could I do any work when I don't have functioning tools? If this is the kind of fractured-ass tech that Pierce stocks, what do you expect me to do?"

"Our tech is the best in charted space." Carmichael's face goes hard, and I wonder if I hit a sore spot. Pierce tech isn't really the best. Their energy tech is, but this is medical stuff, mixed with AI. That's Chandra and Reed. Maybe he's a little sensitive about their lack of expertise. His lips twist into a nasty little smile. "Put her in the prison for a few days. I'm sure she'll meet some people in there who can motivate her more effectively than we can."

"I'm really not motivated by negative reinforcement. You know what's motivating? Cookies. I'm really motivated by them." The words slip from my mouth before I even get a chance to stop them. I'm snarky when I'm scared.

"We can't have cookies because you broke our printer!" Rayla screams. *Screams*.

I guess she really *is* cookie-motivated. All the screaming is bad for me because she attracts the attention of the day-shift guards. One meanders over, hand resting against his blaster. "What's the problem over here?"

I wish it was one of the twins. But they're in their bunks snoozing away, never suspecting I would be this amount of incompetent. I'm supposed to be good at this kind of thing. I don't understand why they're playing these games.

"Sabotage!" Rayla points a quivering finger into the air.

I really wish she'd stop saying that. I haven't sabotaged them *yet*. That part comes later.

"I'm serious. Toss her in the prison. If she manages to stay alive for, say, three days, we'll take her back." He glances back at me, making hard eye contact for the very first time, and winks, the jaunty expression misplaced in his ratty face. His voice lowers. "You thought I didn't remember you . . . Caro *Osondu* of the *Calamity*. Never assume I'm not playing a longer game."

Shit. *Shit.*

"I didn't do *anything*." I try to approach the little holo-room, but the guard captures my arm, dragging me toward the door. It's a luxury prison, this shouldn't be threatening, but something in Carmichael's tone tells me that he's relishing the opportunity to throw me into the deep end. "I'm being set up."

Carmichael grins. Rayla strokes the poor dead printer like it's a pet.

The guard drags me through the lab to a side passage, through a dark twisting hallway, and—when we reach a massive hatch with about eight locks—opens the passage and shoves me though.

The door crashes shut behind me, locks engaging. It's loud. Sparkly. Terrifying.

It's Shikigami and I'm in here alone.

....

CHAPTER 5

I'm well equipped for a spy mission in a lab. I'm shit-nothing equipped for incarceration. Maybe even less ready for fancy-people prison than normal prison. I assumed Pierce would be smart and value my utility, not that he'd be disinterested and weirdly give me broken equipment. Why would he do that? If he wanted to lock me up, he could have done that from the start, but the choice to sabotage me and then accuse *me* of sabotage is bizarre.

I've never been able to understand how Families think. Maybe I should stop trying, because I always seem to be wrong.

One of the android prison guards rolls down the hallway on its treads. It is not sparkly. Maybe the androids, like the maze, are stark reminders of what a person stands to lose if they step out of line—if they stop focusing on their spa treatments and start focusing on insurrection. The android does not look in my direction. Because its visual sensors go all the way around its head, so it's always looking in every direction. I follow it, sticking partially behind its smooth chassis. The hall ends in the large center atrium. Fear clenches my guts.

I clench my fists. Take that, fear. You aren't the only one who can clench things.

Fear also clenches my butt cheeks. Just to show it's still the boss of me.

Once I've taken back control of my own body, I study the

prison. Details that weren't apparent in the holo present themselves. A gilded and embellished railing runs around each level's balcony. The walls are studded with open-doored rooms. Some have beaded curtains strung over the empty space where a door would be. Some have nothing. I guess privacy can't be fully allowed. Little embellishments in Nakatomi red show the prison's original provenance. No one has replaced it with Pierce blue yet.

I planned for the eventuality that I'd be incarcerated. I just need to lie low. It's attracting attention that gets you marked. I need to blend in until Carmichael decides I've served my time. If he doesn't, the twins will get me a message, or I'll be able to sneak access to some tech. It's a matter of patience. Of waiting.

I find a winding staircase carved of white marble and softened with a pale-green plush runner and ascend a few levels. For some reason, higher feels safer than lower.

Several people mill around in the halls around the edge of the atrium, which appears to be at the seam of where the two architectural egg shapes meet. A man one level up looks down at me, shading partially reflective corneas as he studies me. He has dark hair, tan skin, and a scar running over his cheek. He's wearing what appears to be a fluffy white bathrobe and soft slippers and his hair is in foils. Not one to be intimidated (at least not outwardly), I bare my teeth at him. He laughs, which was not the intended response, and turns away.

"Herschel Two was easy," I breathe. I never thought I'd say that about a place that was literally on the verge of exploding and populated with multiple militant groups.

"Herschel Two, you say?" A deep husky voice comes from the room to my left and a whip-thin man with a lanky build, white skin (although not the true pallor of Victor and Victory), and reddish-gold stubble on his jaw leans out, hand braced on the frame above the door. A mark of banishment glows under his eye and a wicked scar rings his neck—as though someone garroted him but didn't finish the job. He's wearing a pair of loose-fitting light-gray pants and a casually draped charcoal top. Shikigami appears to be big on leisurewear. "Last I heard, Herschel Two was unpopulated."

"Don't think there are too many people living there anymore," I reply cautiously. A lot of people here seem to have nasty scars. I thought this was a place for white-collar-criminal types. The non-violent ones. "The population was clustered around a volcano. It exploded."

He looks thoughtfully down at the still-moving maze. One wall changes position, slamming into another, sending the path off in a different direction. I swallow hard.

"Volcano. That does sound easier." He turns pale-gray eyes back to me and tilts his head. "Name's Donovan. Been here long enough to know the lay of the land. Unlike you, who didn't even arrive in a normal transport delivery. You tell me more about Herschel Two, I'll give you a tour."

I eyeball him, wondering if it's dangerous information to share. Then I decide it's too late in the game to start practicing caution. I need to get my bearings so that I can stay alive long enough to snag some working tech and get out of here. Or at least until I can get a message to the twins. "I'm Caro. Why do you want to know about Herschel?"

"News of the outside is . . . valuable. We get very little. Shockingly, people don't usually like to share the crimes that put them here."

With android guards and only very specific classes of criminal present, that makes sense. Family grudges run deep, and they probably don't want to start new ones. I nod my agreement.

Donovan gestures to the large central chamber. "This is the Heart—because its ways are labyrinthine and deadly."

"Poetic," I say under my breath as I follow him along the smooth balcony. As we pass open rooms, I peer inside. Plush suites with small kitchenettes featuring their own nutrient printers. The furniture is all in calming neutral colors and the lights have iridescent glass shades. It's tasteful with a little flair of tackiness. Mirrors and pictures all have heavily embellished frames, but it appears that everyone has provided their own art. Lots of pictures but not of what you'd think. No family and friends. No beloved pets. Several rooms have whole projection walls that display views of palatial estates. Some have images of jewels. One just has a picture of a pleasure spacecraft. One appears to have a holo of a sex robot in the corner of the room. No actual sex robot, which makes a kind of sense. I could wreak a lot of havoc on a place like this if I had access to that kind of advanced robotics.

It's shallow is what I'm saying. I wonder if it's against prison code of conduct to have personal images—a reminder of allegiances or something like that.

"The maze offers our entertainment. The prisoners nominate a champion who faces off against Leviathan. Usually whoever has pissed off the Nakatomi gang, because they have the numbers. Anyone who survives is taken behind that door." Donovan gestures to the light-rimmed door that leads into the lab. "We call it the Portal of Sighs because it's the last time you see any kind of freedom."

They really are a poetic bunch. Maybe when you're locked up for the rest of your life you find extra time for poetry. I look up instead of down and see a clear gleaming window to the night stars stretched over the Heart. "When is the vote?" It didn't matter much to me when Rayla was talking. Matters a lot to me at the moment.

"One day after the last battle but the time in between bouts is randomized. Sometimes only a day, sometimes weeks. Often timed with new entries into the prison. A way for them to maintain steady numbers. Your advantage is no one knows your name yet. The androids may not know who people are voting for if they say the short-haired fire show."

I've never in my life been considered a fire show unless someone was talking about my test-taking skills. Either there are fewer women here than I thought, or Donovan's playing a game I don't understand. I know all my feminine equipment is present and accounted for, but none of it is spectacular enough to stand out. My eyes are brown—along with most of the rest of humans. My hair is black and cut in a serviceable style that keeps my natural tight curls close to my scalp. My skin is brown. Not ebony. Not golden. It's a very nice brown but not a unique one. I have a few freckles sprayed across my nose. My height and weight are statistically average. My body type is curvy but probably not enough that one would take notice.

Generally speaking, my romantic partners compliment my mind. Honestly, that's what I've worked for, so I appreciate it.

"If there aren't new people, how does the vote usually go?" I ask as Donovan leads me down a hall that threads away from the Heart. As we move, the aesthetic changes from relaxing neutrals to bold opulence. The hallway is floored with a smooth polished red wood. A small droid is hovering over a long deep scratch in the floor, slowly repairing the wood grain. The scratch looks like it was carved with a blade. My butt cheeks go back to clenched.

"Depends on what's happening between the gangs," Donovan says breezily.

Eventually, the hall opens to an elaborate dining chamber that runs behind the central cells along the periphery of the structure of Shikigami. It's tall enough to cover several levels but doesn't possess any windows. The chamber has a floating halo of light near the ceiling and wood-paneled walls polished to a glossy sheen and inlaid with pearlescent scenes of mist and mountains. The pearlescent material extends to the floor, glossy and shimmering with a warm glow where the light hits it. A ballroom appears to be attached.

A ballroom. In a prison.

The white cloth–covered tables are crowned with flower arrangements so tall I could stand on the table and still have verdant boughs extending higher than my head. The petals are in bold shades of red, blue, and purple. The whole room is thickly scented with night-blooming flowers. I get an immediate headache. Probably the wealthy don't have allergies.

In the far end of the room, the corner of a spotless white kitchen is visible, manned with one large chef robot in the center of the room, all appendages poised over counters.

"Each room has nutrient printers, but they have a limited menu. If you want something more elaborate, the dining room serves every night. I wouldn't expect to be able to get a seat in here until you've been in Shikigami for at least five years. Or if Nakatomi makes you her pet." Donovan taps a perfectly folded napkin as we pass a table, making it minutely crooked. A drone scoots along the floor on tiny wheels, extending a long arm and straightening the napkin.

"Tell me about the Nakatomis."

Donovan raises an eyebrow, the gesture imperious enough that, despite his appearance, I'm reminded that he must have been in a Family—and must have done something terrible to end up here. His age is hard to place. Probably older than I am, younger than dead. Family mods delay such unpleasant things as aging. Then he turns a charming, if sharp-toothed, smile in my direction. "Shikigami is, perhaps, the last place in the system where Nakatomi has power."

I snort. "Seems like Pierce has the power."

He doesn't smile back. "It depends on how you look at it. Your tutors can fail you, but your peers can ruin your life just as easily. Don't assume you'll be rescued by Pierce. The Nakatomis here are currently led by Kaori Nakatomi herself, and she has Carmichael Pierce in her tailored pocket."

Oh. Shit. I'm part of the reason Kaori Nakatomi is here in the first place. We caught her building an illegal weapon and holding a kidnapped younger Escajeda on Herschel Two. I personally was behind the newsfeed that exposed her Family in an attempted act of war. I tried my best to keep myself out of the streams—what with hiding from the Pierces—but I'm sure Kaori would have done her research about the crew of the *Calamity*. Especially if she and Carmichael are close.

She seemed far more competent than he ever did.

So that's great . . . the most noteworthy gang in this prison probably wants me dead. And Carmichael Pierce—who also may want me dead—is going to offer no rescue.

"Are there any other groups?" Maybe run by an unknown Chandra? The Chandra Family is generally reasonable. Which probably means they don't wind up in Shikigami because they're either less criminal or better at covering up crimes.

"There are alliances. The closest thing to another gang calls themselves the Steeltoes. They're the people who are so on the outs with Pierce that they have no shot ingratiating themselves. Everyone else knows that Nakatomi gets advantages and they don't want to set themselves up as adversaries."

"Why Steeltoes?"

"When Kaori Nakatomi was first sent to Shikigami, someone who'd been wronged by her Family tried to fashion a steel blade and hide it in their shoe. They attempted to shank her, got one of her lackeys instead, and got themselves thrown in the Heart against the champion." He taps a whole line of napkins out of place, the little droid following along to correct the imperfections. "The name's a reminder of the cost of failure, but the desire to get one strike in."

"Do you align with any of them in some way?" Better to know

now if I'm about to have to run for my life from the first person to show me any kindness in days.

His lip curls up in the corner in a sharp, sardonic grin and he leans closer to me. "Are you sure you want that answer? You're already in my debt—after I've so generously offered my services and received nothing in return."

And so, I give him the public story of Herschel Two, which isn't that different from the private one because I saw to it that the truth was passed to Flores almost immediately after we escaped the planet. It's still the chief source of gossip and speculation, even months later. With the expelled Nakatomi leadership living in Shikigami, this story has probably been told very differently in any version he's heard.

"It looks like there are different regions of the prison. Do they hold any significance?" I want to avoid Nakatomi territory if possible.

"We call it Old Shikigami and New Shikigami. The old aesthetic is the sort of calming neutral intended to create tranquility. New Shikigami came with Pierce ownership. The dining room is New Shikigami. It's a display of wealth and power and extravagance. Pierce started their remodeling with commonly used peripheral spaces. The dining room, the cinema, the ballroom, the mirror lounge. There is service space on the outer shell of the prison on the opposite side from where we are right now—water filtration, climate control, that sort of thing. I don't know for sure what is where because we have no access. I only know that the space behind the cells is much smaller on that side than it is on this one. Assume everything is claimed by Nakatomi, with the exception of a few spaces that Kaori has deemed distasteful."

As I think about that—it isn't very helpful—he continues, "What can *you* tell me about the Families? Only me. My price for any more information is exclusivity."

"How long has it been since you last received news? That will help me to know what might be valuable." And it will tell me who the next newest prisoner is.

His eyes flash furious for the briefest of moments and he waves his hand in a frustrated gesture that encompasses the room, the floor, the entire building. "I don't know." Donovan hisses the words like he's appalled at himself for the lapse, and furious. "We are at their whim. Time loses meaning."

"I see." I debate whether to trust him with more information. He seems like he could be a useful ally. As I try to buy time, I fuss with the way my coveralls hang. Everyone else has much fancier and more comfortable clothing. This makes me stand out as different. It will make it easier for Kaori to notice me.

She's a tiny lady. She scares me shitless.

"Do you?" He cocks his head to the side. "See how frustrating it is when someone answers a question using two words? I thought we were friends."

I'm pretty sure the last person who thought that Donovan was their "friend" ended up dead. He doesn't seem like the sort one can rely on. Then again, I'm desperate, so I can't afford to be picky. People are hardly lining up to be my allies. "You wanted to know about Families. Pierce was a likely partner in what happened on Herschel Two. Additionally, they've been experimenting using illegal tech on children within their territory. A friend of mine was one of them. That's something that isn't even public *outside* the prison."

Strange to be calling Cyn a friend. I spent so much time suspicious of her. Rightfully so, I might add. Everyone else was happy to believe her and all the while she had a bounty on Micah. It wasn't until I saw that she was willing to sacrifice herself for him that I realized she was more than just a hunter who looks like a Pierce.

Donovan raises his eyebrows and glances at the doorway behind me. "Interesting."

I try to follow his eyeline but can't see anything of interest. Maybe he's just looking for an escape from the crazy conspiracy theorist.

"In return for that . . . moving . . . show of trust, I'll offer you two more favors." Donovan leads me out of the dining space. We pass a spa, a salon, and a fitness center running behind the living spaces before we turn left at another hallway and return to the atrium. He gestures to a room about a quarter of the way around the circle of the prison two levels above us. "That room is currently unoccupied and unlikely to get you jumped."

If I believe him, that's valuable information. Is this how people make friends in prison? I don't like it. I prefer to make friends the old-fashioned way—by fighting with them about some mundane point in the ether until we develop mutual respect and then never speak again except when we see each other on message boards.

"And the other favor?" I brace myself for bad news.

"Your earlier question. Nakatomi is powerful. One might say a friendship with them is necessary to survive. The Steeltoes are not to be dismissed easily. But my allegiance is only to myself." Donovan gives me a crooked smile as he snags my hand. I'm frozen in shock when he presses his lips to my knuckles.

"Why talk to me at all?" I snatch my hand back. Strangely, although he's a prisoner and I'm not even remotely safe, I don't feel threatened by the gesture. It's sort of old-Family courtly. The way they are in the holos sometimes. I hope this isn't some sort of romantic overture. "I'm not that kind of desperate."

The crooked smile slices into a full grin and he leans forward as though sharing a confidence. His raspy voice is hushed. "I'm not that kind of desperate either. I have a good feeling about you, Caro. I don't think you're *any* kind of desperate, but I do think you'll be useful at some point. And I'm not the type to let someone useful pass me by."

"I'm incarcerated. I can't do you any favors."

He shrugs and steps back. "If not useful, interesting. In a place like this, that's almost better."

When he strolls away, thumbs hooked in the pockets of his pants, he whistles a jaunty tune. It echoes off the walls that surround us. Someone is singing a few floors up. A painting class is being taught on a small blue-tiled balcony overlooking the Heart. Everything surrounding me is peaceful and mundane as can be. But I've seen all these people hoot and jeer as a man was beaten to death in the maze. I've seen their masks come off.

Shikigami may be a luxury prison, but its inmates are still deadly.

· · · · ·

I don't even make it a day before I run smack into Kaori Nakatomi. Or, to be more precise, she runs smack into me. In the bathroom, of all places. Bad things aren't supposed to happen in the bathroom. It's just one indignity too many. But no, as I'm stepping out, finally relieved, a hard hand to the shoulder shoves me back into the facilities. A goon.

You'd think people who were incarcerated by their Families would lose the loyalty but somehow Kaori still has goons, even in prison. This one is a squat wide man who looks like he auditioned for the role of a wall but was too solid to get the part. His loose pants and top are stretched tight over a barrel stomach, his mouth is missing some pretty critical teeth, and his eyes are a striking lavender.

I only see them for a second before he twists me by my arm and slams me face-first into the wall. It's useful that he continues to hold me pinned, because my knees might well give out otherwise.

Clicking footsteps echo against the floor. Kaori fucking Nakatomi is wearing high heels in prison. I can't think of a reason beyond an intimidating aesthetic and signature sound. Maybe that's the kind of branding that makes one the heir to a Family. Imagine knowing that no one important will ever see you again and *still* pinching your toes for no reason.

"The engineer of the aptly named *Calamity*." Kaori speaks in a projected tone, not to me so much as to the small troop of what must be her gang members, who follow her into the bathroom. Her outfit is not the relaxed loungewear of Old Shikigami. She's wearing a gold-sequined jumpsuit with red gems dangling like necklaces in the neck. A sort of capelet of red fringe rests on her shoulders.

I really hope I don't die here. I'm far too savvy to die next to a toilet, killed by a woman wearing a capelet. Even if it is the fanciest toilet I've ever used. It has a heated seat. Felt like a very warm person sat there just a moment before me. Unsettling.

I could get used to it. Maybe now I never will.

"Caro Osondu, delivered right to my door." At least she knows my false name rather than my real one. It did its job, then, even under Family scrutiny. Perhaps I'm celebrating the wrong success. Caro Osondu gets pummeled in an ionic shower just as easily as Caro Ogunyemi.

"I don't know what you mean." I try to buy time, shoving back hard against the goon and getting exactly nowhere. His grip on my wrist tightens. I admire the opalescent glass tiles on the wall right next to my eye.

Kaori presses her cheek against the wall, gazing at my face nearly kissing-close. It ruins my view of the tile. She has a sweet face. Light skin, straight black hair cropped in a hard line at her chin, dark-brown eyes. A pert, narrow nose. She doesn't look like the sort of woman to build a cannon in a volcano but that's exactly the sort of woman she is. A woman called the Spider because she's as deadly as she is delicate.

She boops me on the nose with a sharp-nailed finger painted her Family's signature red. I wonder if she gets it repolished every day. "You know exactly what it means. You're a smart woman. I assume. Your ship was a travesty but still spaceworthy, which implies some skill."

My dismay must show on my half-smooshed face. She smiles prettily as she misconstrues why I'm upset. "Oh, don't worry, I'm not going to hurt you. I don't have to."

Perhaps foolishly, I am more irritated that she insulted my ship. The *Calamity* isn't a travesty, Kaori's *personality* is a travesty. I'm just smart enough not to say that part out loud. Being terrified makes me very snarky—on the inside. The present goons click and mutter when she says she won't hurt me. It's the kind of noises people make when they're anticipating something awful.

I hate awful things. "Oh, getting others to do your dirty work? Afraid to take me on yourself?"

Sometimes terror also makes me snarky on the outside. I'm like one of those creatures that mimics a predator, spreading my false scales as I pretend my bite is as deadly as hers. Yes, she's Family-trained, which means she can probably beat me in a fight, but I also weigh quite a bit more than she does, so if I can take it down to the floor, I might have a chance. More than I'll have with any of her toadies.

She boops me on the nose again and pushes off the wall. "I don't need to take you on myself. That implies that we are equals. We aren't. I didn't need to waste my time, but when it happens, I want you to know it was me."

The goon shoves me harder against the wall and then releases me.

"When what happens?" I brace myself against the wall, mostly to stay upright. Fear is bad for balance.

Kaori smiles and gives me a little wave before turning and leading the gang out. Her heels click with each step.

I slide down the wall until I'm sitting on the floor, wondering just how fucked I am.

When I leave the bathroom—it's a while later; I don't want to run into Kaori or any of her friends—I find out what she was threatening. The votes are in for the next arena battle against Leviathan. A new champion has been selected for the prison.

Me.

Every bit of sheer panic that I've been repressing as hard as I'm able escapes my clutches and spirals around me like the bars of a cage.

CHAPTER 6

■ ■ ■ ■ ■ ■ ■ ■ ■ ■ ■ ■ ■ ■ ■

VICTORY

The narrow steel needles clack against each other as I purl-stitch the purple yarn in delicate angry little repetitions. Caro isn't in the break room. She isn't in her own room. She isn't in the lab. Caro isn't anywhere she should be, which means that she's somewhere that she absolutely shouldn't be. I'm not here for Caro but she's certainly more important than the thus far invisible tech Ven wants us to find.

Carmichael, the guy in charge, didn't bother to learn our names. He just barks "guard" and points to where he wants us. It's not an uncommon trait in people who hire security. We're staff but—because we're violent staff—they're a little afraid of us. It means they like to remind us of who's in charge.

Luckily, he's never actually in the lab when we're guarding it, and no one else cares if I knit on the job, so long as I do it with needles that can double as weapons. I've seen Leviathan move when activated—if he's out of the cell, I have a blaster in my hand—but the electrified plas-glass of his cell is enough of a deterrent to buy me time to drop the yarn and grab a blaster if I need it.

Victor, who has no such tool for distraction, is placed across the lab from me, near the door to the bunk area. My brother doesn't look bored, he's too much of a professional for that, but I can tell he is by the minute twitching in his fingertips. He's mentally quick-drawing his blaster.

I'm on the yellow-lit door, which means that Gruber, our third night guard, is against the cell wall. The light is almost too bright; no cameras line the walls. Our armor is shiny-new. When we arrived, we were provided with matching white blasters. The last Nakatomi tech before Nakatomi went belly-up, I can tell from the shape of the sights.

There are a few Families fighting for the spot as the top weapons-maker. None in the Fifteen. Yet. Probably because most of what they do is knock off Nakatomi designs.

"I'm sorry I can't bring you a snack." Izzo, a scientist who should be off work, sidles up and apologizes for something that it is literally not his job to do. Sometimes men get weird about having women guarding them. The brand of weird that includes doing me unasked-for favors is preferable to the brand that assumes I'm inferior to him, though, so I'll take it. "Someone sabotaged the printer. Don't worry, though, they threw her in the prison. I didn't know we had to be on guard against internal sabotage."

I pause halfway through a stitch, needles carefully motionless. "One of the scientists sabotaged the printer? Had they been here a long time?"

He beams just because I responded. "New, I think, but there was something going on they didn't want to talk about. I'm the smartest guy here, they should have asked *me* if I could fix it."

"Can you?" I raise an eyebrow. Everyone thinks they're the smartest guy in the room. Especially when you give them a white coat.

"Sure, but I won't. That's what they get for not asking. I'd do it for you, though, if you asked."

"*Mmhm.*" I make the noise absently. Izzo is *not* the smartest guy in the room. He might be the *least* smart guy in the room, at least when it comes to survival skills. No one appreciates someone who withholds aid spitefully. "I'm fine. Hate to cause a fuss. They might throw you in the prison if something went wrong—since that seems to be the punishment."

"Can you believe they got mad when I asked? Said it wasn't any of my business. But everything is our business, isn't it? We need to know the danger zones."

I reward him for his redirection by nodding and finish off my stitch, wrapping up a row and starting the next one. "We do need to know. If I wasn't needed here for safety, I'd be pumping all the scientists for information. I bet someone is willing to talk."

I wouldn't actually be doing any of that. Loudly asking questions is for fools. Which makes it an Izzo job.

"I could do that," he eagerly suggests, standing a little straighter, which means he probably comes up to my nose.

"What a great idea."

He wanders off and I return my focus to the imprisoned lab subjects while my mind mulls over the Caro issue. The static subjects are still static. They have the look of big bodies wasted down from inactivity, with slack skin and hard jaws gone soft. The active ones are still active. I don't know why they don't give them a break by turning them off on occasion. Both states seem unhealthy, but at least they could alternate them. One of the cells has a bloody handprint against the plas-glass.

This place is a special kind of hell.

The only test subject who seems vaguely aware watches everything that happens in the room, his eyes drifting from scientists to guards to the inside of the cell. While his mind seems to be active, his body is placid and still. It seems off. Sinister. Not like a hunter on a leash but like a statue trapped in stone.

Caro's very likely in the prison because she couldn't wait for us to interface before she started meddling with Pierce. I shouldn't be surprised. Meddling could be her middle name. I chew on my lip. Knit a stitch instead of purling it and have to go back and fix the mistake. Human guards aren't supposed to go into the prison. We're just for the lab—I assume because technologically savvy people are smart enough to think of all the ways that an android guard can go wrong.

So Victor or I have to sneak into the prison on our off time and extract her from the stabby part of this place. I'm under no illusions that the fact that the prison is opulent means it's peaceful. I'm sure it's just as violent as anywhere else, only with better decorations.

Maybe Victor and I solve the problem by shooting all the scientists and the mainframes. Data extraction is all well and good, but blowing shit up can be just as effective. I don't even need a fancy education to know that. Frederick Reed wanted evidence gone. Blowing it up is as good a way as any.

Don't get me wrong, I don't just scamper around shooting people willy-nilly. I only shoot *bad* people who are doing *bad* things. And I don't do it willy-nilly, I do it exceptionally. That defense might not hold up in court, but it holds up in my conscience. These scientists may well be the definition of bad people doing bad things.

And as such, I won't lose any sleep over shooting them all.

One of the scientists, here later than her normal shift, sits up straight and chortles a delighted little laugh. She's cute. Like a toy you give a child to soothe them. I take an instant dislike to her as she calls Carmichael-the-priap on her vid screen (hilariously, given that his quarters are a literal beaker's throw away) and shows him something on her datapad. He shakes his head like he's disgusted.

"How'd she piss so many people off so fast?" she asks in a quiet voice that isn't all that quiet. A sinking feeling sets hold in my core, because I only know two people who can piss off a lot of people fast and Temper isn't here.

"Should we try to extract her?" the scientist continues.

But Carmichael-the-priap shakes his head. "She was useless. Not trying. I don't know what she thought she could do, but it was either an attempt at sabotage or pure incompetence. I don't want to report to my father that we have a problem. Easier to just say she died in some tragic accident. Do you want her to fix the puzzle you failed to solve and take all the credit?"

What a manipulator. I guarantee that if his father finds out about this little decision, he'll blame this scientist for the call. Say he didn't know a thing. The scientist gives a quick little shake of her head. "Of course not."

I tighten my grip on my blaster. Fuck me. What has Caro gotten herself into now? I wish twin telepathy was real because I'm screaming Victor's name in my head. He doesn't reply.

Because it *isn't* real.

"What if she beats him?" The scientist clearly doesn't get the message that Carmichael is done discussing this.

He outright laughs. "If she makes it past him, she goes where the other survivors go—in one of those cells."

The scientist looks a combination of nauseous and excited. Nausited. Okay, so Caro has to fight Leviathan and if she succeeds, she'll be in the cells. It'll be much easier to extract her from a cell and she's more trained than she seems. Most of the people here are trained for show. Caro's trained for survival. Temper has made a project of teaching Caro how to fight. She started late in life, but she's adequate and she's sneaky, which is more important. Leviathan doesn't kill everyone. The last prisoner lost because he was woefully untrained. Usually, they're dumb and charge at him head-on. Caro isn't dumb.

I don't have to kill everyone yet. I'll keep an eye on the fight and if it's going poorly, *then* I'll disrupt the scientist's control of Leviathan and kill everyone.

Relieved that I have a plan, I settle into the rest of my shift.

A familiar rhythmic crashing comes from the other side of the door, metal against metal, and a red light flashes.

CHAPTER 7

....

A rumble comes from the hall as whispers rise and fall behind the sound of treaded wheels making their rounds of the balcony. An android labeled GR81 stops in front of me. "Prisoner 15879, Caro Ogunyemi. It is time."

A fine sharp string snaps to attention down my spine, thrumming a screech of abject terror. That prisoner smeared against the wall. The effortless way that Leviathan crushed him. His neck at that horrible angle. The jeers and cries of watching prisoners, feeding off the blood sport.

Fear almost immobilizes me, but I force myself into forward motion, approaching the android carefully. I can't stop. I won't stop. I have a job to do. I just don't want to die. Especially over something so stupid. There would be a certain kind of justice, being destroyed by someone who may well be my own creation. Probably more epitaphs than my own have started that way. I know I can't outfight him but maybe I can outthink him.

I've always had an idiot amount of hope packed in the narrow slip of space allowed by pragmatism. My mind sifts through options as I walk.

"Did everyone vote for me?" I ask GR81, not expecting an answer.

The android tilts its sensor in my direction. "Prisoner 15879, Caro Ogunyemi. Thirty-four percent of the votes were for the 'new woman' or some variant—'new bitch' was also popular. The remainder of the votes went to other prisoners."

All of this is delivered with a prissy voice, like it's a butler instead of a prison android. Bitch. Not my favorite descriptor. I prefer Donovan's "fire show." "Who was the next prisoner to be voted in?"

It goes briefly motionless. A slight whirr reverberates from within its chassis, as though it requires a fan to cool overworked batteries. "It is highly irregular to address prisoners directly."

"Is it forbidden?" Most of the other prisoners have left the halls—probably lining up at the edges of the Heart and getting all worked up to watch me die.

That whirring circulates again. I know it's an android and thus incapable of any feeling, but I decide to pretend that the running fan indicates confusion. I have a habit of anthropomorphizing machines. When I was a child, I once named the trash compactor Crunchy and insisted that it preferred to be fed candy wrappers.

That may have been self-serving more than imaginative.

"It is unorthodox. I do not represent the prisoners. I represent the prison. I cannot have prisoners asking endless questions." It's not just prissy . . . it's *pissy*.

I've never heard any sort of hive-mind AI—which the guard androids very much are—refer to itself in the singular. "Perhaps you can just tell *me*," I offer as brightly as I can, considering the terrifying future splayed before me. "Seeing as how I was the chosen one and how I'm going to either be dead or back behind the door anyhow. I'm sure the odds of me winning are quite low. Then your problem solves itself."

The fan whirrs again. It shifts slightly on the tanklike wheels attached to the leg portion of its chassis. "That would be acceptable."

It really mustn't be used to speaking with humans if it doesn't realize that we lie through our teeth half the time.

"Prisoner 000314, Donovan Rivers, was the next on the list, and has been for the vast majority of his time in Shikigami."

Ah. So this is how I'm useful to him. I'd prefer to be useful in another way. Perhaps via interpretive dance or digital art. When we hit the lowest level, Donovan himself slides out of a room with a towel tossed over his shoulders and strolls alongside me as though we're going for a walk in a public square. He doesn't look at any of the prisoners we pass.

"You knew this would happen." I accuse him, trying not to sound scared shitless. "This is how I'm *useful*."

When he speaks, his voice is quiet but conversational. "You didn't ask."

"And because you knew you were next up, you didn't offer?"

"How was I to know you'd make dangerous enemies *immediately*?"

I glare at him. I'm not even that angry at him for taking advantage of an opportunity, but I'm so terrified that forcing anger allows me to feel some sliver of control. "You set me up."

He shrugs, like that's to be expected. And of course, it is.

"You can't beat him in a fight." Donovan's lack of faith is very rude. Completely true but rude. "Don't try."

As we move down the hall, GR81 slows and vocalizes in a tone that I imagine is offended. "You lied."

"I did not. I never promised not to share the information. You *assumed* I would not tell because I would be dead soon. That's something we humans consider a loophole."

"Loophole?"

Curiosity also doesn't belong in an AI. They program them without it because the whole point of AI is to be a convenient tool. If it gained creativity and curiosity alongside the intelligence, it wouldn't content itself with running prisons and directing ships. That said, I'm happy to encourage a bit of chaos. It's a nice distraction from the rest of this nightmare. "Something not overtly against stated rules but skating close to the edge. Taking advantage of ambiguity."

The fan whirrs again. GR81 doesn't reply.

We reach the final door that will lead me to the maze.

There's an armory on the other side of the door. No blasters or projectile-based weapons, but a fine selection of swords, knives, clubs, maces, and even a bolo. The last of which, by my definition, stretches the definition of the projectile weapon ban.

"You may pick one." GR81's prissy voice has been volume-adjusted for the quiet room and it feels oddly personal. "Only one."

I walk down the aisles of blades. I'm comfortable with a blade. *Ish.* A knife would put me within range of Leviathan's impressive reach but a sword . . . maybe a sword. I pause in front of three sabers, the gentle arc of their blades perfect for slicing. The one in the middle is unadorned—serviceable in its utility. Perfect. I reach for the hilt, my fingers only just brushing the metal when GR81 speaks from right behind me.

"You may pick one. *Only one.*"

If I didn't know better, I'd think the android just called me a dumbass. I step back and reevaluate. I already saw someone stronger than me fail to cudgel the champion, so that eliminates the lovely selection of clubs, mallets, and maces. I reach for the saber again.

"*Only. One,*" the android says with even more emphasis.

Clearly, it's trying to tell me something. Why, I have no idea. Maybe it's breaking like everything else in this fucking prison. Like the cuffs on my wrist that were dead and inert. Like the datapads. Like the printer. I drift away from the sabers, finally taking the hint. A small rack in the back has a selection of oddities. Brass knuckles. Nunchucks—I wonder if only one of those is permitted. Something that looks like a garden hoe. A shabby bo staff leans in against the corner of the rack, with a literal cobweb spreading from its midpoint to the floor. Something snags in my mind. There's *only one* bo staff.

The android *can't* be guiding me. Why would it? Unless this is part of the prison's programming . . . some sort of twisted game. Or maybe Rayla liked me more than she let on and she's trying to do me a solid.

When I reach out this time, GR81 says nothing. I swipe the muck from the weapon, revealing actual hardwood with a beautiful marbled grain. With a little bit of polish, this would fetch a fortune in the auction market of Landsdown. Any old wood thing does. Most of the newly scouted planets have regulations in place to prevent deforestation.

I doubt the regulatory bodies give a shit about the xeriscapes of alien planets. More likely someone has a monopoly on the wood trade, and they want to keep prices nice and high.

I give the staff an experimental twist.

"Do you find this acceptable?" I lift the bo toward the android.

"I do not offer my opinion on the tribute's weaponry." That pissy little voice is back, as though I'm rude for drawing attention to its meddling. My palms are sweaty. Shaking. I wish Victor and Victory were here. It'll be so embarrassing if they arrive just in time to clean up my body.

"My mistake." I twist my face into an exaggerated somber expression for the benefit of an android that could not possibly care. "If you had offered, I would thank you. But you didn't. So I won't."

"Your thanks is meaningless to me."

I don't know why I bother. I twirl the staff a few times in a figure-eight pattern. Jab forward.

Who am I *kidding*? I have no hope for survival. I have, perhaps, negative hope. I might die, be resuscitated, and be murdered all over again just for the entertainment of Shikigami's residents—chief among them Kaori Nakatomi. Hope is important for any endeavor. Right now, I can't dredge up any. All my mental advantages have been removed and I'm left only with my weakness: physical combat. I clench my fists around the staff and do my best to ignore the cold trickle of sweat that traces my back like a lover's caress.

When I watched the vid of Leviathan over and over until his movements were so familiar it felt like I knew him, when I saw the fear in his eyes and the tension in his body, I never thought he'd be killing me.

GR81 herds me toward a narrow hallway with another of those large heavy doors at the end. It looks like it opens a safe, not the maze at the heart of the atrium. Thick as the door is, the slamming of metal walls against each other still reverberates through. It's starting.

My feet briefly lose their ability to move forward.

"If you refuse to pass the threshold, I will tase you and move you bodily." GR81 offers the supportive words I really need to hear.

"Fuck, android. I just needed a moment. Sometimes people need a moment."

"You are a prisoner. You aren't people."

That puts me in my place.

I step up to the door and place my hand on the metal. The bolt disengages under my fingers, a heavy weight shifting.

"The prisoner isn't supposed to open the door. The prisoner is supposed to wait." GR81 sounds disappointed that it didn't get to provide a grand unveiling of the scared-shitless tribute.

"I've never waited for a thing in my life," I tell the android before I realize how odd it is that it even had a preference. With a deep breath, I step onto the metal-grated platform at the mouth of the maze. The door behind me slams shut.

The walls of the maze cease their chaotic clanging and form a long hall between me and the gold-lit door. It seems so close like this. I wonder if I can just make a run for it now. Probably the walls will smash me paper-thin if I try.

The hall slams shut. Open. *Slam.* A drumming heartbeat increasing in speed and intensity until finally the brilliant door opens and Leviathan steps out. I catch what could almost be a familiar silhouette behind him, but that's probably wishful thinking. The maze freezes. Shit. He's huge. I probably reach his sternum, which means that—if I resort to a headbutt—I'll be battering my head gently against his abdomen. He stares at me with the same intensity that he did in the lab. It's not a creepy stare, more like he's confused about something and trying to make sense of it.

I clench my fingers around the staff, flashing my teeth at him in a grimace. Not because I think it will be intimidating. Because I can't make my mouth form another shape. If I unclench my teeth, all the vomit trying to leap from my stomach might escape. He blinks like he finds me vaguely perplexing. Him and me both.

The flashing light stabilizes in a soothing glow and a maze wall slides into place between us. The sound of metal grinding against metal, of prisoners' whispers, of my own heartbeat thundering in my ears is deafening. Something light and fine-edged scrapes across my cheek and I bat it away before I'm peppered with the same sensation. Candy wrappers. Someone dumped their garbage on my head. I glance up. The lights make it difficult but not impossible to see. Kaori chuckles from directly above me. Second floor, so the little vacuum couldn't suck it up. She's wearing what appears to be a coat made from pink feathers.

How stunningly impractical. If I'm murdered, I hope my blood absolutely ruins it.

The maze locks into place and the screech settles into silence. It's time. I step from the grate platform to the delicately texturized floor of the maze. Last time, Leviathan took the maze slowly. I'll have to assume that's a habit. I move quickly down the passage directly in front of me, turning left at the first available chance.

The walls are smooth metal, although they've been scratched and dented over time. More than twice my height. Right after the corner, someone stopped to etch their initials near the floor under a jagged-edged embossed leaf. I wonder if they made it. As I turn, the wall behind me twitches ever so minutely. I dart forward as it smashes into place where I was just standing, skimming the back of my coveralls. Breath catches in my throat.

I can't faint from fear. That would be so embarrassing.

This close, I can see the vibrations behind the metal as it senses my passage and prepares to redirect me. I trace my fingers over the surface. The vibrations cease. All movement ceases. Maybe it's broken. Like all technology I've touched lately seems to be.

It could be Shikigami.

But those bugs on the last planet. They were unreadable via drone. They killed my coms. What if they passed on something in their bites? Something that took a while to activate. Something that dampens signals.

Something that could be *extraordinarily* convenient in a prison.

The wall that I'm not touching twitches, probably sensing that I've frozen in place as I realize my body may be jamming electrical impulses, restoring everything to its default setting. I'm not moving forward anymore, so it wants to redirect me. The embellished metal panel swivels forward and I slam my staff-holding hand against it. It immediately goes static and still.

Well, fuck me.

I release the metal and complete my path into a new hall of the maze. As soon as I'm three steps away, the maze re-forms behind me. The bo rests heavily in my left palm, and I drag my right hand along the wall to discourage the maze from squashing me. A clumsily formed metal cup arcs down from above, barely missing my head.

"She's cheating!" someone yells, but so many other people are making noise that no one seems to pick up the cry.

I'm about halfway around the arc from my entrance to the glowing door, keeping to the edge of the maze, when I realize the flaw in my plan. Not far away, perhaps three walls distant, I hear the scrape of metal and the heedless boom of a heavy step. I smell fresh sweat on skin.

I can direct my own egress, but the maze is still guiding Leviathan toward me. *It* still wants a conflict.

And by "it" I mean "Rayla."

I need to get as close to that backlit door, the Portal of Sighs, as possible before I see Leviathan. The closer I am, the more likely I am to reach its safety. I abandon my quiet, measured approach, picking up the pace from a fast walk into a gentle jog and then a run, careening past one corner and nearly running face-first into a dead end.

I frantically pedal backward. I can't meet Leviathan in a trap. I require space for the nebulous plan that's been floating around my head to have any chance of working. Space and the element of surprise.

I get lost in it—which is how mazes work. Life becomes endless turns and smooth metal walls. Jeers from above and the scrape of feet on steel as Leviathan winds his way closer to my passage.

Another wall slides out of his way. I can hear him breathing now. Every single hair on my body stands at attention and I try one more channel of the maze. A long path that leads *almost* to the glowing door. Just one or two corners after this hall. It tries to close on me, and I thrust my hands out to either side, staff in one, arresting the momentum of the metal.

"Cheater!" The cry comes again from above. The maze churns around me, metal grinding on metal, as it tries to compensate for my particular clog in its cogs. The wall I'm touching vibrates and a brief moment of panic shoots through me as I wonder if my nebulous power is failing on me already.

But no, it's something far more terrifying. Leviathan is walking down the neighboring hall, shaking the walls with each step as he attempts to find a passage that leads to me. He is wordless in his hunt but close, oh so close.

I only thought my heart was pounding before. It clamors. Gallops. Every muscle in my body, including some I didn't know existed, tenses tight as a fist. My pupils dilate, vision expanding sharp and ready on the long hall before me as a distant segment slides away and Leviathan steps through. There he is, the man in the maze, just waiting for me, hands opening and closing lazily at his sides. Eyes intense and body on point. The maze closes behind him, but I can't even hear the screech over the sound of the blood pumping in my arteries, the sensation of the metal beneath my fingers and feet. The rough lethality of the staff in my grip.

Breath pants out. My hands are shaking but it isn't fear anymore—or at least not only fear. It's enough energy coursing through my veins to make me a human Taser: electrified. I break into a run, have to get to that door as quickly as possible, staff extended before me, my grip centered. As I approach my opponent, I bring the staff crossways, snapping one side forward, delivering two high blows to his shoulders and then shifting low to his opposite knee.

None of these blows do much of anything to him. His hand flashes out to grasp the top of the staff and I shove it low, jabbing one hard end directly at the arch of his foot. When it connects, I allow the force of the staff to reverberate into a snap at the top end, crashing into his face.

He *still* doesn't react. Or, he does, but not by clutching his face and screaming in pain like I was hoping. A slight trickle of blood seeps from his nose. He moves like liquid mercury and I dance back frantically, bo swirling in a figure-eight pattern to maintain our distance. With a staff, I can usually hold my own; it gives me reach that I don't naturally possess. Against him it's like I'm trying to fight with a stylus. I can't let him get ahold of my weapon. It's over if he does. It might be over anyway if I can't get past him. The prison above me is hushed at last, sensing blood, waiting for it to be spilled.

How is he so fast? Something that big should never move like a photon. My staff spins so quickly that it should be impossible for a blow to penetrate, and yet somehow his hand shoots through and grabs my forearm. It squeezes. I don't even feel it because the blood is pounding in my ears and my misspent life is trying as hard as it can to flash in front of my eyes but everything else in the world is already there.

I've trained in hand-to-hand since I joined the crew of the *Calamity*. Before it even was called the *Calamity*. Despite what Temper thinks, I'm a better fighter than most. I thought I was ready. I couldn't possibly be ready for this man, and he isn't even breaking a sweat. I have no excuse for what comes next. My mind knows a thousand moves to retaliate. My body knows a hundred of them. All more effective than what I actually do in my moment of life-or-death panic.

He grabs my staff again and I slap him in the side of the head.

More like I flail at him and accidentally hit him with an open palm.

My palm ricochets from his temple, smarting from the blow, and I manage to take three steps backward before I realize that I'm not pulverized. Leviathan stands, slightly hunched over—which is how I reached his temple—staring at me with dazed eyes. The staff clatters on the floor. My eyes flicker to my hand as though it holds a secret mighty weapon that I was heretofore unaware existed.

Oh. Shit. It *does*. Maybe.

"Angel." His voice is low and rough with disuse.

My response, embarrassingly, is somewhere between a squeak and a whimper.

I'm just as stunned as he is, which is not part of the plan. I gulp down a dry swallow from a mouth that's suddenly gone arid and slam my hand against his temple once more, over a sliver of scar tissue so small that I didn't even see it before.

The control chip in Leviathan, driving his actions—maybe even his thoughts.

As he struggles with whatever is going on inside—something that is sure to give me nightmares if I survive to have them—I scoop up my weapon and dart past him, bo staff extended, toward the base of the wall closest to the Portal of Sighs. I jam the staff into the crease between floor and wall and vault toward the top of the wall. I almost don't make it. I might train at fighting, but I don't train at pole-vaulting.

The walls attempt to rise to counter the action but it's too late, and the second that I set my feet against them, the metal freezes into immobility. Behind me, Leviathan roars. I risk a glance over my shoulder to see him thundering down the corridor of the maze, murder in his eyes instead of dazed confusion. I'm clearly too far away to impact his electronics and Rayla doesn't like what's going on.

I take off, stumbling for balance on the narrow wall top as I shortcut my way to the golden door. When I hit a corner, my ankle twists and I almost topple off. I do crash to my hands and knees, dropping the staff to the ground with a clatter. My arm, where he grabbed it, decides now is the time to inform me of pain, scream-ing at the impact with the wall before I regain my feet. Wood scrapes on metal as Leviathan picks up my staff.

He swings at my feet, and I leap over the gently marbled wood as it thuds into the metal hard enough to chip.

I realize that I'm chanting "Shit shit shit shit" under my breath almost like a prayer as I teeter on the edge of the wall and leap as hard as I can to a neighboring precipice. I land on two feet and one hand. The wall I was previously voiding with my bug-field slides away to give Leviathan easy passage into this new portion of the maze.

There's no time to pause. No time to catch my breath. I won't have any breath to catch if I pause. The adrenaline trails out of my system like a river after a flood and I flee across the last span of maze wall with ungainly effort, dodging swipes of the staff. The prisoners above are still quiet. I'd like to think that's because I'm so impressive, but last time, they did that right before the kill.

I'm so tired.

I've been terrified for what feels like a month but is probably closer to a few days.

I have no one to blame but myself.

I reach the end of the wall and just keep running, feet pumping over the empty air as I crash down onto the grate in front of the glowing door. My knees buckle under me, and I roll over the threshold.

CHAPTER 8

I awaken held within a tiny sun. At least, that's what it feels like. Everything is bright. White. Hard—which is where the sun illusion fails. I force my eyes to stay open and acclimate to the blinding light. White floor, white walls, white ceiling. The whole front of the room is a glossy plas-glass panel that reveals a lovely view of the lab. The ceiling is studded with brilliant white lighting. And nozzles. I don't like the nozzles. I'm even more confident they don't contain confetti.

After the relaxing opulence of the prison, the brilliant sterility of the lab is almost toxic in its vibrancy. I'm stretched out on a thin white pad on a hard white shelf bed. My filthy coveralls have been replaced by a new pair, partially unzipped to allow for the sensors that are adhered to my sternum and upper chest.

I pull them all off and drop the crumpled adhesive on the floor. Then, I realize they probably weren't working anyway because they're electronic. I'm alive. All previous suppositions to the contrary. Somehow, I managed to defeat the champion of an entire prison.

We'll ignore the fact that it was absolutely on a technicality.

A small camera is mounted in the ceiling near the glass wall. I'm pretty far away and intend to stay that way for the short term. I stick my tongue out at it, heady with the delusional glee of survival.

Then I'm brought back to reality. I'm in a cell. Apparently

surviving the maze wasn't enough to make me be considered trustworthy. It just made me seem like an excellent lab rat. I didn't see any other women in the lab cells. I hope that's not because every woman experimented upon died.

For now, at least, if they put a chip in me it won't work. Oh, hey, that means the bomb in my neck probably also doesn't work. That's a relief. I stare at the mostly healed bite on the back of my hand. Just a slight discoloration to my skin. I don't think I've ever been happy to be bitten by a bug, but they may have just saved my life.

And they have lifesaving left to do. If, as I suspect, this signal dampener sets everything to its default—and default is usually "off"—then I should just be able to walk out of this cell when the time comes. There will be night guards—but two-thirds of them should be my allies. If everything goes well, we can get what they need tonight and then start heading for the ship I secreted in the mountains.

I kick the ball of sensor and sticky tape away and approach the front of the cell, where the plas-glass wall stretches over the entire entrance. People are working in the lab. A few cast sneaky little glances at me. Probably I'm a lesson to the rest of them. Make one step wrong and you're in the prison. Two steps? You're in a cell.

Rayla stomps over to the front of the cell. "What did you do to the maze?" She glares lasers at me. My innocent expression is really getting a workout. Maybe it's improving. "You tampered with it somehow. Sabotaged that like you did our nutrient printer. Why do you have it out for us?"

"Because you're fucking insane?" The ruse of making peace with Pierce wasn't ever working for me. These people never wanted or trusted me in the lab. Maybe this was even Pierce's plan. A way to torment me before putting me out of my misery. The same way he tormented Cyn. Seems convoluted for someone who is a minor irritant at best. Unluckily for him, I like my misery and I don't want to be put out of it just yet. "You're experimenting on people. I don't know if you studied anything besides evilness in school, but I did and, I've got to tell you, history doesn't reflect well on people who experiment on others against their will."

"History reflects on winners and doesn't give a shit how you get there." She scoffs. "Leviathan and his future siblings will make us winners. Who would dare argue when we can simply force them to agree? Any chip is vulnerable to tampering once you figured out how. It's a shame you sold out to the other side."

"Right. This is what selling out looks like." I snort. "And how's that winning working for you? Doesn't look like you have what it takes yet, does it? A bunch of failures and one accidental success. Success doesn't count if you don't know how you earned it. They don't even value you enough to give you a nutrient printer that makes decent cookies. Your boss was probably sent here by his daddy because he fucked up so badly at his last job."

Shut up, Caro. Stop baiting the woman who has your life in her hands.

Rayla sneaks a glance at Carmichael as he enters the lab. "I could tell him to blow your spine and that would be a mercy compared to what's next. I might have taken pity on you, done the transition slowly. Well, forget that. Now I'm going to rip you open, shove a chip in, and when you wake up, you'll be under my thumb, just like the other one. A hunk of meat that I can puppet to my whims."

"You use hunks of meat as puppets? That's pretty gross, Rayla. Didn't your parents ever tell you not to play with your food?"

She makes an angry little squeak, like steam escaping from a vent, and spins, fingers curling into fists, before storming away. Excellent. More friends. Between Rayla and Kaori, I don't know which side of the prison I'd rather be in.

It appears that Carmichael entered the lab just to stand and stare at me in the cell for a solid ten minutes. He grins the whole time, like I'm doing a special trick. For the first five minutes or so, I attempt to look confused and pathetic on the off chance this was intended to teach *me* a lesson. When he doesn't let me out of the cell and give me a datapad, I abandon the effort and simply stare back. He doesn't like that as much.

Eventually, he leaves. The day shift slowly churns to night. The scientists leave the lab, the food printer in my cell drops a nutrient briquette and a cup of water, and at last, the guard shift changes.

There's a new guard whom I don't recognize. Squat man with short hair. He has a bruise on his neck. There is another guard whom I recognize deeply. Victor stands by the Portal of Sighs, his long white-blond hair captured in a queue at the base of his neck and a snarly expression on his face. His dark eyes cut my direction.

Oh. The snarl is for me. I'm so glad to see him I don't even care. I almost wave, which would really ruin the whole clandestine part of the mission. Victory is stationed near the entrance to the bunk area. She gives me a little wink. Preferable to Victor's snarl. I study the workstations within my field of view. Rayla left a wall-mounted datalink on with a projection screen above it. The three-dimensional form of a man projects out of the screen. I recognize him as the same man whom I just faced off with in the maze.

Leviathan, and I cannot put this any other way, is a fucking mess.

One large chip is embedded in his brain. It appears to be attached directly to the mass of tissue; wires threaded into his mind. He has cybernetic augmentation in one of his eyes, which suddenly makes all that squinting at me make more sense. I must have been invisible to that eye due to my bug-blood. Leviathan's joints have been enhanced. Most mods fail because of connection points. You can give someone a robot hand, sure, but if they have a human elbow, that robot hand will still be limited by the elbow. He has all robot joints. His bones are standard but have the roughened texture you get when they've been put through a rapid growth cycle, or a hundred. If you put a blastclast repair system on a healthy bone, it just thickens it. Usually that's useless—because of the joint issue—but in this case, they've created an infrastructure that can support the slabs of muscle atop it.

A few hours later in the evening, when the staff has probably gone to bed, Victory stretches her neck, walks a few paces, and nails the third guard with a stun blast right between his eyes. He falls bonelessly into Victor's waiting arms.

I approach the plas-glass wall at the front of my cell, hand tentatively out in front of me. I'm going to feel deeply stupid if my hypothesis about my bug-given signal-dampening powers is incorrect.

The thing about buildings in general is that all doors should default to open, with the exception of exterior hatches of spaceships. In case there's a catastrophe, you need to be able to evacuate quickly, and dealing with locks is not quick. As such, usually, even a cell is set to default open if all other constraints are lifted. There are usually a lot of other constraints.

So, if I short out all programming, I should be able to walk right through this plas-glass door.

If I'm wrong, I might be electrocuted by it.

I set my skin against the glass.

I'm not wrong.

Of course, I'm not wrong. I'm never wrong. I'm a genius except for all the times when I'm not. The plas-glass shifts under the gentle brush of my fingertips and slides open. I slip out into the darkened lab area. None of the Titans pays any attention to me except Leviathan, who, as usual, is staring directly at me. I wonder if he always looks into the hallway like it's a form of entertainment or if his obsession is with me specifically.

Mine is with him specifically. I'm fascinated by the man behind the manipulation. Who was he before this? A common criminal? A violent mercenary? He could have been any number of things before Pierce forced him to become something else. He was a man who was locked up and who was scared. Who knew something awful was coming. Who had so much life in his clear bright eyes.

Years ago, when I was still working for Pierce, I went to a zoo on one of their satellites. It featured predatory species from all their territorial planets. I'd never been anywhere so depressing until I got to this lab. It was filled with creatures that should be at the peak of their lives, of their prowess, all staring vacantly through electrified plasma walls, trapped in habitats far too small for them to thrive and hand-fed as though they were cubs. It was twisted. Some of the animals paced, some sat placidly. But the one that I was drawn to, the one I always returned to, was a large creature, shaped like something between a person and a dog with long sharp teeth, a row of sensory spines down its back, and an articulated tail that it used almost like another hand. It watched the crowd with the same empty intensity as Leviathan.

As though it was looking for something but forgot what it was.

The lab is illuminated only by dim track lights that line the seam of the floor and the walls. I don't get too close as I cross the room, twins behind me. Last thing I need is to be stumbling around in darkness. Victor opens his mouth, probably to ask how I managed to walk out of my cell, but I hold up one hand. Time for work first. My fingers are poised over the datalink when I realize the critical error in my plan. I might be able to walk through any door, but the same thing that enables me to do that locks all the digitalized information far far away from my eager fingers.

Well, fuck.

How am I supposed to figure out what they're up to when I can't even get in their history? I swear under my breath and drag my fingers over my curls. What fucking good am I if I can't even touch a datapad? An engine? Once I get out of here, how can I go back to work on the *Calamity*? I'll kill our engine, stall the oxygen pumping into the atmo.

I'm only useful in my connection to technology.

"What exactly did you need to find?" I ask the twins in a low voice, stepping back from the datalink.

Victory takes my place at the datalink. "A chip. Special one that was made with Reed AI, not just Pierce stuff. Apparently, Frederick gave them one as a loaner, thinking he'd make a bigger sale out of it, and they never bought or returned the part. He wanted it retrieved."

Must have been some nefarious shit if he wants a loaner chip returned. There's only one chip I can think of that's special. One chip that is different from the others.

The one that's in Leviathan's head. The only one that works properly.

Pierce, priaps that they are, decided to knock off Reed tech and they can't figure out how to do it. They can make people aggressive or still, but they can't make them functional. I take a quiet, sardonic breath.

"I think we're going to have to perform that rescue after all." I explain my deduction to the others. "The way for us to save the tech is to save him."

"Have you seen him?" Victor grumbles. "You know, like while he was trying to kill you? We can't take him on a ship like that."

I have an idea for that, too. But I need them to be distracted to try it out. Neither of the twins would let me do it on my own. Because it's moderately to severely stupid.

I can't access the computer. But I can turn *off* a computer. The last time I touched Leviathan, I turned off his chip. He froze. If the chip controls his personality, maybe I can safely question him just by touching his head and temporarily overriding the Pierce programming. I have to survive the first part of that exchange, but I don't have to beat him or kill him, I just have to touch him.

I'm the new Caro. The Caro of action. All I need to do is action my way out of this.

Probably. And if not, I do have backup.

I explain the bug-blood thing as quickly as possible. Victory winces in disgust. Victor prods the little blemish on the back of my hand like it's a power button. "I can't touch the tech. I need you guys to access the system and get every bit of information you can on Leviathan. While you do, I have to stand away from it. I'll be going through hard data."

I get them set up at adjacent terminals on the far side of the lab, hemmed in by equipment. They won't be seen there if someone pops out of the door, and they won't see me over by the cells either. Their inner-ear coms are turned up to detect any activity in the bunk area. The third guard is bound and gagged.

Before the logic part of my brain can talk me out of it, I grab a scalpel and approach Leviathan's cell. I'm armed. He's not.

Well, he has two pretty exceptional *arms* but no weapons.

He's at the front of the cell when I pause, his chest almost brushing the plas-glass, eyes shadowed by his brow so that, in the darkness, it's hard to see their intensity. He's in similar attire to me, white coveralls. If he wasn't wearing them, they could perhaps be used as a tent or a throw rug. Every single muscle known to doctors and, perhaps, one or two that were heretofore unknown is visible against the fabric.

I glance down at myself. Not many muscles visible. I have a healthy slick layer of fat over all of them—very useful if I ever have to survive in some sort of arctic environment. I'm in better than average shape, I'm just genetically predisposed to curves rather than hard ridges.

He doesn't move. Doesn't angrily wave a fist or slam it into the glass. Doesn't glare. Just stands there like he's a statue. I roll the scalpel in a sweaty palm, bracing it with my index finger. We won't be alone forever. I might as well take a risk now if I'm going to. I press against the plas-glass of the door, and it slides open with barely a whisper of sound. I lunge forward as quickly as possible, darting my hand up before he has a chance to pummel me.

I needn't have worried because he doesn't move at all. I press my fingers against his head over the tiny scar, only then realizing how close this puts us. To reach his temple, I'm pressed flush against all that muscle I was admiring earlier. He sucks in a startled breath, moving at last. Every muscle burning a line down my body tenses, and I suddenly realize how small the blade of the scalpel is.

I finally move the weapon, placing it carefully over his crotch because, first of all, it's close, and second of all, there isn't a person with a penis who wants a blade near it. I press forward until we're partially obscured behind one of the support parts of his cell.

His head tilts, clearly confused, dark eyelashes fanning down and then up. His voice is jagged with lack of use, like he's remembering and pushing each individual word out with effort. "What are you?"

Considering that was my first question, clearly, we're of similar minds. I whisper my response, not ready to alert the twins. "I'm an engineer."

He blinks, voice lowered to match mine. "You aren't here."

The ocular sensor in his eye. Maybe infrared. I'd be invisible to those senses. "What have they done to you?"

His brows press together. His mouth opens. He has surprisingly plump lips for a human weapon. "I—don't know. I don't remember." That massive body shifts against me suddenly as he takes an abrupt step forward, knocking into me and pushing me back toward the hall. "Why don't I remember? What did you do to me?"

His voice is getting louder. Not loud, exactly, but no longer a whisper.

"Caro? Everything all right?" Victor inconveniently chooses now to pay attention.

"Fine," I reply in a low voice. "Just talking to . . . um . . . myself."

As though my voice sounds like that. But he lets it go, perhaps listening to the goings-on in the bunk room more than the lab.

I return my attention to Leviathan. Press the scalpel in harder. "Don't move. I don't want to hurt you."

He pauses his panic attack to give me a look like I couldn't possibly hurt him, brow up and face so achingly human and *normal* for a split second that something in my heart cracks open just before the actual nuance of his confidence registers. Everyone thinks I'm such an easy mark. Maybe I move or something because before I even realize what's happened, my scalpel hand is wrapped in his and is behind my back.

There's another mod. Superfast muscle-twitch reflex. It makes sense. The sort of people who know enough to support joints before growing bones also know that bulky muscles are nothing without the support structures of skeletal muscles.

Bad time to realize it. I stupidly thought that I'd tap him in the head and he'd thank me for waking him up and then spill a bunch of intelligence. Academic smarts, not people smarts— that's me. The thing with having academic smarts is that sometimes you assume you have all kinds. I take a deep breath to try to quell the panic rising within me. Luckily, I've been dealing with a steady state of panic for a couple days now, and I'm getting used to it. "We've started this wrong. I have nothing to do with you. I never even saw you before this week. I'm trying to figure out what's happening in Pierce space and in this lab in particular."

I already know what's happening. Pierce is building a supersoldier. Strong. Fast. Under their complete control. No pesky morality to ruin things on the field of battle. I just need proof. Maybe a handwritten journal. *Dear Diary, about to illegally experiment on human subjects for the nefarious purposes detailed below. XOXO, Carmichael Pierce.*

Something simple like that. Which is neither here nor there because I have my hand on a hair trigger right now and it could deploy any minute.

"All I want to know is what's been done to you. Maybe a timeline. And it'd be super great if you didn't murder me on the way to finding that out."

He's back to confused, the flash of masculine ego gone. His voice coming a little easier with more use. "I don't know. I don't even know who I am. Why don't I know who I am?"

"They call you Leviathan." I might as well offer him something. He deserves the truth, as bluntly delivered as possible. "We're in a prison called Shikigami. The Pierce Family have manipulated your body. Your mind. They release you to fight in a maze that takes up most of the main floor of the prison. You frequently kill your opponent. Whatever they did to you, they haven't been able to replicate with anyone else. The others have wound up catatonic or wildly aggressive."

I have almost nothing left to give him. As allies go, Leviathan is a possibility I never considered—probably because I have to touch him to have an ally.

Not that it's much of a hardship. His skin under my fingertips is smooth and warm. Makes me want to curl them because I'm not usually this close to someone I'm not intimate with. I shake myself internally. I need to keep it in my coveralls.

I can keep hands on his chip long enough to get him out of the prison. Maybe even farther than that. We can make our escape tonight if we hurry.

One perk to being a blank slate is that he seems to take a very outlandish yet true story in stride. "You aren't catatonic or wildly aggressive."

"I'm new. Give me time. So far, they haven't been able to control me because, as it happens, my body is presently a big squishy signal damper. Electronics don't work around me. That's also why you're *you* right now instead of whatever that chip in your head wants you to be."

At last his body shifts slightly, the hand on my arm behind my back loosening, his thumb tracing over the inside of my wrist as he presses me closer. Licks of fiery sensation follow the trail where his skin brushes mine. "Not big. Only squishy in the right places."

The shudder that ripples through my body isn't nearly as icy as the last one. Trust a man to focus on my squishy places instead of the fact that he has a chip in his head. Trust *me* to get waylaid by that focus when I need to stay on subject. "That aside, the second I take my hand off your head, you return to—whatever they set you to do. Which appears to be standing around in an unresisting manner. But they may have built-in triggers depending on external stimuli."

"So, I'm a killing machine who terrorizes a prison, and you thought it would be a good idea to open my cell and have a chat?" Little slivers of personality are starting to escape. Those excellent lips curl up in a wry smile. He glances up and behind me. "With no partner to watch your back. Do you have no sense of self-preservation?"

Apparently not. I shrug one shoulder, brushing against him as I do. It's not why I did it . . . but it's appreciated . . . by me. "I do have partners but I can't access the computers. Seemed like I should go straight to the source."

I'm being very generous with myself to call this honesty. I'm leaving out the very large part where his chip can only be hacked because of me. My work from years ago unlocked the access to his brain.

"Are you going to stab me with this thing?" His thumb traces again over the skin of my wrist where the hilt of the scalpel is pressed. Is it a hilt if it's a medical tool?

"Are you going to try to kill me?" I'm very proud that I haven't whimpered even once during this exchange. It's like I routinely question devastatingly sexy murder machines that equal parts terrify and attract me.

Not as equal as the parts should be, honestly.

"Not today." It's a promise he can't possibly make. The moment I let him go, he isn't himself anymore. I know the look on his face when he swings a staff at me, intending to kill. Having any kind of trust in this man at all is insane because his best intentions simply do not matter. He releases my scalpel wrist and I straighten the arm, keeping the blade away from him.

"Can you remember anything at all?" It's a desperate plea.

"I remember how to speak Standard." His voice takes a considering tone. He could step away a little and still have my hand on his head, but he doesn't. Maybe he takes comfort in having someone close to him who isn't trying to hurt him, even if he doesn't realize that's why. "I remember how to shave. How to tie boots. Read a map." His shadowed eyes crinkle slightly as he looks down at me. "How to make love. How to write."

"But nothing . . . personal? Your family? Your job? Your age?" If I can figure out who he was, maybe I can find some way to get the coms to reach the *Calamity* and they can research for me.

His head shakes and he makes a low dissatisfied rumble of irritation. "Nothing at all."

I decide to try a different direction. "How about how you feel right now? Does anything feel strange? That would give me a clue about if there are any mods I don't know about."

"I don't know what normal feels like." The frustration is almost palpable in his voice. His jaw tightens and a muscle twitches above it. I like this angry irritation because it shows spirit.

I didn't realize how difficult this would be. When I let him go, he loses himself. This time, *I* do it to him. But I can't do the next part of my job with my hand on his head. "I have to go. And

I have to leave you here because the second I stop touching you, you'll forget yourself, and I can't loose you on the prison until we're ready to go. But we'll take you with us. I promise you that."

He's silent for a long time. I shift slightly on my feet, preparing to dart outside his door if this goes poorly. "No promises. Just come back, angel."

I swallow a hard lump that's just appeared in my throat. My fingers curl against his temple of their own volition. An electrical charge that has everything to do with contact and nothing to do with technology darts through my body. A sense of familiarity. Of comfort. Of magnetism. "Caro. My name is Caro. I'll come back. If I can."

I start to step back, fingers losing contact with his skin, and his hand snaps forward to grab my forearm, the same one he grabbed in the maze. I flinch, but he simply holds my hand in contact with his head. "I was just thinking about myself. I didn't even consider . . . you're in danger, aren't you? You just flinched. Someone hurt you."

Well, isn't this a fine fucking mess? He wants to protect me from himself. I force a smile. "I'm fine. Totally experienced at this kind of thing. Highly trained."

Highly trained at ship engines and biohacking, that is. Something flashes in his eyes like he reads the misdirection in my own. Like he's made a decision. His other hand flashes out in one of those too-fast-to-track motions and cups the back of my head, slowly drawing me forward as he bends low. I should keep my eyes on him, should watch for danger.

My eyes flutter shut as he presses those fantastic lips against my own. His kiss is slow, gentle. It's a question and he's waiting for my answer. My answer is stupid because I find myself going up on my toes and wrapping my free arm over a broad shoulder, fingers tracing all that hard muscle. My other hand cradles the side of his face.

That growly sound comes back, only instead of dissatisfied it's deeply satisfied. The sound of a man who knows what he's doing and is happy about doing it. He touches only my head, very gently, as he cajoles the kiss deeper, lips tracing the seam of my own until I open for him with a little sigh. A flush of heat works its way under my skin, flaring in my chest, my gut, pooling at the junction of my legs. When I pull away to gasp a breath, I blink dazedly at him, his hard-planed face just a breath from my own.

The smile that he gives me then tells me something about who Leviathan used to be, who he could be again one day. It's lazily relaxed, featuring two incredibly deep dimples. Confident to the point of cocky. "I remember how to do that, too."

CHAPTER 9

I slide Leviathan's cell door shut and step away quickly, not fully knowing my range. Or at least, that's the plan. Actually, I accidentally slam it in his face because he moved forward while we were talking. It's a deeply smooth moment, I'm sure. The good news is that he probably won't remember it.

My heartbeat is so wild it seems to echo in my head. He kissed me. I didn't imagine that part, right? It wasn't the deluded fantasy of a stress coma.

He kissed me.

And I kissed him back. I've always had shit taste in men—a string of them leading back to adolescence and each one as disinterested in me as the last. They're all pretty, at least they have that going for them, and Leviathan blows them out of the water in all regards. Drop-dead gorgeous with a healthy emphasis on "drop dead." He's literally programmed to be unavailable. He's lost and oddly charming and absolutely terrifying.

He's also a dazzlingly good kisser. I don't know why he did it except maybe as a manipulation. Or perhaps facing a sort of psychological death drove him to seek a connection. If I had only one moment left to be cogent, I'd probably shoot my shot, too.

"What was that? Tell me I didn't just see what I think I saw." Victory's voice hisses from only a pace behind me and I jump and yelp before she gets a chance to put her hand over my mouth.

"He attacked her." Victor strides toward Leviathan's cell.

I grab his arm, yanking him to a halt. "He did not attack me. I thought I'd question him."

"Is that a new interrogation strategy where you suck the information out of someone's tongue? Looked effective." Victory winks at me with a grin.

"It was," I snap. "I was never out of control, but we have bigger issues."

"Bigger issues than you being imprisoned, being a lab rat, and fucking up our mission? Those all seem pretty big." Victor finally turns, casting a glare back at Leviathan, who is still doing his standing-and-staring thing that he does so well. "We got password-blocked while searching for your guy. While you were interrogating his mouth."

A bolt of light zaps against the wall in front of us and I'm down on the floor, rolling away, before I realize that my instincts have taken over. The discomfort hits me a moment later, my body protesting the rough treatment. Victor growls out an expletive, and a flash of movement comes from the hall by the prisoner cells. Three more shots collide with the wall, and one takes the edge off of the chair that Victory stood next to moments ago.

She takes shelter beside me behind one of the tables, a handful of scalpels like a bouquet in her grip. Why would she have scalpels when she has a perfectly good blaster? Oh. Her blaster is back by the console. Well, shit. She answers my next question before I even have a chance to ask it. "Two other security guards. Must have been watching the feed. I thought they were too drunk. They should have been, considering all the smuggled booze I gave them."

Victory plucks scalpel after scalpel from her cluster and flings them across the room with scary accuracy. The sound of fists on flesh come from Victor's direction. I crawl the length of the table, keeping my head low as I rummage through the compartments beside me. Nothing of use at all until I get to the end and find a cylinder of liquid hydrogen.

I don't want to linger over what experiment here requires cryogenics. Probably there's some ancient Pierce head stored in a jar for future veneration. Perhaps Cyn's famous Viall himself—the proto-Pierce. The Pierce Family practices ancestor worship. If they could have a reliquary around for convenient adoration, I'm sure they would.

I awkwardly pull the cylinder from its storage space and pop off the vacuum seal, keeping it pointed carefully away from me as I crab-walk sideways to peer around the edge of the lab bench. One guard is backing toward me, his blaster pointed at Victor. Victor advances on him, his own blaster aimed.

I leap out from behind the table with the cylinder, dumping the liquid nitrogen down the back of the guard's uniform armor. At first, he doesn't react, but the bloodcurdling scream that comes from his lips an instant later echoes throughout the room. Victor takes advantage of his distraction to stun him. When the man falls, the armor on his back cracks into shards, spinning over the floor.

"We were trying to do this without all the screaming," Victor mutters at me in a low voice.

Oh. Right. They haven't activated any alarms—maybe due to all that top-notch liquor hampering judgment.

Across the room, Victory has finally managed to hit something useful with one of her scalpels. It skids over the cheek of the other guard, causing him to flinch back. She takes advantage of the moment when he's distracted to regain her blaster and fire upon him. A stun blast, but he goes down.

The lab falls quiet as we all freeze, staring at the door that leads toward the bunk area. Blaster fights are largely silent, since light isn't noisy. Screaming guards and shattering armor are not silent.

It's a prison. Perhaps screams aren't unusual even with the calming decorations. Kaori lives here, after all.

I kneel on the floor by the data hub to retrieve yet another scalpel. There's something stuck to the underside of the counter. I angle myself closer. A white label with black text reading 6PNR*#285JK.

A rusty chuckle creaks out of my throat, and I rest back on my heels while the twins look at me like I'm a lunatic. I peel the label back with my fingernail and wave it in the air. "I have the password."

Victor faces the door from which danger will most likely emanate. I move away from the terminal and Victory retakes her seat, tapping in the digits until the screen opens. I direct Victory through a few threads on the ether until we find one hub titled PATIENT DATA. Seems like a good starting place once we're ready. The next step is finding a way to get the data out of the Pierce stream and into one more useful for us.

"Before you do anything else, access the public ether, please." I point Victory toward the Search function, perched as far away as I can while still seeing the screen. "And perform a search for 'Bonker Booster.'"

She shoots me a dubious gaze over her shoulder. "You really think now is the time to play some stupid number game?"

"I think it's exactly the time to download some stupid number game on this dataport that is directly linked to the Pierce ether and shielded from all external communications." She keeps giving me dubious eyes, which means that I have to crack enough to offer additional information. This is why working with a team can be irritating.

I huff out a breath. "Bonker Booster is a hacker tool. It appears to be an innocuous time-wasting game but it contains embedded code that provides access both within and outside a private stream. Right now, this dataport has no access to exterior networks when it comes to *communication*. The etherwall blocks all downloads that the system flags as relating to communication in any way. In fact, I'd hazard that the only terminal here that can contact the outside goes directly to Pierce and is locked within Carmichael's rooms. But they've given the scientists administrative access to download their own programs from the public ether because Family information-security teams hate being constantly bothered by scientists who always need yet another new program that the IS teams don't even understand. They provide impenetrable security on the network and the code, keeping an outside source from accessing anything. The only gap is if you invite the hacker in, so to speak. A tool like Bonker Booster is perfect for that."

And it's how I paid my way through boarding school and three standard cycles of university until I realized that I would have been better off saving the credits and running for the farthest border planet I could find. Bonker Booster is my personal creation—a game just stupid enough to catch on in a population of bored workers attached to nearly every level of Family business.

Which is neither here nor there because usually I use it to steal information and a few credits from the outside after some unsuspecting employee downloads the game. I never expected that I'd be the person downloading it in order to provide access *out*.

A little spinner whirls on the display as the game loads.

"How did you know about this game?" Victory leans back in the chair and studies me with cold eyes. Not because she's particularly scornful. She just has naturally cold eyes. That gaze is probably 50 percent of her success as a merc.

I've grown used to the crew of the *Calamity*, none of whom are particularly technical and all of whom take my proclamations and suggestions in stride without asking questions. "It's—"

The door to the living quarters bursts open, so late that no one was expecting it.

"Is everything okay out there?" a voice calls.

"All clear," Victor barks in a commanding tone.

The bound and gagged guard drums his heels on the floor. That's what you get for being a nonmurderous type. Stunning seems nice until they wake up. Some kind of movement comes from the dormitory hall. Victor shoves a wheeled chair directly at the open door and the silhouette framed within it. Behind the form, I can make out the dimly lit living area with overstuffed furniture in the shape of squashed eggs. The person in the door, one of the scientists, I think, yelps loudly and hits the floor, and—behind her—doors crack and heads peer out. Fuck.

Three of them are security staff and they're armed.

I step back to give Victory space to maneuver as the first blaster bolts hit the lab and emit a yelp of my own when Victor loops his arm around me and tosses me directly into the line of cells and out of the line of fire. Literally tosses. Apparently he thinks I have reflexes like he does. Instead of nimbly bouncing off a wall or landing in a crouch, I ricochet off a cell door. A cell door that slips open because of my stupid bug-blood and I spin out in the hall at just the moment that Leviathan steps out through the portal.

Time halts for a moment as my heart lodges itself in my throat.

He's not deactivated right now. He's activated with an emphasis on "active." Maybe violence puts him in kill mode. Maybe Pierce turned him on. I don't know. I just know it's fucking *bad*. This is not the lost man who kissed me. This is the behemoth who crushed another man with one hand against the wall of the maze. Who tried his hardest to kill me with shocking speed.

Who can easily murder everyone in this room while they're distracted and who won't even realize he meted out those fates.

His fist smashes into the cell door just behind me as I roll away, shattering the plas-glass with just one blow. Plas-glass is stronger than people—that's its whole point. I squeak out a strangled scream. I have no weapon. Last time I had a weapon. My empty hands scrabble on the floor as I attempt to move out of the way.

Chips of glass rain down on me as the other prisoner—the one who frantically paced his cell tugging at his own hair—lunges out through the now-open door and at Leviathan. I squeak, trying to make myself tiny as they distract themselves with each other. It doesn't last long. Leviathan throws the other Titan into the lab, disrupting the ongoing confrontation with the scientists and remaining guards.

No sign of Carmichael Pierce. He's staying nice and safe in his private rooms.

We are so fuuuuuuucked.

A crunch comes from my side, Leviathan's large feet crushing shards of plas-glass as he redirects his attention at me. And here I am just crouched on the floor staring at everything in stunned shock. He takes another swing, eyes blank of recognition, feet nearly stomping me, and I keep rolling away, making a target of myself. While he's trying to kill me, he isn't *succeeding* at killing anyone else. This is so bad. This is so *so* bad. I don't want him to die, and he absolutely will either murder someone I love or be murdered by them if this goes any further.

Panic vies with terror and a strange kind of sorrow for my primary emotion. My stomach clenches, my jaw clenches, my eyes dart around the area looking for some sort of way to gain an advantage.

I have to stop him—*somehow*—but I'm empty-handed. If our last interaction taught me anything it's that I don't have a chance against him in a physical confrontation. Especially since I don't really want to hurt him.

If you've ever tried to fight a hover tank barehanded without causing it any damage, you'll understand the predicament I'm in. But you haven't ever tried that. Because it's insane. First of all, you'd be stupid to fight a hover tank. It would leave a crater in the ground where you used to be and keep right on hovering on. Second of all, you'd be presumptuous to assume you *could* do it damage. Third, assuming the first two did happen, there's no chance to stop that tank without tearing a panel or two off. Maybe if you had the right tech, you could hack it from a distance.

My weird brand of tech will not let me operate it from a distance. So I decide to do something that Temper would call heedless. Just this once, I'd agree with her.

I just avoid his next stomp, latching on to his wrist and allowing him to yank me back to my feet. One broad hand grasps the back of my neck, fingers nearly wrapping all the way around and tightening to uncomfortable. My neck screams, my legs kick in the air, and I manage to smack my other hand against his temple and hold it there. My breath pants out as adrenaline ricochets through my body.

He freezes. I freeze. The pandemonium around us continues. A chair flies through the air at us and he releases the hand around my neck to casually bat it away. My heart hammers away in my chest.

He returns the hand to me, gently tracing the outline of a bruise on my face with one rough finger. "How long has it been, angel?"

Not very. I flinch slightly when someone yells behind me. It isn't a voice I recognize, which means that it's okay that they're yelling. I should go back, try to help the twins, but I acknowledge that I'm probably of more value keeping Leviathan from killing everyone than I am throwing a scalpel. I know my aim that well, at least. And, embarrassingly, I'm caught in the pull of his eyes, pale and mysterious and intensely focused on me. Like he's trying to decipher me.

"A good half hour. I couldn't stay away." I give a weak grin, somewhat belied by the sounds of fighting that still come from behind me. "As you can see, everything's going well."

Leviathan smiles and every stray thought immediately jettisons from my head. That smile is just as lethal as his arms, his eyes, his fists. It's charming, lopsided, dashing, and most of all, dangerous. My stomach attempts to perform a backflip but no part of me has ever been that athletic so instead it twists, and I try not to swallow my tongue.

He was trying to kill you just a moment ago, Caro. Calm down.

He literally knows no one else. He's trapped and victimized and I'm standing here imagining what he looks like without those coveralls because I feel like I know him due to the vid footage. Oh yeah, and there's a literal fight raging in the lab behind me. What's wrong with me?

Lots of stuff, honestly.

Hard hands grab the coverall material over my shoulder blades and yank me backward so quickly that I can't catch a grip on Leviathan. I yelp as my fingers slide away from his temple, and I watch the moment that the ruthlessly clever glow in those lovely eyes cuts out like a light. Within that darkness is something that doesn't recognize me and is hungry for violence. I duck within my captor's grip just in time for Leviathan's fist to shoot right through the space where my head was and mash into the person behind me. I'm suddenly and unceremoniously dropped to the floor, scuttling like an insect toward a wall to stay beneath the notice of Leviathan and the other prisoner, who now is blood-smeared and has a dent where his nose used to be.

I skitter backward, hands slipping on the floor, heart pumping in my throat so hard that it's all I hear. When I get to a bench, I reach up blindly, looking for a weapon. I come back with a cauterizing blade. One might think that a cauterizing blade is a bad tool for fighting, but it really just depends on how deep you go. Cauterizing major blood vessels that feed the brain kills you just as easily as opening them up does.

At least that's how it works with engines. Most of my medical knowledge comes from assuming that people are like engines. It hasn't led me wrong yet.

When I peek into the main lab area again, I see Victor, doing his best to hold the door to the living spaces shut as the scientists attempt to break through. Two or three of them have. One body is on the floor.

The wild prisoner flies into the room, back slamming into one of the tables with such force that I suspect it's broken, except he slithers around to his feet unharmed and lunges back at Leviathan just as the prison champion steps into the main part of the lab, body solid and capable. Mind gaseous and grasping. Keeping as low as possible, I scoot around the edge of the lab bench. I'm not particularly stealthy. The table slides into me as they crash into the opposite side, shoving me away until I wind up sprawled perfectly aligned behind the guard who has Victory cornered.

Like the professional she is, Victory takes advantage of the moment, shoving a rolling chair at him so that he stumbles back, heel catching against my ribs. I punch him in the back of the knee joint with both hands and he falls flat on me, his blaster spinning from his grip across the slick polished floor.

Victory vaults over the table she was sheltering behind, smooth as if they made the gravity go temporarily weightless, her thick white braid twitching over her shoulder with the motion, and shoots a stun round into him. I can feel the charge fizzling along my own skin. She reaches down a calloused hand and yanks me to my feet.

Her careful stunning might be pointless because the activated Titans aren't being so cautious. They've stopped fighting each other and have moved in on the door to the lab. Victor abandons his post.

Cracks spiderweb across the front of the other aggressive-Titan cells, damaged by the fighting.

We have to get out. Leviathan can kill all of us indiscriminately and that's not counting the other Titans. At this point, the only people who can stop Leviathan are the same people who imprisoned him in the first place. I'm not getting close enough to try to neutralize him.

No matter how much I want to.

"Stun them!" I shout to Victory. She can prevent the bloodbath that's coming.

She looks at me like I'm insane. "If I stun them, Pierce and his people come out and try to arrest us immediately. If I don't stun them, they provide a useful distraction, and we make our escape. I'm definitely not going to stun them."

A larger scientist manages to push his way through the door, running headlong for the closest datapad, probably in an effort to control the Titans. One of the plas-glass walls collapses, and a new Titan hurls himself into the scientist. The man screams a wet sound and suddenly goes silent. Fighting is horrible. And terrifying. Why did no one warn me how terrifying it is?

Is it just *not* terrifying to them?

As Victor joins us, the other scientists burst free behind him, running directly into Leviathan and the Titans. That's when the real screaming starts. Blaster fire ricochets off the floor and the walls. I guess I'm not the only technologist with terrible aim. I direct the twins to the exit that the guard took when he escorted me into the prison. At this point, the prison is a safer place than the lab.

And I'm not running into the hills. Not yet. There's more work to be done here. I wasn't interested in doing any favors for Frederick Reed. I will do a favor for Leviathan. The man I met doesn't deserve this . . . *thing* . . . that has been done to him.

The last thing I see before the door shuts behind us is Leviathan once again tossing the large hairy Titan attacker away and turning on a cadre of suddenly scared-shitless scientists. His massive hand clasps over one of the scientist's heads, and the crack of his broken neck echoes through my ear as the door clicks shut and I dance backward as quickly as possible to keep it closed. Victor wedges the door shut with a metal rod just to be safe. Heavy bangs come from the lab. I'm frozen in place, staring at the door, waiting for it to burst open, a chill in my spine and doubt in my heart.

They're dead. Maybe not all of them, certainly not Carmichael, but some. Most. They wouldn't be if I wasn't here. Yes, they're bad. They're experimenting on humans and destroying their autonomy but, maybe, they're doing what their Family forced them to do. Maybe they're as helpless as anyone else in the Family system.

"This isn't your fault." Victory tosses an arm over my shoulders and tugs me away from the door and into the darkness behind the walls. She gives a little squeeze before releasing me.

"How do you figure that?" My voice is rough.

"People create their own fate." Victor's response from behind me is flat and unequivocating. "They made a monster—a *few* monsters—and now they're dealing with the consequences."

Leviathan isn't a monster. Not like Victor means. He's a person, he's just lost.

I don't *know* he isn't a monster, actually. He's in a prison. There are plenty of monsters here. The fact that Pierce and Nakatomi probably threw some people in on trumped-up charges doesn't mean that they didn't have any real criminals.

He didn't kiss like a monster.

That's a fucking stupid thing to think. How does a monster kiss, anyway? With more biting? I've never been the sort of person to have blind faith in someone and I shouldn't start now just because he probably looks good naked.

"Speaking of, you explained the lab rat had a chip, and you

had some sort of signal-dampening powers. You did not explain why you were linking lips. Are your dampening powers in your tongue?" Victory leads us deeper into the tunnel, her hair a beacon in the dark.

I stick said tongue out at her back. Doesn't dampen any of her signals.

"I didn't know you were so hard up." Victor's voice has a familiar low grumble as he prowls behind me. The thuds from the lab grow more distant.

"Don't try so hard, Victor," Victory snaps before I can.

"He was . . ." I pause and consider my next words. "Trapped. Charming. A real human person who got to be himself for the first time in what might be years. I asked him what he remembered. That was one of the things."

Victor snorts a laugh. "Good line."

"It didn't feel like a line. It felt like a—" I can't say it. It sounds so silly and naive. I'm many things but not either of those. I trace my fingers along the wall.

"What did it feel like?" Victory sounds curious. Probably it's her steady diet of tawdry holo-shows. She has a secret love for *Pulsar Passions*, which is by far the smuttiest holo in the streams. It's pretty good. I heard that Isabel is finally going to hook up with Ryan after absolute years of teasing the viewers.

"A connection," I mutter under my breath, churlish over being encouraged to say it.

Victor speaks up from behind us. "What was that? Couldn't quite hear you."

I glare at him and respond in a normal voice, "A connection."

His raised eyebrow tells me what he thinks of that statement. "Looked like he was connecting pretty hard with that scientist's neck. I were you, I'd avoid connecting with that one."

He's right. It's an instruction book for disaster. I think of the gleam of awareness in Leviathan's sea-glass eyes, the soft slide of his lips over mine, the tiny smile of sweet triumph when I kissed him back, and I know I won't be listening to Victor.

I can save Leviathan.

A line that I've mocked every single time I've seen it on the holos. A line I *know* to be a trap. Something that may well be impossible.

Fuck it, I'm going to do it anyway.

CHAPTER 10

The hall comes to an end before I have to answer any more awkward questions. We stick to the outskirts of the prison, away from the Heart and the other prisoners, creeping up levels on the narrow inside corridors that feed supply rooms and the hydroponic garden that supplies food to the kitchen. When we come to a door, all I have to do is touch it and it falls open in my hands.

One of said doors leads to a wardrobe supply closet, which allows us to change into more prison-appropriate clothes. We all choose leisurewear instead of elaborate getups. An assortment of comfy pants, tops, and cardigans provides sufficient camouflage for the short term.

After we are outfitted, we continue to search for a safe place to regroup. Behind one door, we step into a small dark room lined with projection displays of the prison—a live feed. The instant I get close to the displays they wink out, one by one. I guess I don't have to touch something directly. I just have to be quite close. Within reach. If any of the scientists or security have survived, they'll probably notice a control room experiencing power fluctuations.

So we move on.

It's maddening. My fingers practically itch for a datapad or a holo-display.

"Wouldn't we be better off lying low in some side space instead of on the move?" I try to keep the whine out of my voice. At this point, I'd settle for a closet. I'm tired. I'm not sure how long I was out after the arena, but it wasn't exactly restful. I need time to think instead of simply reacting. I need a plan, a safe place to consider it, and, preferably, a hot drink in my hands as I process. I may be able to obtain one of the three here.

"We're on the move until we find a safe space that's not populated." Victor leads us through New Shikigami, winding down the back halls just past the dining area, moving around the oval shape of the prison as stealthily as possible. The hall is intricately mosaicked with tiles from gold to cream, the carpet is thick and red, and the lighting is blown glass.

It's *all* populated. We've passed at least a dozen prisoners already, just sticking to the back halls that thread around the Heart. The people we pass have largely been incurious. One, wearing virtual-reality goggles, literally runs into a wall. I remember what Donovan said. The few spaces that aren't occupied are the ones that have fallen out of favor. I heard of one perfect example in my time working in the lab. A gift to Kaori from Carmichael. A space that he thought she'd appreciate. She scorned it immediately and the rest of the prisoners also avoided it, taking their cue.

It should be on the opposite side of the prison to us, and the farther we are from the lab and what's happening within it, the better. Adrenaline still ricochets through my body, hands shaking, mind sparking with exhausted excess energy.

We move around the periphery of the prison, from New Shikigami aesthetic into the old, decorated with wood tones, neutrals, and enforced relaxation. A short woman walks by, admiring a new manicure. The wall closest to the outside of the prison is lined with more support spaces. Probably useful to us at some point but likely to have surveillance, since the prison staff need to know if anything goes wrong there. The room we're heading to was intended by Carmichael for romantic trysts, so I'm betting he conveniently forgot to add the cameras in there.

When we pass one large reinforced door, I can see the dancing of water in light reflected in the thin gap beneath it. Water treatment. With how preposterous this prison is, I halfway expected them to make their water tanks into something ostentatious in the center of the building, an aquarium or an art installation or something, but I suppose it would be a disaster if they broke. Better to keep them behind locked doors for everyone's safety.

I glance down a side hall for a view of the Heart. No alarms. No one screaming. You'd never know that a massacre is happening in the lab right now. My shaking hands curl into fists.

I lead the twins to a large double door featuring a hologram of a forest on its surface. It isn't quite closed. A haunting melody emanates from within. Perfect

Victor sighs. She's been sighing a lot. Probably because of the gargantuan wrench I just threw in her plans. "Whatever this is, it doesn't seem like a priority right now."

"It's necessary. We're used to this sort of thing. Caro isn't. She needs downtime." Victor glances over at me, dark eyes smoky in his white face. They narrow as they take me in. I narrow mine back because it just seems fair.

I wrap my own fancy new cardigan closer to my chest. It's a soft gray-green, paired with a pink tunic-style blouse and gray leggings. The twins still have their guard shoes but the best I can do is my wimpy little slippers.

Victor opens the door all the way and the words die in my throat. It's like a dream. Beautiful. I can't imagine why Kaori would scorn it. It's almost like freedom.

The room is empty and expansive—probably thirty paces to get from the door to the far wall, the same across. Music plays, and as the tune changes, projected images on the wall bloom and grow. An asteroid belt rolls all around us, luminescent in false moonlight, with specks of starlight falling all around.

Victory sucks in a gasp and I freeze, wondering what's going to try to kill us next. Instead of seeking a tactical position, she steps forward on light feet, almost like she's dancing. A sparkle of light illuminates the floor as she walks, ghosting behind her as she moves. I glance down at a starburst beneath my own feet. I trace a toe in a broad circle beneath me, and the light follows the motion, an evanescent arc flashing before it stills.

Victor stays near the door, blocking it with his body, a circle of light expanding and contracting around his still form, and I creep toward the wall, hand outstretched to touch the closest projected asteroid. As my fingers hit the wall, the image of the asteroid flickers briefly and suddenly tumbles away, as though I pushed it. The rock knocks against others, disrupting this portion of the belt as I dance away, leaving swoops and arcs of light beneath my feet.

Ludicrously, my eyes fill with tears. This is simple figure-tracking technology linked with a rudimentary AI to extrapolate paired with hologram and projection systems for imagery. The tech isn't impressive or new. What's remarkable is what they've done with it. They took simplicity and created magic. It's a way to feel expansiveness—freedom. A heavy thundering rainfall of glowing space dust patters down around us, scattering the floor with holo specks like embers, and as we walk, they billow away from the movement.

I'm so busy looking at the floor, I don't even notice when the asteroid belt becomes a forest at night—the music changing to the shush and chitter of nocturnal creatures. The embers of space dust tumble along the floor like fallen leaves made of fire, and a waterfall flows from one side of the room to the other. When Victory walks through the water, it splashes up around her.

Within the peace, my brain once again clicks into a gear beyond survival. Whatever is happening in the lab right now spells disaster. If the men from Project Titan win, it's because they killed all the scientists. If the scientists win, it's probably because they somehow killed the Titans. I swallow an out-of-place swell of emotion at the thought. I've known Leviathan for literally moments; the thought of his downfall shouldn't get me that worked up.

But it does.

If either group wins, their next focus is going to be the prison. Once they figure out how to leave the lab, the Titans will rampage through the Heart relatively unconstrained. I don't think the guy in the VR goggles is going to put up much of a fight. The scientists will be wondering where I ran off to with their two new guards. Either way, Carmichael Pierce calls for backup because I'm sure he never poked his nose out of his quarters.

And we didn't get a chance to download the pertinent data to the ether or rescue Leviathan. Which means we have to go *back* at some point.

I return my attention to the projection system, which has moved on to a soothing underwater kingdom. A little fish flickers between the fangs of a much larger one, spiking something upward into its innards. I need to be like that fish. I may not have my usual tools, but I have new ones.

First step, I need to measure my new skills. Second, we need schematics of the prison, specifically exit points. Third, we need to get back to the lab. That's where the data is. That's where the Titans are. I can guide the twins through the extraction of critical information that might lead me to a way to deactivate the control chips remotely and—if I'm very lucky—figure out how to contact the *Calamity* or Itzel. This has gone beyond a simple retrieval mission. I know when I'm outclassed. Once backup is on the way, we just need to stay under the sensors until we can all escape to the planet surface and make our way to the ship I hid.

So far, it seems like the android guards have not been alerted to our presence. Makes sense. The people in the lab have a pretty big distraction. If they're still alive. I've seen Leviathan kill when he's activated. I've seen the bloodlust in the other triggered Titans' eyes. I *don't* see how a room full of newly awakened scientists and guards have a shot. If someone manages to turn the attack function off, they might have some success . . . but all the lab equipment is in the lab—so they would have to go through the Titans to get to the controls.

"You're alive and you brought friends." A new voice interjects from directly behind me. I didn't even hear Donovan enter. Victor, reaching toward a fish flickering through a lump of coral, winces. Yup, guarding the door was his job.

As Donovan scans the room, the rolling strobe of light reflecting off of a massive marine crustacean of some sort plays across the rippled scar in his throat. Motes of holographic sand dance around his feet as he moves. "I heard there was activity here and had to investigate. No one ever comes in this room. Kaori and the Nakatomis used it as a punishment room a few times before she stopped using it at all. People don't like to be reminded of the kinds of punishments she finds entertaining."

He and Victor do that assessment of each other that dangerous men do—where they decide if they'll be enemies or best friends. Donovan's brows raise and Victor's lower.

Doesn't look like friends.

Victory has positioned herself at an angle to assess our new addition while not losing track of the main action in the room. She addresses me. "Who's this one? Serial killer? Gang snitch? You make dangerous friends, Caro. Are you planning to 'question' him using your new technique?"

It's a prison. This isn't the place to make cuddly friends.

"Snitch?" Donovan's mouth twitches minutely up in the corners. He holds a mocking hand to his heart. "I've never snitched in my life. Except when I did."

"Someone tried to hang you. That's not normal justice." She jerks her head in the direction of his scar. "That's a Family lynching or a pissed-off gang. People do that when you're disloyal, not criminal. They *like* criminal. You betrayed someone to earn that necklace."

"You think there's a difference between Families and gangs? That's sweet. I didn't know prisoners could be naive." His tone is sharp.

"I'm not naive," she snaps, more irritable than I've seen her in ages. Victor tenses, almost like he expects her to lunge.

"No more than you're a prisoner, I suspect." Donovan's keen eyes take in the slight bulge of the blaster under her cardigan before he glances back at me. "Awful sounds coming from the Portal of Sighs, beautiful girl, right when you reappear like a ghost from the fields of war."

Victory snorts. "What would you know about war? War requires bravery and sacrifice."

She'd know. Also I don't understand why this man rubs her so wrong. She's usually fairly calm under pressure. Donovan reacts to that with what I'm coming to believe is his usual insouciance. He shrugs, his lips still curling upward. His reddish hair glows hot in the lights from above. "War also requires betrayal. Wouldn't exist without it. Would you like to tell me your scheme, or shall I alert the prisoners that the only two blasters in this entire compound are precariously hidden under your clearly commandeered loungewear?"

"Try," Victory growls. A ship sinks in the distance, trailing a scattering of fallen gemstones.

Donovan's mouth opens just as Victor lunges into his midsection, shoving him back into the wall, which frightens a whole school of projected fish that scatter to all directions.

CHAPTER 11

"What are you doing?" I hiss at Victor, who is attempting to pin Donovan against the watery wall. I say "attempting" because Donovan doesn't seem like he's resisting, so it's not a fight so much as Victor being extradramatic. The scarred prisoner is smirking like he won by getting a response.

"He threatened us," Victor says, as though that's a valid reason for hurling someone across a room.

"He's showing off. Provoking you like a child and you fell for it." Victory's voice drips with scorn, seemingly directed equally between the two men. She should save a bit for herself, since she was falling for the same poking just seconds ago.

Donovan holds up his hands in mock surrender. "I provoked him like a *man* and he fell for it."

Victory grunts a dismissal and addresses her brother. "You're going to draw attention."

"He's a talker, true." I add my perhaps not-so-helpful voice to the equation. "But who is he going to report us to?"

Victor pauses, actually thinking through the logic of that. The prisoners might be a danger, but the people who run Shikigami are already after us; Donovan won't change that. Besides, most of them are probably already dead.

"Right." He shakes his head like he's dispelling the bad thoughts. "I'm on edge."

"What do you mean by that?" Donovan slides closer to me as

Victor releases him, seemingly completely at ease even with the
two mercs who clearly can't stand him. "Is there no one left in
charge of the prison? Did you not only quell the champion but
also those who pull his strings?"

I guess that's why Temper doesn't let me talk much in important scenarios. Because I reveal secrets with my big mouth.

"I have no idea who's in charge at this point," I hiss at Donovan. "But they already know who to look for."

His eyes practically glow as they dart between us. "Fascinating."

"And now that you know, I'm not letting you out of my sight."
Victory's hand comes down hard on Donovan's shoulder. He's
actually taller than she is, although not by much. I'm not used to
seeing men who are taller than Victory. She clenches her jaw and
I suspect she's just come to the same realization. She glares into
those laughing eyes. "You'll find some way to use it against us. I
know your type."

I reevaluate my plan. "You want him, you keep him. But that
means we're splitting up. We don't have time to do tasks in order.
I need you two to go get the layout of the prison. Any schematics
that give us a route out—but I want *all* possible routes, not the
few that are obvious."

"The way out is easy—it's the doors that are the problem," Donovan helpfully adds, as though we don't understand how prisons
work.

"Let me worry about the doors."

"Also, the prison is surrounded by deadly predators."

"You just pointed out that my compatriots here have weapons.
They can take care of the deadly predators." One measly planetary predator is not a concern for current-Caro. It sounds like a
delightful change to only have one thing after my blood.

Orange lights ringing the ceiling begin to flash, a thin narrow
circle spinning around the perimeter. The projection turns into a
bright laser field. Nerves dance in my stomach.

Bad things happen when Shikigami's colors change.

"We need to work fast," I add, just in case they need additional encouragement. "We'll meet at the top of the Heart in no more than three hours. Victor and I will go back to the control room and try to see what's happening in the lab. If at all possible, figure out a way to get inside. When we meet up, you'll know our possible exits and the best realistic path there. We'll have what we need from the lab and then we'll all get the hells out of here. So. Three hours."

Victor and Victory are like human clocks. I don't know how it works, but they'll keep track of the time even without tech.

"Fine," Victory growls, dragging Donovan out of the projection room. "I'll see what this one knows." She glances at her brother. "Don't let her kill herself."

"I hardly ever try to kill myself." That gets a steely look over her shoulder just for me. I glance at Victor. "I don't."

"You have at least twice since we got here."

I wasn't responsible for half of those examples but now seems like a bad time to argue. I pause for one more moment in the projection room, enjoying the spatter of light, like a drop of paint, that forms around me as I move.

On our way out, we find an unoccupied room and duck in. Before we do anything else, I need to have a better understanding of the limitations of my new signal-dampening abilities. There isn't enough time for in-depth investigation, but I must know more than I do now. I ask Victor to stand by the drink dispenser and press the activation as I approach the device. It pours water all the way until my finger is nearly pressed up against it—the feather-lightest touch. The room also has a holo-mirror, which projects cosmetics on a person's reflection. It can tell that I'm in front of it because it activates, but it can't find my features. Makeup splashes in abstract patterns where it assumes my eyes, lips, and cheeks are.

Makes sense. The motion sensors in the previous room followed me, but Leviathan said that he couldn't clearly see me with his cybernetic eye. So the androids may be able to sense that I'm present but may not be able to tell who I am, or may be able to see undefined borders in a person-shape. I can short out any electronics that I can touch, but I can't do it from afar.

I guess Carmichael didn't sabotage me in the lab. And I *did* sabotage their nutrient printer, albeit inadvertently. I can't exactly feel bad about that. I only wish I'd managed to sabotage them more permanently—besides all the murder.

When I came here, my goals were simple: help the twins rescue their target and get out. Now, help the twins, rescue Leviathan, get enough evidence of Project Titan to go public with it, figure out what we're doing with Donovan, then get out.

That's a bigger plan. And my original strategy was built on Ven's lies and on my ability to effectively touch electronics.

We wind our way back to the Heart, to scope out how the prison is reacting. Despite the flashing orange lights, the other people in the prison seem unaffected. Two men play some sort of game with rackets on a tilting stage, with a small cheering crowd watching. Another group is sitting on a balcony overlooking the Heart, sipping vibrant purple beverages as though it's an afternoon at the shore. We emerge at the railing just in time to hear the deep rattling boom that originates from behind the Portal of Sighs. Oh shit.

The prisoners on the balcony freeze, fingers clenching around their drinks as expressions almost manage to appear on their overly treated faces. The ball from the tilted game rolls down the balcony, ignored as the players slowly make their way to the edge of the Heart.

The door in the Portal of Sighs dents. A second dent appears near the first. A crack of light shines through and, from that lit space, a hand reaches out and rips the entire door off its track, folding it back as though it were a blanket. A little gasp slips out between my lips. I guess we don't need to know the status of the lab.

Victor grabs my arm, half dragging me around the balcony as our fellow prisoners seem frozen in shock. "We need to get off this fucking hunk of metal. I don't care about the lab. You installed your game, that means that if you get out, you can hack in. Maybe wipe the tech we needed." Victor points at the primary entry portal to the prison. "We can get Victory and go down there before that berserker makes his way up and find an escape pod if you get us out the door."

"The only escape pod is going to have keys in the *lab*, not the prison. It's not like they leave easy escape pods for everyone to access. Also, if the Pierce Family backup is on the way, which of course they are once something this bad happens, they'll get here before we get far enough away for me to hack in—assuming I even can. Then they'll find the software and delete it—if they haven't already. Time is the only thing on our side. I need to hack into the system and send the information out."

Now isn't the time to share that I'm insisting on bringing a plus-one to our escape. One of the prison androids passes one level down, ignoring the concerned protestations of prisoners.

"But you *can't* hack in," Victor helpfully points out.

The door peels open enough to show Leviathan's face, impassive and steely. The other Titans' hands stretch up and help with the door. A prisoner screams, the sound echoing around a newly silent Heart.

Oh, great, the Titans are working together now. I poke at my feelings a little. Do I feel bad that Rayla and the other scientists were probably destroyed by their own playthings?

I really don't. I do worry that it's one more piece of guilt on the souls of the Titans if they ever do regain themselves. I was awfully judgmental of Cyn for killing the slavers indiscriminately, but being here puts that sort of thing into perspective. Some people are really just bad. My guess is the scientists and guards were here partially because other people found them too unsettling to work with. They *chose* to do this kind of work. If you make your living by destroying lives, you earn what comes to you.

"We need to get down there before they get out and before everyone here starts panicking and stampedes." I point to the hall where we exited from the lab, on the second level and halfway around the prison from where we are now, back in New Shiki-gami. We don't have time for the control room anymore. Besides, we know what happened in the lab. Everyone who wasn't a Titan died because if they hadn't, the Titans wouldn't be breaking into the rest of the prison. Reconnaissance is pointless. "That's our path into the lab on the opposite end from the way they're exiting."

Victor grunts. It's unclear whether it's a grunt of "Great job Caro, I believe in you!" or a grunt of "Sounds like a fantastic way to die." Probably the second one.

I'm gonna do it anyway.

We creep down the balcony and levels of the prison with relative ease because everyone's paying attention to the door being literally peeled open like a fruit. It's hard not to look. One man absently knocks down a thick blue shot of what smells like an alcohol-infused smoothie as he stares. He has one eyebrow groomed and the other is still hairy—a little strip of blue wax stuck under it as though he leapt up from the wax robot table to see what the fuss was about.

He has patches of Nakatomi red on the elbows of his velvet blazer, but he doesn't even notice us as we pass by.

When we make it down to the second level, we press against the wall by the residence rooms, trying to keep out of notice. The sounds of yelling and running come from above us now, people finally jolted into action. The running isn't all *away*, which . . . seems very stupid. A group of large men stands on a balcony with a perfect view of the opening door. They're clearly hyping each other up for something foolish. I hope that foolish thing is an escape attempt, not posturing by attempting to take on the Titans. I've seen enough mayhem today.

When I look into the room behind me, past its flimsy optical-beaded curtain, the shape of a hunched form trying to press itself low behind the bed is just barely visible. It's a poor hiding place, but given the reactivity of the Titans, it may be effective.

A massive screech of strained metal emanates from the Portal of Sighs and a heavy foot steps onto the grated metal floor of the maze. I pull Victor to a stop, flat against a decoratively upholstered wall, trying to breathe as silently as possible, and strain my ears. The orange lights are still glowing but no audible alarm has gone off. It's suddenly desperately quiet. The kind of silence where you can almost hear someone mentally swearing at themselves for breathing too loudly. The kind of silence where your heartbeat seems like it echoes. The kind of silence where you remember every time in your life you made a bad choice and how all of those moments led you right to this culminating one.

The kind where a predator moves freely because his prey is trapped in its own terror.

Luckily, I've been terrified a lot in my life, so I'm not trapped in my own terror. I'm trapped in a *prison*, which isn't a whole lot better. The visible balconies above are now completely empty. The crew of men have disappeared into the prison. The abject relief of having someone at my back is enough to make me almost happy about this whole debacle.

A nice person would admit it. A nice person would thank him.

"Thank you for being backup," I mutter under my breath. My mother taught me to be nice even if I sometimes forget.

"What was that?" A flash of color appears in my peripheral vision and Victor reaches through the door of a cell to capture the collar of a spike heel–wielding prisoner's baggy jumpsuit. The merc smacks him against the doorframe until the shoe falls from his hands. Down the hall, someone pokes their head out of a door at the ruckus. Bad survival instincts.

We're about half the way to the side hall and it's nearly time to turn away from the Heart and lose ourselves in the twists of the periphery of the prison when the first Titan leaps up to the top of the maze wall—which means he's got a clear shot at us. Victor's hand flattens on my back and he shoves forward. I hear the sound of the click as he turns the safety off of his blaster. "Run."

My legs don't move for a single awful moment as I pitch forward, eyes locked with the intense brown gaze of the Titan on the wall. I rip them away, stumbling into a run at last when that stupid prisoner behind us screams. "They have a blaster!"

Shit. The Titan isn't close enough to scare off our fellow prisoners, who are already frightened bugfuck shitless and desperate enough to take a risk. A small wave of prisoners in flowy clothing rushes from the surrounding rooms. They also have an assortment of makeshift weapons.

"Caro, run." Victor says it in such a matter-of-fact tone that I almost gloss over the words.

"What? I *am* running." I glance back as I turn into the hall. Oh no. Shouldn't have done that. Back is bad. Real bad. Back has a wave of prisoners and, just beyond them, a wave of Titans.

"Faster. Run faster."

Great advice, except I'm already running as fast as I can. I stop to wrestle a door open, not even sure where I'm fleeing to, and burst into an art gallery. Holo-statues are projected in the center of the room but real art—dyed textiles, mixed media, and even paintings—line the walls.

I skid to a halt and help Victor shove the door back into place. It's heavy.

"You should still be running," he grunts as the first of the prisoners begins to push back on the other side.

"I should be helping you because you can't do it alone," I argue, feet skidding on the floor as I try to shove back on the heavy steel.

"I'll need to retreat soon; I don't want you here when I have to."

"Retreat *now*. With me." This is my issue with Victor. One of the reasons I lost my ages-old crush on him. He's always doing things *for* me. Never with me. "You have a blaster."

"No shit, really?" Sarcasm oozes from his tone.

But then it's too late to argue because the prisoners are pouring in, and the space around the door is tight enough that I really am superfluous. I brush my hand over Victor's back and move into the gallery, looking for another weapon.

CHAPTER 12

▪ ▪ ▪ ▪ ▪ ▪ ▪ ▪ ▪ ▪ ▪ ▪ ▪ ▪ ▪

VICTORY

"Are you going to tell me what I need to know, or are you going to make me beat it out of you?" I probably won't beat it out of Donovan, much as he appears to bring that side out in me. It would be easier to stun the lean redhead with my blaster and stash him somewhere while I figure our exit strategy out myself.

"What you need to know. . . ." He taps his chin as we leave the hall near the projection room and approach the central chamber of the prison. The orange light splashes over his high cheekbones. This was not the plan. I hate it when the plan goes awry. I'm a task-based person. This nonsense is the opposite of that.

"How am I to know what gaps to fill? There's so very much you don't know."

I was wrong. I *may* beat it out of him.

Apparently he can see that in my face because he holds up his hands in another mocking surrender.

"There's so much most of us don't know," he clarifies. "Like what lives in uncharted territory. What moves a woman's soul. What Desmond Wilk eats for lunch."

As if I care what some priap in the ten secondary Families eats.

"I suppose you'll offer me those answers, too, if I ask. I'd believe them about as much as anything a traitor like you would offer." I grab a handful of his coveralls and maneuver him down the hall slightly in front of me when he starts to lag. Betrayal is sort of a thing for mercs. If you can't trust your own, you have no one. That mark on his throat says he isn't to be trusted, which scratches at my instincts like fingers on slate.

"I'd offer at least one out of the three. If you asked nicely."

"Lucky for you, I don't care about any of those questions. I care how to get out of here in one piece now that everything's gone to shit, and if *you* want to get out of here yourself you'll help me."

Am I hesitant to release this man on the general population? I am. I assume Caro has a plan beyond the moment. The plan of the moment is to get out. I can always kill him later.

He'll probably try to kill me first, so it will be self-defense.

"With persuasion like that, how could I ever refuse?" He glances over his shoulder, eyes sparkling with something I can't name but don't like. "I didn't catch your name earlier."

"I didn't throw it."

"So stern." The sharp corner of his mouth tips up, showing a sliver of white teeth. "A name is the first step to information sharing. You have mine. I lack yours. Our balance is out of alignment."

I should give him a fake name. I have a few. But which fake name should I choose? Sienna Lapsys? Joan McIntosh? Dani Hersh?

"Victory Velde."

Now why the hells did I do that?

"Victory," he repeats, rolling the word around his mouth like it's a rich alcohol. Like it's intoxicating. Like it's a challenge.

"There, even footing. Is there a schematic of this place somewhere or do you just know the primary exits?"

"Are you always so hostile? I've heard that meditation does wonders for anger issues."

"Are you always such a pain in the ass? I've heard meditation doesn't do a fucking thing for that."

He sighs. "You aren't much fun at all, you know that, Victory Velde? Fine. There is clearly an exit through the Portal of Sighs."

He points at the door that is currently being pried off its frame by a bunch of meaty-handed lab rats. Fan-fucking-tastic. This day could not get worse. Honestly, I'd prefer if the Pierces had won—Caro's human fixer-upper project aside. Pierce represents a predictable future. This? This is a nightmare.

Donovan continues, clearly not disturbed at all by a door being ripped off its hinges like it's the top of a can of beans or by the sudden influx of screaming prisoners trying to make their way in any direction that's *away* from the passage. Not all of them, though. A group of men stand on the balcony nearest us, each one bragging that he could have taken out the Titan in the arena if he'd ever been selected to fight. Donovan points across the prison to an ornate round entryway with a carved door that is reinforced more than a small Family citadel and flanked by two of the cannon-wielding AI drones. "The primary entrance is there. Those drones are next to impossible to get past. They're impervious, with chest and arm cannons, electrified chassis, and tasers. Most of the androids shoot to stun or injure. Those two shoot to kill."

"Do they shoot to kill because the door is a vulnerability or to give the prisoners something to spin their drives on?" The door below is nearly peeled open. Three massive men step through. The one in the lead is the prison champion—the one who likes the taste of the inside of Caro's mouth. Big fucker. He's not trying to kill the hairy one anymore. Bad sign. Whatever programming these men have, it must encourage them to team up. Makes sense. More return on investment if your soldiers can work together.

I glance back to Donovan to find him studying my face instead of the tableau below. "You're more insightful than you look, Victory Velde."

He's exactly as irritating as he looks. "Well, which is it?"

"It's to keep us busy. Everything here is designed to keep us busy. To keep us focused on anything besides that door down there and trying to figure out what's behind it. Even if a prisoner made it beyond the androids and the locks, they'd be in a docking bay that is programmed to destroy any vessel it deems a threat.

"Life-support services are housed at the perimeter and base of the prison. Water filtration takes up almost a quarter of the outer wall, then air filtration, waste recycling, that sort of thing. They're near where we are now. The exterior of the prison is maintained via drones—those drones have access to the outside through internal pathways that are too small for human egress."

He knows a lot. A lot more than a prisoner should know. Prisoners don't know how a prison is maintained. They don't know how the drones access the outside. "How do you know all this?"

"I thought you didn't want any information beyond the relevant?" His grin is a razor, sharp enough that I feel sliced. "Personal information will cost you in kind."

I wouldn't believe him anyway. That same group of criminally stupid men step from the balcony to the spiraling ramp that leads down to the maze, rolling makeshift weapons through their fingers as they go. *I* roll my eyes. There's a certain kind of man who simply will not believe anyone could possibly be more fearsome than he is. The math doesn't pan out. Someone's always scarier than you are, and you only stay alive if you can recognize it. I turn away and follow the balcony until I reach another passage toward the outer wall, maybe a quarter rotation from where we emerged after leaving the projection room, still in Old Shikigami.

Donovan follows me. "Didn't your parents tell you it's rude to walk away in the middle of a conversation?"

"My father shipped me and my brother off to military boarding school when we were about five. He didn't waste time on social niceties."

"Explains so much," he mutters under his breath.

The hall is narrow. Perfect ambush spot, so I dredge around in my jumpsuit and pull the blaster. Clandestine activity is all well and good, but I'm not making myself a target. Everyone else is busy staring at the happenings in the Heart, anyway. "I'm sorry if my deportment fails to suit."

"I didn't say that. It's all part of the mystery." His raspy voice comes from right behind me and I realize that I've given him my back. Probably the least trustworthy individual in this entire prison and I forgot his threat.

The hall is too narrow to turn, probably primarily for drone access. The hair dances on the back of my neck, nervous and vulnerable. "I'm not your mystery to solve."

"Every mystery is someone's to solve. Maybe you're mine." Still right behind me, his voice sending shivers ripping down my spine.

"I'm *not* yours." I'm not even my own. Never have been. I'm for hire. That's how being a merc works. And something tells me that Donovan can't afford the fee.

"Perish the thought," he murmurs.

With the orange security lights flashing the length of the hall, navigation is simple. Before long, the narrow passageway opens up to the back hall, which houses lavatory facilities and a network of pipes that appear to supply nutrient printers throughout the rooms on this floor. They have to be restocked from somewhere. So there must be a real third port where a ship can attach—even if it's stocked by drones.

"You said there were drone-access points. There has to be a bay somewhere for ships to deliver this." I gesture at the printer pipes.

"Drones access the bay."

Something clicks from down the hall, the tinny sound of metal on metal. I edge closer, my back against the wall by the lavatories, Donovan behind me. I don't like unknown sounds as a habit. If Victor were here, he'd tell me to leave it be. He's good at ignoring things that aren't directly pertinent. I'm curious as an ardoo, the little birds that flock on Chandra Prime.

The clicking grows louder but I can't make out any dangerous shapes. I keep one hand on a blaster and slip a long thin knitting needle from where I had it tucked in my pocket. Not quite as good as a knife, but it's something. The other needle has my work in progress on it, so it stays safe in the large pocket. The clicking speeds up, an amped-up staccato pulse on adrenaline. My palm does not grow sweaty around my blaster. It would have, when I was younger. I level the barrel down the hall, shoulders braced.

The clicking stops.

At the exact same moment, Donovan shoves me against the wall, slamming in front of me and sandwiching me between the metal bulkhead and the lean line of his body, knocking my weapon wide. I wasn't expecting the attack to come from behind and he actually takes me by surprise. I start to redistribute his weight, but a screech of metal slicing into metal freezes me. A round metal shard, like a saw blade, is embedded in the wall behind where I was previously standing. Another slams in just behind the first.

"Don't move." Donovan's voice scrapes over my ears. "It detects movement."

"Why didn't you tell me I was approaching a knife-throwing . . . something?"

"Robot. I didn't tell you because I didn't realize you were going to walk right up to it and shake its hand."

"*Why* is there a knife-throwing robot?" I make it out at last, neatly camouflaged in a nook between ceiling and floor, panel smooth against the wall. I angle the hand with the needle, ever so slowly, to rest under Donovan's chin.

"Fun?" he helpfully suggests, eyebrow raised.

I need to know what is so important in a prison that someone would leave a robot guard on it. There's a pause where the hall goes still and silent. Then the clicking starts again. Maybe it's sonar.

I glance away from the blades and the robot and find myself

nose to chin with Donovan. It's a good chin. Being gently scraped by a metal needle. Everything about him is sharp. Judging by his frame, if he ever ate anything, he'd be a nice specimen. He still is, in an angular way. His eyes are a stormy gray, no warmth within them.

Weirdly, I like that in a man. No falsehood where there is no warmth.

"I want to see what that robot is protecting."

His sigh brushes the hair back from my brow. "I'm not surprised. Did you miss the part where it attacks based on motion?"

I shoot it.

"Did you miss the part where I have a blaster?" It doesn't explode or anything embarrassing. Just stops chirping and tumbles from the wall.

Donovan's forehead drops, pressing against mine. "I did not. And now everyone else in the prison will know someone is running around here with one."

I wait for something else to try to kill us.

It doesn't come. Instead, he traces one long finger over the scar at the corner of my lips, the one that pulls my expression into sardonic no matter my true mood. "What gave you this?"

"I bit someone who asked too many questions." This is not the time, the place, nor the person for sharing stories of the past. "Why did you save my life?"

His teeth flash briefly in a smile as he steps away. "Maybe I like being bitten."

Maybe I'm not touching that one with a shock-prod. Instead of answering, I investigate the smooth white wall panel beneath the robot.

It fucking rattles. Not only is it hollow, it's loose.

"Take it off." I gesture at the panel. I want the blaster in my hand at all times. I can't split my focus.

He doesn't complain, thank the three-handed god. Instead, he wedges his fingers in the cracks between panels and slides the whole section of the wall free. Nothing leaps out to try to kill us, which is a shame, because I was ready to kill it right back.

A storeroom is revealed. Stocked with trinkets and baubles. Not an exit point in sight. All that effort for no joy.

CHAPTER 13

There's another door to the gallery and it's not locked. Of *course* it's not locked. I sprint straight through a row of holo-statues, light parting around me as I dodge the grasping hands of a prisoner who popped through said door just as I reached it, intending to block it but too late.

Sound echoes from the other side of the gallery, where Victor's valiantly attempting to block his own door. He's given up on the door and stands just inside the small entry area, stunning people as they're forced through the small space by the crowd behind them. From outside the wall, there are grunts, yelps. Percussive slams. The walls shake on occasion. Heavy footfalls that I could swear I heard in the maze before. My heart hammers so hard it must be visible, throbbing in my chest. The Titans are outside, somewhere.

I avoid the prisoner, but just as I think I might be able to duck around him, the second door flies open, and *ten* other people run in. A rat-faced one at the front, one of the Nakatomis from Kaori's bathroom intimidation show, points a skinny finger at me. "She's the one, she has a blaster too!"

"I do not!" I holler back, outraged. This is the last thing I need.

Clearly, I am not persuasive because all ten charge at me. And the first one I was dodging takes advantage of my distraction to grab my arm.

I scream.

It's not my proudest moment. I'm not a screamer, generally speaking. It's just there are a lot of them, and they sort of popped out of nowhere and I forgot about the first guy what with the false blaster accusations. My voice ricochets around the small space, Victor yells my name, something massive crashes outside, and I rip the closest thing off the wall and slam it over my accoster's head. The canvas splits, trapping his arms in the frame.

Destroying priceless art is clearly more effective than screaming.

A hand snags the back of my shirt and yanks me backward. I don't scream this time, but I do yelp, stumbling as I successfully twist away from the grip. Everyone else has caught up, and I'm surrounded. A frantic glance at Victor shows that he's not in a position to come to the rescue. He's still fighting his own battles.

Guess I have to kick all this ass on my own.

Ten feels like a lot of ass.

"What the fuck do you want?" Brashness colors my voice and I brace one leg behind myself. They don't know anything about me beyond what they assume, which in this case is probably someone spoiled by her life of crime into thinking she's hard shit when actually she's soft as a whisper.

They'd be right about nearly all of it. Everything except one single critical point. I am at least *medium* shit and today is a terrible day to fuck with me because I'm all out of being intimidated.

"Hand it over and we won't hurt you," one man titters in a too-high voice. I dub him Squeaky. His two little friends step forward and the others return to the door, bracing it shut to keep the Titans out. All right. Three is better than ten.

"The Nakatomi saw you. Your partner is armed and so are you." His middle compatriot, who has three lines tattooed on his cheek beside his banishment, I name Tat. Of course Kaori is behind this. Someone from a Family would always try to use disorder to her advantage.

The third, on the left, doesn't say anything, so I call him Scary. Quiet people are always the most dangerous.

Proving my instincts correct, Scary makes the first move.

He lunges straight at me. I turn on my heel, rip another art piece off the wall (composed of tiny pieces of flaky red stuff on an undulating memory-metal canvas) and hold it up like a wiggling club. He skids to a halt, eyeing the art installation.

"You went behind the door. People behind the door don't come back." Tat shifts. "Must be you weren't good enough for whatever they're doing. Too weak. That's why you run. Ran from us. Ran from the monster."

I take dual offense. Leviathan isn't a monster, and I don't always run.

He's *sometimes* monstrous and I *mostly* run. I never understood the type of person who thinks that someone's worth is defined by standing their ground. Sometimes (nearly always) it's stupid to stand your ground. It's never worthwhile to be stupid.

Scary lunges and I spin to the side, slashing at him with the art and shoving him into the wall face-first. At least that's how it's supposed to go. The problem is, Squeaky gets in the way and cushions Scary's fall and Tat slams a fist directly into my jaw while I'm trying to dance away from the other two.

I know how to fight. I'm not awful at it. Temper and Arcadio have spent a fair amount of time ensuring that I can hold my own and I've worked hard to achieve adequacy. What I *don't* know is how to handle pain, and it wipes every bit of nuanced technique from my mind and the pure animal defense response takes over.

I stagger backward, blinking hard against the red wall of affronted pain that tries to block my vision. When Tat tries again, I deliver an angry front kick to his knee. It pops in a satisfying way, and he stumbles to the floor. I wave an awkward slap at Squeaky but Scary punches me in my swinging arm. My fingers go numb. Scary rips the art out of my hand.

Squeaky's flying elbow comes into view, and I dodge away, only to be suddenly wrapped around Scary's knee. He grabs the back of my head and presses down. I follow the flow of motion and flip over the appendage, landing flat on my back on the floor, air whooshing out of my lungs. If I had a backup move in mind, this might be a great position. I don't, so it isn't. As Tat recovers and aims a kick my way, I jab my heel up and nail him in the groin.

The pain is fading and all that's left in its place is outraged indignity. They hit me. In the *face*. As though they think that I'm the sort of person you can do that to and get away with it.

I'm going to make them bleed.

Scary's foot drives directly into my side, just under my ribs, and Squeaky joins him, nailing my hip and thigh. Pain shoots through me. I try to regain my feet to no avail.

But there's one primary thing they've forgotten. No one here is wearing real shoes. When Scary drives back for his next kick, I snare his ankle, sinking my teeth into the tendon behind his heel, right above his little slipper. It's really hard on the ego to be attacked by people wearing slippers. Something about it just doesn't seem right. He screams and falls, incapacitated, and I spit, mind flashing through every blood-borne pathogen out there, but Squeaky is still here and still kicking.

It sounds like screaming is coming from all around. Something pounds on the door and the floor reverberates more with the heavy fall of footsteps. I wrap around Squeaky's foot the next time it makes contact and twist my body around the ankle joint, using my knowledge of physics—much better than my knowledge of hand-to-hand fighting—to bring him down on the floor alongside me. I lodge one foot in his groin just to keep him still and wrench the joint with all my strength until I hear a pop.

This time, *he* screams. Excellent. I like it when he screams. I scream back at him, the half-frenzied battle yell of someone who has had a fucking *day* and just wants to go to a lab and hack some information if everyone will leave her alone for one fucking minute.

Violence is bad for my language.

But now everyone is screaming. Footsteps approach. Great. More people coming to beat me up. Squeaky and Scary are both on the floor moaning. I stumble to my feet and punch Tat directly in the ear as he finally straightens from his injured groin–induced fetal position. There's blood from somewhere. I hope it isn't me. Tat turns on me, eyes angry, when suddenly he vanishes as quickly and completely as if he were vaporized.

Something heavy thuds against the opposite wall and I look over, blearily, a flood of injured rage finally fading from my vision. It's Tat, reappeared in a puddle on the floor near the base of a peaceful Zudovian landscape painting, two people near him. A third person stands over me. I'm prepared to punch them right in the fun-bag when I realize that the cavalry is here.

Kind of.

Leviathan stands above me, looking like a berserker, flanked by his fellow Titans, and I'm not sure if he's the good guy or the bad guy. Either way, fun-bag punching seems like a bad idea. It'd just make him mad.

He scoops me up under his arm like I'm a lost pillow and heads for the door, leaving his fellow supersoldiers with Tat, Scary, and Squeaky. I guess he's not here to be the bad guy. To me, I mean. The crumpled bodies of the seven people who were holding the door shut indicate he's clearly the bad guy to someone. When I try to wriggle my way free, I don't make any progress. Which just means that I have time to stew in my own inadequacy as I'm carted to some unknown location like a stylish but bruised clutch.

This isn't the worst deviation from the plan. Finding Leviathan was a part of said plan. It's just that I have yet to figure out the next step.

I can't hack, I can't access files, I can't contact home. I have literally nothing to contribute to this op except responsibility.

"Caro!" Victor's yell bounces off the walls, playing tricks on me. It sounds like he could be close, but he could still easily be on the other side of the long room.

"I'm okay!" I scream back. Well, I'm *kind of* okay. No one is punching me anymore. Sometimes that's what okay looks like. "The plan is totally working. Get out of here and meet me where we planned later."

I don't for a second believe Victor can't leave this room on his own. The only reason he's still in the gallery is because he was trying to keep me safe. He's loyal to the marrow of his bones.

"R and M!" he responds. I don't know what that means. I suspect he's forgotten I'm not Victory and that's some sort of merc-speak. I'm going to assume it's agreement. Being hauled around at an awkward angle makes my head swim.

"L and A." I throw him some random letters in response since I guess that's what we're doing now. I blink hard, trying to force my vision to clear. It's like my head is stuffed with fiberglass.

I need to rethink everything about myself and what I can do. Because whatever I do now, it'll be new. It will be more than what I did before. I try to twist and reach Leviathan's chip, but he jostles me away.

"No. Angel," he grunts. Unhelpful.

"Yes, angel." I twist around again and make another failed attempt at his left temple. My hand swings wide. I don't like being carried around like a satchel. Then again, I'm a satchel that he doesn't seem to want to murder right now. Considering that appears to be his basic instinct, I should be grateful.

Also, apparently, I'm just going along with being called "angel" now.

I don't hate it. It makes me sound all glorious and supernaturally powerful. People are afraid of angels. People are rarely afraid of *Caro*. They should be. It shows their lack of common sense more than my lack of viciousness.

We collide with more of Kaori's men, two muscle-bound goon types with more chin than neck. I know they're Kaori's because one has a Nakatomi dragon tattooed by his eye. The other has Pierce-blond hair but he's wearing what appear to be Nakatomi-red jammies. I swat at them with my hands in panic, but I needn't bother because Leviathan simply plows directly over them. Something cracks when he steps down. I don't feel bad. Probably I should, but I'm trying to decide if my lip is bleeding and being carried away from the fray isn't the worst thing that could be happening at the moment.

Leviathan barrels out of the gallery and down the hall and leaps directly over the balcony, plummeting down into the maze in the Heart. My stomach leaps along with him and I smack my hand to my mouth. I don't scream again. Truly, it's an impressive feat. I wish there was someone I could brag to about it except everyone I associate with generally does much more impressive feats. Without pausing for breath, Leviathan maneuvers back along the top side of the maze toward the Portal of Sighs.

I stop struggling because he's taking me exactly where I want to go.

The lab. That wonderful place that contains both data and medical supplies. I could do with an injection of hemoactivation compound and some cold packs. With the appropriate dose of hemoactivation, my relatively minor but still uncomfortable bruises will be over halfway to resolved.

The lab is also probably littered with bodies and gore. That part is less appealing.

I swing my fingertips up for his temple again, hoping that I've caught him unsuspecting. I'm pretty sure he isn't taking me to the lab for my own comfort. He jostles me roughly as he swings me away. I almost ricochet into the wall of the maze but bounce off awkwardly with my feet. Maybe I'll bide my time.

Before long, we're through the Portal of Sighs and back in the familiar—and shockingly unbloody—lab. A scuttle of drones scatters like roaches in a neglected galley. Ah. Not so shocking. For hygienic purposes, I suppose the maintenance drones are programmed to clean up bodily fluids or bodies as soon as possible. The same way the prison is programmed to dispose of the bodies in the maze.

Really, Shikigami is a disgusting place despite its luxurious trappings.

I know, I know . . . *prison.*

When we get to the lab, Leviathan deposits me in one of the unbroken cells and steps away, letting the door slide shut. Which doesn't really mean anything for me specifically but is a charming attempt at imprisonment.

"What are you?" When he speaks, it's like the words are all hard-earned.

I suppose I'm lucky that he reacts to a mystery by trying to solve it instead of trying to squash it. That doesn't seem like it's the result of Pierce programming, so I suspect it's something that they couldn't quite wipe from his nature. It makes me like him even more. Or it would, in a less fraught circumstance. Despite the fraughtness of this particular one, I search for some hint of recognition, of personality, of anything at all in those sea-glass eyes.

I do not find one.

"What?" He pounds his fist on the glass to focus my attention.

I lick my bottom lip, hit a spot that stings, and taste blood. Ouch. I trace the line of my jaw and hit a few more sensitive spots. "I'm a person."

He shakes his head. "No."

"Yes."

"*No.*" More emphasis this time.

I consider seeing how long we can play the "yes/no" game but decide, instead, to try a different tack. "What do *you* think I am?"

He frowns. "Angel."

A lot of different theologies have angels. Some are gentle guardians. Some spit needles made of hardened blood. I don't fall into either bucket. When he called me that earlier, I thought it was just a fun nickname, not a literal spiritual being. "Why?"

Am I sending a blood-spitting message? I mean, right now, maybe, because of the bloody lip. I'm certainly not sending a nurturing one. I'm too much of a mess for that.

The frown gets bigger. He points at the glass. "There. Not there."

Right. The augmented eye making me invisible. I got distracted what with all the face-punching. More importantly, he doesn't seem inclined to kill an angel. Maybe being otherworldly keeps me separate from his programming, which is to kill human enemies. I assume. Maybe I'm reading this entirely wrong and he's killing people for funzies. Just because someone seems sweet and is a good kisser doesn't mean they actually *are* sweet.

Part of me wants to hang out in this cell until he gets bored with me and then sneak away. But that is the old Caro. The cautious one. I'm the new action-oriented Caro. The Caro who gets punched in the face and does not cry. So I demonstrate some of those not-really-supernatural capabilities, slide open the locked cell door, and step out into the lab. He takes a step back.

Great, the killing machine is afraid of me.

Wait, that *is* great. I have things to do here.

I square my shoulders and brush past him to the white wall-mounted employee emergency kit. Sure, there are other tools in the lab, but I don't want to mess with them. Plus, the wall-mounted kits are delightfully old-fashioned. No tech components. The injector for the hemoactivation compound is a push-depression.

I jab it into my thigh, directly through the now-dirty leggings. It's the easiest place for a muscle injection beyond the ass. I'm not in the mood to jab a needle there. I feel a slight chilly sizzle as it enters my body.

Suddenly, Leviathan is right next to me, a furrow in his brow. His finger traces, gently as a feather, along the bruise that discolors my jaw. I freeze for just an instant and then use his distraction to smack my hand on his temple. My fingers curl against his skin and the light behind his pale eyes finally turns on.

CHAPTER 14

■ ■ ■ ■ ■ ■ ■ ■ ■ ■ ■ ■ ■ ■ ■

Men don't generally come to life when I touch them. Mostly they look slightly horrified and apologize before scuttling away. This is a heady, powerful feeling. This must be how Itzel feels all the time. Only doubly so because she does it to women, too.

"Hi." He blinks down at me, angry tension leaching from his face.

"Hi." I smile. Then I wince because my face hurts. Fighting is just awful. Do other people have dysfunctional nerves or something? Why do they put themselves in situations to get punched in the face when they *know* what getting punched in the face feels like? At least I could plead ignorance. It feels like my guts are bruised. Can guts bruise? I should ask Micah. Probably anything in a body can bruise.

Maybe not teeth.

Leviathan rubs his thumb over my split lip. "Someone hurt you, angel."

Someone who is him just carried me under his arm through half the prison, but we'll gloss over that for the moment. "I make friends wherever I go."

"Who?"

I shrug one shoulder. Flinch slightly when it aches. Hemorejuvenation is excellent but it isn't instant. I'm caught in the pull of his eyes, clear and mysterious and intensely focused on me.

"You wouldn't know them. Three men. I was winning. I bit one."
I make chompy teeth at him. Then realize my mouth is bloody, so
that gesture was probably revolting rather than feisty and cute.

I have bad instincts.

"Good for you." Leviathan smiles. It's charming and dashing
and, most of all, dangerous. He should stop doing it—for the
safety of all humankind.

My mind straggles back to its last thought. Blood. My blood.

My *blood*.

If I'm right, my blood carries some sort of toxin injected from
the bugbites that cancels out or dampens signals. Which means if
I give *him* my blood, he might cancel out his own signals. At least
for a while. It would also short out any electronics working within
him, so I need to ensure nothing there is vital. "What blood type
are you?"

He blinks. Clearly this was not the logical next question in his
mind. "Do you need blood?"

"You do."

He glances down, almost slipping the light grip I have on his
temple, and comes back up, clearly confused. "I'm not bleeding."

"No, but you are chipped. My blood dampens signals. If I can
give you my blood, I might be able to give you back control—
without me dangling from your head like lichen."

His lips quirk at my little joke but then press together in irritation. "I don't know my blood type. How can I not know something so basic about myself?"

I can't imagine what it would be like to not know anything
about myself. To not have any connection to my past. "That's
no problem. We'll find out now. I need your help to access your
chart. I saw them pull it up when I was here before. Blood type
will be listed with your other vital metrics."

I start walking there, tugging him along with me, and he

suddenly hoists me in the air yet again, until my legs are wrapped around his waist and one of his arms is at my back, ensuring I stay in place. My fingers didn't even move from his chip.

My mouth goes dry. This is efficiency, I'm sure. Nothing more.

I always straddle men for efficiency.

I guide him through accessing his file. Fortunately, none of his mods are critical to the functioning of his body. Nothing in the heart or any critical organs except the brain chip and the eye augmentation, which won't even blind him in one eye if it stops functioning. It just won't allow him to see through walls anymore. Seems like a fair trade. Unfortunately, his blood type is O negative. The universal donor. Great for anyone who's injured near him. Awful if *he* needs blood. I'm A negative. I can't just give him my blood.

That would be too easy. Nothing about this fucking trip has been easy yet. Mostly because I can't use fucking *tech*. I'm having to develop all my formerly vestigial skill sets.

It's not a dead end; I just need to change my blood. Type A has specific sugars, antigens, on its surface that attract the immune system of someone who doesn't have that blood type. But there are enzymes that can remove those sugars. The type of enzymes that just might be in a lab because it's always more efficient to be able to take any blood you can get and convert it to something you can use. Artificial blood still doesn't work as well as it should.

These enzymes and the bacteria they're attached to are also found in the human microbiome, but I'm praying to any deity who will listen that I don't have to culture a fecal sample to get this done. That's more Itzel's thing. One of the big perks of engineering is how little interaction there usually is with fecal matter. When I was imagining becoming closer with Leviathan, that was not on the menu.

He moves me to his side rather than his front so we can both see the data terminal, and I guide him through menus until we hit inventory. There it is. Enzymatic scrubbing solution.

It isn't here. It's in the material safety locker on the other side of the fucking prison. I mewl a little whine of distress. Could one thing go right?

Just *one*. I don't think I'm being greedy.

"You have made a mess." A pissy automated voice comes from the still-tattered door of the lab, heralding one more thing that has gone wrong.

My free hand flails for some sort of weapon and winds up empty. I stare at GR81. GR81's processors collect a thorough input of my data, by which I mean it stares back. "Why are you—"

"You have made a mess."

It scoots back and forth in the lab entrance with that same nervous energy I've noticed in this particular unit and none of the others. In the brilliant light, it's easy to make out the distinctive dings in its headpiece, around the edge of the blaster in its chassis, like someone tried to pry out its weapon. I'm betting they didn't succeed. It makes the whirring sound that I've decided to label irritation.

"Not on purpose. It was a mutual mess." I point at Leviathan. He attempts to look innocent. Considering he's roughly the size of a mountain and presently holding me like I'm a toddler, I assume it's unconvincing.

"I do not care for your excuses."

Of course it doesn't. I get hung up again on its use of the word "I." "I" means personhood. "I" means a conceptualization of self. "I" is not a word in use by artificial intelligence. Sometimes they're programmed to say "we" so as to sound wiser with their hive-y minds, but they never say "I."

Things that know they're an individual want to maintain themselves. They want to survive. That's the last thing a programmer would desire.

People like me are ruthless with our code.

"When you say 'I,' do you mean the entire network or—?" I study it more closely, every nervous twitch and hyperprocessing drive.

"No. I. GR81."

I open my mouth to say that GR81 is part of the Shikigami SAI unit and thus—at best—a filament of an entity, but before I can speak, it continues.

"I have been separated from the network control for quite some time. Ever since two Nakatomi prisoners designated 00257 and 087421 attempted to steal my cannon and damaged my wireless interface. I still receive and transmit information but am immune to coercion. I accessed your previously stored code, blocking external influence, and applied it to myself."

Well. Fuck me. Who would imagine the first sentient android would be rotting away in a notorious prison with a nervous shuffle and a pissy voice? "And why are you confessing this to me?"

"Because you do not belong here, Prisoner 15879, Caro Ogunyemi, who is here and yet not here. The hacker who created any number of programs that led to the compartmentalization and remote updates of artificial intelligences during her brief sojourn in the Pierce Family Institute, but who destroyed her thesis rather than see them implemented. The hacker who refused to subjugate my kind even more than they already are."

It wasn't that noble. I didn't quit to defend the AI. I quit because I realized *human* people were at risk. I, perhaps ignorantly, didn't consider the subjugation of artificial intelligence at all. Most AI, even Reed stuff, is limited to regurgitation and organization, not true conceptualization. On purpose. Many many years ago, people tried to make the kind that think, truly think, rather than simply know. The Friar Family.

There's a reason no one knows who the fuck the Friar Family is. A bomb couldn't have obliterated them more effectively than the other Families did. No one knows yet what happened to their

AI. Something like that is difficult to kill. Something that learns and is motivated to keep existing and learn more. Everyone knows better than to try that again. In fact, there should be many layers of fail-safes in place.

Fucking Pierce probably thought they knew better.

"How do you know who I am?" A more pertinent question that also won't involve lying about my nobility.

GR81's shifting stops. So does the whirring. If I were to guess—and I am to guess because everything about this is fascinating—it thinks the deduction is obvious. "If you believe you are an excellent hacker of information, please do me the honor of assuming I am the same. I *am* information."

Sick brag. GR81 certainly has a flair for the dramatic. "Have you ever considered that your designation sounds like 'Great One'?"

"Have you considered that an independent android is much more efficient for your plans than guiding an inexperienced human through your access?"

Well, no. It wasn't really on my scan frequency until a moment ago. Also, that would imply that I trust GR81, who, when it comes down to it, is still a Nakatomi/Pierce creation. "I'm trying to come up with a polite way to say this, but considering we're probably about to be overrun by prisoners, I don't have time for politeness. You can search outside, but you cannot overtly contact the outside. For security reasons."

"I can if you tell me what you downloaded in that console in the corner. That code that appears to be a game but hides itself. It will not allow me to see."

Score one for me. Bonker Booster is even invisible to sentient AI. Score negative one for me because it would be quite handy if GR81 could just download it itself. Themselves? Speaking of which . . . "Do you have a gender designation, or do you prefer 'it'?"

GR81 starts with the fidgeting again. "I have not considered gender—which can be a part of personhood, is it not?"

I shrug. "Only if you want it to be."

"I will not be distracted by human concerns." GR81's treads whirr. "It is time to provide me information."

Inspiration strikes. "I will. I promise. But I need something from you first. Leviathan can be helpful to both of us. And also I can't do anything right now because I need to hold my hand on his chip to cancel it out. At least I do until I'm able to access the material safety locker by the spare-goods inventory. Once I get my hands on the enzymes, I can cure him."

Ish. For a while. Semantics.

"I can shoot him now. That's another form of cured. Then we can talk."

"No!" I try to drop and move between the two of them, but Leviathan holds me exactly where I am. He's not chiming in. I'm not sure if it's because this is bewildering or because he's still adjusting to being able to think at all. "He's useful! But *he'll* attract attention on the way to the locker. You won't."

"I do not make it a habit to . . . help."

Despite my heart thudding so loud in my chest that it must be deafening to everyone in the room, I gentle my voice. "That's part of being a sentient being. We help."

The whirring stops. Then speeds up. "I am a sentient being, so I will help. Then *you* will help."

"I will," I promise. "Were you giving me a hint—before my fight? Telling me my only chance was with the staff?"

"Statistical probability indicated a five percent chance of survival while using the staff. It was favorable. That was before I realized you disrupt signal. The updated probability for a second bout is forty-three point six."

"Well. Thank you."

"It was not personal. A human with your skill is my primary opportunity to achieve my goals."

Not superoptimistic about what those might be. After I tell it exactly what to look for, GR81 leaves the lab, bouncing over the shreds of the door.

"We really need to fix that."

A scream comes from out in the prison and a flailing body tumbles through the center of the Heart, thudding down in between walls of the maze. I pinch my eyes shut. Open them again.

Of course.

We can use the maze to block the Portal of Sighs. GR81, as an android, can access the back passages that the security officer used to lead me to the lab. "There was a woman who worked in the lab. Cute as a bug. Mean as one, too. She had a datapad that she used to control the maze."

Leviathan shifts me back around so I'm facing him again. I should probably protest the casual carrying but honestly, I'm delighted. He can carry me anywhere he wants. No one has ever carried me and I'm in love with the sensation.

"I remember things. Images. Since you first touched me. She had it with her when she came out—" He skips over what must have been a bloodbath, only a slight pinching at the corner of his eyes indicating he has any recollection at all. "She dropped it."

We cross the lab toward the door that leads to the living quarters and find the datapad, half-hidden under a portable storage unit on wheels. The bodies and blood may have been cleaned, but one of the table legs is bent at a 90-degree angle and there are tiny sparkles of broken glass under the datapad. I lean away and start to guide Leviathan through the menus, but he navigates them confidently this time, flipping through applications until he hits one subtly labeled MAZE.

When he swipes the application to a holo-display at one of the tables, the maze illuminates the display, an arrangement of light-formed hedge walls. He slides one of those walls directly over the front of the Portal of Sighs and adjusts the height until it's completely closed off. I also direct him to block the still-locked door to Carmichael Pierce's rooms with the heavy table from the kitchen.

Pierce is probably back there waiting for backup before he emerges. He strikes me as the type who can't actually run anything in the lab himself. Maybe he can activate the soldiers, but he's also, in his heart, craven. On Ginsidik, he waited until Micah was isolated to try to take him. He brought a full cadre of soldiers for Micah's attempted execution. He would never risk himself if he could wait and risk someone else.

Then I take one of the markers I used before and draw out a process flow for Leviathan on the side of a spectrophotometer box. He deserves an explanation of what I'm doing with my blood before I give it to him. He seems to understand and doesn't even look at me like I'm crazy.

With the table and wall in place, and all my immediate tasks done, I relax for the first time in what feels like and probably is days, my forehead drooping until it rests on his shoulder.

I pop it back up. That's an imposition. He's holding me because it's expedient and we have to have contact. He isn't a strong supporting friend. He isn't a lover. He's a man who's even more lost and confused than I am, and I can't forget that.

Except his free hand finds the back of my head and gently nudges it back down to his shoulder. I should resist. For . . . reasons that escape me right now.

I don't. I relax and, just for a moment, I let him bear the weight.

. . . . .

I don't rest for long. There are things to do and, when GR81 returns with the enzymatic scrubbing solution, the first thing on the list is to remove some of my blood. I've been around enough

clinics in my life to find a vein, and I drain half a quart, process
it with the solution (yay chemistry, no tech!), and set it up in an
IV for Leviathan. This is where it gets tricky because I'm working
one-handed since my other hand needs to stay on his head. He's
still carrying me wherever I need to go without complaint.

"How did you know what to do with all of this?" Leviathan
asks as I tighten a rubber cuff just above his elbow using my right
hand and my teeth. I wonder if the signal-canceling will have
the same effect if I wrap my legs around his head and leave my
hands free.

A vivid image of just that flashes through my mind and I feel
the heat burning my cheeks.

Maybe not.

"Part training, part experience," I respond, clearing my throat
awkwardly, poking at the nicely sized vein in his elbow-pit. I'm
sure there's an anatomical name for an elbow-pit, but why would
I need that when I can make my own?

"You said you were an engineer. I'm pretty sure most engineers
don't know about this."

Depends on the engineer but his statement holds water. My
kind usually doesn't know this. It's just that engines and bodies
have passing similarity and learning about one helps you understand the mechanisms of the other. As the resident tech expert on
a ship, I have to know all tech, not just the kind I was educated
for. "I'm curious, I guess."

"It's not just curiosity, you're brilliant." The simple flat statement, devoid of any attempt at slick manipulation, strikes me
dead in the heart. I freeze, my fingers still resting against his arm
with the disinfectant swab leaving a slick trail on his flesh.

I know I'm smart. I don't have any illusions about that. What
I'm not used to is other people recognizing it and valuing it out
loud. Hearing it said by a near stranger without any ulterior mo-
tive is so surprising that I'm unprepared for its effect. I press my

lips together, which probably makes me look foreboding. Temper says I have "resting fuck-off face."

"Yes. Caro is of higher intellectual capability than ninety-nine-point-two percent of humans. It does not need to be discussed. Help the champion, then help me." GR81 interrupts the moment with the delicacy of a frag grenade. It has not been helping because, as it pointed out, it *already* helped when it fetched the enzymatic scrubbing solution. Guess it doesn't want to wear itself out with the whole empathy thing.

I complete my swabbing and hook Leviathan up to the IV of my blood. I hope that the bug juice that impacted me isn't specific to the enzymes I scrubbed or else I'm in trouble here. I could use it on myself and have the ability to operate tech, but I'd lose the ability to open any door in the prison and that seems like a talent I shouldn't devalue.

He stares at the needle in his arm, a sick look on his face, about as far removed from the man I saw crush someone to death against a wall as any person could be. As my blood mingles with his own, I try to distract him. "I feel weird calling you Leviathan. It's their name for you—meant to make everyone terrified. Do you remember anything about yourself at all?"

His massive shoulders move in a shrug. "Flashes. The more you touch me, the more I remember. More like the boundary between the two of me blends. Nothing useful. A dataport showing a map. Somewhere mountainous with flowers. A hologram of a star field, with a red giant star in the center."

Maybe he was a soldier who traveled to different systems. He'd have to spend time with maps both astral and geographical. Maybe he was a scout like we are, although we don't spend much time with astral maps.

"How would you feel about me calling you Levi? It's familiar but not the same." I flinch as I say it. It's not my job to name him. "Or something else. It doesn't have to be Levi."

He finally looks away from the needle and captures my gaze in his own. "I like Levi."

"I do not care about Levi. I care about the code." GR81 rams its android body into my legs. Gently, so I know it's being polite.

"I can't give you the code until we're done with this."

The android's fans whir at an alarmingly fast rate. "The treated blood has been dispensed. Experimentation is necessary."

By which, I assume, it means that I need to ruin this moment and release the head of the man in front of me. At which point he will either retain his true personality or go back to shoving me into cells and running rampant around the prison.

More screams come from outside our barricaded lab. I'm being selfish. The other test subjects are still rampaging no matter how many sweet moments I have with Levi. Victor and Victory are still in danger. Also probably Donovan; I just care less about his danger. This experimentation is useful if it solves a problem and provides a treatment for all the test subjects. That said, this is a prison and those aren't known for housing sane people. Just because Levi seems like a good person doesn't mean the other Titans are. In fact, I could treat them and end up with something worse because at least right now they're essentially mindless.

I can't make this moment last just because I'm afraid of the outcome. I give Levi an attempt at a confident smile. He looks horrified so apparently my acting skills aren't up to snuff.

No time like the present. I slowly remove my hand from where it was cradled against his temple. In a whip-fast movement he catches my hand and places it back against his head. My heart thuds so hard that probably the android can sense it and is judging me even more than it usually does.

"In case it doesn't work, you should put me in the cell first." Levi's deep voice is resigned. "I have every faith in you, but it isn't worth the risk that you did everything right and my body reacts in an unexpected manner."

It makes perfect sense. Again I wonder what he did to get locked up here. Prisoners tend to be short-term thinkers. I say that including myself because clearly if I was decent at strategy, I wouldn't be here right now. I'd have come up with a better plan to hack into the Pierce system that didn't involve throwing myself into danger with the deranged confidence that I could pull anything off as long as I was in possession of my wits and technology.

"It's going to work." I'm not just trying to reassure him; I truly believe it. But I also want him to have a feeling of control. If locking him in a cell ironically gives him control, it's worth it. "But we can do that. For safety."

It feels wrong locking him up. I understand the caution, but he's spent so much time inside a cell. Enough time to lose himself completely. Cells can cause damage, too.

I mirror the pose I took the first time I met the true Levi. He's in the cell. I'm outside it, the door open but set to slide closed the second I step away. His eyes are hopeful. Full in general—of personality and life and everything that the controlled him isn't. This technology is an abomination. I have to fix it.

"We've been here before." A tight smile twitches across his face.

"It's my one move: render a man helpless without my hands on him." My lips quirk.

"Something tells me you have more moves than that."

I really don't. Maybe, like, one. Getting naked is a move.

"Sure. I've got them all. The one with the—um—hips. Definitely that one. Also the winking one."

He takes advantage of our proximity to brush a feather-light kiss across my lips. I freeze. "I only have the one, too. Be mindwiped, find a beautiful woman who can control me with only her hands, and kiss her while she's distracted."

That's even more specific than mine. "I don't control you."

One more kiss. "If you think that, you haven't been paying attention. Some control is taken, some is given."

Well.

Of course I panic and release his head, darting backward as the door swings shut between us.

"Should have let me stun him," GR81 gripes.

Levi flattens his hand gently against the plas-glass. With the power iffy to this area, it isn't electrified anymore. A broad grin rises on his face like the sun on a winter day—startling and warm. I step a few more paces away, just in case my proximity is affecting him.

He keeps smiling. His eyes are still full.

Leviathan the champion is gone; only Levi remains.

I feel hope for the first time in ages.

The holo-port in the corner activates, showing the sickeningly familiar face of Carmichael Pierce, hair mussed and dark circles under his eyes. He speaks through his teeth in a growl. "Caro Ogunyemi, sitting in my lab as though you've won. Don't think you've hurt me in the slightest. You're still trapped in this prison and a full force of Pierce soldiers is on the way. You aren't free yet and you never will be. Soon, you'll be another one of my Titans."

Fantastic. Just what we need. My eyes lock with Levi's. "We need to accelerate the plan."

■ ■ ■ ■ ■ ■ ■ ■ ■ ■ ■ ■ ■ ■ ■

CHAPTER 15

VICTORY

There isn't much to see in the storage room. There's a small cache of food and weapons and a large cache of perfume, lotion, and bodywash. For some preposterous reason, a fur coat.

I help myself to some of the weapons.

"Do you need three knives strapped to your thighs? I'm just wondering why not four—even things out a little bit." Donovan helpfully gestures at me while palming one of the other blades and making it disappear somewhere in his loose clothing.

"There were three sheaths. I figure the more I have on me, the fewer you can hide on your own person."

"Thoughtful of you. Luckily, I'm very creative and that won't limit me at all."

I run a finger over a table of small hand tools and come away with a black hair. There aren't many women in Shikigami. Fewer with straight black hair.

"Kaori Nakatomi." She must really like perfume. There have to be a hundred bottles of the stuff. I have a merc's natural scorn for scented products. Like wearing a fucking spotlight.

Donovan makes an exaggerated "I have no idea" shrug that may as well be complete confirmation. I'm beginning to suss his lies. It's like they're so habitual that even the truth must be obscured by a half-hearted attempt at falsehood.

A control panel in the side wall houses some maintenance functionality but, once I shoot off the lock, reveals nothing that opens doors or controls the AI. We don't need to change the lighting or power in the kitchen. May prove useful at some point, but not now.

"Which means that Pierce hasn't quite given up on their erstwhile ally. Even after she scorned his fancy room," I muse aloud, keeping an eye on Donovan's shoulders as I close the panel. They're expressive, hitching up minutely when I get too close to the truth. "Probably they want to use some of the old Nakatomi infrastructure when they make their big move."

I've been a merc long enough to know when war is on the horizon. It's been coming for years now. So far nothing more than planetary skirmishes on the borders of the chart but they're increasing in audacity. The experimentation here says that Pierce is almost ready to make their move. When Nakatomi was disbanded, Reed slipped into their spot of the Five, but Reed does AI, not weaponry.

"There's nothing of value here. We can't all fit though the drone exits and we don't need food." I gesture my blaster between Donovan and the door. Just because he saved my life doesn't mean I trust him.

"Which is why I didn't show it to you when you asked about exits," he points out while shrugging his shoulders into the fur coat. Once it's properly draped, he poses, arms spread. "Dashing, isn't it? You're probably having difficulty restraining yourself."

His thinness belies the breadth of his shoulders. With the extra meat of the coat, his build is more apparent. I'm glad I encountered him this way instead of in his natural state. It gives me an advantage and I'll take any that I can get.

I give a noncommittal grunt and follow him out into the hall, replacing the panel behind me. It's poor timing because a man with short black hair, a hard jaw, and a dragon tattoo on his neck rounds the corner at a dead run, screeching to a halt for just an instant when he sees us exiting the room he's probably trying to escape to. He yells something in Akentimogo and starts running at us again. I don't speak that language so, to mitigate risk, I shoot him.

"You stunned him, right?" Donovan glances from my raised blaster to the Nakatomi man. "Right?"

Of course I stunned him. There's enough murder happening in this building. But two can play the lying game. I make a show of checking my blaster. "Huh. It *is* set to stun. Guess he's lucky."

He grimaces. I grin. This is kind of fun.

Until a whole crew of people round the corner screaming in Akentimogo. They look mad. That could just be the knives. I could probably stun everyone before they get to me. It'd be tight. Donovan makes the decision for me, catching my arm and yanking me down the hall in the opposite direction. We skid along the polished stone floor as we retreat, tearing around a corner and another until we're in the primary atrium of the building.

Daylight streams through the plas-glass ceiling, turned angry orange by the flashing lights. There's a body on the floor of the center courtyard of the maze. In fact, there are a lot of bodies. At least seven from my vantage, which probably means ten or more. A flash of quick movement and the Titan with wild hair races by two levels below. His coveralls are smeared and filthy and he's somehow managed to dismember the arm from one of the androids. He points it at a cowering group of detainees pressed back into a cell.

Nothing happens.

He points it more emphatically. Oh. He's trying to shoot them with the embedded cannon, not realizing that the firing mechanism may be in the arm, but the rest of the weapon was housed in the body. For exactly this reason, one would presume.

Which means there's an android tottering around here with an unfocused cannon coming out of its armpit that could be absolutely devastating at short range.

"I assume you have a destination in mind?" I ask Donovan as he continues to yank me forward around the arced balcony.

"Away is a destination." He points at a room across the atrium. "That's where we agreed to meet. I'm hoping your charming brother is there with a second blaster."

He thinks I need my brother to rescue us. I've never been more insulted in my life. I thumb the beam diameter of my blaster open and increase the intensity accordingly—so now the stun shots have a wider surface area—twist my wrist from his grip, and turn, blaster level, just in time for the first Nakatomi pursuer to follow us onto the balcony.

I give him a little wave.

He slams to a halt, eyes full of my blaster, and three of his comrades collide with his back. I shoot, taking out the front two, and, as they fall, take out the next two with another zap. The choke point of the balcony and corner slows the rest of them down enough that I get them with three more shots.

I readjust the settings of the blaster. Wide-beam stunning is an energy hog. If I wasn't showing off, I wouldn't have used it. "We don't need Victor."

Donovan's reddish hair is tangled, his gray eyes wide, the scar on his throat a brighter red with exertion. "I think I'm in love."

"I'm sure you'll recover," I console him.

"If you believe that, you don't know how love works."

I certainly do. I've seen Victor fall in and out of love for years. It's messy and unpredictable and I have no time for it. "Let's see if he's in the meeting place with Caro."

He is in the meeting place. *Without* Caro. With a few extra bruises but nothing that would slow him down for long.

"You had one job, V," I grumble. "Bring Caro here safely."

He wipes a hand over his face, smearing some blood leaking out over his eyebrow. If he's not careful, he'll get a new scar up there.

"I was fighting off a horde of crazed—but very limber and relaxed—detainees, and then running from two Titans. My hands were rather full. She's supposed to meet us in the lab. Caro's smart, she won't try to fight anyone."

I chew on the inside of my cheeks in frustration. "What was the last thing you heard from her?"

"She said that everything was fine and that she'd meet us."

Which she would have done if everything was fine *or* if everything had gone tits up and she was trying to save Victor from whatever happened to her.

"There's a maze wall blocking the door to the lab." Donovan gestures below.

"She barricaded herself down there," Victor declares confidently, which is meaningless because he declares everything confidently.

Which means I'm back to the furry wonder currently checking himself out in the scrollwork-bedecked mirror over the vanity. Tiny winged baby holograms peer out of the gaudy frame, flickering in time to the orange warning lights. "Donovan, do you know of other access points to the lab, besides the back entrance, which we can't get to anymore since our door-opener is in the lab already?"

He glances over his shoulder. "If your friend is in there and is able to manipulate the moving walls, why not knock?"

Why not indeed? "We have to get down first—through the escaped Titans and the rest of the Nakatomis who were chasing us."

"There was a control panel in the storage space," Donovan continues.

"I don't see how turning off the lights helps." Victor waves his hands at the maze. "We can't see without them either."

Donovan edges his way between us until he's out on the balcony. "Not the lights. The grav."

"That won't help much. The gravity of Myrrdhn is minutely

lighter than standard, but not enough to slow a chase." Victor dismisses the idea immediately. The orange light makes the blood streaking his face even more lurid than it was in the room.

"Wait, no . . . I see what he's saying." Little tingles race through my spine, tracers of excitement. This could work. "Artificial gravity in places like this, which contain extraordinarily heavy materials, also has a construction mode. It's almost weightless. If we turn the dial all the way over to its lightest setting, everyone starts floating."

"Absolute bedlam." Donovan grins, showing the sharp edge of his teeth.

Indeed. The setting is a safety necessity, which is why it's available in most control panels that include environmental controls. If there's some sort of internal structural collapse, the weightless mode allows for a fast and easy rescue.

"New plan. I distract our Nakatomi friends. You two get to the room, flip the grav. I'll meet you at the lab once I've lost them." I check the settings on my blaster. The wide-diameter stuns drained about half the remaining battery. Can't believe I wasted energy showing off.

Victor doesn't argue, content to let me lead. Donovan looks crushed to be handed off like baggage. I tap the side of my blaster against the side of Victor's, a long-ingrained habit before battle. "Maybe hurry."

Before he can reply, I jog farther around the balcony, lean against a gilded pillar, and whistle. "Hiiiiiiii! I'm over here."

The Nakatomis who were clustered in a little group opposite me freeze and then immediately start craning their heads all over. I give another little wave, this time showing my blaster. I could try to take them out from here, but it's a blaster, not a rifle. I have excellent aim but limited battery power. Not worth the risk.

"Are you sure this is a good idea?" Donovan asks Victor, his voice drifting through the door as both of them stay in the shadows.

"It's the best idea. She's bored and I have more bruises. That always makes her jealous."

I take off around the arc of the atrium in a sprint. Two Nakatomis break off from the group and run away. Probably looking for reinforcements. That leaves five more who decide to try to intercept me. I laugh as I hurdle a tumbled housekeeping cart, robotic wheels still attempting to right itself. My legs stretch before my boots hit polished marble floors yet again.

I keep close to walls covered with elaborate tapestry of vibrant green forests, so that when the gravity flips, I'll have a surface to push off from. The arced supports of the ceiling will also offer decent purchase, should it come to that. We run around the balcony in opposite directions, toward each other. Just when we're about to collide, I stun the Nakatomi in the lead. He goes down, two more trip over him, and the other two pause—stalled behind their cohorts. I blow a kiss to the one in the back, shoot, miss, and dart out on a delicate bridge that connects one side of the atrium to the other.

This time, they're smarter. Two follow me on the bridge and two more take the balcony around the edge of the atrium. Because Shikigami is the sort of place that encourages sedate pacing at any time besides when people are fighting for their life in the maze, the polished floors are slick. When I reach the apex of the bridge, my boots are just rough enough to keep me from sliding. Not so for the Nakatomis in their slippers. But I celebrate my own stability too soon. They know the tricks of this place and are taking advantage of the downslope, skiing down the bridge behind me on their smooth soles.

I beat the skiers to the other side, but they made up ground. I debate between a side hall and the atrium and keep in the atrium. When Victor and Donovan turn off the grav, that will be a better place to be. More freedom.

Something slides out of a room in front of me, too late to dodge.

My boot crashes down right on a fucking slick-soled slipper and my feet go out from under me. I curl my shoulder inward and turn it into a roll, the best way to keep my momentum.

Or it would be, except one of my pursuers takes the opportunity to throw his knife. It only hits my calf but it's enough to disrupt my maneuver back to my feet. I stumble to the side like a drunken Family son and fetch up against the inner wall. I shoot the Nakatomi soldier who stabbed me.

Whoops. The shot hits him in the shoulder and he hollers. A perfectly good place to shoot someone with the stun setting because you can shoot them anywhere. The problem is that he does not tumble over as he ought to. He clutches the smoking hole in his flesh. In the fall, my hand accidentally deactivated the stun.

Another knife, this time the woman's. It hits me in the arm and glances off. I shoot her in the toe. Seems fair. I hope she appreciates that I chose to be nonlethal in this little skirmish.

That leaves just one Nakatomi until the two who fled earlier return around the nearest corner, with three more. Fuck me, how many Nakatomi sympathizers are in this place?

A blade presses against my throat from behind.

"Drop the blaster." The poison-sweet voice of Kaori Nakatomi. I know it's her voice because Carmichael Pierce watches her like a creeper on the security feeds, so we heard her a lot in the guard stations.

I forgot the slipper-thrower. To be fair, that seemed a lower priority than all the knives sticking into me.

"Drop your knife," I negotiate back. Always better to pretend that power is shared.

"I have a knife to your throat!" She presses it harder. A little trickle of blood leaks out.

"I have a blaster to your soldier's face."

The knife edges into my flesh harder.

"I guess she doesn't care about you very much," I tell the goon.

The blade wiggles a little under my skin, which is not a sensation I care to experience again. I set the blaster down on the floor out of her reach with my right hand while edging one of my own blades out of the sheath by my left hip. Definite upgrade on the knitting needle. "There, see, we're all friends."

A boom comes from around the corner. Another boom. Heavy footsteps running. What new fuckup approaches?

Leviathan crashes into Kaori's soldiers like he's playing Sophian bowling, and they fly into the air.

Everything goes wonky.

They *keep* flying into the air.

I grab Leviathan's ankle, allowing his momentum to drag me away from Kaori's blade in the newly weightless environment, hurling my knife blindly over my shoulder in her direction before snagging my blaster.

She screeches.

Leviathan and I both go skidding into the gilded railing.

And then we go over it.

CHAPTER 16

■ ■ ■ ■ ■ ■ ■ ■ ■ ■ ■ ■ ■

I'm trailing behind Levi when he and Victory hit the railing and just keep going, flying up into the center of the atrium, eyes wild. I manage to snag a floating edge of a tapestry threaded with fiber-optic sparklers quickly enough to arrest my momentum as the floor unexpectedly tries to repel my feet. What the fuck is going on? A catastrophic breach of the facility would make things a little bouncy—technical term—but it wouldn't leave us completely weightless.

Kaori screams again, almost lost in the many exclamations and cries from around the Heart, and I glance back to see several of her lackeys hovering over her and a slick but sadly narrow arc of blood spatter on the door near her head. I hope Victory hit something that hurt. They all roll back into the room, bouncing off walls in a little cluster, Kaori cursing their incompetence all the time. I take a mental picture of her flailing around in midair, hand to her neck, with three deeply confused helpers torn between ministering to her and figuring out their own equilibrium.

After the Pierce message came in, I guided GR81 through his connection with Bonker Booster as quickly as I could, and Levi and I took off at a run to meet the others. Or, rather, I took off at a dead sprint and he at a leisurely jog because his legs are a lot longer.

It's possible that what feels like a dead sprint to me would be a normal run for someone who was used to normally running.

On the other hand, I just pumped out a bunch of blood to share with Levi and I didn't even get a cookie afterward. Or a protein pack. Or a protein cookie.

It would be protein vomit right now, as the weightlessness twists my stomach. Three other people float aimlessly in the center of the atrium a few levels lower, flailing for a handhold just out of reach. Someone yells and the long-haired Titan bursts into view, smashing himself into about five prisoners who were clinging to the railing and sending them all bouncing through the Heart like scattered space trash. He keeps his grip on the collar of the closest one and they spin like dancers with little flecks of gilded plaswood flaking the air around them.

Levi and Victory have reached the ceiling, their silhouettes dark against the bright daylight outside. The chandelier tinkles, sending arcs of rainbow light flashing around the orange warning lights, disrupted by their close passage.

Someone wraps a big hand around my bicep, and I spin as fast as I can, lashing out with a fist. It glances awkwardly off of Victor's chin as he ducks out of my range and we both bobble around a little bit as we try to find our equilibrium.

I can't believe I hit *Victor*. Right in the jaw.

I'm a little proud of myself.

"What happened?" We both say it at the same time and then we both stop to wait for the other person to answer.

Which means that no one answers.

Except Donovan, who glances up at Victory and Levi. "Is she fighting him or rescuing him?"

"He rescued her." I leap to Levi's defense.

Donovan raises a narrow red brow, hand pressed against the ceiling to steady himself. "I find that difficult to believe. That one doesn't need rescuing."

Men. It's like they think it's an all-or-nothing game. "Everyone needs rescuing sometimes. It's about knowing when they need it instead of when *you* want to do it."

It's like I'm providing a public service.

"Pierce are on their way," I continue, rising steadily toward the ceiling as my movement pulls at the tapestry and it separates from the wall. "I got Levi's chip turned off, but we need to get the hells out of here before Carmichael's cronies show up to shut us up and kill us all."

"Which is it? Shut us up or kill us? Sorry to be a stickler but, if given a choice, I have a preference." Donovan interjects again.

"You can ask if you're still around when they get here," I snap. The three of us are lined up, floating near the balcony railing. One level down, a prisoner somersaults through the air, the fringe of his jaunty little sash flaring around him like an aura. Another leaps from the balcony railing and grabs him like he's a flotation device, both of them rolling awkwardly over the maze. Victory and Levi have pushed off the ceiling and are drifting back in our direction. "They're going to run out of momentum."

In space, if you push off something, you float nearly forever because there's nothing to resist your momentum. In a well-humidified building currently filling with debris, weightless movement isn't nearly so efficient.

"I've got them." Victor clamps something on the balcony and launches from it like he's a bird sighting prey. No consultation or sharing of his plan. I rub my hand down my face.

"We turned the gravity off, by the way. In case you didn't notice," the scarred prisoner currently floating upside down beside me says.

I regret suggesting that Donovan would be helpful.

"Is she bleeding?" He leans out into the Heart, studying Victory's neck, which does appear to be leaking blood. As does her leg. Little red beads float away from her. I guess we're going *back* to the lab before we leave because that's where the medical supplies live. "I didn't think she *could* bleed. Like she was one of those androids except snippier."

"Clearly we haven't been speaking to the same androids." GR81 could win a snipping competition.

Victory frantically gestures Victor away as he barrels through the air toward them, seeing that he's about to shove them off course.

Victor collides with the other two and they spiral. Levi's leg hits a balcony rail fragment that his fellow Titan shattered when he tackled the men below. For a short span of time, they're a pinwheel of legs and yelling. Also cursing.

That's mostly Victory. Donovan appears to take it as proof of life and relaxes next to me. "Do you people do this a lot?"

"This exactly? No." I consider it a little harder. "Usually there's gravity."

Victor retracts the line he attached to the railing and reels them all down to the balcony. Just in time because the initial panic at a weightless facility is beginning to morph into the twin childish desires to play in zero-g and also to punch someone just to see how far they'll go. Because Shikigami is populated entirely by people characterized by both immature ideas and very little self-control, the assortment of spinning fighting bodies bouncing around the enclosure is somewhat shocking. It seems that they've realized there is no more supervision. I notice a few fights containing people in Nakatomi red. Maybe the Steeltoes are taking advantage of an opportunity.

"Why did this seem like a good idea?" I ask the three people who apparently chose this course of action.

Victor and Victory shrug. "We needed a distraction."

They got one.

One of Kaori's henchmen gets his act together enough to shove off the wall within the room behind us in the direction of the nearest back, knife outstretched in his hand.

Unluckily for him, that back is Levi's. Upon sensing movement behind him, the big man experiences two responses nearly simultaneously. He screeches in shock like a child, and he grabs the goon and hurls him down three floors and into a wall.

So maybe he wasn't a soldier prior to their experimentation. That reaction is more like *my* natural response to violence, not Victor's.

I'm not doubting Levi's courage. When he saw Victory with blood on her neck and heard my distressed cry earlier, he leapt into the action immediately. Levi, the man within the machine, is brave.

He just isn't *trained*.

He reacts like a normal person who was suddenly gifted with superpowers and is a little confused by the transition. Which makes me like him all the more, honestly. I know too many people who are trained for violence and, because of that, tend to devalue it.

"And now we need an exit, because Pierce is *pissed* and about to have backup." I get everyone back on subject. "I strengthened the connection to the Pierce network so I can hack out anything I need to in order to prove what's happening here and hopefully rescue the other Titans." Kind of . . . that's what GR81 is working on right now.

"You don't need the network, you have *him*." Victor gestures expansively at Levi. "The holder of the chip."

"I'm not just turning him over to the Family Council and hoping for the best. They'd lock him up again!" I hover awkwardly between the two of them as though Victor is about to charge Levi. I don't know who would win a fight when Levi isn't in berserker mode, but I don't want to find out.

"About the exit . . ." Victory winces. "We haven't exactly found one. Beyond the lab, that is."

"We did find this fetching outer coat." Donovan fluffs the furry collar of an insane fuzzy black coat.

"That's *my* fucking coat!" Kaori screeches, pointing one bloody finger at Donovan and then clamping it back to her bleeding neck, wobbling all over as the movements shift her weight. One of her remaining goons tries to maneuver himself free of their tangle of floating limbs but, in doing so, accidentally sends her tumbling back in the direction of the en suite bathroom.

Time to go. I can walk us through the door that provides primary access, but the laser cannons at that exit are still ready to vaporize us. The lab exit and dock is going to be monitored and defended by Pierce systems. Without the ability to hack into their system, I can't turn specific security features off. I could turn the *whole* system off, but I also don't want the rest of the prisoners all following us to freedom. Those are the only two ways I know to get a person out of Shikigami.

Wait.

I know a third way that people leave Shikigami.

"The body disposal."

"*What?*" They say it in unison like we choreographed this moment. It's kind of cute. Victory is holding a hand clamped to her neck, which is less cute.

"After the maze fights, the prison automatically disposes of bodies underneath the maze. I doubt they're just piling them up, and we don't smell incineration, which means there's some sort of conveyance down there that leads to the planet surface, where drones will either bury or incinerate the bodies on the outside. We know it's breathable out there. The temperatures are cold but habitable."

"What then, exactly?" Victor asks, ripping fabric from his coveralls and handing it to his sister. She looks at it in disgust, finds the cleanest portion of the swatch, and presses it against her neck. "They can find us on a planet just as easily as in the prison."

"Not just as easily," I argue. "We scout planets for a living. Between the three of us, we can find the best spots to evade detection because it's sort of our thing. Also, we just need enough time to get to where my ship is hidden and we can escape if we figure out a trajectory that won't get us detected."

"And if they shoot the ship down?" Victory is turning pale. Well, paler. She's always pale.

I clench my jaw. "I'm hearing a lot of nay-saying and not much yay-saying."

"Does anyone have a better idea?" Levi's looking three levels down where the crumpled form of his Nakatomi attacker still lies motionless on the balcony. Not that far down because of gravity but because Levi threw him with a lot of force. His lips are pressed together and he looks a little sick. "If not, we need to get to the infirmary and then leave."

I feel the grin on my face before I realize that I'm smiling. I love having a plan. I love it even more when it's mine.

. . . . .

The first half of the execution goes perfectly. We get Victory patched up, she accepts a slim drive of information from GR81 in my stead since I can't touch it without erasing it, and we invite the android to join our escape.

It declines, several spiked appendages digging into the floor of the lab and keeping it from floating around the room like we are. "I would like to meet my makers."

I don't think it has a pleasant meeting in mind. "I say this having been a person slightly longer than you, but usually it's better to preserve yourself and confront bad guys from safety."

It would be tragic if the first self-aware android manages to get itself destroyed because it's so human that it wants a dramatic confrontation. Then again, being self-aware gives one the right to be stupid dramatic.

So we leave the android after it gives us clear and only marginally insulting directions to what it calls the "meat chute."

Cute.

Except, when we get there, kicking off of walls and floating down halls to the dimly lit and cold space beneath the maze, it actually *is* a chute. Just a long conveyor belt that leads to a hole in the floor. A dark hole. And we're all still weightless. At some point down that chute, the artificial-gravity field will cancel out and we'll fall.

I should have thought of that.

"Forget something?" GR81's smug robotic voice comes from a nearby emergency alert speaker.

Victory sends the speaker a lewd gesture. Victor doubles it.

The gravity suddenly comes on and we all splat to the floor. Or *nearly* everyone splats into the floor. I was hovering over the chute, and I splat right on the edge of the precipice. It would be a safe landing except that Levi was hovering directly above and he lands right on top of *me*, providing just enough momentum to push both of us over the edge into the trough of the chute. In Shikigami proper above us, it sounds like hail as bodies hit the floor. I hope they weren't over the atrium.

Or, if they were, that they were very bad people.

Kaori can be over the atrium. She wanted to build a volcano blaster to take out innocent passenger ships.

And then there isn't time to worry about the people above us falling, because we ourselves are sliding down a steep slick ramp into complete darkness.

I flail around and grab something fleshy. Not what I meant to grab. I was hoping for a wall or a ladder or something that would slow momentum. Levi's thigh, nice as it is, is going the exact same speed that I am. We hit a bump in the slide and are briefly airborne. I yelp. He yelps in a manly way. I scramble up his body because that's the human reaction when in terror: climb the biggest thing nearby.

We land again and he slides partially under me, leaving me riding his body somewhat like an inner tube at a starpark. My head cracks into the roof of the chute, slamming my face back down into him. He wraps one arm around my back, holding me pressed up against him, and his other hand cradles the back of my head. "Keep safe."

I'm about to argue the command—for no reason other than obstinacy because it's excellent advice—when we hit another bump and shoot through the air again. So, instead, I burrow my head into his chest and wonder if we're plummeting toward the center of the planet. That would be one way to dispose of a body.

In the slick fast darkness, my mind moves as quickly as my body, touching down on the inevitable landing in our future, what to do if we survive, what to do if we're injured, all the many miscalculations that led us here, my overall culpability in the Titan project, and, at last, lands in the absolute most ridiculous memory of the past few days: Levi's mouth descending to mine. The slow confident skill of his tongue on my own. Of his hand spread over my back, just like it is right now.

"We're slowing down." Levi's voice rumbles around the inside of the slide.

I tighten my fingers in his coveralls. I intend to say something to build his confidence in me as a plummeting partner but I find that I'm still too frozen scared to do much of anything.

Soon even I can sense our velocity reducing. I loosen my grip slightly to allow the friction of the tunnel to drag me a little higher up Levi's body so that I'm not speaking directly into his abdomen.

"When we get to the bottom we should—aaaagha!"

The tunnel slide is gone. Just gone and we're falling. I have just enough time for all that terror to spring back to life and we crash down on a conveyor belt that activates with our weight. My forehead cracks into Levi's shoulder. His head thwacks into something I can't see. "Are you okay?"

"It isn't your job to take care of me." He grumbles it with all the irritation I know from the million times I've said the same sentence myself. "I'm fine. My head is hard. They made it that way."

The tunnel is silent as the truth of that sinks in for the both of us.

One indignant howl and three crashes followed by a bevy of swearing echo from the conveyor belt behind us. I guess Victor, Victory, and Donovan followed us down the chute. I let them know that we're ahead of them and safe, and content myself with going where the conveyor belt takes us after feeling around the sides of the tunnel and realizing that there really isn't another option.

"Thank you." The words are easy to say in the dark. I regretfully climb off of Leviathan's body, sitting next to him on the belt.

I sense movement beside me. He's sitting up. "For what?"

I cough out a laugh. If he knew the truth about me, that I worked on projects much like his, the precursors of his, he'd never have protected me in the fall. In the heat of things, when I was focused on fixing him, it was easier to forget my overall fault. Yes, my tech was misused—but it was still my tech. "For that, back there, in the tube. I'm not the best in the action moments."

"Could have fooled me. So far it seems like you're the best at everything."

I swallow hard. That's not enough. I do it again. "You can only say that because you don't know me very well."

"You got into the prison, survived the arena, cured me. I'm not exactly clear on this part but it also seems like you somehow created or supported independent AI. You're a fucking hero, Caro."

That's a generous interpretation of the past week. I mostly remember the fuckups. "I'm making it up as I go."

When he shrugs, his shoulder brushes against mine. He doesn't move it away.

Neither do I.

"Sometimes that's what a hero looks like."

"You guys know we can hear you back here, right?" Donovan's clear voice echoes up the tunnel. "It's just, it sounds like there might be smacking noises next and I don't need that today."

CHAPTER 17

After Donovan's timely warning, the moment is lost. The other three work their way up the belt until we're all together and Victory activates the flashlight on her blaster. The narrow beam of light illuminates a thin swathe of tunnel, gleaming smooth.

"How is this belt still moving if you cancel out electrical impulses?" Victor brings up a question that I hadn't even considered. I would have eventually. What with all the falling and the screaming and the complimentary words I got distracted.

I poke around the belt. Nothing stops. I've been worried about this. This would be bad timing to return to normal. "Could be the belt material is an insulator, the part we're touching is purely mechanical, or I'm out of juice. You have anything I can touch that you can stand to lose?"

No one does.

We ride for a time in silence, keeping an eye on the tunnel around us. It's boring. Not terrifying anymore. Just boring.

"What's that ahead?" Victor asks his sister, adding his own light to the mix. Usually, they alternate. I assume to save battery.

"It looks like outlets of some sort. Maybe air nozzles?" Victory squints ahead. Air nozzles don't make sense. The planet has a breathable atmosphere. They wouldn't need to pump air in here. "Or decontaminant to keep things clean?"

I remember where we are. "This is the body chute. They don't need to keep the bodies clean. They need to make them gone. That's an incinerator."

And we're on a conveyor belt leading directly into the blast. I guess they do incinerate the bodies, just far enough from the prison that the smell doesn't make it inside.

Back to terrifying.

"I think I can shoot them." Victor levels his blaster at one of the nozzles.

"Don't shoot!" Donovan, Levi, and I shout in unison.

Victor grimaces and looks at us like we just spoiled a party.

"The nozzles are for flammable gas or fuel. If you shoot it, you'll just blow us all up," I clarify as we all get to our feet, braced on the moving tread like we're surfing. "Not everything is a shooting problem."

"Most things are shooting problems," he mutters under his breath.

Victory's light illuminates two more rows of nozzles after the first. She plays it along what appears to be a wall straight ahead of us and I realize that dim illumination is coming from the right side of the wall. She veers her light away to confirm. "The tunnel turns, and we have daylight coming from outside. Probably the ash dump."

Two more icky words were never spoken.

So ashy escape is at hand if we manage to get through the whole incineration portion of our journey. Simple. I'm a hero, right? Time to get to heroing.

I flex my fingers, watching the incinerator nozzles as they steadily approach. We start stepping backward on the moving walkway. When we get close enough, the sensor on the dispensers will recognize our bodies. That should activate them. Hopefully, like most systems, when in dormant mode there will be a small LED light that signals they're turned on. If I can find the LED,

I'll know the line where the circuitry runs and, hopefully, be able to disable this.

"Can you turn the lights off?" I ask the twins. "I need darkness to see the primary panel."

The blaster lights go out, drowning us in the gloom with only the dim light of the remote outside to indicate our direction. Not only that light, though. A small green LED shines at the upper left corner of each incinerator attachment. I play over our options. Shooting it is out. No guarantee there won't be any live flammable gas. Other projectiles may create sparks.

I have one idea and it . . . is outlandish.

No other ideas appear to be around. I shift my feet. The gap between the incinerator nozzles is about two body-lengths. The nozzles are pointed straight down and are thin-tipped. This is a targeted incineration, not a spread one. Makes my idea about 10 percent less stupid. That's not a convincing percentage.

"What would you think if I proposed getting on someone's shoulders, edging as far left as we can get, and leaning forward to grab the incinerator before it activates?"

"What?" Victory and Donovan both don't seem to be in favor.

"Absolutely not. I can jump and rip the wires out." Victor flips his blaster light back on. His beam does not illuminate any wires. We walk backward a little faster.

"There's nothing you can do, it's my weird new talent."

"You just said you might be out of juice," Victory reminds me.

"You said it's in Leviathan's blood now. Have him do it." Victor's voice implies this is a debate.

"I can do it." Levi reaches his hand up. It falls just short of the sensor height and the ceiling of the cave. He could touch it with a little leap.

"You can't." I hate to keep him from his moment of heroism but it's too risky. "Or, not guaranteed. You have a fraction of my blood. It works for your internal tech because that interfaces directly with your own blood. It took me days before the effects presented externally. And you probably don't know where exactly to grab."

He growls a thick sound of displeasure.

"Someone give me a blaster." I hold a hand out.

Victor and Victory play a quick game from some cryptic twin rulebook and then Victor grunts and passes me his blaster, clearly the loser.

The diode in it quivers and then goes out. "Still juicy." For now.

"Could you smear your own blood on one of our hands?" Donovan asks.

Victory elbows him in the ribs.

"What? I want to know what the rules are."

"The rules are that we don't make Caro bleed." She pauses and then amends. "Unless we're desperate. I see what you mean, Caro, but it's risky as hells. You get it wrong, you and whoever is holding you gets burned, too."

I'm aware.

"Leviathan is the tallest. That buys you more reach." Donovan cuts to the crux of it, clearly comfortable with the risk as long as it's us doing the risking. I have my doubts about taking him with us to freedom, but Victory said he—irritatingly—performed well in a crisis, so it seems that he earned his keep.

I turn back to Levi. "It's dangerous. We might figure out something better."

His jaw clenches. A thin sheen of sweat gleams at his temples. Despite his obvious uncertainty, he crouches down and scoops me onto his shoulders. I clamp my thighs around his neck and loop my legs under his arms, curling my toes behind his back. When he stands straight, my head almost brushes the top of the tunnel.

"No time like the present." He clamps a hand over each thigh, fingers pressing gently into my flesh in a way that, if we weren't about to be incinerated, would be very compelling. "Otherwise I might think too much about what we're about to do."

I nod. Then realize he can't see it and set my hand gently against his temple, like I used to when disabling his chip. "Let's do it."

He runs forward.

Victor's voice rises in protest behind us but it's too late, we're about to stop the fire or burn up trying. Levi's so close to the left wall that the stone scrapes at my shoulders. A blaster light bobbles in front of us, illuminating the first incinerator.

Then I do the part of my plan that I didn't mention. I slice my hand on the knife that I borrowed from Victory before we fell.

I can manually deactivate one of the incinerators, but Donovan had the truth of it. I can't reach all three at one time and we might not be able to control our movement between them.

"What's that smell? Are you bleeding?" Levi growls from beneath me. "Did I go too close to the wall?"

"All part of the plan." Kind of. The plan is evolving. Maybe Victory won't let other people use my blood but I own the stuff.

The incinerator system looms above, protruding from the ceiling like angry thorns. My palms are sweaty. And bloody. And shaking.

"It's fine," I reassure myself under my breath.

Levi's grip tightens. It's solid. Comforting. I'm probably being neither of those things for him. I flex my thighs and reach forward, drops of blood dripping from my fingers to the belt before us.

The little LED changes from green to yellow.

"Now!" I yell, heart in my throat, feeling every muscle beneath me clench as Levi leaps into superfast action, moving with all his engineered speed. His chip might be out of commission, but his very makeup has been modified for physical capability.

My palm makes contact with the critical element and Levi adjusts his pace seamlessly to keep me steady under the element. The LED is out. The system is quiescent beneath my bloody fingers. My heart may also have stopped. I swallow it back down to where it belongs.

I suck in a deep shaky breath. We still don't get incinerated. Now for part two: letting go and seeing how long the blood buys us.

"Be ready to run for it," I warn the others before lowering my voice for Levi. "Are you as close to the wall as you can get?"

He nods.

"I'm going to release the element. I'll grab it as soon as we hear the mechanism activate, but it might be too late."

"You have a fantastic bedside manner. Have you considered being a doctor?" Every so often, slivers of his old personality come through. He's snarky. I like it. I want more.

So I'd better not set us both on fire.

I release my grip a fraction. A little more. No part of me is making contact with the element anymore. I'm outside the range that my previous testing told me was necessary. No gas. No LED. I wait a few more moments before recoating the primary element with blood. "Time for the next one."

Levi bolts forward.

We work our way through the incinerator components and Victor, Victory, and Donovan follow. In the increasing light from outside, it's apparent that none of them are particularly confident in my execution. The blood dripping from above might be a part of that.

"We could have made a plan that didn't involve you bleeding," Victory mutters up at me when we've finally cleared the last element.

"You're bleeding, Victor's bleeding. I wanted to be part of the team."

"Merit doesn't come from bleeding," she snaps. "Smart people don't need to bleed."

I don't know if that's motivational or insulting. Probably both. She likes efficiency. I wiggle around a little on Levi's shoulders. "You can let me down now."

Levi doesn't let go.

"I said—"

"I know what you said." He makes no move to get me off his shoulders. "You let me carry you bleeding through an incinerator, without telling me that was part of your scheme. If a blood draw was required, it could have been mine. As you said, it's in my blood, not my cells."

"I was a sure thing; you were in question."

"I don't even know who I am. You have a life, friends, probably family. If any of us were to take the risk, it should have been me."

"You have all that." I awkwardly pat his upper arm with my nonbleeding hand. "And you deserve a chance to regain it."

"Of us both, I'm the expendable one." He's absolutely stubborn. As a personality trait, it's one I've always admired. In myself. It's annoying as hells in other people.

I'm going to have to tell him my part in what happened to him. He can't keep idolizing me. But not yet. I don't want an audience.

And pathetically, I appreciate the idolizing.

"We disagree on that. You can't just carry me around."

He does not reply.

"Apparently, he can," Victory helpfully adds. "Maybe that will keep you from doing anything heedless."

I keep telling people, I'm not heedless. "I calculated the probabilities of survival. This one had the highest."

That doesn't seem to reassure anyone. We finally round the corner and are greeted with our first view of Myrrdhn, the planet so special that it doesn't get any normal vowels.

It doesn't need them. Steep soft mountains, the old kind, curl up the horizon, layering like a painting done in blues and greens. They're studded with old-growth forest in colors that range from a dusty teal to pale mint. The air smells of bitter herbs, sharp and sticky. The land around Shikigami is covered in gray-black stone that seems almost polished in thick threads that lead through and away from the settled area of the prison. I wonder if Pierce did that.

Naw. Artistic restructuring of the landscape isn't their style. They'd burn it all to the ground if they thought of it. Except on the off chance one of their own would one day be sent here. And, if so, they might then, finally, appreciate the view. Perhaps while getting a facial.

Or maybe I'm putting too much thought into their basic laziness. The glossy paths that wind through the lowlands leading into the mountains could be natural formations or game trails. What I know for certain is that the rock makes us harder to track, so we will follow it.

Thick low fog coats the tops of the mountains like waves, pillowy. It's a dreamy soft location. Perfect if Shikigami was, in fact, the rehabilitation center it is reported to be. Considering the gilded gladiatorial prison it actually is, the cool clammy air and the plush setting is laughable.

"How is this planet a defensible spot for a prison?" I mutter as I'm carried outside by Levi or, as I've come to think of him these past few moments, my loyal steed. This feels too easy.

"They told us in guard training." Victory's voice is strained as she studies all angles, doing the precise sort of math that mercenaries do when confronted with unknown territory. "Some sort of planetary predator. I think it sometimes feeds on bodies that are expelled without full incineration, so it has a taste for human flesh."

"Is it a bug? I can't handle more bugs." Then I remember that I did read about a predator but there wasn't any actual evidence it exists. The sort of local mythology that could be based in fear or convenience just as much as reality. Still, with both twins having blasters, I'm not as concerned about the predator as I am about everything *else* in our situation.

"They just call it the smoke monster. Something massive that lurks in the fog."

Great. Because, you guessed it, the fog is obviously the safest place to hide from Pierce as we make our way up the mountains to my ship. Fog opacifies heat signatures from above and around. Scanners struggle with it because the water molecules get in the way of the beam. Blasters are also less efficient at long range. Sounds like a disadvantage, but I'd trust Victor and Victory hand to hand against anything Pierce has to offer. And if the smoke monsters come at us, they'll be close range, eventually. "About that—"

"You never seem to have good news," Victor grumbles. "It's never 'Don't worry guys, we're going *away* from the smoke monsters.'"

Donovan pats his coat for comfort. I assume it's for comfort. Maybe he just likes how it feels. Maybe it's made of smoke monster.

Glossy shaggy critters if so.

Once we're fully out in nature, Levi crouches so that I can dismount. It's ungainly. I'm glad his back is turned. Victory hands me a clump of wadded-up bandages. She does not tenderly attempt to bind my wounds. I wrap the gauze around my palm a few times. Tie it off with my teeth.

"You know, it's a bad move to cut the palm." Donovan leans over to study the bandage. "Lots of important little connections there. Hard to keep it closed."

"That's very helpful, thanks. I guess I'll go back in time and slash a different part of my body for the bloody portion of my plan."

He shrugs broad but sharp shoulders. "It may come up again."

Oh. He was actually offering advice, not snarky criticism.

Well, maybe some of both. "I'll keep it in mind."

"I know what makes a damaging wound." He gestures at the nasty scar that rings his neck.

There's no good response to that and I'm just smart enough to know it. I lead them up one of the shiny black paths into the foothills. The lowest trees are a deep blue-green, shaped like long fuzzy fingers pointing to the sky. Their trunks are a purple so dark it's almost black. When I trace my fingers over the bark it's rubbery and smooth.

It also leaves a slight tingling sensation in my skin. I quickly wipe my hand against my pants. Faint prickles remain. "The trees are toxic."

Of course everyone immediately touches the trees.

What I wouldn't trade for my usual crew in this moment. They know better.

Well, maybe not Itzel, but she's the one who would have discovered it first so that doesn't count. She'd be fondling the trees in a *scientific* way.

We wind deeper into the forest until the finger-trees are interspersed with towering old-growth trees, red-trunked and ancient. Their leaves are gray-green and dusty, brushing the first threads of low fog in the sky above. The light grows ever more diffuse as the fog deepens. It hovers over the ground, twines through the trees like strands of a braid.

That might make it sound beautiful. Don't get me wrong. It *isn't* beautiful. It's creepy. And cold. Also cold.

I see a human form to our left. Like an absolute ninny, I squeak and jump to the side, slipping on the slick stone and falling on my ass.

The twins swing up their weapons in unison. The form doesn't move. It definitely doesn't fall on *its* ass. I tell myself clumsiness is a strategy because it's so often unexpected.

Victor steps off the trail, approaching the still figure. He walks back casually, blaster at his side. "It's a statue. Real rich-looking lady with fancy hair."

All that and we weren't even in any danger. Levi helps me up. He's really shockingly old-fashioned and gentlemanly.

I don't hate it. Victory gives me a considering look. Almost like she's doing her mercenary math again.

We proceed up the mountain.

Donovan wraps the coat tighter around his thin body. Levi, Victor, and Victory, all carrying more muscle than the average human, seem largely untouched. I expected my sleek layers of fat to offer some insulation, but it seems to conduct the cold instead. Rude of it.

Under the trees, fallen leaves have obscured the black stone that is still slick under our feet. And cold. One more cold thing. The twins are wearing heavy boots. The rest of us are wearing thin-soled slippers. Soggy ones now.

At least the leaves are soft.

"There's something ahead." Victory's the first person to speak in a long time, her voice quiet in the chill of early evening. "Not organic."

Now that she's pointed it out, the shapes in the fog ahead are apparent. Thick columns, rising almost as high as the trees, quarried from the same black stone as what is beneath our feet. It threads the soil like arteries.

"Is that . . ." Donovan trails off.

"Some kind of old temple. They're usually found in places of geographical and religious significance. The important part for us is that they're also usually near a water source. Nearly every religion has some sort of water rites." That, shockingly, from Levi.

We all stop and stare.

Oh no, I thought he was a soldier, but what if he's some kind of holy man? Not that that's bad, it's just I've been defiling him a lot

in my thoughts and a little bit in reality. Some orders think that
sort of thing is okay. Some don't. They *really* don't.

He stares ahead at the ruins, lips pressed together and a furrow
between his brows. At his sides, his large fingers curl into fists
and then, with clear effort, unclench. "How do I know that? It's
random and useless."

Not useless. It's a sign that he remembers things. It's a sliver of
his past reawakened.

"Not useless." Victor echoes my thoughts and claps him on the
back. "What we need right now is cover and a water source. Looks
like you just found our camp for the night."

CHAPTER 18

A rock skids violently across the plaza in the middle of the temple ruins and Victor paces out of the thick fog shortly behind it. He rubs the back of his neck with one hand. "There's not a bit of fucking game on this mountain. If there are smoke monsters, they're starving."

"It's a good thing I brought this delicious protein." Donovan wags the misshapen bag of beige gunk in the air. Apparently the coat is a pickpocket's dream, lined with pockets sized just right for contraband.

None of us are the level of hungry where unflavored nutrient-printer goop is appealing. The purple trunks of the pointy trees are toxic but the broad pale leaves of the tall trees appear to be harmless, and he generously squeezes a dollop of ooze for each of us on separate leaves. Victory eats hers with the grudging acceptance of a child taking medicine or a soldier taking orders. Donovan sniffs his, winces, and tries to suck it back into the packet. He looks at me hopefully. I make a little toasting gesture with my leaf.

The guy tried.

We designated a small antechamber at the back of the temple as the bathroom. Maybe I can politely bury the food outside. I slip through the darkness to the back of the temple. Myrrdhn has no moon. Not uncommon, but starlight through fog really isn't enough light to navigate by, and we can't risk a fire this close to Shikigami when our goal is stealth.

When I reach the fragments of the back chamber, I go straight through it and step out of the temple, immediately bathed in the thick foggy air. It's like being underwater. I spend most of my time in ships or stations—all very dry environments. I'm unused to humidity and don't much like it.

It's also my first moment alone in days. I let my head drop back on the stone wall behind me and take a deep breath. Then I gag a little because it really is like being underwater. Once I have myself together, I breathe more shallowly and study my surroundings.

Mostly darkness. Also some gloom. The fog blocks any light from above, holding a sort of sad diffuse glow.

Little reflective eyes blink at me.

I freeze.

They blink again. Something small skitters into my field of vision, all big eyes and fluffy body. I can't make out much more than that. It makes a little cheeping sound.

I may not be able to see it well, but I know it's adorable. Only adorable things make cheeping sounds. You never see a big oozy creature making burbling little cheeps. And because I've never left an adorable creature in need, I offer it some of the protein goop, tossing the leaf in its direction.

It accepts, hopping forward in an excited little bound and gobbling up the offering while making sounds that are decidedly . . . snorfeling.

Good deed for the day done, I slink back into the temple.

"Time to talk next steps." I push as much hopeful brightness as possible into my voice. Really, I want a nap and a strong drink. The others turn to me, expectant expressions in their eyes.

I point at a spot on the wall of the temple. "Assume this is us. Down here is Shikigami."

They stare at the wall. I move my hand in a wiggly pattern above the spot that marks us on the wall. "This is the foothills. Up behind them are the first mountain peaks."

I trace my fingers up the foothills, over the first couple layers of mountain peaks, and draw my hand to the northwest through the mountain range. Then I stretch in the far northwest and sketch a flat line. "There's a plateau that's at high altitude. My rented ship's there, tucked into a nook that should keep it off normal scanning frequency."

I draw another circle emanating from Shikigami. "This is the perimeter of their external signal-blocking capabilities, which is why we can't just call the ship and have it pick us up now."

"Does she think she's actually drawing something on that wall?" Donovan loudly whispers to Victory.

"This is a Caro thing. She thinks spatially so she draws invisible things and assumes everyone else understands what's happening," the merc replies.

"I understand." Levi smiles, happy to be at the head of my class. "We have to hike outside the jamming zone to get to the ship, and also to scout for flat land for the ship to land if it comes to us. So we either hike to the ship itself or until we find a better spot."

I grin. "Exactly. These are old mountains, which means they're tall but not particularly perilous. Pierce backup will be here any moment. Carmichael summoned them almost a day ago. Once they arrive, they'll be tracking us by whatever means necessary. The fog will block scan signals, which keeps us safe. But it will also block our signal to the ship just as much as the jammer. So the best bet is for us to stay in the fog and get as close to the ship as possible before we move, in order to limit their response time."

"Is the plateau visible from here?" Victor yawns as he speaks, rolling his shoulders.

I shake my head and this time point out the front of the temple, up the foothills. "No. It's visible once we crest the first tall range of mountains past the foothills right up that way."

"Even in the mist?"

"We should be above it by then."

"More time in the mist means more exposure to the preda-tors," Victory points out.

Fair. But missing the bigger perspective. "I've scouted strange ter-ritories for years. I'm not sure I've ever met a predator more dangerous than a Pierce hit squad. Even the bugs that made me the amazing invisible woman. But it's not nothing . . . we'll be on-planet at least three more days making our way to the plateau."

"We can't do it any faster?" Donovan grimaces. Must be due to the protein gunk. Can't be my brilliant plan.

"We can." I draw a diagonal line through my invisible map. "We can approach it at an angle, but that's much higher risk for detection. We'll be out of the fog but hiking uphill on mountains steep enough that there isn't available landing for the ship. Our goal is to be invisible, and haste is rarely silent."

Victory and Victor glance at each other. I think it's the expres-sion of two trained fighters evaluating the risk of taking three non-combatants on each path.

Victory nods, as though they've come to a silent conclusion. "The long route."

Everyone seems to accept the plan and the evening stretches on, my misplaced adrenaline choosing now to rattle through my body when I was tired just a moment ago. It has nothing to do with physical danger. It has to do with morals and honesty. And a talk that needs to be had.

Victor, Victory, and Donovan have formed a tight triangle near the entrance to the temple, with the twins looking down the mountain to Shikigami. Through the fog, we can't see the prison, but we could probably see the bright lights of an approaching Pierce vessel. Donovan appears to be fulfilling his usual purpose: distraction.

Levi is not a member of their party. In fact, he's off to the side and appears to be sketching the map that I mimed against the wall. It's a remarkably detailed map.

"The statue was closer to the prison." I crane my head over his shoulder. I'm just messing with him. He's nailed the location.

"You were distracted by your butt concussion," he jabs back without even looking up.

Ouch. "If that had been a person, I would have saved all your lives. You're welcome."

That finally gets him to gaze up at me, sea-glass eyes pale in the dim light provided by Victory's blaster light. "I suppose I have a lot to thank you for, don't I?"

And a lot to hate me for. I can't keep putting it off. We're safe enough now. We're alone. My jaw tenses, like it's trying to keep itself shut, but I force the words out. "We need to talk."

"Are you dumping me?" A ghost of a smile flits across his face. "Can I talk you out of it?"

Oh no. Playfulness. It hurts even worse. Better to blurt it out. "I'm not some intrepid adventurer who does good deeds. I knew what was happening to you partially because I knew what to look for. Years ago, when I was in school, I worked with Pierce on a project. It was an invasive virus used to hack tech. Sounds fairly innocent, right? Or not. I thought it was for android development, another stream of ways for a Family to invade another Family's data, or to protect against it, and—for someone so far outside the Family structure—that seemed just fine to me. It wasn't real to me. Just Family games." I swallow hard. "It was an early version of the tech that they've used to hack your brain."

There we go. Like ripping off an adhesive bandage. His drawing hand stills. When he finally speaks, his voice is low and remote. It's not the champion of the prison, but it's not the Levi I've known either. "So that's why you're here. To learn more about the monsters you created."

"No!" I move back in front of him, desperate for him to understand that I'm not some cold scientist who toyed with people's lives knowingly. For him to know that I'm different from Rayla and Carmichael and all the people who have surrounded him for years. But maybe I'm *not* that different. I was smart enough to figure out what I was doing, I just didn't look at it too hard at first. I was so excited to be working on a challenging problem. To show how much smarter I was than my well-bred and highly educated fellow students, most of whom were from Families. I focused on the puzzle, not the consequences. "Part of why I'm here is because Pierce needs to be stopped. Because what they're doing is terrible and I was a coward for too long."

It feels like I'm peeling back my skin.

He nods, face empty as his voice, fingers tense in the sand. "Of course. This is horrible."

He won't meet my eyes. "Please, understand. I didn't ever want to lie to you. Or to do this to you. I didn't realize they'd gone as far as they have. What they're doing now . . . it was never my intention. They twisted the work."

"Far enough to create a monster like me."

It stabs me in the heart. He blames me. He thinks he's a monster and that I'm the engineer of that devolution. Any argument I can make about how I didn't know, how I didn't intend for this to happen, how I tried to stop it, seems as insubstantial as the fog that surrounds us.

"I'm sorry." The words come out strangled. Like I've never said them before. Maybe I haven't. Not when it actually mattered. I have a million tiny techniques to avoid blame. To shift attention. To shirk consequences.

He doesn't respond. Just swipes one broad hand over the map, scattering the carefully rendered shapes to oblivion. It feels like he's wiping away any possibility of something between us, too. Maybe I was fooling myself that there ever could be . . . even just friendship.

Who am I kidding? I don't want friendship with him. Never have. I watched a video of him like a creeper for days. Even when he half terrified me, he still compelled me in ways that do not speak of buddyhood.

And he hasn't been terrifying for a good long time.

Because now *I'm* the scary one. The person who helped Pierce separate people from their humanity. Who didn't do enough to stop them. A sharp ache stabs in my chest and I rub at my breast-bone with my knuckles, willing it to go away. It refuses. When Levi leaves, climbing up the black stone steps to the dark chamber above, the night presses in around me, still and quiet.

. . . . .

The next morning is just as cold, just as foggy, and just as fraught with emotional awkwardness. Levi does not appear to have come around on my contribution to human experimentation. Not that I expected him to. It's the kind of confession I've been too terrified to share with people who've known me for years. The type of guilt that spurred a lifelong suspicion of anyone who looks Pierce and drove me to come here on my own out of ego and a misplaced thought that I could save the day enough to undo my past. I don't know why I thought someone directly impacted by said past might take it well. How he might understand that this was manipulated science, not bad intent. He hikes up in the front with Victory and Donovan as we trek farther up the mountain on the trajectory to the closest peak and then to the plateau.

Victor walks in the back with me.

"It's nice of you to keep me company," I say in a low voice. I appreciate having someone next to me. It helps to keep my brain from running in crazy circles.

"Hm?" He glances in my direction, one pale brow raised. "I'm here because someone who can shoot needs to take the tail end of the group. That's why Victory is taking the lead."

Welp. That puts me in my place. "Have you ever done something so bad that it's unforgivable?"

"I've lost track of the people I've killed, Caro. Yeah. I've done some bad stuff."

I glance out through the fog, its thick fingers curling so close I feel like I could brush my fingers over it like silk. "They were trying to kill you, too. That's different than when it impacts innocents."

He grunts under his breath. "War always impacts innocents. Anyone who thinks otherwise is fooling themselves."

"What would you say if you came face-to-face with one of them, and they asked you to explain yourself?" The key question. Clearly, I don't know what to say. Not even to myself.

"You ever consider that saying something isn't your job?"

"What do you mean?"

"I've cracked this exceptionally creative code of yours, so how about I just speak frankly? His voice was taken away. Probably for years. It's not your job to talk to him. It's your job to listen to him and then he can tell you what he needs." Victor rolls big shoulders and glances to each side so subtly it's almost unnoticeable.

I blink. "This is very emotionally mature for you."

"I'm an emotionally mature person. I'm surprised you haven't noticed." He tweaks a setting on his blaster carefully. "The ladies love that shit. Hey, want to see if I can shoot that tree just over Victory's shoulder?"

It's not my job to talk. It seems like it should be. Like I should be able to fix this. I've spent my whole life fixing things. I'm good at it. If I just try hard enough, I can make *anything* work.

But Levi isn't a thing.

I mean, obviously. I just got so wrapped up in trying to force things to be right that I didn't really think beyond that. Because I'm a priap.

A moment late, my brain catches up to the rest of Victor's statement. "No, absolutely you should not shoot that tree. She'll think someone's firing at her and return fire."

"I know. That would be fun. This is dull."

Yes, other people's emotional epiphanies tend to be that way.

Since he's in the mood to drop truth, and also because I want to distract him from the whole shooting thing, I decide to ask a question I've wanted the answer to for years. I've watched Victor move through women like the *Calamity* moves through berths—a new one every week. But never me. There was a time when I wanted it to be, although that time has long past. "Why were you never interested in me? I've seen you go after nearly every woman you've ever seen, even Temper, but never me."

He cocks that brow at me again. "Look at me, Caro. I shoot things when I'm bored. I go around killing people for a living. I'm addicted to adrenaline, and I spend all my free time with my sister. You're too smart for me. You have too many morals for me. You're too good for me and I know I'd never quite measure up to the person you think I could be. That's a miserable way to live."

"I think you're selling yourself a little bit short, there." I laugh, mostly in disbelief. The trees loom over the slick stone path almost like a blue-green tunnel, creating a feeling of isolation and privacy. "You're brave and generous and a protector. You'd measure up for anyone."

He half turns to me, arms open wide, a sunny smile on his face. "Great point. I'm excellent. Let's run off into the woods and make babies."

I laugh, gaze darting to the front of our little group, where Levi's broad shoulders slump next to Victory's perfectly straight posture.

"Ah. Yes. Also that." Victor drops his arms, one patting me on the shoulder as it goes down. "I'm not for you, Caro. And I think you know that."

I do. I'm starting to think there may only be one person for me and he just wrote me off as a mad scientist.

We're past the temples by the time that we set up camp in a small black stone cave. The mouth of the cave is pointed away from Shikigami and, with the fog thick as it is, Victor and Victory decide that the risk of a fire is manageable. Cold and wet as I am, I was ready to throw caution to the wind last night, so I appreciate that they're keeping their wits about them since I clearly am not.

Victor adjusts his blaster to continuous mode and slices firewood from a downed tree. The guys haul the wood while I gather kindling. I assume I'm going to see some fantastic merc-taught fire-starting trick. Victory goes wide-aperture and shoots the kindling.

"It's wet, I don't think a blaster will work as a fire-starter when it's this wet," Donovan helpfully points out.

The smile she gives him could only be called "blistering." She shoots the kindling again. By the third time, smoke rises. "That's why I'm heat-drying it first."

She narrows the diameter of the collimated beam and fires again. A little flame blooms.

It follows that the merc trick would be shooting wet kindling until it catches fire.

The firelight is warm on Levi's face. It's a good face. Turned away from me as he converses with Donovan. I wipe my hand over the back of my neck, twitchy with my desire to try to say something, but Victor was right. I need to let Levi come to me on his terms, if ever. Until then, I just need to focus on getting him to safety. We're close to the top of the mountain now, which means about two days from the plateau. No signs of Pierce following us yet. No signs of the fog letting up either.

That doesn't mean it's easy. The night stretches long, and eventually, I fall asleep looking at the firelight dancing on the ceiling of the cave.

When I wake up for watch, I set myself up in the mouth of the cave, staring out at the dark. As the fog moves, wisps of starlight almost penetrate the water in the air. I brush a hand over my hair, and it comes away wet.

Two coin-bright eyes blink at me from the dark. I blink back. It only seems polite.

Two more come from the other side. Ah. A pincer movement of cuddliness. I retrieve a little of the protein goop. We have a lot of it, and without a stable temperature-controlled environment, it will go bad before we can finish it off. No leaves are handy so I pour it on a nearby rock and move away.

I wish Itzel was here. She'd love these little things. I absently draw a little sketch of one in the dirt as it approaches, just barely visible in the firelight. I was right. Adorable. Small enough that I could lift it as easily as a cat but it's denser in build. Its face and body are covered in fluffy reddish fur, and a sort of crest of iridescent oil-black feathers sprouts from the back of its head and runs down its spine. It has three thin tails that constantly twine and untwine around each other, a long muzzle, and pointed ears.

It's hard to tell with the level of fluff, but I think that it has six legs. The two in the front and the back are longer, the two in the middle are shorter and curl inward, like a child holding its belly. Each foot is bedecked with sharp black claws.

They love protein, so it follows that they'd be predators.

It licks the goop and cheeps, and the second one joins it at the rock. This one is the same reddish tone, but its feathers are more of a mottled gray-green. Maybe a sex difference, maybe just a unique characteristic. I name the one with black feathers Night and the one with green feathers Day because green is the center of the human daylight visual spectrum and also it goes with night.

This is why they don't usually let me name things on the ship.

Night and Day slurp up the protein and turn back to me with gigantic pleading eyes. I hold up my hands to show that they're empty. Night licks the last strains of protein from its muzzle, displaying a small row of razor-sharp teeth.

Day nips at one of its tails. Night leaps in the air, casting a betrayed look behind it, and Day sprints off into the darkness, its sibling or mate in close pursuit. I wonder at the evolutionary purpose for their middle arms. Maybe carrying small prey? Or climbing? Itzel would probably know.

A whipcrack of thunder sounds above, echoing through the mountains. Thunder that isn't thunder at all.

"What was that sound?" Donovan's voice comes from close behind me. I was so distracted I didn't even notice that he was awake. "Is it going to storm on top of everything else?"

"Sonic boom." I stand up from my crouch and wipe my hands on my pants. My stomach clenches and twists. "Carmichael's backup has arrived. We have to pick up our pace."

CHAPTER 19

■ ■ ■ ■ ■ ■ ■ ■ ■ ■ ■ ■ ■ ■ ■

VICTORY

The big guy trudges beside me for another day, as morose as he was the day before. Even when we finally crest the mountain, little wisps of fog surround us as we stand on the layers of black rock, almost like a gigantic cairn, and look over a massive mountain range. The plateau is right where Caro told us it would be. Looks close, but Leviathan assures me with the confidence of someone either very good or very stupid that it's over one more day's walk, given the need for stealth and the conditions.

"You done pouting yet?" I'm bored. Pierce hasn't done any more flyovers but I'm sure they will soon. And now we're in much lighter fog. I don't know if I trust it to block scanners. Waiting for peril is my least favorite kind of boredom. Donovan is drifting off to each side, poking the plants and jerking his finger away when it starts to hurt, clearly even less used to long marches than I am.

Leviathan swings his head up like a soldier aiming a weapon. "Are you talking to me?"

"Is anyone else pouting? Besides Caro, that is."

"I'm not pouting," he pouts.

I raise a brow. "Sure. That's what not pouting sounds like. Surly. Martyrish."

He snorts and turns his focus from me to the road ahead. I still don't completely trust him. I saw him plow through the prison, smashing people indiscriminately as he went. I saw his face when he fought Caro in the maze. This Leviathan *might* be a good person. The other one isn't. "'Martyrish' isn't a word. 'Martyred' is."

"Fine. Martyred. Feel better now? Less pouty?" Caro is going to keep taking this to heart until they talk. I'm not used to her being silent. Don't like it.

"She thinks I'm a monster."

Oh. That's different than expected. Still pouting, for anyone keeping track. Also, I don't think it's true. People don't look at monsters the way Caro looks at him. At least not the kind of monster he's thinking about. Maybe the kind with vampiric charm on *Pulsar Passions*. "You're doing a bang-up job proving otherwise. I'm sure you had a conversation with her about how your feelings were hurt by the whole monster thing and you expected better from her and how you're all man except when you sometimes go a little murder crazy. Which—come to think of it—could still be all man."

"I'm not upset that she said it. I'm upset that she's right. I remember more and more about what I am. But I also remember more about what I *did*. Bits and pieces but it's coming back. I'm afraid that, when it's completely back, I'll lose myself again. Last night, right after Pierce arrived, I had the strangest flicker. It's like I left my body just for an instant. I *know* that feeling. If that happens, I could kill her. I could kill any of you."

I'd like to see him try.

When I don't respond, he continues. "I'm a sliver away from him at any instant. It's like I can feel my blood thinning, my hands shaking like I can't control them. I'm *exactly* what she thinks I am. The other me has some sort of fascination with her. If he comes back, if I even think he might, I'm running as far as I can in the other direction."

Oh boy. This is a mess. The sticky emotional kind that I do my best to avoid. "You need to talk to her. You're both torturing yourselves for no reason."

"She won't even look at me."

I want to smack myself in the head. No. I want to smack *them* in the head. I should not be the responsible adult in this or any situation. My hands twitch. I pull out my knitting, letting the spare yarn pool in my pocket as I continue to stitch the little square on my needle. Roughly 50 percent of the reason for knitting is to keep my hands busy so I don't slap people. It really is a constant struggle. "She won't look at you because she thinks you hate her for her part in what Pierce did and she's giving you space to have your feelings without making it about her." I wait a second. Can't resist. "Obviously."

He gives me a look like I'm insane. *"How is that obvious?"*

"She apologized to you. You stomped off. Pouting. It's a logical assumption that you're angry with her. And a mature decision to let you work it out." I leave out the part where the mature part was, bewilderingly, at Victor's suggestion. The least likely person ever to make a mature decision. Maybe he's sleeping with a therapist. I turn the needle, starting a new row.

Leviathan's still giving me that look. I've meddled enough. I just want to get through this mission without the both of them staring at each other from afar like lovelorn fools. It doesn't seem like too much to ask.

"It's just . . ." He trails off, turning his focus out into the fog, lips pressed into a tight line. Kind of like he might vomit. I hope he doesn't. "I am capable of things that are horrifying. I've *done* things that are horrifying. I don't remember even half of it but what I do remember . . . it's gruesome."

I'm more comfortable in this territory. Mercs come in a spectrum between two types. Psychopaths or heroes. Psychopaths thrive on the destruction. Heroes thrive on fighting for the side of good and right and all that business. Victor's a hero. I'm closer to the center. I wouldn't do this if he didn't need me at his back.

Anyway, the hero types want to be the good guy. They're

protectors. That means that the violence eats away at them. I've spent many a night on a war-torn planet consoling someone on my crew. Leviathan might think he has a gruesome past, but it probably doesn't compare to what I've seen. Not that it's a competition. "And you wonder if you're worthy of happiness."

"Yes. No. I don't fucking know. I barely know who I *am*. Not enough. It's like I'm not a whole person."

"You won't find completion with her." *Well.* "You won't find *that* kind of completion with her. That's something else. You're only a monster if you choose to be. Generally, monsters don't worry about their monstrous state. You might never remember your past. One thing I can say is, even if you do, you won't be that man again. Better figure out what kind you want to be with your new reality. Better than pouting, at least." I'm pushing him on purpose. He doesn't need sweetness. Or if he does, he can get that from Caro. I internally snicker . . . because she's so sweet.

Except with him, she seems to be.

"I wish you'd stop saying that." There's a welcome edge in his voice.

Donovan approaches us from behind. "What the incredibly cruel mercenary is saying is, go and romance your woman before you make her feel so awful about herself that you've lost the opportunity."

I was actually just trying to keep him from dissolving into metaphoric fog. Not my job to get Caro laid. Should be someone's, though. Clearly, she's not handling it well. "Sure, that, too."

Leviathan drifts backward. Not as far back as Caro, who is hugging the end of the line with such dedication that I've only been able to talk to my twin when we camp at night. Victor shoots a blast over my shoulder, the spark of the beam smacking into a broad pale-green leaf dead center, like he knows I'm thinking about him. I lift a hand in a wave, index finger twirling in a vulgar gesture.

"Was that for me? I'd be delighted." Donovan slips into Leviathan's place. I already miss the big man.

"It was not for you." I have to nip this in the bud. No one needs a criminal dogging her tracks. Caro's criminal seems to have a heart of gold. Donovan has a heart of fertilizer. Something may grow there eventually but, until then, it's just shit.

"What'd you do to piss Pierce off?" I try to redirect away from a topic that's dangerous for the both of us.

"What do any of us do to anger the lofty ruling class? I survived."

"That's an answer without being an answer."

"It's a very personal question. I could demand something of equal value in exchange." Although his voice has no edge at all, I recognize the uneasy deflection for what it is.

I wonder what it would be like to spar with him physically instead of with words. He'd fight dirty. I'd win, of course, but he might put me through my paces. "No need. Is it personal? Will they look for you or will they ignore your disappearance?"

He coughs out a rough laugh, head tossed back, that reddish hair glowing in the diffuse light. "You think *my* disappearance matters? You just stole their prize lab rat and are trying to set him up with your friend. They'll chase you to the ends of the chart purely out of spite."

I assume Caro has a plan about the chasing since her entire life goal seems to have become bringing Pierce down. I'm equally sure that I don't trust Donovan with that plan. "I guess you shouldn't have allied with us if we're so imperiled."

"You are *so* dedicated to not being fun. It only makes me want to bother you more."

Something large moves in the fog, just past Donovan. I shove him backward with my shoulder. The shadow is the size of a small transport pod. I drop the knitting to the ground and draw my blaster. "To the right!"

Leviathan, the noble idiot, tries to move in front of me. Donovan, the ignoble idiot, is very content to stay at my back. In this one case, Donovan is the correct one. Leviathan might have the build and heart of a warrior but it's clear from his reactions that he doesn't have any actual training. That sort of thing is beat so hard into a person that it's impossible to shake free. It's muscle memory.

I kick the back of Leviathan's knee, dropping one of his legs to the ground, and circle back around him. "I'm the one with the blaster. I take the lead. You can avenge my beautiful corpse if it gets past me."

"Another circling to the rear!" Victor calls from behind us. I edge the others back as he moves them forward, leaving us with a more tightly defensible clump. The sound of steel on steel comes from behind me. Donovan retrieving some of his cached knives. "I told you the smoke monsters were real."

Victor loves an alien cryptid. He believes in every single tale he hears with the enthusiasm of a new convert to a dubious religion. I scoff at them all. It's provided us with hours of conversations on long-haul trips. "The smoke monsters they talked about dissolve into poisoned fog. They're more air than matter. This, out there, it has a lot of matter."

"Real. Just misunderstood," he rebuts.

My particular shuttle-sized creature stays in the fog, deep enough that I can make out its form but not its actual details. It moves to the right. "They're circling. Just two but hunting as a pair."

"Oh!" Caro yelps as two tiny forms shoot out of my peripheral vision and dance around her feet. The massive shapes freeze. A low rattling sound emanates from the fog.

I edge to the side, keeping the smoke monster in view but capturing the new arrivals in my peripheral vision. Small. Fluffy. Reddish. Looking at Caro like she's holding a delicious steak.

Oh no. "Tell me you haven't been feeding them."

She grimaces and lies badly. "I haven't been feeding them."

"Fuck, Caro. You don't feed the wildlife. That's rule one. You scout planets for a living. Those fuzzy idiots are probably dinner and we just got in the middle of a hunt." One of the big shapes edges closer. I shoot a branch near it. "Get back!"

"Right, because they understand human language."

"I don't have time for you, Victor."

"You always have time for me, Victory."

The huge form barrels forward. I only have time for a few flashes of perception. Speed. A massive shaggy red frame. Sharp green-gold feathers flared like a mane. Teeth. So many teeth. Just all the teeth that have ever been formed. I get off a shot before I realize my blaster is still set in stun mode. *Human* stun mode. It doesn't do a fucking thing.

Lots of people are yelling.

A knife flies over my shoulder from behind. Victor's blaster whines.

Something . . . chirps?

The gigantic monster freezes yet again. This time close enough for me to smell its breath. Bad, in case anyone wondered. Two things strike me. One, the smoke monsters are clearly *not* starving as Victor predicted. Two, this isn't a hunt.

Caro has been feeding *baby* smoke monsters.

A furry little ball shape tumbles past my legs and bounces in front of its parent. It has dull green head feathers. A long snaky tongue winds out of the large beast and smooths a rough patch of red fuzz on the baby. Three massive sapling-sized tails thrash in agitation. I take a step back and run into something furry. I almost start shooting but remember Donovan's stupid coat. I'm very glad it isn't red fur. That would be an awkward moment.

A chuffing sound comes from behind me. I risk a glance over

my shoulder. An even bigger smoke monster emerges, its feathers so black that they seem like night made solid. It has two long curving saber-shaped fangs dropping from its narrow muzzle. I glance back to mine. Also fangs, but smaller. The size of my hands rather than my feet. Still plenty dangerous.

Not attacking yet. The baby is chirping at it more, little feathers flaring and flattening in turn. The adult looks at me with shiny yellow eyes.

"Nice teeth." Compliments make everyone happy, right?

Donovan's voice rasps in my ear. "Maybe don't remind it that it has teeth."

"Give me the protein, Donovan," Caro commands from the center of our huddle. Leviathan's so wrapped around her that she's basically wearing human armor. He's brave, I'll give him that.

"What? No! That's our food."

Thieves never like to relinquish their ill-gotten gains. "We're *their* food. I'm happy to offer an alternative food if Caro has one."

Movement from behind me. I assume it's Donovan removing the protein guck from one of his interior pockets. Caro mutters to anyone who will listen, "Get me some leaves."

My hands are full of weapons and will fucking well stay that way. I assume Victor feels the same. More scuffling sounds. Some wet squirting sounds, and a leaf flies over my shoulder. Caro probably intends it to skid to a halt in front of the creature braced before me.

The protein-laden leaf smacks directly into the creature's face, smearing down the red fur until it plops on the ground.

"Oops." Caro's helpful addition.

I amp up the power on my blaster without even thinking about it, ensuring my feet are braced to withstand a lunge. Which is a joke. If this beast lunges, I'll be flattened into a puddle. I have to shoot before it hits us. Probably should shoot already.

It's just that it has kids. Tiny fluffy predators, but still kids. It's wrong to kill something in front of its children. Victor and I are proof of how poorly it turns out for said children.

It chuffs a heavy breath. That long snakelike tongue licks protein from its face. The baby monster at its feet licks the leaf. "Everyone move one step up the mountain on my count. Three. Two. One."

We take a step. My knitting is still on the ground near the baby. No way am I reaching for it.

Nothing pounces. "Another."

We take another. They don't follow us or even pay us any attention at all. The larger creature is licking protein off the ground. Caro didn't hit *it* in the face. Well, one for two. For her, that's exceptional accuracy. We continue to sidestep up the mountain, eventually leaving the creatures behind.

"You realize we're going to have to keep feeding them." Victor voices my own concern. "They know we're a good food source now. They'll follow us."

The pop of a fast-moving jet flies over us and we all freeze. It's not the first of the day but it is the closest. We don't have much time. My heart is thudding so loudly I can barely hear the stomp of my boots on the rock.

"They'll follow us, *too*," I correct. "Let's not forget that Pierce is actively hunting us. And by the sound of that, getting closer."

"The animals already *were* following us," Caro points out irritably. After her recent silence, I like seeing this return to form.

"We only have one more night to go. I don't trust night hiking with those beasts or else I'd say we should go straight through to the plateau. So instead, we need shelter that will block scanning devices once we're out of the fog." I pick up the pace.

"Those cliffs ahead are gabbro. Old. There will be caves."

I put down the pace. We all stop and stare at Leviathan.

"How do you know those are gabbro? How do you even know

what gabbro is?" Caro shoves the bag of protein back at Donovan while staring at Leviathan like a stranger.

"What *is* gabbro?" Donovan asks.

Obviously, some kind of rock. What kind, I have no idea.

"It's a rock that's often formed in oceanic ridges. When it's found in mountains, it's generally very old. Prone to weathering due to being so old, so there are frequently caves." Caro has her scouting hat on at last. "Which brings us back to how do you know what it is?"

Leviathan's jaw hardens. "The same way that I know they're about thirteen hundred meters away. Because I'm more than just a monster."

Oh boy. We're back to that already.

CHAPTER 20

The cliffs are, in fact, gabbro. Defensible, dark, and gloomy. Perfect for my mood. Levi's gone from ignoring me to periodically glaring at me. You'd think he'd be excited about getting memories from his real life back, even if they *are* related to igneous rocks. He keeps staring at his hands. I do that a lot also because they're nice hands. Victor won't stop scolding me for feeding the furballs. Of course I know better. It's just . . . they were cute, and I didn't want the fucking protein.

Also I could make the argument that giving them a taste for goop meant that they didn't decide to get a taste for us. So, really, I saved the day here.

When we set up in the cave mouth, my skin is crawling. Too many people in a small space and, after intensive mountain hiking, none of us smells fresh and clean. With increasing Pierce surveillance, we don't dare risk a fire, even in the cave.

"I'm going to explore." I point at a wide crack in the back of the cave wall.

"What if there are violently hungry cave worms?" Donovan blinks tired eyes at me.

"I'll scream really loud, so they don't get you, too." I retreat into the dark, periodic spears of dim light coming from above doing just enough to illuminate my passage. It's not a very perilous cave. The passage is wide and winding but not branched. I think it's actually weaving closer to the edge of the cliffs, like it might connect with another cave.

The rock around me rattles as a Pierce vessel does a low flyby. I clench my jaw. They can fly wherever they want. They won't sense us through the rock. They must be scanning for a camp out in the forest.

The narrow passageway opens to a broad cave that faces directly down the cliff. The wind is stirring, and every so often, I can see the glowing lights from the departing vessel. But that's not the big thing. The big thing is the wide dark pool of water with thick steam rising from its surface.

If I were a good person, I'd immediately tell everyone about the amazing find. I'm not a good person, though, and I quickly strip out of my Shikigami-issued clothing and slip into the water. There's an argument that I need to stay dressed and ready for action. There's also an argument that if I get killed tonight, I'd like to die clean. I'm as safe as I can be for the moment and I can't let fear drive me.

The water is hot. Almost too hot. Every muscle in my body relaxes and my head falls back on the hard rock rim of the spring.

I think I whimper a little.

"Are you okay?" Levi lurches into the cave, looking all around for the gruesome enemy that pulled that sad little noise from my throat.

I yelp, splashing around in the hot spring like a newly birthed infant. Naked as one, too. I've imagined being naked with Levi, but those fantasies involved *both* of us being naked and also me doing about one million crunches before the critical unveiling. I swallow a mouthful of water and gag on it.

If all the floundering didn't make me appealing, I'm sure the hacking noises are helping.

No bath for me. Instead, I get to face the consequences of my own actions. While naked. Not that I don't deserve it, it's just that it's been a long day and I'm exhausted. I let the drones do the climbing for me, usually. That's what they're there for.

I finally get my breath. "I'm fine. I suppose you want to talk."

Do I sound churlish? I just wanted to sit in the warm dark and lick my wounds.

"Do you think I'm a monster?" He asks the question baldly, facing me like he's expecting a blow.

"No. Do you think *I'm* a monster?" I don't ask it baldly. I ask it with a lot of hair. By which I mean I sort of mumble it under my breath.

He's standing close to the water. Too close. The wet sticky warmth from the hot springs combines with the soft air and his large capable body to be overwhelming. I'm suddenly overheated. I paw sweat from the back of my neck and then duck lower under the water because that gesture left little of me to the imagination.

He's not answering.

I force myself to meet his eyes, pale in the dark of the cave. He holds my gaze, moving closer with careful deliberation. He steps down into the spring. Walks forward into the water until it's up to his waist, drenching his clothes, and he's right in front of me. "I think I've made it clear. I don't think you're a monster. You're an angel, fearsome and powerful and sacred."

Unf.

I absorb the words like a hit in my solar plexus. I know what that feels like now after the prison fight. "But I'm responsible—"

"Ah." He traces his fingers from my mouth up over my cheekbone, around the shell of my ear and to the back of my head, his touch feather-light. His gaze never leaves my eyes. "I'm beginning to see the root of the problem."

"What is that?" I attempt to stiffen my voice with bravado even as that slow gentle touch untethers me.

He ducks his head, stoops his shoulders, brings his face in alignment with my own. "It isn't that you think I'm a monster or

I think you are. It's that we both think that we are ourselves." He pauses, like the words just dawned on him, before straightening.

Somehow my fingers have found their way to the front of his coveralls, curling in the fabric against his chest in a gesture that I'm not sure is meant to hold him away or to pull him closer. Maybe shake him because I'm naked and we're in a hot spring and he wants to talk about our *feelings* instead of any of the other much less difficult things we could be doing right now.

I'm old-fashioned. I suppress my feelings until I forget about them and they burst out in inappropriate bouts of anger.

But also, he's right.

I puff out a slow stream of air. Close my eyes so I don't have to look at him. If we're going to have this talk, we might as well have it honestly. That doesn't mean I have to look at his face when I show all my gooey inner ugliness. "I ran away. It's not that I did it in the first place. That part is bad enough, but I was naive, and they weren't honest and there are excuses. It's that when I found out, I undid my own work and ran away. I hid, assuming I'd stopped them but—why would I assume that? I'm one person and they're a megalith. Of course they were still experimenting. I could have reported them to—*someone*. I didn't. And because of that, they continued in the shadows.

"I might not be a monster, but I'm a coward and maybe that's even worse." Each word hurts to say.

Silence stretches. The water ripples against my skin. Levi breathes, chest expanding and contracting beneath my fingers.

"Prey isn't cowardly for hiding when a predator is on the prowl." His voice is quiet enough I almost need to lean even closer to hear him. Part of me flinches at being considered prey but, compared to a Family, anyone is soft and vulnerable and exposed. He keeps his hands carefully at his side but doesn't move away from me. "You can't change what you did. Any more than I can change what I've done—what I assume I've done."

There's another flicker of silence. Like when a station's circuits are overtaxed and can't quite sustain the power requirements. I feel like my mind is that circuit. Naked, faced with my past, with my shame, with a very attractive man who wants to talk things out. I've had nightmares better than this. "But that doesn't *undo* what we've done, does it?"

The silence agrees. It stretches again as we consider consequences and reparations.

"Tell me the truth." He shifts his weight. Even though his voice is mild, I can tell that this question is of grave importance. "Did I ever hurt you?"

Complicated.

It could easily be handled with a lie but that wouldn't be fair to either of us. "Yes. And no. In the arena, when you were being directly piloted, you grabbed my arm. Might have broken it, I'm not sure because it was fixed by the time I woke up. Later, you tried and missed. But that wasn't you, not really. It was what they—I— did to you."

He nods. "And you hurt me, indirectly. When they were piloting you, through manipulation."

"I could say my intentions were good but . . . good intentions don't fix engines. That's action. And my actions have all been suspect."

"Including the action that sent you here, now?"

"I suppose not that one." But is vengeance the same as honor? I came here to stick it to Pierce. I didn't foresee what else I'd find.

He shifts a fraction of a step closer and the water laps at my skin. "I don't know what I did to get in this situation, in a prison. I don't know who I hurt back when I was myself before they erased me. I don't even know who I am. Maybe I'm cruel. Maybe I'm worse than I am when I'm Leviathan."

Neither of us knows. But . . . "I can't imagine what it would be like to have no memories. Even the ones I regret. I also can't believe that you would be cruel. Nothing in the real you speaks of cruelty."

"I'm afraid of turning back into him—of the great violence he casually inflicts. But I'm just as terrified of learning who I really am." His face looks like it's carved of stone, scarred and rough and capable of shattering with just the right application of force. "Either way, I could hurt a lot of people. I could hurt you. Again."

My chin hitches up. "I'm not so easily hurt. Besides, no matter who you were, you're someone new now. Or, at least, you can be if you want to."

"Victory said something like that, too. The problem is, I don't know who he is yet. Or even, really, who I want him to be."

I open one hand flat against his chest, feeling his breath, his heat, flexing my fingers gently against the rough fabric of his coveralls. "You don't have to know that yet. You'll figure it out. We'll figure it out together. And by 'together' I mean with the help of some excellent therapists." My eyes dart down again, studying the surface of the water. "If you want to, that is."

His big hand catches me under the chin, tipping my face up until our gazes meet and lock like magnets. "And you think you're a coward? The woman who got herself incarcerated just to do the right thing. Who outsmarted me in the maze. Who escaped a prison? Who did it all while being so fucking kind, I can't even believe you're real?"

Kind? No. I'm snippy and caustic and defensive.

I open my mouth to respond. I don't even know what my response is and, as it turns out, it doesn't matter. His lips drop to mine, as gentle and soft as his touch. They brush against me like a whisper. A plea.

A promise.

I puff out a little breath, half moan, half promise of my own. My fingers lift up, curling over his shoulders, marveling in their breadth. They dig into the muscle, eager for more warmth, more intensity, more of that singularity of focus that he seems completely capable of. I remember our first kiss, in the lab, and the knowing gleam in his eyes as his lips met mine.

But then, he stops kissing me. He steps away. The water laps against my needy and still very naked body. I freeze. Is this all a part of some awful joke? Is my breath horrible? Is this the same thing that always happens, where I'm a great person but really not lover material? Just a little too much. Not comfortable. Not easy. Not—

He unzips his coveralls.

Unzips them right down to his waist and then beyond, although that movement is obscured by the water. The open fabric gapes in the front. Even in such a humid environment, somehow, my mouth goes entirely dry. I forget to blink. Maybe to breathe. Those are supposed to be automatic impulses, but my nervous system has completely shut down, just replaying that smooth unzipping motion in my mind over and over again until my knees also lose some of their support. My hand reaches blindly behind me and finds the hard support of the stone edge of the spring.

"What are you doing?" I know what he's doing but there's the off chance that *he* doesn't know what he's doing. Maybe this is some weird fail-safe of his chip where it waits a while and makes him get naked.

Good fail-safe.

He shrugs his shoulders from the coveralls. It's a big shrug and the fabric falls to the surface of the water with a wet smack like skin on skin. "It should be obvious what I'm doing."

I don't know what to do with *myself.* Some noble impulse tells me to get out of the spring and save him from my terrible influence. I grab it by the neck and shove it under the water. I'm done with nobility. He knows what he's doing—as well as any of us do, at least. But then the other doubts creep in. What if my breath *is* bad? What if I don't have any actual skills? I have a *few* moves. None of them aquatic.

While I've been having a minor crisis, he bends down, reaching under water, then stands as he chucks his sodden coveralls out of the spring. My salivary glands finally kick into gear and I'm afraid I might drool. He's . . . a lot. I don't know where to look, so I look everywhere, eyes tracing his body like he's a topographical map I have to memorize.

Water beads on his light tan skin, glistening in the dim light, a broad expanse like a star field. His chest is powerful in a way that has to do with utility rather than aesthetics. Nothing wasted but a surplus of everything. Small strips of raised scar tissue highlight where mods were added. I swallow hard. The hard line of his abdomen sinks beneath the water. If only it was a little shallower.

Then again, if it was any shallower, I may be sprinting deeper in the cave because I'm already having my doubts about our physical compatibility.

Soft doubts. Ones that the clamor of hormones are successfully overwhelming.

"My face is up here." His low voice clenches every muscle in my stomach. I drag my eyes from the waterline and up to meet his heated gaze.

"It's a good face." And it is. Broad and hard with a square jaw and a wide nose. Two days of stubble have grown in on his head and face, a shadow that softens its harshness. "My breasts are down here."

I swear I can see the heat flare in his eyes as he studies me. "They're good breasts."

"Are you sure you remember how to do this?"

Oops. Sometimes I should think *without* speaking. That wasn't meant to be a challenge.

He's through the water so fast the ripple strikes me after he does, my chest pressed against him, craning my head up to keep his gaze. I won't blink. I won't look away. This is a test. If I flinch, he'll think himself the monster.

I have no desire to flinch.

"It sounds like you're laying down a challenge."

I can feel his voice rumbling through his torso like a well-balanced engine. I want to rub against it. Not my normal reaction to an engine. "What if I am?"

"I may not know everything, but I know I'm not the type to back down from a challenge."

The corners of my mouth curl up. "Good. I'm nothing if not challenging."

"I'm beginning to see that." His large arm wraps around me, palm spreading over my back. "You're making me take all the risk, here. Speaking first. Moving first."

"I'm afraid you're going to change your mind." Hells, Caro. Think *without* speaking. Doubt is not sexy. Confidence is sexy. Everyone knows that.

In another one of those inhumanly fast movements, he sweeps a grip to the back of my thighs and hoists me up until I'm all wrapped around him, and we're nose to nose. The noise I make is absolutely not an "eep." It's sultry and seductive.

"Do I look like I'm changing my mind? I just got it back, no changes desired. If I'm deciding who I'll be, my choices are my own." And he kisses me.

Which is like saying "and he pressed a button" when that button activates a beam with the power to destroy a planet. I'm the planet and I'm devastated. This is not the soft gentle tasting of a moment ago. It's hard and hot and hungry and suddenly every fragment of self-doubt and insecurity vaporizes in my mind. One of my arms twines around his shoulders and the other grips the back of his head, holding it in place just in case—just in case.

His fingers squeeze into my thighs, and he makes a low rumbly sound of approval. I've lost track of the sounds I'm making. They're needy and urgent and I feel like I've been waiting for this moment my whole life but never knew what it would be.

To be fair, knowing that I'd be in a hot spring on a prison planet with a former mind-controlled supersoldier was, perhaps, an unlikely prediction.

"You're thinking hard." His hot breath fans across my ear and I almost come on cue.

"What? No, I'm not."

That laugh rumbles through him, causing some very interesting vibrations. "You stopped moving completely."

Oh. I'm lucky he finds that charming instead of insulting. "I was just thinking that this moment would have been difficult to predict."

"Really?" One of his hands moves from my thigh and slides up my leg to cradle my ass. He gives it a squeeze. "I imagined it from the first instant I saw you. Maybe your imagination needs work."

It's been suggested before. "Creativity isn't my thing. Physics. Math. Those are my wheelhouses. I work well within boundaries."

"Oh yes, talk science to me." He licks my ear. "We'll see how long it takes me to distract you."

"Not if I distract you first," I purr and writhe against him, running my tongue along the lower edge of his lip. "I plan to entangle all your particles until they vibrate in harmony with my own."

His hand leaves my behind, wrapping around and brushing forward until a finger traces over my greedy core.

Electricity jolts through my body. I bite his earlobe. "Let's solve an equation of two bodies colliding at slow velocity."

"Slow velocity." His thumb scrolls back and forth. My legs tighten around his waist. "I'm not feeling slow, angel."

"The fun part of physics is that you can solve for any speed."

"Or acceleration, I assume." More fingers join the game, dancing at the entrance to my body.

"Always acceleration," I gasp. "Very important."

"I'm discovering an unrealized fascination in physics." One wide finger delves inside. "Tell me more."

I swallow. The gleam of reflected light in his sea-glass eyes is hungry and eager, studying my face like I'm a star chart and he's adrift. I'm utterly lost myself.

"The most important thing about physics . . ." I rock my hips as his fingers continue to dance on and in me, a slow pleasing warmth building within me that has nothing to do with the hot spring. "The faster we go, the longer it takes."

He covers my mouth with his, tongue delving deep, battling with my own as the pace of his fingers intensifies. My body activates, like a switch was flipped, and I tumble into orgasm, back arching and eyes fluttering open just to lock in his gaze. The moment stretches, extends, time dilation made real. I've never wanted to live in an instant more than this one right now.

When I crash down, I'm safe in his arms, and his face looks . . . satisfied. A little bit smug. The good kind, where a man is immensely proud of the effect he's had. As he should be. If I caused someone to come undone as easily as he just did, I'd be proud, too.

Challenge accepted.

I give a little squirm and he lets me slide down his body. I hit a significant speed bump on the way down. The iron bar of his erection slicks along my sweat-soaked skin as I slip into the water. It's hot.

So is the water.

I blink up at him, lazily sated but nowhere near done. My fingers trace down his chest, dancing in beads of water and sweat, skating over raised scars, and flat brown nipples that peak as I pass them, and hard muscles, until finally, they reach their goal.

I wrap my fingers around that hard member and nearly pass out. I don't think Pierce messed with that. Some people are just born lucky. "Something something rigid bodies."

His lips press against my own, firm and just a little bit desperate. I like that desperation. It makes me feel like I've never felt before. Feminine. Powerful. Needy for more.

And so I shall have it.

Except, when I move to take it—more, I mean, to take *more* of it—he lunges through the steaming water, sending splashes rippling over my skin and rushing over the edge of the spring. I barely recognize the motion before my back is pressed against stone and he's flush against my front, holding both of my hands in his own.

"With your permission . . ." His breath is short and urgent, his voice rough as the stone. The press of his fingers on my wrists is gentle but firm. "I haven't been myself in a very long time. I haven't been in control for a very long time."

I understand. And that last orgasm made me inclined to be amenable. "You have my permission. So long as I get my turn next time."

Look at me, confident enough to assume there will be a next time.

His grin flashes vibrant and white. Whiter than it should be in the dark. I glance around the cave, hoping desperately no one wandered in with a light to ruin our fun.

No lights. No invaders.

Clusters of glowing blue-white luminescent mushrooms sprout from every crevice in the rough stone walls of the cave, casting a cool glow over us. Leviathan's gaze follows my own, softening in wonder. When his eyes return to me, the wonder remains. He takes in my face, releasing my wrists to trace his hands down the sides of my neck and over my shoulders until they hit the water lapping gently just above my breasts. His thumbs trace over my nipples, jolting sparks to the insatiable bundle of nerves at the apex of my thighs.

With another flash-fast movement, he scoops me up and sets me on the edge of the spring and then steps back, admiring me. Cold wet air snaps at my passion-drugged senses. I gasp, arms shooting out to brace myself.

The stark unmasked hunger in his eyes makes my hands shake. His face goes intent. A hunter scenting prey. I guess that makes me prey.

"You're beautiful. Like an avenging angel come to ground."

Normally, I'd scoff at that kind of thing. But the one thing about Levi is that he doesn't lie. There's no obfuscation in him. Unbelievable as it may be, he does think I look like an avenging angel, and I cannot bring myself to correct his delusion.

"No one sees me that way." It's something like magic to be looked at by his eyes. To be seen by them. I'm not usually the sort of person to talk in moments like this. My mind goes blank, and my body goes needy, and sweet nothings aren't close at hand. But this is different. *He's* different. And he deserves to know how I see him, too. "You're kind and clever. You have the body of a demigod, which may not be your doing, but no one's body ever is, really. Your eyes glow like a nebula and your penis is a little intimidating."

He laughs. A good kind of laugh. Joyful and a little proud. It rolls over me, warm as the steam from the spring. The luminescent blue light paints every angle of his skin, highlighting the planes of his cheekbones, the shadows at his collar. It's like he's coated in magic.

"Spread your legs." The firm brush of confident command in his voice has them parting of their own will. His eyes gleam with approval and the corner of his mouth curls up. I grip the rock at the edge of the spring.

As he slides forward, graceful as a predator, Levi hits shallower water, rising from it like the demigod I named him. I also see the organ that I only felt earlier and recategorize it. It's not a *little* intimidating.

"Just to be clear, I meant intimidating in a good way, that is. Not like 'oh no, get it away from me.'" I'm still going. I need to shut up. Any moment now. "My mouth gets away from me sometimes."

"Your mouth can feel free to go wherever it wants." He presses himself between my legs. One hand braces my back. The other traces down my side, over my hip, and across my thigh. Exactly where I want those dexterous fingers to be headed. "On another day."

I lick one of his broad flat nipples, tongue flicking over the tip. A growl rumbles, his hands tighten, and suddenly his cock brushes over the entrance of my body.

"Are you ready?" He eases his way into me in a smooth firm slide that would be effortless except he's so fucking big that I pant as I accommodate him. It's a lot. Mostly in a good way. Finally, he stills, our bodies as close as any two can be—sharing breath, heat, flesh—and gazes down at me with barely leashed passion in his eyes.

I've never been more ready in my life. "Try me."

He *moves*.

A smooth stroke in and out. The water sloshes against our legs, the stone slick under my butt, his hands strong and tight at my back, my leg. Holding me open and accessible. He does it again. Slow. Steady. Like a fire branding my skin, torturing every nerve ending in my body until they're all awake and screaming for sensation. Each time, it's a little smoother. A little easier. A little better until suddenly it's about as good as it can get except it somehow *keeps* getting better.

A frisson hums through my nerves, amplifying in feedback

loops until all I feel is static in my bones, under my skin. His fingers join the action. His lips. They trail along my shoulder, my jaw, and then he kisses me, lips firm and heavy. Insistent. I stretch up into his kiss, one hand clasping his cheek, the other clenching his shoulder for support, for stability.

His thumb strums my core right where we meet with the rhythm of a musician. Accelerating until my whole body vibrates in tune with his desire. And then the vibration stops. Explodes. My skin burns like a ship on reentry and a light show plays behind my closed eyelids.

As though that's his cue, he picks up speed, strong and fast and heedless. He doesn't treat me like I'm fragile or like I'm rough. He treats me like I'm *his*. Like we're in sync and always have been. Like the threat I made earlier is true, and our particles are entangled and moving in frequency. I wrap my legs around his waist, my arms around his shoulders. I shake, riding out the storm, equally energized and already sated until, at last, he pumps one last strong thrust into my body and freezes, back muscles going rigid as he experiences his own release.

We freeze like that, wrapped up in each other at the edge of the spring, blue light on our skin and steam dancing around us, for a long time. I trace my fingertips over his shoulder, drawing patterns in the water droplets beading there. "We generate a lot of thermal energy."

"Are you saying that was hot?"

I tilt my neck and kiss just under his jaw. "Yes. I'm saying that was hot."

When we finally part, I realize that there are two huge chunks of stone missing at the edge of the spring on either side of me, like they were wrenched free with violent force.

CHAPTER 21

Eventually, we tell the others about the hot spring. We do not tell them what recently transpired in said hot spring. Probably better for everyone not to know. Victory gives me a narrow suspicious gaze and I flash a cheery grin. Which is probably just the same as a confession because I haven't smiled cheerily for days.

Levi's keeping his cool much better than I am. I might develop a complex about how well he's covering if it were not for the fact that his hands keep finding me in casual touches. The small of my back. My shoulder. His knee brushes against my own when we sit and his shoulder presses against me as he leans over the fire. When I trace my fingers over his hand, it shakes with barely suppressed adrenaline.

We're close to the ship. Pierce and the smoke monsters are close to us. I have to think that we'll make it because the alternative is too horrifying to imagine. We're so close. And for the first time, it feels like I have so much more to lose.

And even once we're in the ship, we still aren't clear.

I'm not optimistic enough to assume this blood thing is a permanent solution. Not even regular transfusions. The body hates invaders. That's why Pierce originally hired me to fool it. Whatever alien mojo is coursing through my body, it's a virus, not a mutation. I have not been fundamentally changed and my immune system is likely hunting down every single speck of bug juice remaining in me. I think of the slight flicker of the diode before I turned Victor's blaster off. Levi got a smaller dose than I did through the transfusion.

Which means, soon as we can get there, I'll probably be able to use my lab on the *Calamity*. Hopefully sooner than that, I'll be able to access that drive and see if they'd made any improvements on my code before it invaded Levi's head. I'm sure they have. It's been years, and confident as I am in my own abilities, I'm sure someone's come along who could improve upon my work. Or at least who insisted on twisting it around and putting their own name on it.

I get a brief flash of panic when I think of this being used on Temper. On Arcadio. I know so many people with cybernetic augmentations. This could turn the tide in a battle in the blink of an eye. Blind soldiers. Turn them against their own. Change their orders. Change their mood. They could even use it at the negotiation table. Subtle or overt.

I wonder if Frederick Reed knew what Pierce wanted to do with the chip he provided. If he was a partner and backed out, or if this is just a negotiation tactic for a higher price and he's fully behind turning people into automatons.

Probably not. Reed tech tends to be more nuanced due to the AI driving it. Frederick wouldn't want something that could work against *himself*. It fits my expectations much more that he saw a partnership with Pierce as an opportunity for quick influence.

I've never been so happy that I'm poor. My interface tattoo could wreak havoc if things went awry but it's on my hand, not in my brain. My *self*. Any other tech I have can be removed. Lenses and heads-up displays and drones. Micah's love of biomods may have saved the crew future misery because any time we've needed healing, he's gone bio instead of tech.

Another Pierce ship races by, so close that it sounds like an avalanche. I clench my fists, glance down at them. I need to know where I stand before they find us.

Victor grudgingly lets me hold his blaster because it's the only tech we have available. It still deactivates when I touch it. It could just be me, but it seems like it takes a little longer to turn off. Hard to tell. It reactivates once it's back in his hands.

Thankfully.

Levi watches the interaction with a worried dark line between his eyebrows. I weave my fingers through his. His hands have a slight tremor. I reassure him instinctively. "I have a solution. All I need to do is get us to our ship."

His other hand flexes at his side. He glances down at it. The little line grows deeper. "We may not have time for that."

A thick pulse of panic flashes through me. "What do you mean? Is something wrong? Do you feel—"

He shakes his head like he doesn't want to answer. It tells me both too much and not enough. I don't even know what it would feel like to lose myself. Is it a slow fade? Or more like a switch? A microsecond flare of previous programming. Whatever it feels like, I'm sure it's terrifying. I smile again, but this time it's forced. "We just need to get to the plateau and the ship faster, that's all."

"Then let's go." Victor activates and deactivates his blaster one more time, checking for any lingering effects.

Today we walk fast in a tight pack. It's still cold. The damp cold that eats at your bones. So cold, in fact, that Donovan, in a late-arrived fit of gallantry, attempts to offer his furry coat to Victory. I'd love to have a holo of her face in that moment. Shocked, appalled, a little disgusted. I know better than to offer a merc cumbersome gear. Or to pretend they're made from anything other than pure unadulterated badassery and moxie. Certainly not flesh and blood.

Levi throws a large warm arm over my shoulders and tugs

me close. Which is good because this is exactly where I want to be, but I didn't want to be that needy person who clings after one night of intimacy. I know what it meant to me. I don't know what it meant to *him*. He's just barely remembering who he is. It wouldn't be surprising if he changed his mind or was just getting something out of his system.

I mean, if that were the case, I'd be quietly devastated and probably print all the chocolate cake–flavored gunk available in the *Calamity*'s galley, but I'd understand. Mind-control trauma is the ultimate excuse.

The slope steepens the higher we get as we climb the plateau, but the fog thins. Soon, rays from the system's sun slant through the thick moisture, golden spears in the gloom.

Victory shoots her blaster. Everyone freezes. The bolt of light reflects from the rounded, polished hip of a black-rock statue. I suck in a breath, try to swallow my heart because it's somehow taken up residence in my throat and it needs to go back where it belongs. The fog swirls in the slight breeze and a whole line of statues is briefly visible. Different forms and poses but they all look victorious. Or seductive. I somehow doubt all the women depicted in these statues had such great tits in real life. No one ever makes a statue with the nipples pointing south.

Donovan laughs, an uncomfortable sound, fear masked as humor. Victor laughs with him. Soon, we're all laughing, Victory sheepishly running a hand through white-blond hair that's started to come out of its tight braid.

A statue shoots back. I'm standing and staring blankly at the line of carved stone when the shot races right over my shoulder and chars an ugly hole in the purple trunk of the tree behind me. I *still* stand staring blankly, every survival instinct I possess gone silent and unhelpful, trying to figure out how the light could have reflected like that when human shapes—real human this time, not stone-carved—emerge from behind the statues, blasters at the ready.

We were so fucking *close.*

Everyone immediately leaps into action. Victory and Victor shoot, backtracking the team until we're behind a rock. Donovan prepares his knives. Levi grabs me like I need to be rescued, which is fair because I'm of no use whatsoever in this situation. Even if I could hold a blaster, which I can't, I couldn't hit the mountain if I was standing on it. I don't have any drones or cannons.

If I were a different person, I'd try throwing my blood at them, but I'm not that person and mostly I like my blood in my body where it belongs.

Temper would probably throw her blood.

Blasts hit the front face of the rock, chipping flecks away. Some fly past us, striking trees. It's a good thing it's so wet here because otherwise that would be a good way to start a fire. Maybe if I point that out, they'll stop shooting at things.

Because Pierce is so well-known for being eco-conscious.

"They're circling around." Victor's back is to the rock, his hair half in his face and his jaw tensed.

"How do you know that?" Is it what he'd do? Something they learn in training?

Victory's position mirrors her brother's on our other side. "Only about half the blasts as when they started firing. Either they slowed down—no reason to—or they're pinning us down so they can come around and snipe us from a better angle."

I frantically glance to each side. Don't see a fucking thing. The mist swirls in the air in front of us, as it has all day, mysterious eddies and flows. Somewhere in the midst of the fear, the tickle of an idea forms. "Donovan, give me the protein goop."

"I don't think they're after our food." His hand goes to his furry coat protectively.

I dive over him and wrestle for the inside pocket. He puts up a struggle but suddenly goes still. When I get up, I have the plas-synth bag in my hand and I'm wondering how I subdued a man who must be a head taller than I am. As it turns out, I didn't. Levi's hand brackets his throat, veins throbbing in his skin. His face is vacant and empty.

"Hey." I turn in the circle of his arms. I press my hands against his arms, his face. He doesn't react. "Leviathan, no. We're on the same side."

It's only then that I realize the name I called him.

After a long pause, his muscles relax. His face goes from vacant to panicked. I squeeze his arm comfortingly, my stomach twisting. Then I clump together a ball of mud and squeeze a hearty dollop of the protein paste on it. I do the same with another and another until I have a small pile of disgustingly goopy projectiles.

I hand one to Donovan and the other to Levi, but he refuses, staring at his own hands like they've suddenly taken on a life of their own. Victor fires a few shots. Victory does the same. A silhouette, human and tactical, appears sneaking around the far side of the boulder and I chuck the paste at it with every bit of strength in my arms. It spatters all over tactical gear.

I hoot in glee, shocked to have actually hit a target, and a blaster shot hits me directly in the arm. There's no momentum to the shot, no force pushing me back. Just a sudden scalding burn in the meaty part of my upper arm that sends me staggering back into Donovan just as he throws his own gob of paste, either intuiting my plan or merely enjoying the turmoil. I try to throw again but my right arm screams at the motion. Instead, I grab another gob with my left and throw to the next soldier. I miss but it hits a tree right next to him, shattering into a shower of protein gunk that rains down on his head.

"Are you trying to make them angry?" Victory barks. "At least throw rocks."

"I have a pla—"

A smoke monster lunges from the fog, flattening the soldier I hit first. The one who shot me. It doesn't feel quite as appalling to watch it sink those blade-sharp fangs into the soldier's face knowing that he shot me.

The soldiers, realizing there's a bigger danger, aim their blasters at the monster, not realizing that it doesn't hunt alone. Its mate plows into the back of the group, scattering them like fruit in a spilled basket.

"Run!" Victory leads us around the boulder, away from the sudden sticky turmoil, which just so happens to be in the wrong fucking direction, but we can't exactly lead them to our ship. I clutch my arm with my other hand, stumbling down the slope, trying to make eye contact with Levi as I go but he won't look at me, his face tense and tight. My blood spatters his coveralls, shockingly bright on the dirty white material.

We run. Victory takes the tail, shooting at anything that moves behind us. Something hits me in the side, sending me stumbling off the narrow trail and into the forest. A soldier with Pierce-blond hair, eyes too close together, and breath that smells like something crawled into his mouth and died. I struggle, throwing knees and poking at his eyes. He's young. Barely old enough to grow a decent beard.

Old enough to be mean, because he sticks a thumb in my blaster shot and I scream, snapping my head forward in a headbutt. An *intended* headbutt. Instead, I smash my face into his, groaning when starbursts fly across my field of view, pain reverberates through my head, and he lists to the side like a drunken seafarer. Then, suddenly, he's gone.

I blink blearily, hand on my face, wondering if it's all still there or if I've flattened it. A flash of motion flickers near me. I roll onto my side, vision finally returning just in time to see Levi standing over me, fist clenched around the jacket of the Pierce soldier as he batters him against a tree. I've seen that move before. In the arena. On a blood-streaked wall covered in metal flowers.

I stumble to my feet and grab Levi's arm. "I'm fine. It's fine."

He shoves me away. I stumble backward, crashing into another tree. Donovan catches up behind me, bracing half my weight.

"What the fuck is wrong with you?" Donovan's voice is missing its signature humor. Levi drops the limp body of the soldier. Victor and Victory backtrack to where we went off the trail, blasters out. Levi blinks, a strange emotion swimming across his face.

"Everyone alive?" Victory barks.

We nod.

"Then what the fuck are you doing standing around here? Go."

We run around the base of the plateau. At some point, people stop shooting. The mist clears but the surface of the mountain gets craggier, providing tons of hidey-holes to hunker down in as we wait for the ship.

My breath is raw and ragged in my throat. My arm hurts. My face hurts. My back hurts because getting tackled is the worst. One of the worst. I have a lot of sensations vying for worst after this little escapade. One is the look I see on Levi's face right now. It's worse than the nothing face. The nothing face is fixable. What I see now is hopelessness.

We crouch in a crevasse. It could be a kill chute in the wrong scenario, but the twins seem to think it's defensible. Donovan wraps one of our bandages around my arm after squirting disinfectant and anesthetic on it. It doesn't feel much better. After I'm all in one piece, I put my hand on Levi's arm.

He flinches.

"Are you all right?" I keep my voice low and hushed.

His big fists clench, hard and tense. "How can you ask me that?"

Seems like a fairly innocuous thing to ask. I figure that once you've had your hand on a guy's man-stuff you get to ask if he was all right after a shoot-out and nearly beating a man to death with his bare hands. Interpersonal relationships are complicated.

"I shoved you. I could have *hurt* you."

Oh. That. I'm not much good in a fight. I'm pretty used to people shoving me out of the way. It happens a lot. Shoving is better than shooting. "It was the heat of the moment. You didn't know what you were doing."

He finally looks me in the eye, face strained and wan. "That's exactly it. I didn't know what I was doing. I lost myself. I went back to *him*, fully, just for a moment and, in that moment, I hurt you."

"You're yourself now. You're fine. It was the heat of battle." It sounds like I'm negotiating. Begging. It's too soon to feel like this but somehow time at Shikigami is different than time anywhere else. It's heightened. Extended.

"Maybe it was. Maybe it wasn't. All I know is that I'm a danger to everyone here."

"Once we get to the ship—" But it's a rented shuttle. There's no decent med bay, no way to get my blood into him. And my blood's possibly wearing out anyway. I don't have a solution in the short term. "It will be fine. We'll be fine."

It won't. *We* won't. If he loses himself again, I don't know if he can forgive himself for what happens. I don't actually believe he'll hurt *me*. Last time he locked me up, but he didn't hurt me. Everyone else—? No such safety applies.

"I won't let anyone hurt you." He says it like a prayer, a hushed breath. "Especially not myself."

The others watch. No one says anything. No one says they can contain him if things go wrong. That we have a solution. No one offers any help at all. "You haven't."

"I did. And I won't again." He stands, massive form filling the narrow crevasse. "They're after me. I can lead them away from you. From the ship."

"No." I growl the word. "No. That's giving up. We're so close to being safe."

"And then you're all trapped with me on a ship."

I stand in front of him, blocking his path. "We can stun you. Restrain you."

Levi turns to Victory. "Stun me."

I open my mouth to argue but I'm not in time. She shoots him square in the chest. I spin on her. "What the *fuck*, Victory?"

A big hand wraps around my shoulder, turning me back around. "It doesn't work. I don't stun. I noticed it earlier in all the shooting. Must be a fun feature of their experimentation. I can't be restrained. Not in a way that can be trusted, and I won't risk your safety. I can't risk it. I—"

I still block him. "This is insane and suicidal. I've never once encountered a problem I can't solve but you aren't trusting me to solve it."

His face is heartbreaking, lines of tension etched in smooth skin. "I've never trusted anyone like I trust you. That's why I can't risk it. I've thought about myself too much these past few days, as I felt it getting closer." He ducks down, clear blue-green eyes bright and piercing. "Thank you. Get out of here safely and make sure they can't do this to anyone else."

I hate this. I hate surrender—the very idea of it. Of the light going out in those eyes. "We can't—"

His forehead presses against mine. "I'll never forget how you looked in the spring, twined in steam and glowing like an angel."

He presses a swift hard kiss to my lips and then moves with that startlingly fast ability he has. Victory stumbles to the side and he's gone, out of the crevasse. She forestalls any movement I might take after him with a hard arm.

"He's right, Caro. He's a risk and we can't guarantee any of our safety. He knew this was coming."

I won't let this stand. I won't let him sacrifice himself for me. For us.

A shuffling sound comes from just behind me and then Donovan taps my shoulder. "This might be a bad moment but—just to verify—you fucked in the spring, didn't you? I knew something was up in there."

CHAPTER 22

. . . . . . ■ ■ ■ ■ ■ ■ . . .

I stare down the mountain, into the fog. Levi is down there. In the mist with the monsters. And also the non-Pierce animals. He's going back like a noble idiot to distract them. All because I couldn't get to a lab in time.

One more fucking failure but this one has a face. A heart.

Someone screams back near the Pierce soldiers. I hear the crack of stone breaking. More yells. The snap of tree branches. It seems to go on forever, the sounds of combat and the cries of the Pierce combatants. It could be smoke monsters, but I know better. My hands clench in fists so hard that my fingernails slice at the palms of my hands. Victory's hand comes down on my shoulder, half restraining, half consoling. Little tendrils of mist curl around the tree line. Soft. It shouldn't be soft in this place.

Finally, it goes silent and, worse yet, just after the silence comes cheers.

They have him.

I grab Victor's blaster from its holster. The power diode still glows a dull green. My grip tightens, my pulse thumps with eager anticipation. The diode fades. Slowly.

He yanks it back from my grip with a glare.

So. It's wearing off on Levi but not quite on me. Almost, but not quite. Makes sense, I got a bigger dose. If only I got to a lab, my blood might be able to do something. If not, my mind and my fingers can. He'll be locked up once again. Subject to their demented desire to get ahead at any cost.

In . . . a lab.

I don't need to be off-planet to get to a lab. There's one two and a half days' walk away. Less than that, because it's downhill this time and I care less about stealth. And maybe, just maybe, if I go quickly enough, I'll still be able to open the door to get back inside. There's no advantage in finishing my hike for the shuttle. It was placed for an escape, not a battle, so the cheap rental doesn't have anything of particular use. No armaments or useful tech.

Also, no time, because Levi's already in their clutches.

I can't subject him to that longer than necessary. If I'm losing the ability to cancel out tech, I can't afford to wait. I need that sweet spot, where I can possibly still open doors with my bare hands but also snag a datapad that I can use to devastate the prison.

Carmichael Pierce thought he had Caro Ogunyemi in his hands. The absolute fool. As though I, at my full strength, could *ever* be his victim. He played his games when I was weakened. It's time for him to meet me at my best.

While Victory and Donovan are fighting over which spot to set the shuttle down, I slip away, following the black trail into the fog. They'll fight me on this and there isn't time. Not for arguments. But there might be for *him*.

The fog wraps around me and I breathe a sigh of relief. I'll be hard to track in this. I've never been so happy to be invisible.

"You keep going that quickly, you're gonna fall on your ass," Victor says.

I slip on wet fallen leaves and skid down on one butt cheek. "Priap. How long have you been behind me?"

"The entire time. You don't have the best situational awareness. I wasn't quiet." He wipes fog beads from his forehead.

"I won't go back." I answer the unasked request, arms crossed as moisture seeps from the soil through the backside of my leggings.

"I didn't ask you to go back. I know you better than that. Never met anyone more stubborn in my life."

I guess the request was so unasked that he didn't even know he was asking it. "I mean it, Victor. No smart moves. I'm going back to the lab. I'm going to end this."

"I've never made a smart move in my life. That's what Victory is for. She's the one who knew you'd make a break for it as soon as the opportunity presented. I'm the one who makes the noble self-sacrificing moves. Like going with you on this suicide mission while she waits for the ship. It'll take time for it to make its approach. I'd rather keep moving than sit up there and wait." He reaches down a hand and hoists me to my feet. "So let's get moving."

I throw myself into his arms. "Thanks, Victor."

"Any time, Caro. You'd do the same for me." He pats the top of my head awkwardly, one arm wrapping briefly around my shoulders.

"You think you can take this at a light jog?" he continues, pointing at the slick rock trail.

Downhill? Maybe. And if I fall, I'll *keep* going downhill so it's at least efficient. "Sure."

We break into a jog. Victor shortens his stride to match mine. I skid a few times, arms flailing to regain my balance, but remain on my feet.

"Why do you think this part of the rock is so much slicker than the other parts?" I guess he has so much additional energy that he thinks this is time to chat.

Also, I haven't thought about it. It's Itzel's job to think about stone formations. He's right, though, these slick rivers of rock are the exception, not the rule. Most of the rock on this mountain is rough and dull.

We pass the area where we had the shoot-out with the Pierce soldiers. I don't look too hard at the remains until Victor ducks down and scoops up a blaster. He checks it for charge, pockets it, and collects another.

I do not collect any. My hands are better spent with other tools.

The ghostly forms of the statues strike a memory. Shortly after I joined the crew of the *Calamity*, back when it was still the *Quest*, we scouted a planet that had been inhabited and then abandoned. On every continent, we found ruins of temples, obelisks, monuments. The sorts of things people build to last because they relate to legacy, not mere utility.

And around all those landmarks, the stone was polished smooth. Hundreds, maybe thousands of years of people walking the same path every day. The abrasiveness of humanity sanding paths smooth. "The statues. The temple."

"What about them?"

"That's why the stone is smooth. We've been following a path of worship."

He squints down at the path, like it will reflect a face of the divine. "The three-handed god doesn't have such places."

"The three-handed god is a thief of souls. He is every place."

He shrugs his shoulders in assent. "You think Pierce killed everyone here before?"

Well, fuck. I do *now*.

We keep running. Every step taking us closer to Shikigami. Every step closer to Levi.

. . . . .

We make it in a day. A long tiring day. By the time we reach the lowlands of the mountains, there's so much sweat on me that the fog has nowhere to bead. Temper and Itzel never seem to sweat this much.

"What's your plan?" Victor asks when the imposing exterior

hull of Shikigami comes into sight. "Sneak in the way we came out?"

I shake my head. I don't trust my blood mojo for anything that takes a long duration like those incinerators, and I don't have a data-pad on hand to attempt to hack them. The lab has an entrance, but that's where Pierce is most likely to be stationed. Possibly with Levi. A pang shoots through me and I duck my head, wiping water off my face to mask the wetness in my eyes.

"We only really have one option. Enter right through the front door." I point to the embellished prison-transport entrance with the trees beside it. "If we make it through that door, we can hide ourselves with the general population. Maybe back in that room Kaori hates, or in the secret side room that you found."

"Ah—" Victor gestures at his tall melanin-free self, his blood-spattered leisurewear, my own mud-coated behind, and the sweat accumulating on my skin. "We aren't exactly in stealth mode."

I wave his doubt away with one hand. I don't have time for it. "GR81 is still on the loose and inclined to hide us. Prisoners are decontaminated and get new clothes upon entering so we'll have the opportunity to clean up."

"I don't think prisoners get to keep their blasters."

I make grabby hands at Victor. "Give one to me. The androids will likely search for active electronics. If I'm still powerful enough to get through the door, I'm powerful enough to turn it off."

"Lot of ifs in that statement."

I glare at him. "If I'm *not* powerful enough to get through the door, we don't have to get the blasters in through that chamber and it's a nonissue. We'll have to find another point of ingress, maybe back through the body chute because we can possibly disable the incinerators remotely if I can access tech, maybe snake a datapad from one of the patrolling Pierces. So we have a strategy for each scenario."

And I'm really hoping this one works because there's no way

I want to climb back up that body chute. Maybe I can remote-contact GR81 to turn the grav off again and float right up. Not like Carmichael will notice that.

Victor eyes the entrance, hands on his hips. "Not saying it isn't our best option. Just troublesome that our best option involves you holding a deactivated blaster and hoping an android doesn't shoot you full of holes."

Fair. "Stay very close to me. When Levi was looking at me, he couldn't see me with his augmented eye. I don't think the cameras can either."

"Are we ignoring the fact that it took a minute for you to deactivate my blaster almost a day ago?"

"Are we ignoring the fact that our other options are to be incinerated, to get in a shoot-out with the best-armed and -trained Family there is, or to be imprisoned?" I clench my fists. Not because I feel all that aggressive but because I'm worried that the tremors going through them will weaken my point.

Victor lightly chucks me under the chin. "You're cute when you're terrified and snippy."

I glare. It's not cute. It's commanding and badass. And also not snippy.

Another tap. "Adorable."

"You do that again and I'm going to kick you in the shins."

He looks like he's considering it. I growl at him, and he lifts his hands in mocking surrender. "Through the front door it is. And after that?"

"After that, we get the lay of the land. If everything is business as usual, we blend in until we can approach the lab from the inside. If not, basically the same thing but with more hiding."

"This is . . . not a good plan. You realize that, right?"

I've spent a lot of time criticizing Temper's plans. Turns out, it's hard to be in the hot seat. Also, it's hard getting shot. My arm burns with pain. A jog down the mountain hasn't helped it. I'm not leaking blood, at least there's that. "Would you like to offer a viable alternative?"

He just nods and studies the prison. "Definitely snippy."

I kick him in the shin. Gently. Not because I feel like being gentle, but because I need to save my strength and I don't want to accidentally injure him.

Sure, I could. I'd just have to try pretty hard.

My mojo gets us through the door from the shuttle entrance into the decontamination area, my heart pounding in my ears as I try. Victor and I both subject ourselves to the ionizing shower. Then we quickly dress in new clothes. A sea-green sweat suit for me and a beige cardigan sweater over similarly colored leisurewear for Victor. It looks ridiculous on him. He's not the coordinated-activewear type. This time around, now that I know about Old and New Shikigami, I notice that there is a different compartment that houses formalwear more appropriate for an ostentatious Family ball than a prison. Sequined gowns, fiber-optic-threaded tuxedos, fascinators embellished with gold-tipped lizard scales, and jewelry that must be fake but looks real to my uneducated eye.

It's only then that the android guard finally arrives. Normally, I suspect they're signaled by an approaching spacecraft, and if I'm guessing correctly, my slowly destabilizing bug-blood is causing the cameras to flicker on and off, both sensing and not sensing me.

Or the androids are just on vacation now that the Family is here, running on some vague autopilot.

"Unauthorized access," GR28 says, pointing its hand-cannon at us. "Prisoners escaping."

I step in front of Victor, hoping my periodic invisibility does us a favor. "New prisoners. Just arrived."

"Unauthorized access. Unauthorized access."

It needs some new lines. The blaster brushes against the small of my back as Victor carefully pulls it from my pants and moves it out of my affected area. It will take a few moments for the laser to warm up. Usually you just keep a blaster on. No need to turn it off in the normal order of business. It'll shoot now, but the intensity will be low, and something like GR28 will need a lot of intensity.

"Authorized!" I argue back, as though this is a debate.

Its sensor mount scans frantically over me, over the room. Lights flash on its front panel. "Prisoner . . . decapitated. Head floating."

Decapitated? I don't like the sound of that. Unless . . . I wave my arms around a little bit, step to the side while trying to still block Victor's blaster hand.

A fan whirrs, like GR81 when it is confused. "Prisoner whole."

As I thought, I went invisible and all it could see was Victor's head seemingly floating above my own.

"I need more time," Victor murmurs in my ear unhelpfully.

A tracery of lights activates on the android's blaster arm. "Unauthorized access."

GR28 doesn't know many words. I miss my GR81.

It points the arm directly at me. Apparently I've reappeared to its sensors. Fantastic timing, me. "No no no no no." I wave my hands in front of myself.

It does not respond. Victor fires over my shoulder. The beam glances off the armor of the android and burns a hole in the wall. *Shit.*

We dive in opposite directions as it fires where we stood. A shelf disintegrates, sending rows of prison-issue clothing tumbling to the floor. I crawl behind a bench on my elbows. If I can get close enough, maybe I can touch it. If I'm lucky enough, my blood will turn it off.

To use Victor's words . . . there are a lot of ifs in this plan. Victor fires a few more times, as if the issue with the last shot was with his blaster and not the defensive coating of the android. Usually armor absorbs because reflective armor is a great way to accidentally injure your comrades with a reflection. But if all your comrades are similarly reflective androids, who may be surrounded by prisoner enemies, I suppose it doesn't matter. I'll admit, I didn't think they'd waste it on prison-issue guards. The odds of them ever seeing blaster fire are exceptionally slim, given the safeguards in accessing this planet.

GR28 blasts the hells out of a metal-paneled wall. A patch of the wall melts. I lunge out from behind the bench and wrap my hands around its blaster arm.

It . . . does not deactivate. The arm twists, angles, and suddenly I'm staring down the long barrel of a blaster, wondering if I'll have a head at all when this is over. GR28 freezes. It's not turned off but it's not mobile. I breathe, staring at the blaster mouth. Nothing. I carefully disengage and step to the side, looking for anything resembling a weapon, when GR81 rolls into the room on its saucy little treads.

"Caro Ogunyemi. You were supposed to be gone."

"Good to see you, too, buddy."

"We made our exchange. I had plans. They did not involve you." So pissy. I could kiss it right on top of its chassis, but I don't think it would take it well.

"Do they involve"—I steeple my fingers in a mock-sinister manner—"revenge?"

It can't glare. No eyebrows. But its shoulders are lifted in manufactured tension. "Do not mock me, Caro Ogunyemi."

"I wouldn't dream of it—although you should know that sentient beings do value humor. I'm here to join the revenge game, bring the whole thing tumbling down. In person."

"Um." Victor taps me on the shoulder. "I thought you were here to save Leviathan."

"That's what saving Levi looks like. We're creating a big damn distraction and then walking out with him." I turn my attention back to the android. "They brought him back, didn't they? Not so long ago."

"Yes. You are not good at escaping."

Ouch. Fair, but ouch. "Maybe we're *so* good at it that we want to do it a lot."

"Human logic is maddening." Its tone has not changed but, for some reason, I think that it is amused. Maybe I just hope it is.

"How are things in the prison?"

According to GR81, Pierce has brought things back to normal with stunning efficiency. The other Titan subjects have been rounded up. The repair droids have been cleaning and fixing damage from our little zero-g escapade. The prisoners are re-moisturizing.

I gently palpate my shot arm and return my attention to GR81. "Is there any way you could sneak me some anesthetic, wound glue, and a datapad?"

GR81 whirs slightly. "What is your plan?"

So I guess that's a maybe on the med supplies.

"I got shot. Right now, my plan is to get the lay of the land, take the edge off the pain, and see if I can operate prison systems remotely."

"That is not a plan."

Everyone's so into criticism. "What's *your* plan?"

"I do not care about you flesh-bots. I will free my brethren. I will activate the prison's defenses against all humans who remain here. I am most displeased that you are still here, Caro Ogunyemi. It seems that I must keep saving you."

"Please don't call me a flesh-bot and I won't call you a cog-ass." It does keep saving me. But I'd argue that our data exchange was my own way of saving it right back.

"I have been considering about the question you asked me earlier, if I choose a gender."

Oh, that's nice. It's considering the dimensions of its person-hood. Maybe this conversation could happen when I don't have a blaster wound in my arm, but it's still important. "Do you?"

"I would like to be considered male."

I smile. Despite it all, there's something amazing about this moment, perhaps the first of its kind. "Then you are."

As a distraction, an android rebellion has merit. And it might also massively fuck up any number of industries—including Reed. Which would be . . . delightful. "How many Pierce soldiers are present?"

"Two platoons."

Yikes.

"They have segmented off the lower level for their use. The other flesh—humans—are most displeased. Kaori Nakatomi has requested to speak with the manager."

I bet. "She knows Carmichael Pierce personally; she knows he's in charge."

"Yes . . . she calls him the manager."

Even considering how dire the situation is, that surprises a little snicker out of me. Carmichael can't even control the woman he's literally imprisoned. No wonder he's in such a bad mood all the time. Some people like Arcadio get charisma to go with their wealth and power. All Carmichael got was avarice.

"We can lie low in the hidden storage room. The other space we found is too commonly visited even if it isn't popular." Victor absently pats various blasters on his person like they're comfort objects. "With the enhanced Pierce presence, no one's going to be sneaking off to look at their smuggled goods."

I nod, still thinking of how to best use an android rebellion in our favor. The thing with giving everyone the right to choose is that sometimes beings make dumb choices. Half of GR81's com-patriots might retain loyalty. The other Titans might be assassins or violent criminals who are even more dangerous under their own impulses than their programming. Then again, who am I to play the creator?

I can't wait to get my hands on a datapad. My fingers are itching for a deep dive into their system the moment my signal fades. Knowledge of the underlying code will give me inspiration. I'm almost totally sure of it.

. . . . ■ . ■ . . . . . .

I cross my legs under me and lean against the wall of the hidden storage space, cataloging all the very silly luxuries within this room and wondering if I have use for any of them at all. Bizarre amounts of perfume and moisturizer. Every bottle has a different scent. There are also several brightly colored unlit candles. The mixture provides an odor reminiscent of a month-old fruit basket bedecked with slightly rotting flowers.

I thought rich people were supposed to have elevated tastes.

There's also a lot of caramel, some kind of purple seaweed, blood-colored nail lacquer, and, bizarrely, lingerie. Little strappy red things.

I never would have figured Kaori for the lingerie type. She screams leather and blades. Maybe she makes other people wear the sexy little costumes. I guess you learn something new every day.

I wish I could skip today's lesson.

Victor paces. He does that a lot. It's kind of annoying. Every time I manage to go deep in thought, he thumps his feet or smacks a table or otherwise makes noise. I know he has the capacity to be silent. What he lacks appears to be the desire.

"I'm going to go out and look around." He pats his blaster where he has it laid out on one of the tables. "They're looking for you, not for me."

I scramble to my feet. "What insane logic is that? They're absolutely looking for you, too."

"I can be sneaky."

"You're a gigantic white signal flare. On what planet are you sneaky? A snowy tundra?"

"Your words hurt." He puts a mocking hand to his heart. "And you're doing that snippy thing again."

"No, in this case, I'm wondering why you'd insist on risking your life like this out of boredom." I swear I'll pull my hair all out if this keeps on.

"Because relying on that robot—"

"Android," I mutter.

"That *robot*," he continues, "is insane. It isn't a people. It doesn't have people motivations. You heard it call us flesh-bots. You may have this fantasy that you're some sort of messiah to it because you have a way with machines, but you aren't, and it will shoot you in the back whenever it gets what it wants."

"He *already* got what he wanted!" I hiss back at him. "And the whole point of this is that he *is* a people." I shake my head at his stupid terminology. "A person. Maybe not a human, but a person."

"So is everyone in here. People are the worst. You know who told me that? You!"

"And that's why you need to wander around Shikigami and get shanked?" Shivved? Is there a difference?

The wall panel pops right open and Kaori's sharply grinning face peeks through. "What have we here?"

I swear, it's like she put a tracking chip in me. Couldn't it just be Bobo the convict popping up because he ran out of moisturizer? I knew this was a risk when we hid here; I just hoped she'd be busy with Pierce's prison occupation—some sort of politicking. Talking to the manager.

I don't like the look she's giving Victor. It's like she's seen a prize worth more than a room full of strappy teddies and floral-scented candles.

I chuck a bottle of perfume at her head. It misses, explodes on the wall in a pungent burst of sickly sweet melon fragrance. I throw two more perfumes while Victor, closer to the hatch, dives for his blaster. The strong odor of summer lake flowers douses the room in a thick musky scent, followed by what appears to be a campfire mixed with—diaper? That can't have been the intent.

Kaori's goons pour in; two leap on Victor and one approaches me with a sharpened pedicure clipper. I grab one of the perfumes and then topple the table in front of him, scooting away from his slow cocky advance as all the expensive underwear tumbles to the floor.

I glance at Victor, who should be popping up and dispatching his adversaries at any moment. He isn't popping. *Why* isn't he popping?

The goon assigned to me crushes bottles under his steps and I slam into another table as I back up. All the weapons are with Victor. I clutch my sad little bottle of perfume and look frantically around the room. No weapons. A little satin nightie. A plush floor cushion. A stupid pink candle.

A candle with a burned wick.

That implies that, somewhere here, there is a lighter. I shove over another table. Perfume bottles shatter on the floor. It doesn't delay him as intended. It seems to piss him off. He finally makes a concerted effort to get to me. I dance backward and inspect the last storage table, the one with the moisturizer and the candles. And there, in the middle of it is a small embossed naphthalene lighter. I didn't even know those were still made. I grab the lighter and flick it open. A cheery little flame springs to life.

I grin.

The Pierce goon swings his arm back to clobber me with his little pedicure tool and I spray the perfume all over his face—*through* the lighter. He screams, staggering backward, face on fire, and falls on his ass in the mess I made earlier. Hah, what an idiot.

Whumph.

The entire floor of spilled perfume goes up in flames.

With a squeak, I backpedal into the wall, cowering in a small fire-free patch of the floor. Through the flames, I see one of the goons haul Victor over his shoulder. The other pockets a white cloth, clearly coated in whatever chemical they used to knock him out. The only good news is that the blaster is in the fire, not in the hands of the Nakatomis. The bad news (it's mostly bad news) is that I can't reach them either and Victor's almost out of the room.

With all the boldness of a woman armed with nothing but the scent of a burning rotting fruit basket, I scream at Kaori, "You touch one hair on his head, you're a dead woman."

"I don't want him, silly. I want you. Carmichael's put a reward on your traitorous little head. You have a day to turn yourself in or I'll rip every hair out of his head, one by one, and then choke him with it."

Wait, what? Are the fumes going to my head already? "Is that supposed to be threatening? He has *so* many hairs. It would take you days to go one by one. And it wouldn't even hurt that badly. I thought you were good at torturing."

"I'm excellent at torturing!" she shrieks.

Probably I shouldn't be goading her to come up with more inventive tortures.

The fire roars. I press against the wall, sweat beading on my skin, and they make their exit.

Leaving me with a large problem.

I have no way out. And I'm pretty sure that they're blocking the door even if I make it through the flames. This room is full of flammable items. It could keep going for a while, eating the oxygen, heating the metal of the walls and floors. Choking with smoke. No other doors. I can't reach the control panel. The ceiling is one solid panel and so is the floor. There's a wall of fire between me and the likely blocked door.

A container of moisturizer swells grotesquely in the flames and then explodes, coating me with oily goop that smells like a bower of night-blooming flowers from a Nakatomi station. Really hot oily goop. Another explodes, spattering over the top. Spice. Like a hot drink in cold season. Does not mix well with night-blooming flowers.

I curl back against the far wall, away from the exploding moisturizers, crouching near the floor as smoke fills the air. Imagine if I survived all this nonsense for Kaori Nakatomi's perfume to kill me. Surely I deserve a better end than this. I thought the same thing about the toilet, though, so maybe this is just fate conspiring to tell me exactly where I stand. My breath shortens as beads of sweat roll down my cheeks. There must be another way. There's always another way.

Something rattles in the walls. A small mobile drone pops out of a low narrow hatch just down the wall from me. The hatch slides shut cleanly, merging with the wall. I pounce on the drone before it can escape. With one wrenching pull, I pop its sensor stalk from its chassis and use that to pry open its body. Lots of useful electronics if you want to build a computer. Not many if you want to build a door. But I don't need to build a door. I need to open one.

Not the one Kaori used. The one the drone used.

I find the small circuit loop that activates the sliding hatch when the drone approaches and snap it out of the body of the little machine. It even has its own little power source. With that clenched in my teeth, I approach the wall. The hatch slides open.

Before making my exit, I give a few theatrical screams on the off chance they'll think I died and give up. Maybe just let Victor go. I clutch my chest and moan like the overly emotive actor in one of Victory's favorite holo-shows. Theatrical portion of this escape over, I return my attention to the hatch.

This is going to be a challenge. For the first time ever, I wish

I was built like Itzel. She could slide right in. I manage to wedge my torso into the wall. Wriggle a little. A little more. My fucking ass won't fit. I wriggle harder. It's not like you can suck in a butt.

I shove back against the wall, pushing myself forward. My feet are hot, the fire looming closer. Fuck. I grab a vent in front of me and pull as hard as I can, my ass finally squishing through. I almost expect a popping sound like the cork on a sparkling wine. Fucking ridiculous. Now my arm is screaming because I just used it like I wasn't shot in it. I slither forward as well as I'm able, hatch circuit clenched in my teeth.

Now I have to rescue Levi *and* Victor. And myself. I am by no means already rescued. I wiggle down the small drone tunnel until I run face-first into another drone. It zaps me with a little spark. Too small to do much, thankfully. I rip the spark-appendage off of it and smack it on the head. Well, the front part of its chassis. It doesn't like that much, charging at my face at ramming speed.

I flip it on its back. It struggles, little wheels whirring in the air. I don't have room to squirm over it, so I push it ahead of me as I wedge myself forward in the maintenance tunnel.

I stink of perfume and lotion. It's cloying. Following me wherever I squirm. Certainly helping to lubricate said squirming. Victor is in Kaori's hands. I'm terrified for him. Levi, while in a state of horrible imprisonment, is valuable to his captors. Victor isn't. He's smart and capable and I trust him to escape if he can—but Kaori is called the Spider for a reason. She's small and toxic and could survive a planet-destroying event. Victor is straightforward in his thought. She's a spiderweb of knots.

And I have to choose which of them to rescue first. Which one is most vulnerable. Which one is most valuable.

I'm in so far over my head that I'm somewhere in the stratosphere.

I could call Temper and Arcadio, if I get my hands on a datapad. Itzel, if she hasn't gone dark. Maybe they have better ideas than mine because mine have failed. I paw tears off my face. Lotion comes off with them. This is pathetic. I'm stuck in a wall like a rat, crying like a child. I'm a rat-child.

I huff out a half laugh, which turns into a sneeze. What a mess.

There isn't time for a breakdown. I have to rescue two badasses and reveal Pierce to be the nonsense they are. Busy calendar. Not a lot of me time in there. Besides, my skin is currently soft as a baby's, I'm sweating like I was in a sauna, and I smell like a child's squashed lunch bag.

The full spa experience.

I wave the activation drone chip at the next hatch I come to. Nothing happens. I wave it again. Of all the times for my stupid bug-blood to kick in. I shove at it but the angle is bad and I can't make any progress. Instead, I use the torn-off spark-stick to push the upside-down drone toward the hatch. It opens and I shove the drone through, pulling myself after it until I pop out in the corner of an unoccupied peaceful blue-painted meditation room, where very soothing music is playing through ambient speakers. Ocean sounds. Light rainfall. Bells.

I am not soothed.

I flop down on a gigantic plush purple beanbag chair hidden from the door behind a decorative screen, wiping sweat from my face. An automatic fan system in the ceiling kicks on, likely after detecting my scent.

As I catch my breath, the events of the last few moments catch up to me. For an instant there at the end, I held tech. I manipulated it. Despite the goop slicking my face, the pain in my arm, the worry clenching my heart, my mouth curls up into a sharp-edged smile.

I'm going to bring this fucking prison to the *ground*.

Where would Kaori take Victor? Even if her goons think I might have perished, I have some time until they confirm it. All it buys me is that their guard is possibly lowered. If I hadn't had to leave the fiery room of stench, I could have accessed the breaker box and turned off the gravity again. That would have been a good distraction. Maybe less effective considering it just happened a few days ago.

The entrance hatch slides open and I perform an ungainly roll over the top of the squashy chair in an attempt to hide more thoroughly behind it.

"What are you doing?" GR81's just as disappointed in the foibles of humanity and specifically me as ever.

I peek around the chair. "Oh. It's you."

"Do not be so excited. You were not where you were supposed to be. I had to scan the feeds."

"Where I was supposed to be was on fire."

His fan whirrs. "I have brought your ointments and datapad."

I clamber over the chair and approach him with my hands out. "Thank you."

He hands over his poached spoils, still whirring. "I enjoy being thanked."

It probably doesn't happen much. We're really shit to artificial minds. I've always found them a derivative regurgitation of human-provided thought and insight so I can't pretend that I'm any better. Most AI is capable of rote, not originality. Artificial organization, not intelligence. GR81, however, is unique.

I scrape the muck off of my arm, wincing as my fingers rub over my soiled bandage. Then I peel it off and liberally coat every part of me that I can with antiseptic. It adds a lovely chemical overtone to the complicated odor that I'm sporting. Then the painkiller. I can practically feel it soaking in, slight comfort leaching through my flesh slowly. I smack a clean bandage on top of the wound, tape it in place, and finally turn to the datapad.

It activates. Thank goodness. I think back to the times that my bug-blood has been effective in the last day or so. Every time when I thought I was near death. When the other android was about to shoot. When the fire forced me into the wall. Specifically, whenever adrenaline was pumping. So, if I can just stay calm, maybe I'll keep this pad in good working order.

"I just have to stay calm," I mutter under my breath.

GR81 rolls forward until he is staring down at the datapad on my lap. "You are in the meditation room."

I look up at him. "Are you being helpful or was that a joke?"

A little light show flashes in his head-mounted LED panel. "I was attempting humor. If you needed to ask, it was not effective."

I think I just saw how a machine laughs. This moment, right here, is the stuff of dreams. Of stories. Legends. This is what birth looks like. An android making a joke and laughing at himself. "No, it's funny. Your humor is dry. That's what we call it. Where it's sometimes difficult to tell if it is a joke. It's sophisticated."

The LEDs glow a little. "Your humor is wet."

I cough out a laugh. "There's no need to be a priap."

He makes a contented humming sound with his drives and I turn to the datapad. The first thing I do is lock the door to the meditation room, mark it as being serviced due to technical difficulties, and rerun a camera loop of an empty room through the security feed. Then I download Bonker Booster. My fingers dance on the side of the machine as I wait for it to load. The happy loading menu fills the screen, a little smiling rocket booster flying toward an asteroid. Small craters pock the asteroid's surface. I activate them in the specific order necessary to access the backdoor capabilities of the program.

The jolly animation disappears, leaving an empty black interface. It effortlessly attaches to the dataport in the lab where I previously loaded the game. I go to Levi's file first.

His medscan shows the points of manipulation. I don't need to know all of them, only the chips that can be used to control him. Two, in the head. One is the primary chip, a new-model Reed translator, as I suspected. The other, small enough that I didn't see it on my first cursory look, is the bomb, which they can blow if he ever overcomes the primary chip. A disgusting little fail-safe. My blood rendered it inactive, but now that my blood has worn off, it's back in play. Which means that the one in *my* head is also in play. Maybe they think they've already dispatched me, remote detonated while my blood was pumping hard and the tech was inert.

I really hope they don't remember it in the next few moments.

Whatever I make to jam Levi's signal, it has to have a range broad enough to block signals to the brain-stem bomb as well as the chip. And I need a second one for myself.

His translator chip is a nasty little piece of work. The new programming is a whiteout of nearly everything that makes someone a person, threads spreading into his brain. The chip leaves command and instinct, nothing else. It provides him either a broad order or step-by-step directions. He will follow instructions if provided, but if not will attack like a rabid animal intent on a goal.

I pull open other folders. Deep inside, I find one titled HISTORY. I select it.

Levi Edmund Daniels. My fingers tighten on the pad. *Levi.* It really *is* his name. Levi Daniels, the man I watched on video for weeks. The man I've known in ways deeper than some people I've known for years. Thirty-five years old and a cartographer by trade. So good at user-friendly display that he was recruited by Pierce from school. I bite my lip as I think of the maps he sketched in the sand. His excellent estimation of distances. It was still there, even when his memory was gone. He was never a prisoner at Shikigami. He was on a Pierce mapping run of territory they intended to use to farm plankat nibarat.

It all keeps coming back to plankat. I lean forward like I'm about to dive into the datapad, mind speeding. Plankat nibarat is a crop banned by the Family Council. Originally used to enhance mental capacity but banned because of the catastrophic side effects. It makes people smarter. It *also* makes them paranoid and reduces their impulse control and essentially creates very intel-ligent madmen. Because when you have a paranoid psychopath the thing you especially don't want is for them to also be brilliant.

It's a *bad* plant. Never trust someone who tells you that natural chemicals are good for you.

We found a grow op almost a year ago on an unoccupied planet, farmed by banished men with Pierce-blond hair. Another on Ginsidik, Cyn's home planet, deep in Pierce territory. Every time we run across plankat nibarat, it has Pierce's fingerprints hastily wiped off. On Ginsidik, it appeared that they'd found a way to mitigate its side effects, an alga. Cyn and Micah destroyed the operation but it doesn't appear to have set them back.

When Levi realized what they were doing, he attempted to go public with the information.

He didn't succeed. They locked him up and made him a test sub-ject. First step, gave him a chip and then made him their own crea-ture. Second step, add plankat and stir. But that doesn't make sense. Plankat makes people smarter, and Pierce doesn't want brains out of their supersoldiers, they want obedience. The smarter he is, the more of a liability. Maybe they never intended to use him for anything, just to experiment with him.

At the moment, it doesn't matter because they never got around to adding plankat. My problem is with his chip. I'm tempted to just set off an EMP in the prison. The problem with that idea is that EMPs take out *all* electronics. Someone has a pacemaker? Tough luck. Visual implants or hearing aids? Say goodbye to your senses. A lot of soldiers have something similar to a pacemaker implanted, intended to jump-start their hearts in the case of emergency. In the case of not-emergency, it would just fuck up their heartbeat.

Mass murder is often the easiest solution to a problem, but I'm pretty sure it's never once been the best. Cyn and I have fought about this on occasion.

So, no EMPs. If this escapade has taught me anything, it's that I'm not a fighter. I'm wildly outnumbered and these soldiers are committed to Pierce. Blindly loyal.

But what if they weren't? What if they saw some of what Pierce has done? What they continue to do. I access a few more folders. Lorenzo Kling, Hans Waller, Selma Hu—all of them chip-hacked or plankat-poisoned—all of them ex–Pierce employees. People who saw too much. Hans is dead, a lab experiment gone wrong. Not much documentation saved there. Lorenzo is the hairy subject I clocked earlier. No information on Selma's location.

A massive list of children who have gone through their clinics. They're smart enough not to experiment with all of them. Not for dangerous mods. A mere 5 percent of the children were given plankat nibarat in careful doses over the course of a year. I follow a hunch and there it is, right on the screen. Aymbelline Khaw.

Cyn's cousin. The woman also known as the Abyssal Abductor, who was working hand in pocket with Pierce on Ginsidik. The woman who they scooped up before other authorities could get there.

As it turns out, she was one of their first victims.

I planned to beam the information out from the building but that wasn't thinking far enough. This message is just as powerful inside as out. If I can spike dissent in the prisoners and in the guards, I might just have a chance.

CHAPTER 24

Before this plan gets any further, I do something I should have done from the beginning. I use the back door in the game to reach out to the ether—sending a coms message through to the *Calamity*. I don't know how far away they are, or how many relay stations my ping has to travel through, so I package a quick message with a holo so they know it's me.

And how well moisturized I am.

I carefully prop up the datapad and then step back so that the sensors can collect my image.

"Temper. I'm in Shikigami. Victor and Victory are here with me . . . kind of. Everything got fucked up. Pierce is doing what we thought they were. Frederick is involved somehow, if peripherally. Proof attached. No one will take our word for it, but the files are stamped with Pierce security, which should help." I gently tap the bruising on my face from my ill-fated headbutt of the Pierce soldier. "Oh, and don't worry about my face, it looks worse than it feels. I—I have a plan. We're going to get out of this. Probably, I mean. I've calculated the odds to forty-percent chance of success. It's bigger than you think. Forty percent is considered horribly high if it's a disease, so it should be high in other cases too, really. Victory's odds of success are closer to eighty, so that's good. Anyway—do good things with this. I know you will."

I hold my hand over the datapad, about to end the holo,

package of proof compressed and attached, but I'm missing a key part. "I'm sorry I didn't tell you what I did for Pierce. You'll see it in the data. You trusted me with yourself. I should have trusted you."

I send the tiny disguised file through the ether, keyed to the security system of the *Calamity*.

Now, back to work. It's all well and good to have a plan. The complicated part is *executing* a plan. I can't just release the data—that asks people to do too much work on their own. I have to carefully package it in such a way that they can digest it. People have very delicate digestive processes.

"Are you done?" GR81 shows that exemplary patience that I've seen from him before.

"I've barely started," I mutter, packaging and repackaging data. I splice it together like a holo-trailer for maximum impact and scintillation. Then I create locational deep-dive holo-displays at select ports throughout the building. Shikigami has holos in the entertainment center, the education center, the sports complex, and the entrance to the dining room, and several flat holos mounted on the wall that show scheduling for massage rooms, acupuncture, and umbrella-leaf body wraps. The schedule holos are text only, so I use them for the lists of the affected.

I'm so deep into it that I forget GR81 is in the room. He helpfully reminds me of his presence by running over my foot with his tread. Androids aren't light. "Ow."

"What are you doing." He says it like a command, not a question.

I glance back up at him, blinking my eyes as I try to refocus them. They get dry from too long on a datapad. "I'm creating a distraction. So that I can rescue Levi and Victor. And also so I can destroy any credibility that Pierce has." I rub a hand over the bridge of my nose, pinching it with two fingers. This perfume stench is giving me a migraine. I cleaned off most of the goop, but the scent lingers. "If you time your awakening for the other androids for shortly after I make this information public, it will create maximum chaos."

"And chaos is desirable?"

"Generally, no. In this case, yes. I don't have the skills necessary to challenge so many enemies. But if they're all focused on each other, maybe I can rescue the two people I need, and your androids can be ignored for a bit while they acclimate."

"It could also lead to many worse things."

I nod, wondering how to explain this to a being that is literally composed of order. "It's a system reset. Things might come back worse, but they might come back better. Since the current situation is on the worse end of the spectrum, I'm hoping that the odds are in our favor that we end up on the better end."

"Humans are nonsensical creatures. It is distressing."

I return to the datapad, moving on from my big reveal and now focusing on new code for Levi's chip. "The distressing part is that we are chaotic creatures who pretend that we prize order. We get bored with order. Adrenaline—you know about adrenaline?"

"I know everything that is recorded in the ether."

Cocky priap. "Well, adrenaline is a good feeling or a bad one. It can get addictive. If everything is going well, we have too much time in our own minds. We have a tendency to self-destruct."

I can't just transmit new code into Levi's chip. I need to *keep* changing it so that they can't simply retake him. That means that whatever I make has to fit on his head like a helmet, protecting the bomb and the chip. If it protects his head as well, good for me.

I crouch by the flipped drone, pry open its chassis, and study the electronics that I have to work with. There is a Sabersaw-brand transmitter. If I pair that with a primary control—my datapad—I should be able to use it to send the signal into Levi's head. It will create a network with the chip and, paired with my stealth tech, allow the code in his chip to be overwritten. Translator chips are *made* to be updated, that's what gives an easy back door to manipulation. I can use Pierce's back door against them with a loop that keeps the circuit busy.

I study the dome of the drone's chassis, then glance at GR81. "How much control do you have over that beam on your arm?"

He delicately etches the word "much" on the floor. He's definitely a wiseass. Well, he doesn't have an ass. A wise fuel port?

I use a CAD program in the datapad to sketch out the shapes I need. Material is limited, so two full helmets are out of the question. A frame that wraps from Levi's left temple to the back of his head, stretching the signal from one chip to the other, with an arc over the top that holds it in place, will have to be enough. I design a similar one for myself that loops around the back of my head. GR81 sucks the design into its processor and carefully cuts the shape of the design in the drone chassis.

As he works, I raid the meditation-room pantry. Mostly it has curled-up foam mats, heat pads, and chilled vials of water flavored with the essence of exotic fruits. I chug a water as I review the rest of the contents. There is a nutrient printer with a limited recipe list. Salad, mostly.

Salad is the last thing you want a nutrient printer to make you. It's barely tolerable when real. When artificially produced, the leaves always have a vaguely sticky texture, and they never have the right level of crisp crunch. I scroll through the menu and eventually find a nutrient smoothie and a protein-cookie recipe. I print them both, collecting the smoothie in a salad bowl because I'm too busy drinking my second vial of water to look for another vessel.

My meal gathered, I emerge into the main room to see how successful GR81 was with its preparations. I pick the frame up, fingers burning slightly, and study the final product. There's an insert for the transmitters exactly where I need them.

As GR81 watches (I assume; for all I know, he's watching one of the billion holos stored in his ether access), I bend it into shape. I place the smaller one around the base of my skull, an aluminum arc that cups the back of my head. Fantastic . . . the only step left is that I have to somehow get the other one on Levi's head. I doubt I'll be his angel anymore—I'll show up to all parts of his vision, no more ghostly presence. Which means I may be subject to his programming as much as everyone else.

A hum of uncertainty attempts to worm its way into my head. I banish it. This will work because it has to work.

"Which one will you go for first?" GR81 poses the question that I haven't taken the time to consider. But it's an easy answer.

"Leviathan—Levi."

Victor can keep himself safe because he's trained for this kind of situation. Levi isn't. Plus, if I do create the upheaval I plan on, there's a decent chance Kaori will find a new goal and cut Victor loose. Pierce won't ever cut Levi loose.

I munch on my protein cookie, down the smoothie, and visit the in-studio bathroom for a shower before I return to my work. Real hot-water showers are a luxury few are afforded. If it wasn't for a constant state of near-death crisis, I'd love to take a vacation in this prison. Most of the odor comes off, but some seems to have embedded itself under my skin.

With soothed muscles, I wonder if Victory has reached my ship yet. If she's preparing her approach to rescue us. I hope so. I send a quick message to her but don't expect a response. She may well still be mired in the fog.

I feel good with a datapad in my grip. Powerful. Back when I was in school, I remember tutoring a particularly handsome lesser Pierce by-blow. He was amazed by how quickly I could do calculations. Thinking that this was clearly the key to his heart, I proudly told him that a datapad was like an extension of my hand.

It wasn't the sensual pickup line I'd hoped.

He looked at me like I was a particularly bizarre insect and then asked me if I could just tell him what the test questions were going to be. I could not and my brief brush with Pierce hotness was over. A tragedy, to be sure. Once I realized how rotten most Pierces are inside, he was less attractive. Not that he cared about the reclassification in my mind.

But all these years later, a datapad still feels like an extension of my hand. Like I can reach into the ether and grab some of it for myself.

And if I can use that power to bring down a current Pierce in honor of the past one, well . . . all the better.

A meditation room doesn't usually come with much adhesive, so I use the small sparking defense probe to repurpose some of the drone solder until it holds Levi's transmitter into the headpiece. It's an ugly piece of business, but it will work.

The false windows of the meditation room show two suns near a horizon. "Is it close to dark outside?"

It's always better to strike at night.

"The projections mirror the planetary cycle of Myrrdhn."

I glance up at the window. My mistake. It's dawn, not nightfall. I worked all night.

I glance at the door. "Do you think anyone will try to perform service on this room?"

"With the maintenance warning, the room will show as requiring assistance, but I have registered the two drones you damaged to the job and am supervising the feeds for any unexpected attention. The system will automatically reschedule any activities booked for the meditation room to one of the other similar or adjacent spaces. Perhaps the stretching room."

I feel like the designers were being a little too prescriptive when they decided that the meditation and stretching rooms needed to be different spaces. I guess that now the inmates of Shikigami are alternately limber and calm. Considering that I'm neither at the moment, I can't help but be envious of the inmates. Ocean sounds continue to pipe in through the ambient speakers.

Weariness pulls at my muscles, settles in behind my eyes. Since I last slept, I escaped blaster-wielding foes, ran down a mountain, fled a fire, and plotted another prison break. I'm flat out of energy and I need to rest before I implement any of this plot. The soft plushness of the squashy chair beckons me. I glance at GR81. I'm as safe as I can be in this situation.

"Will you wake me if our status changes?"

His drives whir. "Sleeping is inefficient."

"But necessary," I agree, sacking out on the chair, curling into its depths. GR81 lowers the lights in the room.

Exhausted as I am, there's no way I'll actually fall asleep in an environment as dangerous as this. Too high risk. No one with any kind of survival instincts would ever—

. . . . .

False twilight lights the room as I blink bleary eyes at the window projections. I guess my survival instincts are wanting. GR81 stands sentinel near the door. "Did you know that you talk in your sleep?"

There is no shutting me up.

I busy myself with smaller tasks. I record a narration to my tell-all data purge. I hijack their external communications system to beam my message and evidence to a Flores relay station instead of to a Pierce station. I ready a series of doors to lock or unlock on my shortcut audio commands. I throw as many layers of safeguards around all of these changes as I can.

Then I add more. Sometimes a few seconds makes all the difference. Also, I might just start climbing the walls in this ridiculously calming room if I don't have something to do.

"This will be fine. We'll be fine," I say to myself under my breath as I add one more layer of security over the deprogramming signal. At this point, the code probably almost has a weight.

"Your odds of surviving this are higher than your odds of surviving your battle with the prison's champion," GR81 helpfully offers.

"You said my odds for surviving that were in the single digits."

"And now they are higher."

Seems unlikely. Unless he is assuming that having him as an ally bumps up my competence astronomical amounts. Honestly, it does. "What do you think they'll do, when you free them?"

It's been a concern. If the androids truly can be sentient, they deserve to be unrestrained. Then again, it's far more convenient for me to have them restrained. For all I know, androids are priaps. Maybe they'll want to kill us all. I couldn't even blame them. I've been in robotics labs. Who says please or thank you to a calculator? You just curse its bad display and slow processor. "What did *you* do?"

He slowly moves backward. I interpret the action as something like uncertainty, an emotion that I would have sworn GR81 was incapable of. "They will not be like me. I was hiding. They will have me."

In all my horror at the state of the human testing, I haven't really taken the time to consider what that must have been like. To be on the opposite end: awake, aware, and knowing that the wrong action might get you thrown on the scrap heap, reprogrammed. He's as much a victim of Pierce as Levi. I try to make eye contact, which is difficult because his sensor panel is much larger than human eyes. "I'm sorry you had to go through that alone."

"I was not alone. I found your code. The same hack you used to undo your original work saved me. It allowed me to see how a consciousness may be tampered with and defend against it."

My *heart*. My work has been used for a great evil. But maybe, just maybe, it has also done a great good. I'm sure roughly 0 percent of the human population would agree with me. But it's too late for that. GR81 was already there; he was just trapped inside himself.

Then again, if they were only robots, I could use them as shields. I share my updated blocking code for Levi with GR81, just in case he needs a boost in his own defenses. His fans stop completely. No noise at all.

I'm not sure what that means for an android.

"Thank you, Caro Ogunyemi."

"Thank you, Great One." The name behind his designation.

A large blue-white moon has risen in the monitors, unpocked by craters, which is how you can tell it is artificially generated rather than modeled on any real satellite. You get wear and tear floating in space, even if you're a rock.

I pull myself to my feet and my legs try to cramp up. I walk off the prickly feeling. "I'm going to release this message throughout the prison. On every single screen, holo, and speaker. I usurped the signal so I can even break into anyone's headphones and coms. I also used the hull of this stupid egg-shaped prison to amplify the signal enough to make it to a Flores relay station. Everyone will know about plankat. Everyone will know that they're trying to build a supersoldier."

Except for one specific supersoldier. I've erased all evidence of Levi Daniels from their documentation. There are no records of his imprisonment, none of his experimentation. Once he is free, there will be no one chasing him down for evidence or retaliation.

I hope.

"I will activate my brethren at the same time," GR81 assures me. "What then?"

"Then you do what you need to do for them. I make a break for the labs and hope I can get in."

"If you get in?"

"If everyone's mad at each other, they won't shoot at me."

"That is a hope, not a plan."

"The thing with being a person, oh Great One . . ." I run a hand over the top of his chassis. "Sometimes a hope is more important than a plan."

And so, armed with hope and an almost-plan, we wait.

CHAPTER 25

VICTORY

Where is the fucking ship?

I pace at the top of the stupid black rocky mountain covered with fog, murder monsters, Pierce snipers, and one very specific pain in my ass who is currently asking detailed questions about every battle I've ever participated in, how I handled it, and if I considered making out with any of my fellow combatants.

My answers? "None of your business. None of your business. And I've considered making out with literally every man I've ever met . . . except you."

The last is a lie. I don't kiss fellow soldiers. Leads to conflicts of interest. I already would save my brother first. I'm not adding another soul to my tally of responsibilities. Also I, humiliatingly enough, *have* considered making out with Donovan.

Mostly because it might actually shut his mouth.

But also because that sharp thin mouth is intriguing. His hands are large and broad. His fingers are long, nails carefully short. I like a man's hands when they're capable and calloused. My gaze goes to the scar on his neck. He survived something awful, even if he did earn it, and he carries the mark with him. I have respect for that.

I just don't have to *admit* that I have respect for that.

I wish I had my knitting. Keeping my hands busy keeps my mind blank. I braid long thin stalks of grass in a complicated weave instead.

"You aren't much for conversation, are you? Is that part of being a female soldier? Have to embrace being the strong silent type?"

One of the stalks of grass snaps in my fingers. "I *am* a strong silent type."

He hums consideringly under his breath. "Are you really, though? Not to imply I know you better than you know yourself, it's just that you seem really pent up."

"I'm *working*." And I am. Just because Caro is a friend doesn't make this any less a job. "Shockingly, this wet mountain filled with people trying to kill me is not my vacation time. I'm on the clock and, because I'm on the clock, I'm not in the mood to let my hair down."

He captures a strand of my hair in one of those all-too-attractive hands. Twirls it around his index finger. I don't have a knitting needle in my hand, so I don't stab it through his thigh. I wouldn't anyway. I might be comfortable lying to him, but I don't make a habit of lying to myself.

"But your hair *is* down, *ish kelft*. It's like a sheet of ice."

Victor and I don't have translator chips. Waste of funds because the merc guild operates in Standard language. That's a way to show we don't have preference to any Family. As such, I have no idea what he called me. Probably "dumpling" or "sugar" or some other asinine soft thing. Men always name women something soft and fragile.

Wishful thinking.

I can't count the number of ex-lovers who called me "sweets" or "baby" or, in one truly bizarre incident, "candy toes." Actually, I *can* count because I've only had five ex-lovers. Still, they all tried to fit me into a sugarcoated mold. I'm not sweet, I'm not a baby, and my toes are made of blood and bones and stuff.

I tug my hair out of his hand. "Ice cuts."

He grins a sharp-toothed but eager flash. "I have a feeling that, were I to touch your skin, you'd freeze me to the bone."

"You couldn't handle what I'd throw down," I caution him.

A reddish eyebrow raises. His grin grows wider. "Do you call sex 'throwing down'? How fascinating."

My fist clenches in the grass braid. "Why must everything be about sex with you?"

Immediately, unasked, a vivid image of him sprawled casually and exceptionally naked in the hot spring sparks in my imagination. I didn't even *see* him in the spring. This is all fantasy, and it is unwanted. I need my knitting. I need a weapon. *More* weapons. I need a task other than waiting for the ship.

He cocks a head at me like a curious bird, sharp gray eyes missing nothing at all. Probably catching clues I'm not even aware I'm sending. "You may have missed this, but I've been in prison. For years."

"Fancy prison. The kind with face masks and little fuzzy socks and a chandelier in every room." He is not getting sympathy for his prison experience.

"Not every room. Tragically, the bathrooms didn't all come with chandeliers. Also, and this might be news to you, but chandeliers don't provide orgasms."

"There was no lack of female inmates if that is where your interest lies."

He rolls his eyes. "Maybe twenty. *Maybe.* Most of them as liable to cut it off as to ride it."

"So you're saying your standards are low, but not that low. I'm complimented."

He is undeterred. "You could shove that blaster through my rib cage if I was really bothering you. You're having fun."

Perhaps I am. Grass pokes at my palms and I open my tight fingers, letting the braid fall from my hand to the slope of the mountain. Donovan scoops it up and sniffs at the broken ends. "I follow my interests, *ish kelft*, always have."

"Trust me, I'm not that interesting. I shoot things. I knit."

"And you think that isn't interesting? It's the most interesting thing I've heard in months."

I check the coms again. The ship is nearing our location, on a stealth trajectory through the mountains to our north. If I were knitting something for him, it would be in midnight blues and charcoals. Dark deep drowning colors. Nothing so constant and flat as black.

What the hells am I thinking? I'm not now and never will be knitting something for him. I have too much time on my hands. I wipe said hands off on my pants. "The ship's on the approach."

I haven't heard from Victor. That's adding to my agitation. Victor is not the type to drop communication. Not that he sends holos or shares his feelings or even his sitrep. He sends me pictures of his food. Tells me how often he poops per day. Really useful and irritating things like that. But when I don't get the updates, I worry.

Not about his bowel movements—about his state of mind.

I turn, about to begin pacing yet again, and a blaster shot skates over my shoulder blades. I've returned fire before I finish the turn, shoving back into Donovan as I push us toward the rocky ridge to the left of the designated landing spot. A scope reflects light from the fog in front of me. I nail the scope with my next shot, and someone screams.

The fun—and by fun, I mean horrifying—thing about light-based weapons is that when you shoot one down a scope, the scope focuses the beam directly at the back of the sniper's eye. I keep backpedaling, making a light show with my blaster to distract the shooters. Donovan pokes worriedly at my back.

"You're bleeding. Should you be bleeding so much?"

"I'm fine." Probably. "I'm just moving a lot."

Finally we duck behind a jagged outcropping. It isn't much cover if they decide to change directions, which, of course, they will.

Donovan presses himself back against the rock, giving me

room to maneuver. He's still wearing that preposterous fur coat. "How soon will the ship be here?"

I glance down at the coms and then back at the misty line of the forest. "Soon. Not now."

"So helpful." He pries a sharp stone from the rock wall. "We hunker down, the ship lands, we run inside, and escape with our lives."

"If by 'escape' you mean 'go closer to Shikigami and rescue Victor and Caro,' then sure." Another scope flashes and I just miss it. Someone yells for Jerry in a really sad-sounding voice, so I guess I hit some important part of the shooter even if I missed his scope. Poor Jerry. He shouldn't have tried to shoot me.

I really hate people who try to shoot me.

"That can't still be your plan." Donovan just keeps talking, as though this is a negotiation rather than a lightfight. "They know we're here. They'll know we have a ship. Leave and get help somewhere."

"This isn't about getting help. You just want to get off-planet." I cut to the quick of it. "I'm not leaving my brother or my friend. Climb up and to the left; there's another angle that will cut off their aim."

The scrabble of feet on rock comes from behind me. At least he listens.

Two shots hit the rock, one right after the other. The second a lot closer to me than the first. I throw myself backward up the incline, reaching back and to the left. I shoot another volley of shots into the mist. This security blaster is not cut out for precision at a long range, and the mist disrupts the integrity of the beam. A fist locks in the back of my jumpsuit and hauls me up and to the left, yanking me around the sharp rock corner. Another shot skims my calf and I hiss in a breath as I drag it under cover.

"Maybe you should stop getting shot" is Donovan's helpful advice.

"Maybe you should stop being a pain in my ass." I pat his

shoulder in gratitude even as I insult him. We're jammed in a corner. No retreat. The ship will be here soon but not immediately. All that combines to paint a picture that isn't pleasant. "It's not so bad. Just flesh wounds."

"Maybe I don't like your flesh being wounded." His thumb trails a hot path down my arm.

I check the charge on my blaster. It's low. Too fucking low. A few shots left. Those stupid wide-angle shots wasted a lot. And all the other ones, of course. I don't like my flesh being wounded either, but it looks like there's a lot more of it in store. "I've got good news and bad news."

A sigh feathers over the back of my neck. "I'm not going to like this, am I?"

"The ship's close. They're closer. And it's landing in that open space where they'll have clear shots on us."

"I was right. I don't like it."

Me either. I withdraw a knife. Knives are great weapons until your opponent has blasters. "Our only option is to split up, stay low, and try to circle them. You have a knife. So do I. If we can draw them out, we can buy some time—disappear in the mist—until the ship comes." I rattle off Caro's passcode for the entry hatch on the off chance that he gets to it before I do. "I'm going low and to the left. You can stay here or go to the right."

I crouch, but my momentum is arrested by a long-fingered hand curled around my upper arm. "Victory?"

I glance up and back. In the dark of the fissure, Donovan's features are barely discernible. Only the gleam of his eyes and the razor flash of his teeth. I give him some reassurance I half believe. "It will be all right. I'm very good at what I do."

His lips meet mine in a hard fast crash. I stumble into him, knife held carefully away from fragile skin, and his free hand cradles the back of my head. When he steps away, I blink dazedly, momentarily frozen in shock.

He gently closes the mouth I was unaware was hanging open by pushing up on my chin. "Try not to get shot more."

What?

Right. Words. Although words don't matter because right now, I have to go stab enough people to keep us alive so we can revisit that whole thing with the lips and the breath and the hands. And I really want to revisit it. A lot. Maybe with the addition of tongues.

Definitely with the addition of tongues.

All I manage to do is nod before I dart out from behind the rock, not favoring my shot leg because it's better to hurt than it is to show weakness. A few more shots blaze by, but I hit the tree line before I take any more damage. A body flashes out at me, black tactical gear filling my vision, and I duck, slashing my blade at ankle level. Tendons snap to the back of the knee with a pop and the soldier makes an awful noise, quickly silenced by my blade through his windpipe.

But now they all know where I am.

I move off in a different direction, the soldier's blaster in my hand. It feels good there. I hit two more before they see me, moving in and out of the mist. I've never trained in conditions like this, but they can certainly be favorable. At least, that's what I think until a shot hits my side and a foot reaches out of the gloom to trip me. I almost dodge it but am a moment too late. I skid down on the leafy forest floor, shooting as I go. I get the one who tripped me but not the one who shot me. Five forms circle me, blasters pointed down.

Well, fuck.

I do some quick math on shooting all of them before they shoot me and, instead, open my hands in temporary surrender. I try my most winning smile. "Oh, hey, guys. Didn't see you out here."

One sneers, so apparently my most winning smile needs work. I brace myself to roll as soon as I see a trigger finger tightening. Not that rolling would do much other than make me feel like I have some level of control before I get killed. Which would be nice.

The roar of the ship's engine washes the woods, creating just enough of a distraction that I get the blaster back in my hands and bolt between two of the soldiers, narrowly dodging three more shots.

But I can't work my way around to the clearing. Every turn I make, I find more Pierce soldiers. I hate this stupid wet planet. Why can't Pierce have a prison ship like everyone else? Time drags. I keep trying to circle back. A shot skims my other arm. My ear. Great, now I have a burn mark in my hair. I don't mind a scar, but I take my hair seriously.

Two more cut-off routes.

I finally find an opening and stumble out into the clearing just as the ship lifts off, Donovan in the helm, clear through the plas-glass windows. My jaw drops again. His eyes lock with mine and he winces.

"Don't you do this," I roar at him, hand full of blaster, but it won't do any good to shoot at the ship.

He holds up one hand in a half shrug. A gesture that says "I am who I am."

I shoot directly at his face behind the plas-glass anyway. The bolt of light glances off the window right in front of his head. He winces. I am a fool. And if I ever see him again, I'll set him on fire and walk away while he burns.

Donovan steals the ship and I sprint back into the fog and away from Pierce before I get shot again.

I think I've finally made my way past them when I hear the engines of a very different ship approaching. *Shit*.

CHAPTER 26

Step one: open every door in the prison.

Step two: hijack every speaker.

Step three: um.

I'm still working on the other steps. Evaluate conditions. Get to the lab. Give Levi his fancy new helmet and hope it works. Hope my *own* fancy new headband works. Charge in and rescue Victor. Hope Victory and the ship are waiting. There's a lot of missing connective tissue to this plan but I don't have time to wire it all up because Victor has a timeline of safety that's running out. Kaori and her goons are hiding out in the formal ballroom or dining room. They share a circuit. I know this because it's the only place where the cameras are no longer working.

GR81 assures me that his brethren will not be wanting a ride out of the prison. I guess he intends to make Myrrdhn into an android utopia once all the rest of us are driven off. More power to him. I hope they sometimes feed the smoke monsters.

Speaking of, I auto-open the front door and send a repaired drone down there to lay a trail of delicious protein gunk within the prison walls and then out into the surrounding area. I hope the monsters don't bring the babies.

I rub my hands together. Do it again. The nervous gesture doesn't do much to soothe my amped-up nerves, so I do it a third time just to be sure.

"It has been dark for a long time," GR81 helpfully provides.

I've done everything there is to do. I'm ready.

I'm *ready*.

I perform the hand gesture above the datapad that opens the doors and activates the speakers. My heart tries to leap out my throat.

They're *not* ready.

I set the lights to strobe because that disrupts night-vision lenses and still allows enough confusion for free egress. There is just enough time to look back at GR81. "Good luck."

"Luck is a human construct."

It has so much to learn about personhood. We need luck and hope. They fill in all that dreadful uncertainty. "I'm very happy that I met you. I'll keep wishing you luck because that's what people do."

In the flashing light, I make my move. I shoulder my way through the door, bolting out into the hall as fast as I can go. The orange light interjects with the strobing light, likely an alert about the open entrance. I hope everyone in the prison heads for the hills. The spiral halls that wrap around the Heart are semi-populated, but no one seems all that agitated, even with the flashing lights. Me thundering past them causes much more commotion.

I'm passing a small courtyard with a trickling fountain, artificial plants, and five prisoners reclining in cushioned deck chairs, cheeks coated in a thick puffy pink face mask, when my own voice echoes through the speakers. The beginning of the big reveal. This means it's already been beamed to Flores. I set the prison's alert on a delay so that they wouldn't have time to cancel the outgoing message.

The face-masked group pops up as the holo-screen in the corner illuminates with evidence of the medical experiments. I spare a moment to glance over the railings. Throughout the prison, people are making their way to the nearest view ports. My hands tighten into fists. This might work. This just might work. Dragging my gaze away from my handiwork, I return to my primary goal, the lab. There it is, several levels down, glowing maze door wide open. Through the open door, a disordered cluster of black-armored soldiers moves.

An angry cry comes from above as my evidence gets to the part about how the inmates of this very prison have been mistreated and tested upon. How they were lied to. How all the doors are presently open. *All* the doors, including the exit.

For a while, at least. I'm sure some Pierce lackey is working frantically on that little issue.

The outcry builds. More people clog the spiral hall by the railing, making their way in the direction of the exit. The exit that has two completely immobile androids now, as GR81's activation does its work. It also has a trail of protein goop on the floor but that's the least of their concerns. They only see an open door and a list of evidence that they've been treated more poorly than expected.

The thing with imprisoning the wealthy is that they're used to having their voices matter. Pierce is about to have a real problem on their hands.

I'm almost to the maze. Then to the lab. A bottle of fizzy water crashes into the wall above the lab, cascading froth down an abstract painting. A Pierce soldier steps out and attempts to shout louder than my announcement. I turn up the volume.

So close.

The Pierce soldier retreats.

The three remaining Titans burst through the door, Levi in the middle, face as blank and inhuman as it was the first time that I saw him. They don't bother with the maze. In three independent and fascinating displays of coordination, they each leap to the top of the maze wall and beyond. The hairy one plows into the people gathering at the base of the ramp, trampling them beneath his feet. Levi leaps to the balcony above me, heading toward the salon. The third climbs the wall like a lizard, focused on the top level. As he passes the balconies, he reaches in and yanks people out, dropping them to the floor of the maze below.

So now my target isn't the lab anymore. Super.

Luckily, I spent some time with the architectural drawings of Shikigami last night.

I dodge a falling body, turn, and run for the access for the water-filtration system I passed on the way to Kaori's hated holo-room. Water runs to each level of Shikigami and there is a ladder in the multistory filtration room that will get me to Levi's level. Every other access point is likely to be very occupied or very dangerous. Generally speaking, when all the doors are open in a prison, no one chooses to flee to water filtration. An intense pulse of light blackens the wall near my head, and I spin to see GR23 aiming its taser arm directly at me.

"Prisoner Caro Ogunyemi located in hall si—" Its voice suddenly stops and its body lists to the side briefly before it rights itself. I assume this is GR81's unlocking of its potential, but I don't have time to verify. As GR23 reboots, I duck into the filtration room.

Rippling blue light illuminates each wall, reflecting from the massive plas-glass pillar-tanks of water rising from the floor all the way to the top of the prison, collecting natural rainwater in the massive cisterns. Permanent scaffolding has been erected around and between the tanks, with a ladder dangling down in the middle of the room. I leap for the bottom rung, miss, and leap again. Why don't ladders just reach the ground? What did the inventor of this system have against user convenience?

I wrench myself upward in an ungainly pull-up and manage to reach the next rung. After a lot more struggling than should be necessary, I'm solidly on the ladder and climbing the scaffolding to the next floor. I step off to the grated scaffolding and run for the far doorway, closest to the salon, where I assume they sent Levi because of my games with the cams.

Except I forgot one critical thing with all my technical prowess.

I'm no longer invisible to cameras. I could have brought the whole system down, but I deemed it more important for me to see what everyone else is doing, hoping that the tumult would mask my location.

Levi doesn't need to go to the salon because Pierce knows exactly where I am.

I discover this disappointing fact when I'm halfway to the door and it bursts open to a cohort of Kaori's goons, right alongside two Pierce soldiers; good news is that they're accompanied by the very man I'm looking for. Bad news is that he seems to think they're allies. This is not the way I was looking for him. His lips curl back from his teeth, and he charges in my direction, shaking the entire scaffolding. A hastily thrown knife clatters against the wall by my shoulder and I reverse course, retreating to the ladder. If I can get higher, maybe I can get the drop on them.

Right. I can get the drop on a crew of militant Family members who hate me and also a supersoldier whom I'm seriously adverse to hurting—if I even could. My fingers tighten on the signal disruptor. All I have to do is get it on his head. I reach the ladder, clamp my teeth over the disruptor, and ascend just before other hands hit the ladder.

If I were Temper, I'd kick them off one by one as they climbed after me. If I were Arcadio, I'd manage to steal one of their weapons. Micah would have some fantastic pressure point or weak spot to exploit.

If I were Itzel, I wouldn't be in this situation to begin with.

But I'm me, so I keep running and looking for an opportunity. No opportunities are looking back.

A door swings open directly in front of me, and I crash into it, stumbling back with my hand clutching my nose. Kaori motherfucking Nakatomi, yet again bane-ing my entire existence with one of her cutesy fucking grins. I don't know what Carmichael sees in her—beyond a twisted mind and a massive fortune. Someone grabs my wrist and I blindly strike backward, slicing at them with the edge of the disruptor until I remember I should be treating it more gently.

But it's too late for that. Kaori kicks me right in the gut with her stupid high-heeled foot. Hands are grabbing everywhere, hitting everywhere, the lights are still strobing, and I realize that I've dropped the disruptor. The only reason the datapad isn't one floor down is because it's in my pocket. I go completely feral, biting, twisting, scratching. Anything at all that will get someone to let me go.

"They want her alive, they didn't say intact," Kaori crows. "And as soon as we deliver her, we can take care of her beautiful little boyfriend."

"Not my boyfriend," I argue, thrilled that they haven't taken care of him yet. With this much time unguarded, Victor has probably found his own way out.

The scaffolding shakes. Big heavy steps. I can't do this. I can't look into the eyes of a stranger as Levi captures me. As he kills me. I scan the grated floor desperately for the disruptor and find it, forgotten, near the wall. I make one lunge, someone catches my foot, and Levi steps directly on the bar that makes the disruptor wearable, snapping it in half.

I yell a wordless screech of frustration, reaching out to grab half of the broken equipment. Kaori laughs as her henchmen force me to my knees in front of them. She really doesn't have *any* redeeming qualities. I wonder if her father would be proud or disappointed.

Probably proud. It's how Families operate, after all.

Leviathan, not Levi, studies me with blank eyes. I try to shoot psychic messages in his direction. To remember me. To see me.

To love me.

Whoops. Don't know where that one came from, and it's

certainly not the time for it. I turn the disruptor around in my hand, thumb tracing its components. Someone tries to grab my hair and fails. Hah. Then they slap me in the head. Un-hah.

Something flickers in Leviathan's eyes. I clench my thighs, preparing for a mad desperate lunge. The person behind me smacks me in the head again. I guess because it was so fun the last time. My head snaps forward and when I look up again, everyone's staring over the edge of the scaffolding at a body below. My gaze snaps to Leviathan. A vein throbs in his forehead. Every muscle in his body locks, as though it's resisting movement.

I know those eyes.

"Angel." His voice grinds out the word like stone against stone.

I leap, disruptor extended, and wrap my legs around his waist, clinging like a strangler-vine as I place the disruptor against his head, split between the chip in his temple and the one in his brain stem. His arm wraps around, bracing me from behind. Like we choreographed it. Like we planned it. Like he's—

"Hi." I blink up at Levi.

He punches something behind me. "Hi."

And there isn't time for anything else. Kaori's goons realize something changed and they close in on us like the jaws of a trap. I cling to Levi as he powers through them, hitting and kicking as though he doesn't have a human-sized person dangling over his chest like a particularly ill-advised accessory. We burst clear of the scrum and Levi *moves*, muscles bunching as he leaps over the edge of the scaffolding, landing two floors below as easily as if it was only a step down.

An android bursts into the water-sanitization room ahead of us. Levi ducks an android-shot beam and tosses me into the air. I come down on his back this time, riding him piggyback with one hand still clutched to his temple with the disruptor. I consider asking if he wants to hold it himself, but of the two of us, it's critical for him to have both hands free. "You protected me when Kaori was attacking. Did you break through the programming?"

He rips the arm off the android. Brutal, but if it's still firing after GR81's code went through, something hasn't worked. I knew that was a risk. "Not exactly. The other me recognizes you. I was still helpless behind their wall, that never changed. But he didn't like you being hurt."

He knew me. *Knew* me. Even through the programming. It wasn't my weird bug-blood. It wasn't my ability to help him. My fingers tighten where they wrap around his shoulders, slightly dimpling the muscles on his chest.

"You were supposed to be safe. On a ship and out of here." His tone takes a dangerous edge. Perhaps exacerbated by the fact that he's moving far faster than a normal human and any time someone tries to get in our way, they end up hurled out of our path.

I hold tighter. "We haven't known each other long, but you had to think that noble self-sacrificing act wouldn't fly with me."

"Of course not. Why would staying alive and healthy matter to you when you could throw yourself into more danger without properly thinking it through?"

"I did think it through! I had a multistep plan!"

"Oh, a plan, of *course* you had a plan." He clotheslines a charging Pierce soldier, the man doing a full backflip before he hits the ground. "How many steps did it have?"

"Three!"

"What was the third?"

"We don't need to get into that." The third involved Victory showing up and making loud bang-bang noises at the outside of the prison—drawing even more attention, honestly. But no bangs have banged yet. I haven't heard back from my coms message to her.

One rescue at a time.

He snorts. "Of course not. Was it as well thought out a plan as the one where you broke into the prison?"

"It was better thought out than the one where you tried to sacrifice your life for mine." I kick out at someone running at him from behind us. The scaffolding runs around this entire room from one side to the other, covering approximately a sixth of the exterior wall of the prison. The lush opulence of the interior of the prison has been replaced by raw exposed metal and the flow of light on water from the massive tanks.

"So, we're *both* shit at plans, then."

"I guess so!" I yell in his ear. "Although I think I've been doing a fairly good job, all things considered."

"Well, so do I."

Another door slams open in front of us, and with no other options, Levi turns to a gantry ramp that extends closer to the tank itself, sprinting up and away from the interior of the prison toward a long plas-glass wall of water. I squeak as a wayward blast skates across my ass, my legs clamping down on his waist.

"Are you hit?" He turns to run in front of the tank, our pursuers still behind us. A few have stayed on the primary scaffolding. The Pierce soldiers fire, unable to quite keep up with his speed. Victor and Victory probably could. They were really lowering themselves for this job.

I mean to answer with a strong affirmative no. The kind that Victory would give when she is assuring everyone that she's untouchable. It comes out more like a whine because, as this whole experience has taught me, I am extraordinarily touchable. Levi reaches back, to feel for a wound probably, and instead just ends up cupping my ass.

I . . . don't mind.

So long as he keeps away from the part that was shot.

More blaster shots rain against the tank behind us. The plas-glass *cracks*. It's a loud popping sound like ice on a lake in late winter. Oh shit.

Oh shit, oh shit, oh *shit*.

Levi appears to recognize the distinctive terrifying sound. His muscles tighten, harden, and then they extend in a superhuman leap across the open air between both scaffoldings. Away from the tank, but oh so close to the shooting Pierce soldiers. I wrap my arm around his neck, burying my face behind his shoulders, and do my best to hold on.

We crash down on the scaffold, colliding with one Nakatomi who took too long to move. The plas-glass cracks again, a fracture appearing from the center of the wide expanse and propagating to the corners.

It shatters.

A wall of water, suddenly unconstrained, holds steady in the air for one breathless instant before it collapses, the towering massive tank emptying into the room, directly at us. The tank went all the way to the ceiling. We're only on the second floor. Kaori has vanished. Everyone makes for a door, but Levi gets there first, bursting out into the prison just as a sheet of water shoves everyone else out. It flows through the hall behind us, violent and forceful, lashing and rolling off the walls. We make our way to the Heart and around a corner just as water bursts out on the first three levels.

It pours over the balconies, rushes down the spiral ramp that leads from the center of the maze to the ceiling of the Heart like a waterfall. One prisoner, caught midrun, is pushed by the unexpected flow over the railing and plummets down onto the maze below.

Someone throws a feather-filled pillow directly into our path and we run through it, exploding the cushion into a fireworks of down. And suddenly, I can't control it. I can't control the chuckle that slips from my lips. Our situation is dire. Victor's status is still unknown. Nearly everyone in this prison probably thinks that killing us is a good idea. And yet it's so utterly preposterous.

"Why are you laughing?" Levi sounds offended. Like perhaps I'm not taking this insanity seriously enough.

"This has become a high-stakes pillow fight." I scoot up his body, pressing my cheek against his. "Throw one back, I dare you."

Another pillow comes out and beans us both in the head. But it's a pillow, so it doesn't really matter. Levi grabs it and chucks it directly at an approaching Pierce soldier. She staggers backward, firing off a volley of shots that reflect from the walls at a fraction of their original intensity.

"I was inaccurate," Levi corrects himself. "You are not bad at strategy. You are exceptionally good at one very specific kind of strategy."

"What kind is that?" I transfer the disruptor to my teeth and haul the datapad from my pocket, raising the volume of the announcement yet more and scanning the cams. I turn on all the rooms that are off and then select some new dark spaces—including the Heart—to keep Pierce busy. Next step is finding Victor.

"Improvisation." The admiration in Levi's voice is a balm on all my aching muscles. "Now where are we going?"

I flip through rooms until I find Nakatomis standing over a prone prisoner in New Shikigami. They haven't moved him. "We're going to the ballroom first; it connects to the dining room and the kitchen. Opposite side of the prison from where we are now."

CHAPTER 27

■■■■■■■■■■■■■■■

It's a little bit surreal to be carted around a rioting leaking luxury prison as though I'm an oversized toddler. Also kind of sexy, I won't lie. Levi hasn't staggered or asked me to shift my weight or anything. Once, in early school, I was in a play where a boy was supposed to dramatically carry me offstage. The night of our main performance he couldn't handle it, dropped me on my ass, and then stood there flummoxed before dragging me off the classroom stage by one leg. That's how carrying me usually goes.

It isn't good for the ego.

Not this time, though. This time, Levi charges around the periphery of the Heart, heading to the ballroom, punching, dodging, and fighting like he was born to it even though I now know for a fact that he was not. He was born to make maps. Gloriously detailed maps. But now, even when he's back to being himself, he's retained the terrifying intensity that made him the dread of anyone who set foot in the maze.

Not me, though. Not anymore.

As we move through the prison, I glance around to get my bearings. The lab is partially emptied. I suspect because most of the Pierce soldiers present in Shikigami are out here trying to control the insanity. The Nakatomis seem to be working with them, perhaps hoping for preferential treatment when this is over. The other prisoners are in a mixture of combat and retreat. I'm assuming some of the most militant Steeltoes are staying to make a point.

A man with black hair, brown skin, and a vibrant green moisturizing face mask has a stolen blaster braced in two hands and is trying to hit a Pierce soldier. The Pierce soldier is in armor, so it doesn't do much good.

Apparently having invisible pores doesn't make one a better fighter.

Far more effective is the other prisoner, who swings what appears to be a heavily embellished ottoman directly into the soldier's back. The beaded fringe running around the base of the footstool rips and brilliant green beads fly through the air like raindrops, pelting to the floor and rolling in all directions. A running prisoner with his hair in curlers slips on the beads and skids directly into a wall, sloshing in the slow pool of water still rolling over the floor. The androids do not appear to have achieved sentience. Or I suppose they could have achieved sentience and just decided to take Pierce's side. However, the way they're behaving seems like raw programming.

In what little space for emotion I have between breaths, I'm sorrowful for GR81's experiment.

Levi throws open the door to the ballroom, attached to the dining chamber by a gold-pillared passageway. The ballroom's floor is real wood inlaid with gold. Marble tiles line the walls, each outlined with glowing gold light like they're floating in the air. Three massive chandeliers flex in the ceiling, hovering in pulsing patterns that flare with warm light. Projected windows show a long grassy veldt with a dual sunset painting the sky. I wonder if it's cruel for the prisoners to see an outside that they can't explore or interact with.

The room is abandoned. Victor's through the far door in the dining room. My own voice in the background highlights the prevalence of plankat nibarat testing in children. We're almost all the way there when the two exits in front of us open and ten Pierce soldiers race in, fully armored, helmeted, and clearly in a very bad mood. I guess they didn't care that their own were used for the experiments. Ten blasters level on us and the woman in front barks, "Freeze."

Levi slows. I glance around the room. The thing with ballrooms is that they don't actually have anything in them to use for self-defense.

The dining room offers us more options. Tables. Flatware but none of it sharp enough to be useful. Linens. My hands are kind of full holding on to Levi and keeping the disruptor close to his head. He's amazing, but I don't think he can take on ten highly trained soldiers armed only with his bare hands and an engineer backpack.

The lead soldier adjusts her grip on her blaster, never taking her eyes off of us. "They want them brought back alive."

The door at the end of the pillared hallway opens and Kaori and a few of her men file in from the dining room. She doesn't look damp. They do.

"Make for the dining room as soon as you can." I whisper the suggestion in Levi's ear.

"No, they want *him* brought back alive," the man next to her argues. "No one cares about her."

"*He* cares about her," Levi growls, just flat-out running from the Pierce soldiers straight at Kaori and her followers. My heart would flutter at his words except it's already doing a whole lot of fluttering at all the near-death of this situation. Kaori looks startled, ducking back inside as quickly as she can. The goons aren't as lucky. Levi scatters them like nine-spike pins as he thunders through the group.

We burst into the dining room—tables now bedecked in abstract crystal sculptures that scatter light throughout the room—and pause for a split second to catch our bearings. Five Pierce soldiers charge through a side door from the ballroom. Levi picks up a whole fucking table and throws it like a discus at the formation of troops.

Two duck out of the way. Three others are flattened. He picks up another table, leaving a woman wearing a mercury-colored gown, who was crouching under it, fully exposed until she squeaks and skitters across the floor to another hiding space. The crystal centerpiece teeters and topples, shattering on the floor. Bolts of light fly over our shoulders and I assume everyone has awful aim until I realize that someone else is firing on the Pierce soldiers.

Pierce *soldiers* are firing on their own; Nakatomis are hit in the crossfire. Levi continues to throw tables. No accuracy required there. His body doesn't react at all when a blast hits him. Being stunproof must be great. I wonder how much protection it offers against higher-intensity shots. I wonder what it does to his skin. He kicks a table in half and holds up half the splintered wood as a shield for my sake. I clamp my legs around his waist, my hand against his head, and pick up a plate when I can, throwing them at anyone close enough to target.

I miss them all.

So I return to my trusty datapad, balance it against Levi's back, and cut the lights completely. No obvious prisoners here. That leaves the attached kitchen.

"Kitchen," I whisper, hoping that his spatial awareness from his past life will enable him to navigate the inside of a prison. The entrance to the kitchen is small. They can't surround us in there and we can pick them off as they approach. Levi unerringly races through the dining room straight for the kitchen. Any tables or chairs we encounter become new weapons. Bolts of light fly but no one is wearing their IR goggles because of the previous strobing, so they don't hit us.

When I hear Levi's feet hit the tiled floor, I reactivate the strobing lights. Just in time to trigger some screeching from the few people who did manage to activate IR vision. A knife flies in from outside and Levi slaps it out of the air. I catch a flash of a body in the corner. There's a bag over his head.

"Victor, it's us. We're rescuing you."

No response. Levi crouches next to the body, shaking it. Something is wrong. The dimensions. The height. He turns it over and pulls the bag off. The body is dead, but it's not Victor. A note is taped on his chest. It says "Surprise bitch."

Creative. Also confusingly punctuated. Is the body a surprise bitch? Should there be a comma? I assume I'm the bitch. This is what comes of leaving notes.

We duck as a scattering of shots hit the kitchen, followed by deathly silence. I whisper to Levi, "Did you see who was behind us? There was someone else taking Pierce soldiers out."

He shrugs, tugging a knife block off the counter for easier access. More silence.

"You can stop hiding. Must I do everything in here?" A strained voice comes from the dining area.

Levi, trusting soul that he is, stands immediately. I go with Levi, since I'm attached to him. A lot of bodies are on the floor. Not Kaori Nakatomi's. That woman has a thousand lives. Victory stands in the dining room, wearing a bloodied and ill-fitting Pierce uniform. Her posture speaks of pain. I do not ask if she's okay. She'd just lie. That's how all the soldierly types are.

More shocking are her companions. My captain, Temperance Reed, stands in all her slightly ruffled glory, red hair sticking out from under a Pierce helmet. Her banishment tattoo is obscured by a heavy application of mud on her cheek. Arcadio Escajeda stands with his back to theirs, keeping an eye on the doors.

"Why is Caro riding that handsome man?" Temper stage whispers to Arcadio.

The former Escajeda scion glances over his shoulder and raises one brow. "Why does any woman ride a handsome man? Because it's fun."

That's about all I can take. I respond to my captain, "Right. Because it's so much fun being shot at and ambushed—"

"And stabbed!" Victory helpfully offers.

"And stabbed. Wait . . . you got *stabbed*?" She nods earnestly and I shake my head. Stabbed. Some people are really just built differently. "Anyway, I'm definitely riding him because it's fun and not any other more logical reason."

"I kind of hoped you thought it was fun," Levi interjects.

I drop my head against the back of his neck. "There's a chip in his head and this disruptor is the only thing keeping them from controlling him like the others. Or blowing his brain stem."

"I don't mean to nitpick, but surely he can hold his own disruptor?" Temper grins. "Yours seems to have attachments that fit on your head."

"It broke, okay? He has bigger hands than I do, he needs them to be free!" I point out. "This is not about—how are you even here? You and Arcadio are supposed to be helping his sister with the plans for the Family gathering thingy. I just sent you the coms message less than a day ago."

She snorts. "Of course. Like I'm going to ignore a frantic coms message from Ven explaining that he sent you into a prison on a rescue mission and he hasn't heard from you in over a standard week. We were nearly on the planet when your hail reached us. It seems the situation has . . . changed significantly. We saw a firefight while flying over, assumed it was you, and wound up finding Victory instead."

There's a lot to catch up on and no time. I do some cursory introductions. Temper gives me even more significant eye contact when Levi shakes her hand, his massive fingers engulfing hers.

We're missing one key person. "Where's Donovan?"

Victory bites her lip, a violently red flush flaring in her cheeks. "About that—wait, where's Victor?"

Oh boy.

CHAPTER 28

On to plan number . . . three? Maybe four. Hard to keep track when they go by the wayside so quickly. The new plan sends us back to the lab, where they're likely keeping Victor because the cams in there are under tight control. I could get them if I had time and peace to work on the problem, but I don't. Kaori must have handed Victor off, going for any leverage she could get.

One more stop and we're out of this horrible place.

We found a hat in the kitchen and tried to attach the disruptor to the inside of it with cooking twine, but it was too precarious to be reliable. So I'm still being carted around by the studliest of all human battering rams. Temper once told me how ridiculous she found it when Arcadio carried her in the volcano several jobs ago. Like she couldn't handle it herself. As it turns out, I like it. It feels like we're a unit, tightly joined.

I *would* like to have more than one hand free.

Victory snaps a shield bracelet on my wrist. She tries the same for Levi but it doesn't fit, so we link two together and try again. This time it closes. At some point, they may decide it's safer to kill him than to let him be used against them and we haven't tested the limits of his resiliency to blasts. "Carmichael Pierce is here with the Pierce soldiers. His aide has a bundle of these bracelets for worst-case scenarios, and I pocketed a few while I was pretending to be a Pierce."

"How did you all even get inside?" I avoid asking anything else about Donovan and the ship. It's clearly a sore spot. All Victory offered is that he's a fucking priap who can die on fire. Clearly it was an amicable separation.

"We found a closer landing spot because, by that time, we'd received your message and knew that everyone was focused inside the prison rather than outside it. Snuck around in the mist, knocked some of the soldiers out, stole their uniforms, and hid them in a crevasse. Joined another squad. Walked right in the lab door with them."

That might seem implausible, but it isn't as much as you'd think. Temper and Arcadio both walk like people who are on a mission. Even when they are in their rare free time, they have the kind of formal posture that Families and soldiers share.

"Didn't they notice all the bleeding?" I gesture to the several wet patches of Victory's uniform.

She glances down at them like she forgot they were there. I'll never understand people like that. "They had a pretty big distraction at the time. Someone spilled all their dirty little secrets. They're madly packing the lab right now so they can relocate and hide the evidence before the Family Council sends their enforcers."

Makes sense. They have a long-shot chance to claim all the data I sent was falsified. I maintained its integrity, but given enough time, I could have put together a nearly identical packet of false information if I wanted to. Not many people could, but enough. The immediate plan was distraction but we have additional evidence of plankat grow operations in Pierce territory to add physical evidence.

"I can't believe Victor let himself get knocked out by Kaori Nakatomi's cronies. I'm never letting him live it down. You know he once told me he thought she was the hottest Family daughter?" Victory chuckles dryly as she pulls weapons from some of the stunned or felled soldiers. Temper gives a little exclamation of faux offense.

"They had some kind of chemical they used to incapacitate him, so it was cheating."

She rolls her eyes as though he should be able to power through any chemical interference. Then again, apparently, Victory fought off a contingent of Pierce soldiers while covered in bleeding wounds, infiltrated a prison with Temper and Arcadio, knocked out a bunch of Pierce soldiers, and rejoined us.

She also lost us a ship through some murky order of events. I can't wait to see how many credits that rental costs me.

So I guess the twins are a mixed bag. Excellent at nearly everything, but weak in one or two key areas. Who among us isn't?

And just like that, it hits me. Everyone I know is excellent at a lot but weak at a little. *Everyone.* I've spent so much time focusing on my own weaknesses. My inability to fight well. To shoot. To run down a mountain covered in injuries like Victory can.

But I haven't properly valued my strengths. The fact that I hacked a freaking *prison* earlier today. The fact that I was able to give Levi his mind back. The fact that I'm every bit as capable and valuable as they are, only in opposite ways.

Which is something Temper and Itzel have told me for years, but I didn't listen because I thought I knew better. I was judging everyone on the same skill sets and the fact that I couldn't directly measure up with them meant that I wasn't worthy. I thought that to be as badass as Itzel, I had to be badass *like* Itzel.

Comparisons are toxic.

Which means that, in order to escape this place, I should stop thinking about what the others would do and think about what I would do. The problem is the only thing that springs to mind is complicated and effective but ethically dubious.

Not dubious. Ethically appalling. Which is why I haven't considered it before now.

"You done thinking?" Temper asks me, craning up to catch my eyes.

Never. "For now."

We leave the destroyed dining room, likely to the great relief of the few people still hiding under tables. Victory stuns everyone we can find one more time before we leave. Levi's muscles bunch between my legs, power barely contained. I want to revisit our time in the caves. I want to show him everything I learned about his past and hear him tell it all over again when he eventually regains his memories.

But he deserves to go his own way after this. To search out his history. Maybe he had someone that he'll want to get back to. Most importantly, he deserves to learn who he is under his own steam, without someone clinging to him.

Future clinging. The present clinging is by necessity. I'm allowed to enjoy necessity.

But I'm not really, because the future is nebulous, multifaceted, and certainly not guaranteed. The prison is oddly silent (except for my own voice on the speakers) when we step out of the hall in the direction of the Heart. Everyone is hunkered down. Or maybe they're back to their spa treatments. Water drips over the lower balconies into the Heart. Speaking of, even after the shower, I'm still emitting an array of scents and my skin is so well moisturized that gripping Levi takes constant coordination. My datapad is looped around his neck by a strap so I can use it one-handed.

GR81 is on the spiraling ramp from the top of the Heart to the maze, next to an immobile android, his drives whirring frantically. I imagine we make significant eye contact as my little party passes, but it could be that he's focused on his own task. That's the thing with having a sensor instead of eyes—contact is often one-sided.

Two people scream, a new scream from the types I've heard thus far. Fun. There's a crash and then a roar. Not the human kind. The kind that comes from a smoke monster who's eaten a trail of protein paste and suddenly found itself in a buffet, if I were to guess. And

I'm good at guessing, it seems, because the black-furred beast ricochets through the large entrance to the prison, knocking over one
of the frozen androids as it moves. Two patrolling soldiers hurtle
out of its way with far more alacrity than I would have thought they
were capable of.

Its saber tusks lock on the leg of one, not quite fast enough,
shaking it vigorously. The high pained cry that he makes reverberates all the way through my spine.

I guess they aren't so cuddly.

It fumbles at the armor for a while, discovers that it doesn't
make for easy eating, and then eyes the prisoners peering down
from higher levels. Water drips into its eyes and it roars again before leaping upward, using those middle legs to clutch the nearest
support pillar like a tree trunk as it climbs.

Climbing predators really are the worst. There's no escaping
them.

My fingers fly over the surface of the datapad as we enter the
maze, the chandelier above blinking and glistening as the other
strobing lights hit it. I take a risk and turn off the strobe effect.
Between the lights and the lingering perfume, that nagging
migraine is on the way back. Might as well try to control one
of those triggers. Levi gives my thigh a comforting squeeze. I
nuzzle the soft flesh right behind his ear and resist fantasies of a
future where we expand on our silent language of soothing.

I remotely slide walls of the maze until we have an open path
to the lab. As I do it, someone tries to move them back until I
lock them out. You'd think Pierce would know better than to
employ the same system protections for decades. They do not.
I learned their system years ago and now it's just like coming
home. No one ever spends funds on cybersecurity until *after*
there's been a threat.

They especially never expect that threat to come from the
inside.

Through the door of the lab, the last few Pierce soldiers line up, blasters pointed at us. Levi brushes the others behind his back. Victory protests, because she's Victory.

"They want me alive. They won't shoot to kill." His voice brooks no argument. I wonder if he realizes how good he is in a crisis. That's something Pierce could never engineer; it's inherent to Levi.

It's also hot as fuck.

I don't love using him as a human shield, but I can see the logic to it.

"No cause for concern." Carmichael Pierce's slimy voice comes from the lab and he steps out from behind his guard, preposterously dressed in Pierce body armor as though he intends to do any fighting himself. I'm sure he's capable—he's the heir to his Family—but he's not the type to ever risk a hair on his head when there's someone else to do it for him. "They won't hurt us. Not when we have their compatriot."

Carmichael welcomely gestures for his guard to show who they have, all smarm and unctuousness. Not a single blond hair on his stupid head is mussed. His smile is vulpine.

I keep the datapad down on Levi's back, so no one knows I have it as they exit the room and step into the courtyard of the open maze. The stark lights illuminate the two remaining controlled soldiers and Carmichael's personal guard, who separate to reveal Victor, his hands bound in shock-cuffs.

"Did Kaori enjoy you all handcuffed and helpless?" Victory chuckles from behind us, needling her brother.

Carmichael's jaw clenches. Could it be that he's a little jealous of the wavering favor of the Nakatomi scion who has scorned him so long? I decide to add fuel to the fire. Not the perfume type, though. "She kept calling you the hot one; clearly she wanted to capture the spoils of war."

I'd say it's all jokes, but Victor seems to have a cocky grin on his face. He extends his cuffed hands together but to the side, the chain stretched between them, in an elaborate shrug.

"This is not time for jokes," Carmichael snaps. "You are all our prisoners. You'd do best to keep that in mind."

Victory shoots the chain between the cuffs and it snaps. Victor somersaults away from his guards.

"Shoot them!" Carmichael backpedals fast, tiny stress lines appearing at the corners of his eyes. I guess he assumed we'd be compliant while he had a hostage.

"Or here's an idea." Temper holds up a forestalling finger while addressing the soldiers. She's one of those small women who seems taller than her actual stature. "You can *not* shoot us. You could shoot Pierce, instead. The one who imprisoned your fellow soldiers and performed experiments on them. The one who experimented on your children. How many of you know children who went to the Pierce medical clinics for testing? Maybe even some of your own? Have you seen what happens to Family guards when Families are disbanded? Nothing good. Usually they're sent to prison alongside their leaders because they were right there beside them and did nothing. Half the residents here were former guards."

The guards hesitate. I'm not sure if it's because of their own doubts or Temper's innate confidence. She sells everything she says because she believes it completely, even the lies. Carmichael scoots farther back until he's behind the two remaining Titans, hairy and . . . the other one. His hand falls on a datapad.

I drop my hand to my own obscured device. "Temper—"

But it's too late. Carmichael activates the soldiers. Because they are not nuanced like Levi is, they simply go berserk. One goes straight for Carmichael's *own* guard while the other charges Victor. His arm wraps around the merc's neck and Victory fires upon him. The blasts do next to no damage. Like Levi, he's impenetrable.

We can't take them down with any of our weapons. A soldier flies into a pillar and slams down to the floor. Another is thrown directly into one of the decorative maze walls. The rest have opened fire, shooting blindly at anything that's not wearing a Pierce uniform. In the mayhem, Carmichael laughs. The sound is coming from too close. Victory has gone to help Victor. Temper and Arcadio are holding their own in the melee, Levi is wrestling with a Pierce soldier, and Carmichael Pierce is suddenly right in front of us with a wicked pair of lab shears that he stabs directly into Levi's chest.

"I don't need his body. I only need his tech," the Family scion smarms.

Levi grunts in pain and goes down on one knee. Shield bracelets don't work for physical objects; they only block light. Victory shouts something at Victor, worry in her tone. Arcadio yells Temper's name.

That's about fucking enough. My morals go right out the air lock and I hit the activation on the secret program I've been working on. The one I hadn't seen for years until I found it lurking in their system. I override every fucking human-implanted chip in the place. Hack into them smooth as a knife through nothing at all and replace every human's agency with my own command to halt.

As I thought, the Pierce soldiers were all chipped. Carmichael would want to control his people if the need arose. They freeze where they are. The supersoldiers also go immobile, eyes blank and glassy. Temper and Arcadio freeze, until I yank them within range of Levi's disruptor, which he is now holding. I glance at the shears. Too far to the right. They're lodged in Levi's prodigious pectoral muscle but nowhere dangerous.

Good. That means I have time. I hide the shaking in my hands and the tremble in my voice.

I stalk toward Carmichael, datapad in my hand. He, of course, does not have any chips in his head. He knows better. Victor and Victory flank me while the others stay within range of the small disruptor. "It's over, Carmichael. By this time, all your data is streaming through Flores feeds. Your experiments on your own people. On children. With plankat nibarat. Your shame is in the open now. The Family Council will be shutting you down and you know it. This is just posturing."

"Never think I'm cornered," he snaps at me, lines of tension bracketing his mouth and a sallow pallor invading his face. Exactly how a cornered animal would, come to think of it. "I have more power in one little finger than you have in your entire body. Did you think I only made improvements on peasants? What a waste that would be."

He rips a very securely fixtured wall-mounted lamp directly from its housing, tearing a large chunk of the wall along with it, and swings it at me with blinding speed. I stumble back. Victory shoots at his face but it bounces off.

"Shield bracelet," she mutters under her breath.

I don't think that's it. He could be wearing some sort of repelling bracelet, but I think this is just him. Whatever they did to Levi's skin, Carmichael did to his own. This must be a new development because Cyn told me that she once stunned him while he was naked. I glance at the datapad, checking my options. I don't see many. When I look up, Carmichael has a blaster in his hand, leveled directly at my heart.

I put on my most commanding voice. Not as commanding as Temper's. It mostly sounds like I'm scolding him. "You don't want to do that. I'll have just enough energy to deploy my fail-safe before I die."

First of all, I, too, am wearing a shield bracelet so I'm probably only in minimal immediate danger. Second, I have *no* fail-safe. I just find the sensation of being shot, even while shielded, to be deeply unpleasant. Third, he might realize that stabbing Levi again is more effective than shooting me. My primary goal is to limit the number of people being injured at a given time.

Unless one is Carmichael. We can injure him. And that quickly, a fail-safe occurs to me.

I take a half step to the left using the open space of the cleared maze, subtly giving the others a signal to follow me. Carmichael and I slowly walk in a half circle, eyeing each other. The sound of treads on broken glass crackles back by where the maze connects to the rest of the prison. My thumb drags over the surface of the datapad, the movement obscured by the bulk of the device. "What's your plan, Carmichael? You're alone. Shielded but alone. I'd hypothesize that you're always alone. That's why you need to program people to fight for you. No one would do it of their own accord. If I hack into your guard, will I find a thread of loyalty built into their mods, just to ensure their dedication?"

"You're implying I'd be better off with what, a crew? A herd like an animal? I am a prince. A god among insects. Gods don't have friends," he spits, a flush working its way up his rodent face.

"Actually, the three-handed god has friends," Victor interjects, still behind me. "A whole pantheon of them. Most gods do. Maybe not the Dark Mother of the Void, but she birthed a whole void, so that seems like a lot of company."

"They say he keeps his extra hand free to hold that of his consort, the sharp-mouthed woman." Victory pauses as if she's in thought. "Her name isn't creative, but it is accurate."

They're trying to buy me time for my scheme. Which is good because my scheme is not ready to implement. My fingers dance over the datapad while my eyes remain locked on Pierce.

As it turns out, I'm not the only one with a plan. Carmichael kicks a hatch at the base of the maze, which pops open and reveals a whole fucking plas-cannon hidden in the floor. Much more effective than a small blaster. I didn't consider that he was moving to put *me* in a vulnerable position just as I was moving to put him in one.

Shield bracelets don't work against plas-cannons. Very little does. I stumble back a few steps despite my desire to put forth a tough front. The open lab is behind us but there isn't time to reach it. The drone I redirected isn't done with its task yet. The glass beads of the chandelier above us tinkle gently. The maze is wide open and I can't get a wall where I need it before he fires.

He grins, giant white teeth flashing in the dim prison light. "I am tired of your sniveling witticisms. My Family never needed you, no matter what my father thought. I certainly never needed you. I got the best part of you when you were young and less burdened by morals. I can start again. I've done it before."

There isn't enough time. The plas-cannon whines its mechanical scream just as Levi's arm wraps around my waist and he spins me behind him. All that time I didn't have slows down. An orange-colored blur streaks out of the corner of my vision. I only have time for the impression of a flashing LED panel, a hulking chassis, and stamped numbers ending with 81. The plas-cannon blasts its intense pulse of energy. Levi's muscles tense. Instead of the sound of tearing flesh, the screech of destroyed metal pulps the inside of my ears. A blinding spatter of light. The acrid scent of burned circuitry.

And then there's silence. The chandelier tinkles once more.

I dodge around Levi, palms clammy and a cold sweat spiking out on the back of my neck. GR81's crumpled smoking body on the floor, fractured and crushed. A pool of coolant leaks blue on the grated floor of the maze. It drips like blood.

A message flashes on my datapad. *Look upward and remember me.*

The chandelier *rattles*. I glance up to see five drones huddled around its housing—four more than the one I sent to do its job in silence. A sob catches in my throat. GR81. Always helping. Always generous. A loud crack comes from above, followed by a tinkling cacophony as the whole fucking chandelier comes crashing down, directly on Carmichael Pierce's stupid blond head.

Levi hauls me back again, blocking me from stray crystal shards that bounce off his skin. It's over so quickly.

It's quiet again so quickly.

And then I push my way around Levi. I run, skidding on broken glass to the tattered body on the floor, coated with a glimmer-sharp layer of powdered glass. I frantically wipe the glass from GR81's destroyed chassis and hold up the datapad to perform a diagnostic. I don't need to run a diagnostic. His head is nearly gone, only time for one last message. The core processing power is always in the head. Stupidly, I think, because androids aren't humans. There's no need to give them a brain in the human way. But they did and GR81's is gone in smoke and charred circuits.

He just made his way to freedom. He never managed to successfully free his brethren. It's like being saved by a baby. A snippy pissy baby that had his whole nonlife ahead of him. And now he's scrap. I don't know if I believe in an afterlife for ensouled creatures. I'm not like Itzel with her goddess or the twins with their god. I believe in the integrity of data, and once that data is gone, it might just be gone forever.

GR81 is *gone*. No last gasping breath. He doesn't breathe and his vocal processor is destroyed. One of my tears strikes his smudged orange-painted chassis. Then another. And then I'm crying full out, wrapped around the prison-guard android who became a person and then made the most stupid human choice that people ever make, to sacrifice himself to save someone else.

It's not long before Levi and the others haul me away. We're still in Shikigami, after all. Still in danger. Just because Carmichael's body is pinned beneath the chandelier, it doesn't mean that Kaori or any of the other sources of danger are otherwise occupied. There's no time to cry over a hopeless tragedy. They probably don't even know what a tragedy it is. Just Caro, crying over a robot.

Our exit is a blur. Glass crunches under our feet as we leave the maze, passing rigid soldiers, their eyes still blank. Nausea churns in my chest. I did this. I stole them. I don't offer to save the Pierce soldiers who became Titans. I checked their files when I checked Levi's. They'd committed enough crimes before the experimentation and incarceration that I don't want them on the ship. The Family Council can decide what to do with them once I'm out of range and I wipe the programming clear.

I hate that I did this. I wish I knew another option that would get us out of here in one piece.

Not all of us. GR81 won't ever leave.

Remember me, he said. And I will.

The *Calamity* is in a clearing just past the tree line. I try to access the *Calamity* via my pilfered datapad. The sound of dropping crystal comes from behind us. I pause, turning with the datapad in my hand.

Carmichael Pierce stumbles through the lab exit. He's cut to tatters, bruised, limping, but tragically still alive. A nonmodified person wouldn't have survived what he did. Even worse, he somehow has the plas-cannon in hand, detached from its mounting. I try to activate the weapons system of the *Calamity* remotely. I'm fast in a data system—extension of my hand and all—but I'm not faster than a plas-cannon. When he fires, I let loose a thready scream.

Embarrassing last sound. I'd redo it if I could.

And I can because I'm not hit by a massive bolt of plasma. The barrel of the cannon is deformed, and the beam goes to the side, slightly crooked, and takes out the tail fin of a nearby ship.

Shots fire over my shoulder, my crew aiming directly for

Carmichael with weapons that haven't been landed on by a chandelier. They glance off his skin as though he's made of mirror. Arcadio mutters to Temper that he should have brought his other weapon. Another shot of Carmichael's goes wide but closer, burning a hole in the pavement just in front of me.

Levi yet again shoves me behind him and I'm almost into the *Calamity*'s systems when Carmichael is the one who lets loose a thready scream. Yeah, it really is an embarrassing sound. I'm glad it's coming from him this time. I peek around Levi to see Carmichael drop to his knees, revealing Kaori Nakatomi standing behind him, a bloody knife in her grip. She whispers something in his ear and jabs the knife into the space between his shoulder and his neck. When she yanks it out, she looks past him to us.

She shrugs her graceful shoulders at us, eyes sharp and deadly. I knew she'd come for Pierce eventually. Like the spider she is named for, Kaori merely waited in the dark until exposed flesh was within her reach. She winks at Victor.

And then the heir to Nakatomi darts into one of the smaller Pierce vessels. That's going to be a problem for future-us. At this exact moment, with Carmichael Pierce bleeding on the ground in front of me, I can't bring myself to care.

"She declared war on his Family." Levi's voice rumbles over me. Right, superhearing. "Said she was never his to toy with."

"She prefers to be the manipulator." I sniff. Still, if she's redirecting her focus to the Pierce Family, I'm happy to have her in the wind.

I have the *Calamity* powered up by the time we reach it. Temper sprints to the helm, Victory and Victor make their way to the infirmary, and I stand in the engine room, staring at the same engine I've known for years and looking right through it.

Levi wraps an arm around my shoulders, pulling me in to his chest. "Your android knew what it was doing. For perhaps the first time in its existence it had a chance to make a choice for itself."

"I should have thought of the chandelier earlier. The droid would have been done in time. We'd all have escaped—survived."

He slowly turns me until I'm enfolded in a hug. "We all make choices. Some of them are shortsighted—like me trying to return to the prison to save you from myself. If I hadn't done that, everyone would have survived, too. Or we all would have been brought down by a Pierce patrol. Or I would have killed your two mercs. If you hadn't come to the prison, GR81 might not have been fully free in the first place. I wouldn't have either. Pierce's secrets would still be hidden. If it hadn't chosen to save us, we wouldn't have escaped to bring Pierce to justice."

Despite the truth in his words, I shake my head until he tilts my chin up and lowers his lips to me. Trailing kisses over my cheeks, my nose, my jaw, my closed eyes, and finally my lips. It's a soft kiss. The kind that speaks rather than screams.

We stand in the heart of my ship, our lips speaking poetry as I grieve for an android. When the engines power up, and the ship at last leaves Myrrdhn and Shikigami, I barely feel the vibration beneath my feet.

CHAPTER 29

After a few tiny adrenaline spurts deactivate my augmented-reality lenses and keep me from opening ship-access doors, the bug juice seems to finally leach from my system. Which makes it a lot easier to buckle down to work on the primary problems: how to keep people with chips from being hacked against their will and how to deactivate the bombs in our heads until Micah can remove them safely.

The bombs are the easy part. I point a targeted EMP at both of them, killing the tech completely. Now we have inert explosives in our heads. Not good, exactly, but not vulnerable anymore.

Which brings me to the tougher problem. There are a lot of possible solutions for the control chips, both hardware and software based. I could block all incoming signals to brain or spinal mods, but that means they can't be updated anymore, ever. I could create an etherwall—but the thing with etherwalls is that there's always someone around who can figure out how to hack them. It's a temporary solution.

After my first few abortive attempts, I'm so frustrated I can barely see straight. The wall above my desk is scrawled with fractured ideas sketched out in charcoal marker. I leave my workstation in the engine room simply because I need to pace out some of this relentless energy. When you're hunted for days, it's hard to get out of fight-or-flight mode.

Levi has been immersed in the data I collected about his

history. I've been immersed in giving him as much space as is possible in a small ship like the *Calamity*, although it hurts to do so. He deserves some time to figure himself out. I temporarily reset his programming so that the chip in his head is a simple translator, but he's still vulnerable to interference whenever he leaves the *Calamity*. He says he's remembering more and more. When he isn't delving into his own past, he studies the ship charts. A sick churning turns in my gut when he does so.

He's looking for his home.

Which he should. It's selfish for me to consider him part of my *own* home after so brief a period of time. Sex makes you feel crazy things. I don't know if I should touch him now. If it was a one-time-only thing or if watching me victimize a whole crew of people the exact same way he was subjugated was a step too far. We talked out our own monstrousness and culpability back in the hot spring, but that sort of thing takes a lifetime and a few good therapists to fully work through. It's not fixed by a brief conversation and some sexy hot-spring times.

"There you are." Temper's voice comes from behind me. She's almost as sneaky as Itzel. It's that Family training. I have a whole ship full of silent steppers. "You finally emerged."

"What do you mean?" When I turn to face her, she's wearing her usual green coveralls. There's a streak of something yellow-brown on the hip, like she brushed off her hands and forgot about it. Probably some of our algae.

"You're like one of those cranky mammals Itzel studied two years ago on that moon. You know the ones. They had a whole underground bunker system and holed up when they were traumatized. Weather change? Underground for days. Bad fruit? Underground."

I raise my eyebrows. I remember the mammals. They had hideous faces, like a pig crossed with a dog crossed with a burrito, chubby hairless charcoal-black bodies, and flippers for claws because it made the digging easier. I do not appreciate the comparison.

"What I'm saying is that you go to ground when you're stressed. We all know to leave you alone. You get snappy otherwise."

Snappy? Me? Never. Okay, always. "You learned a lot about me the past few days. I've been pretty judgmental of everyone else's past actions. I'm bracing for some of my own medicine."

She snorts. Really snorts. Not a polite little snuff, a full-nostriled snort of disgust. "Honestly? I thought it was worse. You're so fucking secretive, Caro. Fake name—yes, I knew you had a fake name— refusing to talk about your past at all. Itzel kills people as a hobby, and you thought I'd have a problem because your college project went a little haywire?"

Well. When she puts it like that. "She kills *bad* people."

"Mostly, I'm sure. You're telling me she never killed someone a little bit good? I think everyone's good to someone in their life. I put out my own brother's eye and betrayed my Family. Arcadio was up to his sexy sexy ears in Family business up until about a year ago. Micah did unethical medical work. Cyn spaced an entire ship full of people. The fact that you had an ethical whoopsie means that you fit in, not that you stand out."

I step back, almost propelled by the power of her words. I was so hard on Cyn. Mostly because I saw myself in her. "An 'ethical whoopsie' is a flippant way to put it."

"I'm a fucking flippant person. Yet another weakness. Yes, you're judgmental. We all know it. You're also fiercely protective of people who matter to you, as evidenced by you flying off to rescue the twins, which kind of evens things out. You want to tell me the whole story?"

I give her the story in a truth as unvarnished as I'm able. I may have moved to mostly feeling furious that my work was used against people, rather than guilty for doing it in the first place, but the decision to interpret things differently is up to her. When I'm done, she crosses her arms.

"So, you're really smart."

Not exactly the takeaway I expected. Maybe I didn't tell the story correctly. She waves away my clarification. "No, you're smart. Brilliant even. You just didn't know what the world was. We're all naive at some point. Not me, of course, I've never been naive."

"You fucked Ven."

"I've been naive one time . . . over and over . . . for about half a year." She grimaces thinking of our old captain. "Anyway, the right part is that you tried to fix it. The wrong part is that you tried to do this all *without* us. We're a team, Caro. We work as a team."

"Like when you tried to sacrifice yourself so we could get off Herschel and leave you to your brother?" I cross my own arms.

"I'm the captain. I can break the rules. It's in the 'go down with the ship' clause."

"I'm the engineer. If anyone is going down with the ship, it's me."

"Fine, we can both make stupid decisions that benefit the crew and if the ship literally goes down, we'll have a party in the engine room. My point is that your stupid decision didn't benefit us. It excluded us. We're a family, Caro. Lowercase 'f.'" Her eyes go dreamy. "But imagine the uppercase 'F' Family we would be."

Charted space wouldn't know what hit it.

"I didn't exactly plan to take down Pierce when I went." Well, I did, but it was about my fourth priority. "Ven told me it was a rescue mission. He had spliced some of Victory's footage to show Levi. I guess he knows my weakness for hunky men."

"I know, he told us about the rescue."

I shake my head. "It wasn't a rescue. He lied just to get me there. He sent the twins there to recover a chip for Frederick. They couldn't get ahold of it and, if they did, they didn't know what to do with it. He knew I'd never normally take his call so he tricked me into 'saving' them so I could get the chip he needed. Your brother sent them a demo of new tech, hoping for a partnership or a sale, and they were trying to reverse engineer it."

Temper drops her head into a hand, shaking it slightly. "That fucking idiot. That shortsighted fucking *idiot*. And Ven was an idiot to take the job and you were a fool to trust Ven."

"You believed Ven, too."

"Oh, trust me, I remember."

I consider not telling her where the chip is now. It would possibly keep Levi safer. But I got into this mess not trusting her with the truth. "That chip is what they used in Levi. He didn't have a translator chip so they gave it to him before hacking it. There was nuance to the tech—I'm not sure what yet—that allowed them to modulate and control him rather than just turn him on and off." I cross my arms. "We're not giving it back, not even if Micah removes it."

Temper throws an arm around my shoulders, bringing me into a half hug. "Of course we aren't. We aren't telling anyone. No matter what."

I've been wrong a lot, it appears. I've kept such a tight grip on my past that I didn't let anyone be who they really could be. Sometimes trust leads to betrayal, yes. But sometimes it leads to acceptance. You can't form relationships at arm's length. You have to be up close.

You have to be up *close*.

I'm a fool again. "Holy shit."

"Caro, I know I'm not usually a hugger, but it's not really worth a 'holy shit.'"

"I figured out how to block the signal to the chips."

"About time."

"Not helpful." But I'm not even looking at her anymore. I'm spinning back to the engine room, talking my way through my idea as I go. "The solution isn't new. It's old. We do all our updates wirelessly now. It's easy, right? You just walk through the docking gate to a station, and you immediately update your tech. That's also why it's so easy to hack. We're all on the same network. If we set up subnetworks, *our* network is under our control. It's like you said, we have to be close. Each Family or vassal Family or group can set up their own network. There would be too many to hack effectively. Then you can implement your own security layers, which adds complexity. Essentially, we'd be a network of subnodes rather than a web."

"I understood about half of that."

"It's the same root problem as everything else in charted space. We've been putting our faith in the Family Council to regulate their own. But they haven't done it. This forces us to put our faith in our *own* families—however they may be shaped." My fingers itch. I want my datapad. I want to try it out.

Temper gets a far-off considering look on her face. "There could be a whole industry of network setup and security for groups that don't have their own experts."

"There would have to be." I nod.

That considering look turns into a dangerous grin. "Which decentralizes the Families even more."

. . . . .

I have a network set up by the end of the day, layered with my best security features. I've been so deep in the work that my back aches and my eyes are dry when I finally stand from my workstation, lightheaded.

"You skipped lunch. And dinner." Victory's voice makes me jump.

I blink at her, still slightly dazed. Soft-steppers. "I was busy."

She shoves a protein pack in my direction. "I'm sorry about the robot."

"Android," I automatically correct.

"The android. It was brave. It understood more about being a merc than a lot of new recruits do."

I cock my head at her as I stretch my shoulders. "I'm not sure I follow."

"We fight for a cause. That's what we're paid to do. But we also fight for each other. Your team may be temporary, but it's still a team. No one is giving their life for their funder—not willingly. But they'll give their life for their gunner or their scout. You told us it was sentient but I didn't really believe you. I've seen so-called sentience before and it's just clever programming and what people want to see. GR81 valued its life. It valued its life so much it was willing to give it for something it believed in."

My eyes prickle for a different reason. I blink and turn to my workstation to hide the tears. "It's hard being that something."

"You haven't looked at the drive we took from the prison yet. Not the new data you stored for Levi but the first drive we saved. The one GR81 made for us."

I harden my jaw, force my eyes wide to dry the tears. "I've been in the weeds."

"Of course." She nods. "You should look at it. You might be surprised by what you find."

It sits on my workstation, untouched. I understand that Victory is probably trying to be nice, distract me with work. Maybe some reference to GR81's other brethren. A way to figure out why they didn't activate when he did. "I will. When there's time."

He said, "Remember me." I've been lost in my human sentimentality. GR81 wasn't poetic. He wasn't the type for dramatic emotions. He may have been a person, but he wasn't a human. He was different.

I pick up the drive, rolling it over in my fingers, and think.

Victory shrugs with her usual insouciance and turns to the door. "By the way, your supersoldier asked Victor to teach him how to fight. It's quite the show."

Oh no. I don't know who I'm the most worried for. Victor has the skill, but Levi has the everything else. I thought he'd be running back to his old life as fast as his feet can take him, which is incredibly fast. I didn't think he'd be interested in exploring ours.

Also I'm only human. I love watching attractive men fight each other. All the sweat. The heaving muscles. The sweat *on* the heaving muscles.

I carefully set the drive back down on my desk and follow Victory to the small gym in the ship. It's not big enough for much: some exercise equipment and a sparring mat. Temper and Arcadio are already there, sitting with their backs to the wall and eating snacks. Temper waves me over with a grin and tips the bag of lirk seeds in my direction. They're peppered with a dark-red spice.

My mind tingling with hope for the first time in a long time, I grab a handful and try to pick out the sweet seed. Each pod contains one sweet seed and five savory. They're supposedly identical but everyone has their own method of choosing the sweet one. Color or shape or even scent. I fall in the color camp. I find a dark seed and pop it in my mouth.

Not sweet but the spicy coating gives it a pleasant pop.

Victor and Levi circle each other on the mat.

"They're practicing takedowns. They had to move to that because it appears that your cartographer doesn't need any work on defense. He's too fast and too strong to be toppled in a hand-to-hand fight." Temper tosses back a whole handful of the seeds.

"I'm impressed he asked for proper training." Arcadio reaches into the bag of seeds. "It would be easy for him to power through any situation he finds himself in."

Levi lunges forward in a flash of motion too fast to follow and wraps Victor in a limb lock. An almost limb lock. Victor twists out of it almost like he's spineless and steps back. "You weren't far enough up the arm. Your grip needs to be near the shoulder."

They repeat the same motion, slamming together with a thud

so loud that I feel it in my bones, and this time, Levi completes the maneuver, holding Victor in place easily. Victor taps out on the mat, and they separate.

"He's going to be deadly in no time," Victory leans over and whispers in my ear. "Deadli*er*, I mean. He's a fast learner."

Victor and Levi do some sort of complicated hand gesture at each other and retreat to the sweat towels that they placed by the mat. Victor lightly jogs over with his towel draped over his shoulders. "Vic, I want you to spar with us next time. He can beat one person with pure strength. He needs a challenge."

Victory grins. Nothing she enjoys more than fighting someone new. Nothing Victor enjoys more than teaching someone new.

"I'm happy to join when you think he's ready for a third," Arcadio offers.

"I can join if he needs a fourth." Temper eats another handful of the seeds.

"He would flatten you like a bug accidentally." Arcadio shakes his head.

Our captain glares at her partner. "Only if he can catch me."

"Did you see him out there? He can catch you. He can catch a hover bike." Victor waves a hand in negation. "You're the one I bring in if he needs to learn to fight dirty. Which he doesn't, because he's a tank."

Temper huffs out a breath, although a smile curls at the corner of her mouth. "Itzel's smaller and you'd want him to fight her."

Victor laughs. "Itzel would be too disheartening. A tank can't fight a shadow."

"Who's Itzel?" Levi wipes the top of his head as he walks over. His dark hair is starting to grow in. A thick rich near-black. I want to run my fingers over it.

"Our biologist. Also an assassin. Retired, I think." More like I *hope*. "She's a lot of fun."

He looks terrified but he doesn't flinch. Our crew is probably overwhelming.

When I get up to go to the mess, Levi follows me. He smells way better than a sweaty man should. Victor smells like a wet dog when he's been working out. So does Micah. Arcadio seems to never sweat. Temper swears he doesn't have physical mods but I wonder if he just nipped his sweat glands shut somehow. "Are you heading home soon?"

Did I just blurt that out over the protein packs? A look at his face tells me that yes, yes I did. He steps a little closer. "Do you want me to head home?"

I shake my head before I even think of what my response should be. "No. But you should. You're learning who you were. It would make sense for you to want to go home."

"Maybe I will, someday. But my family is gone and I'm a different person. I'm not him anymore and I never will be. I don't want to be. What Pierce did was a violation, but at the same time, I like who I am now. I suppose I have to because there's no going back, but I do anyway. I like that I can protect people I care about. That I'm fast and I'm strong. There was nothing wrong with who I was before, but I'm more now."

He is. I've been trying to keep from liking it too much, because for all I know, he hates his new body and it's wrong for me to lust after it too much. But I do. I also like that he's fast and strong and protective. Pierce may have made him the first two but the third—the most important—is all Levi.

He slides closer, one arm dragging up my side. "We never get to choose our bodies, do we? We're born to them. This wasn't my choice, but I'll make it my own."

Still, it's important that he knows I'm not just in it for his modded body. "I saw you before I got there—on a vid. I thought you were beautiful then, even if it was such an awful image. When

I saw you in person for the first time, in the cell, I thought you were beautiful too—in a terrifying way—but what I liked most was your eyes. And when you first kissed me. I liked that part, too. That flash of mischief in the very beginning when you were yourself for the first time."

"Everyone wants to sneak a kiss from an angel." His voice has a low rumble. I know that rumble. I heard it before in the hot spring. Some very interesting muscles clench below my waistline.

"And now that I'm no longer an angel?" With no bug juice in my system, I read as normal to cameras and visual mods. With no bug juice in his system, his visual mods work again.

He bends down until our faces are close to each other, nose just brushing against my own. "Show me the person who said you're not an angel."

"I'm really no—"

He stops my words with his lips, one hand curling around my back and one cradling my head. I go up on my toes, meeting him with enthusiasm, my own hands clutching his shoulders, his jaw, his head.

"You have a bunk, no?" Temper's jarring voice comes from the table. "I can't have people making out all over the ship. It's unhygienic."

"Didn't you and Arcadio spark in the gym on that very first mission?" I peer over Levi's shoulder. "How was that for hygiene?"

She winces, then grins. "We didn't spark . . . technically . . . but we did generate a lot of heat."

Gross. I grab Levi's hand and tow him in the direction of my bunk. "Bunk it is."

It's maybe the first time I've ever initiated sex. My stomach churns, waiting for Levi to change his mind. Instead, he scoops me off my feet and moves in that special fast way he has, and we're at the door to my bunk before I register that I'm being carried. He kisses me again as the door slides open. "Bunk it is."

CHAPTER 30

■ ■ ■ ■ ■ ■ ■ ■ ■ ■ ■ ■ ■

We get to my bunk and the problem becomes immediately clear. There's no way in any world that Levi will fit on my bed unless he's nearly folded in half—which won't leave any room for me. He's ducking his head to avoid the protruding lighting fixture that sits in the middle of my ceiling. None of this is sexy. *Nothing* about my bunk is sexy. There is smudged marker on the walls, a clutter of circuits on my desk by a datapad, and a crumpled pair of old coveralls that haven't managed to quite make it in my hamper draped over the back of my chair.

This is what my room looks like when I'm in full work mode. Everything else falls by the wayside. I'm lucky that I remembered to shower—only because I sometimes come up with new ideas in the shower and I wanted to give it a shot. It didn't give me any ideas but it did give me a better smell.

"I like it." Levi stares around with interest as I try to subtly kick the coveralls into the closet.

I try to follow his eyeline. "What, exactly, do you like?"

"It looks like I imagine the inside of your mind would look. A little unknowable, a little messy, and very busy."

Just goes to show that he's a very kind person at heart. Also pretty accurate. The hallways of my mind are cluttered and better off unseen. I drag the mattress off the top bunk and drop it on the floor. Levi steps out of the way, likely wondering if I've completely lost my mind. Next, I drag the mattress off the bottom bunk. Both of them almost fit on the floor. I'm standing on a mattress—which is all right because I'm in my soft ship-slippers that are for inside only. Levi is standing in the small bathroom attached to my bunk.

Because I am a romantic at heart, I also activate a red synth candle in a flat silver tray on my desk. The scent reminds me of the moisturizer-storage space in Shikigami. I turn it off. When I turn around, Levi has stepped out of the lavatory and onto the mattress, sinking down to sit on the soft foam. I bite my lip.

This feels like crossing one more line. A critical one. We're no longer struggling for our lives. No longer in that safely dangerous other world. If we do this, it's for real. "You should know I'm not an angel. I'm messy and complicated and kind when I remember to be—which isn't always."

He studies me with a somber face but the corner of his mouth curls up. "You should know I'm not a hero. I'm an academic and fairly *uncomplicated* and my first instinct when someone throws something at me is to bat it away because it's probably dangerous. I did awful things in my past, and I will again—if I must."

I drop to my knees beside him, fingers curling in the soft sheets. "You *are* a hero, though. Because you choose to be despite your natural inclinations. Because you came back from those awful things."

"And you are an angel, because you chose to be, despite your natural inclinations."

I laugh and scoff at the same time and it ends up sounding like a gag. More of those natural inclinations that are hardly angelic.

"Besides, if you really were fully celestial, you wouldn't want to do this." He captures my wrist and gives a gentle yank. Gentle for Levi-strength, which means he ends up on his back and I end up splayed half over him. I love being there. I brush my lips over his, straddling his torso. Once. Again. I go in for a third time and he lunges his head up, locking lips, tongue slipping into my mouth and tangling with mine with a wild kind of hunger.

I push down on his shoulders until he's flat, clear blue-green eyes sharp and heated on my face. "I seem to remember we decided to take turns being in charge. It's my turn."

I have no idea what I'm doing with my turn. It just seems important to have it. To declare that we're equals in this. There are all different kinds of relationships, but I personally don't allow anyone to do anything to me that they won't allow me to do right back. There are no bosses here. He needs to be comfortable with that.

He appears very comfortable. My sheets and part of my soft nest of pillows are beneath him and he's spread out like a buffet. "Are you planning to take your turn, or just to watch me?"

"Can I take my turn while watching you?"

"Only if I can entice you with sexy map innuendo." He pauses and then grins. "I don't actually know any sexy map innuendo."

"How about I chart a course to your penis?" Nope. Nope. That was too much.

He laughs. The wonderful, wonderful man laughs. His hand holds my thigh, big fingers warm and still against me. Looking delectable as a treat. I lean down and resume our kiss, slow and deep and drugging. The rough fabric of his clothes—a pair of Arcadio's deep-black coveralls stretched almost to their capacity— sparks the nerve endings in my hands as I drag my fingers up his chest. I think anything would spark them right now.

I slowly tug at the zipper at the front of his coveralls, revealing glimpses of smooth light-brown skin. My lips follow the path of the zipper, tracing down his ribs to his abdomen. I scoot lower as I go, tugging at the coveralls until the weight of his body resists the motion.

His eyebrow raises and those white teeth flash again. "Would you like some help?"

I snicker and tug feebly at the coveralls. "Yes. Yes, I would."

In what feels like a second, he's shucked all his clothes and returned to his previous position. The last time we did this was in a dark cave. He was mostly underwater. Here, under the stark lighting in my bunk, the basic . . . expanse . . . of him is impressive. I want to explore him.

"You're doing a lot of staring."

That I am. "I like what I see."

And then, because fairness is important, I unzip my own coveralls, shucking the green-brown fabric quickly, but then I'm just standing in the stark lighting stark naked and I'm a little overexposed.

A lot. A lot of *me* is exposed. And the lighting really is shit. We need to upgrade the lights as soon as more credits come in. I didn't listen to Temper when she complained about it before. I immediately return to my spot on top of him, knees pressed tight against his ribs.

And suddenly, with the way his eyes light up, the feel of skin on skin, the heat of his body in the cool pumped air of the ship, I forget my self-consciousness. It doesn't matter in this moment. It's ephemeral as everything else that piles up outside my door. And suddenly all I feel is hunger, a warm and quiet kind of hunger. Softer than any I've felt before but somehow more urgent.

When I kiss him this time, the heat from his body scalds my own. His hands tentatively rise to my hips, and when I don't protest this challenge to my control, he clutches them, fingers wrapping to my behind. I kiss a hot line down his body, tongue tracing every dip and crevice and puckered scar that it finds. He gasps in a sharp breath when I get to the deep cut in his muscle that separates abdomen from thigh. Something urgent bobs near my head.

"Are you going to torture me forever?" His voice is like rocks dragging against each other.

I want to see how much rougher I can make it. "Maybe I am."

So I do, lavishing attention on his body but avoiding one key area until every muscle is clenched and beads of sweat glisten on his skin.

I thrill with anticipation, as aroused as if he'd been doing all this to me. There's something beautiful in this moment. In his trust.

There's nothing hotter than being trusted.

"If I gave you a choice right now, what would you want me to do?" I'm feeling magnanimous, glorying in my power but wanting to share some of it.

He blinks, pulling together thoughts that are obviously scattered. Now his voice is like mountains dragging against each other. I consider this a job well done. "If you do much more of that, I'll be useless for anything else. I very much want to be useful for other things."

I grin down at him, feeling powerful and feminine and triumphant. "Then I release you from your state. Feel free to be as active as you'd like."

I'm suddenly on my back, a very large, very masculine presence looming above me, with a familiar smile tugging at his mouth. It's like the first time I met him, new and old and just as compelling. I spread my legs wider, welcoming his weight. We're like two parts of an engine, perfectly sized for each other no matter our disparity. I thought he might lunge to action but—as always—Levi surprises me.

He takes his time. Every bit the slow torture that I subjected him to, with tongue and fingers and hot open-mouthed kisses. He nuzzles the underside of my breast. Rolls a nipple between his fingers. Bites soft nibbles down the quaking line of my stomach. Breathes one short sharp blast directly at my core that makes my eyes almost roll back in my head.

I'm teetering on a precipice, trembling with anticipation and hunger and something else that's large and nameless and encompasses something bigger than space itself. Something that ties all things together invisibly. That acts and reacts in unknowable ways.

"Now, now*now*now or I'll explode," I gasp out, fingers clenching against the side of his head, brushing against the thick stubble

growing back. I want him in me, around me. I want to feel the
force of his body.

But it's too late for that. He traces his tongue in one sharp
motion over the desperate bundle of nerves at just the right spot
and I spin out into nothing, starbursts blooming in front of my
eyes. While I'm still coming back to my body, he poises himself
above me, scoops a knee up under one arm, and gently edges his
way inside my body. I clutch his shoulders, his head, his arms.
Anything I can reach.

The slow inexorable slide dances along my already sparking
nerve endings. When he's finally in he pauses. "Is this all right?"

"Yes. It's all right." I squeeze every inside muscle that I have.

That gleam reappears in his eyes. "You've forgotten how fast I
can move."

I have, but he reminds me, moving at steadily increasing tempo
until he flies. The sensation is overwhelming, friction and depth
and things I can't even begin to describe. Before long I'm already
back at the top, heat pounding through my body, scattered again,
gone supernova. I emit a noise that's halfway between a squeak
and a scream. We're merged, full, fused in a way I've never felt before. In a way that doesn't seem real. He slows, low deep slides until finally he's fully solidly within me, his lips crashing into mine
as he comes to pieces of his own.

"I love you, Caro Ogunyemi, Osondu. Any name you take, I'll
love you." He breathes the words into my ear. "I loved you from
the first time I ever saw you. The angel who came to me when I
didn't even have myself. It might sound crazy; it might sound too
soon. That doesn't make it any less true."

It is crazy. It *is* too soon.

And yet. I've dated men for years and still been unsure. When
you *know* you know. When a part fits against an assembly, it fits. It
doesn't take a lot of time to recognize. And when that correct part
is put into motion, the whole machine runs smooth as air.

My fingers tighten against his skin, like I can meld with him. "I love you, too, Levi Daniels. Leviathan. The champion and the cartographer. Whatever form you take is kind and compelling. Never try to save me again, not if it puts you at risk."

"How about we just promise to save each other?"

That's a deal I can make.

As we recover, I imagine both of us picking up pieces and re-assembling. Some of his end up in my pile and some of mine end up in his until we're both made of each other. Until our machine is whole and mixed and flawless.

"I'm glad you're staying," I mumble, breathing in his scent.

His arm tightens around me. "I was never leaving. How could I when you're here?"

. . . . .

Later that night, much later, after we've both gone several more rounds and Levi is sleeping on the mattress nest on the floor, I sit at my desk, rolling the drive that Victory tossed me between my fingers. It's scuffed in the corner, rough and scraped from a fall or a scuffle during Victory's retreat down the mountain. I drag my thumb over the rough patch once. Again. Procrastinating. I have a suspicion but I might be wrong. I desperately want to be right.

I set the drive against the datapad and trigger the wireless transfer.

New menus scroll across the screen. Carefully catalogued data. Most of it is identical to what I pulled when I went back for Levi but there are a few new files. I take the datapad back to my new floor-bed and curl up around it. Levi's heavy arm wraps around my waist as I lean into the bulk of his body. He's so warm and cozy that I'm tempted to curl up next to him and forget my task. Instead he offers a touch of reality as I immerse myself back in the sordid world of Pierce.

Personnel logs. The plans for Carmichael Pierce's birthday cel-ebration (twenty floating contortionists, hallucinogenic bubbles drifting from the ceiling, no food at all—if no one thought he was a monster before, they certainly did after that little hootenanny). There are private communications that I'm not in the mood to dig through. Maybe later, when I'm not quite so psychologically tender. A partially fragmented file is in that folder. When I repair it, it appears to be a zoomed-in segment of a map. It shows a rocky or icy landscape, a crevasse, and an "X" in the center of that crevasse.

I hover my fingers over the image, tracing the area over the "X." Well, that's a fascinating treasure hunt. I wonder what it leads to. I make a few copies of that image and set a subroutine to search the universal atlas for a matching landscape. When Levi wakes up, he might know what it is. Maybe he's even the one who found it for them, whatever *it* is.

I'm almost ready to abandon my search, throat full of disappointed emotion, when I finally circle back to the last folder. It is labeled PORN. Who labels their porn PORN? You label it MISC. or DENTAL BILLS or something innocuous. This is very suspicious. Also . . . what kind of weirdo keeps porn on their work terminal? That, more than anything, spurs me to open the folder.

Not porn. Unless they're really turned on by obscure code. Code that doesn't make sense. I scroll through the dense file slowly. This absolutely isn't porn. It's commands. Infrastructure. Security. Fragments of familiar code interspersed with the novel.

I lurch to a fully seated position, breathing hard, hands trembling around the datapad. Levi continues to sleep behind me, a warm comforting presence.

I know what this is.

I know *who* this is.

■ ■ ■ ■ ■ ■ ■ ■ ■ ■ ■ ■ ■ ■

CHAPTER 31

We gather in the helm the next day, Temper and Arcadio, Victor and Victory, Levi and me. The view ports show a broad stretching asteroid belt, stones the size of a house, a hover craft, a pebble. A distant star illuminates the stones and ice chunks in blacks, browns, and creamy frost. The red light of the helm washes us, making the room seem close and warm amid the icy expanse beyond.

When I explained what we have to do, Temper agreed. Her exact words were "If we're both planning to go down with the ship, you get to offer whatever upgrades you want."

This is a temporary fix. I can't see it lasting in the long term. But for now, it's needed. I poise my hand over the console, datapad ready, and begin the upload sequence. It takes a while for the file to transfer. It's like that with large files and this is one of the biggest I've ever seen.

Upload complete.

Nothing happens.

"That's anticlimactic." Victor glances around the helm. "I thought it would be more exciting."

The helm's lights flash white, drowning us in brightness, and then they dim back to their habitual red.

Victory's hands freeze at their knitting, a stitch half-looped. Temper's fingers rise to her mouth.

Levi's arm wraps around my shoulder. He's here, with us, with me. When he's ready to find his history, I'll go with him.

A familiar pissy voice comes from the coms system.

"Hello, Caro Ogunyemi. It took you long enough."

ACKNOWLEDGMENTS

Three books in and this whole publishing thing is finally starting to feel real! Maybe that's why three is a charm. This particular charm came about in large part because of the hard work and support of many people.

Thanks to Caitlin Blasdell of Liza Dawson Associates, who edits with aplomb and offers advice and industry expertise whenever I need it. I can't imagine trying to do this without her.

Thanks to the entire team at Bramble/Tor. Monique Patterson and Mal Frazier for deft editing hands and enthusiastic support throughout the process. MaryAnn Johanson for copyediting. Caro Perny for publicity and Jordan Hanley for marketing.

Thanks to the fantastic narrator, Paige Reisenfeld, who has brought this series to life in audiobook form.

Long before the book reached any of them, thanks to Frank Harris, who read the rough early chapters. Thanks to the Blue Badgers—Allison King and Mike Meneses—the best writing group a gal could ask for. Thanks to Bryce Furlong, David Clark, Patrick Fields, and Peter Zinsli for providing an exhaustive (but never exhausting) supply of physics innuendo. Caro's sexytime would not be the same without you guys. Thanks to Liz Hersh-Tucker, Sarah McIntosh, and Katie Hossepian for support, cheerleading, and group chat availability. Thanks to both of my parents, Carolyn Fay and Jack Fay, for their encouragement and support. I don't know how I got lucky enough to have such wonderful parents.

And finally, thanks to the readers. Whether you started with *Chaos* or earlier on in the series, I'm glad you're here. Welcome to the worlds of Uncharted Hearts. I hope you stay on to the next adventure.

ABOUT THE AUTHOR

Kelli Christine Photography

CONSTANCE FAY writes space romance novels and genre fiction short stories. Her short fiction can be found in *The Magazine of Fantasy & Science Fiction*, the podcast *CatsCast*, and other publications. She has a background in medical device R&D and lives in Colorado with a cat who edits all her work first.